JEWBOY OF THE SOUTH

This book is a work of fiction. Names, characters, places, and incidents are either products of the author's imagination or are used fictitiously. Any resemblance to actual events or locales or persons, living or dead, is entirely coincidental.

ISBN: 1546923667
ISBN 13: 9781546923664

ACKNOWLEDGMENTS

Though *Jewboy of the South* is a novel, I could not have written it had I not grown up in a small Southern city with only one hundred Jewish families and had I not worked at my family's store, started in the 1880s, selling clothes to farmers and working-class blacks and whites. No college education could give the experiences or teach the lessons of Abe Koplen Clothing Company. I thank them all for a diverse, often difficult, and rich rearing.

I am grateful to Jody Berman, Renni Browne, and Shannon Roberts for reading the manuscript and offering excellent editorial advice. Alice Levine and Amber Byers also edited various chapters and taught me fine points of punctuation. I am indebted to Robert Gatewood for his creative writing class tutelage. Tom Gilboy, a writer who should be famous, never wavered in his observations, support, and appreciation of my budding skills. Thanks to Tom Gilboy for cover ideas and JKoplen Design, which also designed my website, for the perfect cover. Michael Horwith, a fellow writer, recognized not only my story skills but also the humor within my perverse Southern mind. Thanks to Chris Snedeker, a fellow writer attempting to make sense of life's strange experiences.

Thank you to deputies at the Danville, Virginia police department, who were kind enough to allow me to tour the jail and to discuss police procedures and attitudes of the time.

The opinions and criticisms of my sons, Nathan Manning and Jacob Koplen, kept me humble and conscientious. A special thanks to Molly Mohseni, several greats-granddaughter of Jefferson Davis. Thanks to my generous and gracious friends who read my many drafts and gave me feedback.

Most of all, I thank my wife, Barbralu Cohen, a world-class journalist and editor, who taught and continues to teach me the craft, however much I resist her usually right-on advice, not to mention her patience over the years of my efforts and questions.

JEWBOY
OF THE
SOUTH

a novel

DON KOPLEN

DEDICATION

Dear Emet-a-la,

This book is dedicated to you, my long-suffering son. As if the strange gold crown covering my big front tooth wasn't embarrassing enough, through the years you defended me against all who attacked me for all of their reasons. I know it was difficult in this small Southern town, but you never wavered. If you're reading this, it's because I always promised you that I'd tell you the why of it before I died, the whole magillah, but I never did.

Love, Dad

The black and...

The South warps men, black or white, good or bad, as surely as rain warps good lumber. You cain't avoid it any more than you can avoid the humidity or a sudden thunderstorm when yer out and away from shelter. Some dry off with the sunshine of their goodness and go 'bout their business. But fer those with a weaker stock, it can twist the structure of their soul into somethin useless, or worse, dangerous.

The diffrence 'tween that ruined piece of wood an a warped man is that the man can return hisself to good, useful, and beneficial condition if he uses his heart like a hammer to straighten out his soul.

I think it might be harder fer a white man to do.

— *Thomas Eldridge*

...white of it

The South grew me like cotton, plucked me, spun me, and fed me into its gin. I could not escape its loom. It formed me into its weft. Its colorful threads basted my life into a twisted tapestry.

With hate and rage toward me, a Jew, and from me, the South fashioned the fabric of my perceptions of life and reality. It was a broad cloth interwoven with strings of sex, violence, and psychic torment. It warped and distorted me from a very young age. It shocked me into seeing and doing things beyond my natural maturity.

At the same time, courage, humor, and loving kindnesses—beyond what could ever be expected from people who had every reason to be full of hate and resentment—stitched my wounded heart. It challenged me to create a canopy, a chupa, *of love under the worst of circumstances.*

– *Don Cohen*

PART 1

Love, sin, and trying to save Mr. E

CHAPTER ONE

The only Jew who could hammer a nail was crucified.
Until me.

At least that's what my hero, Mr. Thomas Eldridge—I called him Mr. E—said once, us both chuckling. Then, he'd say something serious like, "There's turnin points 'round which yer life's purpose gets spun an whittled, like this hunk of tree on the lathe. It's never fer sure whether you'll carve a piece of junk or somethin beautiful."

Learning carpentry from Mr. E was one of those beautiful turning points.

My love affair with Clara, the Baptist minister's daughter, was the other. Still, she didn't appreciate me laughing when she called my penis "the staff of the Lord's kin."

"Donny, I know this all might sound strange to you, but I do consider myself a good Christian, and I do love Lord Jesus," she'd said months before the fire. "If I didn't think he'd be okay with my lovin a Jew," her blue eyes twinkling against her carnation-white skin, "I wouldn't do it."

On the afternoon before the fire, about dusk, I stood goose-bumped-butt-naked, my back to the breeze coming in through my bedroom window, blowing my tenor sax. Playing along with Miles Davis's *Kind of Blue* on the hi-fi, I was anything but blue—even though the small bells braided with red ribbons into seventeen-year-old Clara's two-foot long ponytail clinked and tinkled discordantly against the music each time she improvised on me.

I could never have imagined it would soon lead to the worst night of my life so far.

As I hit a low C, she hummed "Jesus Loves Me." I didn't care if *He* did as long as she did. When she hit "so", at the ending of "cause the Bible tells me so," my brain and legs went wobbly from the base vibrations.

I took the horn out of my mouth. ("Take tha horn out of yo mouth," Miles Davis would say to Coltrane after an interminable solo.)

"A hymn-job," I said.

"What?" Clara mumbled.

"You're giving me a 'hymn job.' "

"What?"

"You know, guys call what you're doing," and I looked down at her, "a 'humm-job.' But you're giving me a 'hymn job.' "

She looked up at me, the rising color on her cheeks matching her pink lipstick. Beaming simultaneously with wide-eyed love—my own Baptist Madonna—and a threatening earnestness she'd display whenever anyone dared not take her carefully-considered convictions seriously, she said, "Donny, with you bein Jesus's kin an all, when I fellate you," pronouncing it 'fee-late,' like a Southern girl might if she had read the word in a book but never really heard it said out loud, "it's almost holy. Not just somebody sayin the blood of Christ and givin you a fuckin cracker. Drinkin you in is real, like communion to me—HIS seed, HIS body, just pumpin in."

I liked her. No, more…I was in love, as much as a high school boy knew of such.

Even though she was not Jewish, a *shiksa,* I figured Clara was as close as I'd ever come to finding my fated true love, my *bashert.* Because finding a Jewish one in Danville, Virginia was as likely as turning bacon kosher.

Even though I thought she was crazy, because who else would even think to mix fellate, fuckin cracker, and holy in the same breath?

Even though some said that her father was head of the county's Ku Klux Klan.

CHAPTER TWO

"What's your fuckin name?" she asked the first day I met her, in homeroom, eleventh grade, a year before the fire. We'd been assigned adjoining seats.

Before the teacher called roll, I'd picked up and handed her a piece of paper that had slipped off her desk.

When I hesitated, she said, "Goddamn cat got your tongue?"

My face beeted. Southern girls, a minister's daughter no less, just didn't come at guys this way.

"Yeah, I mean no. Donny, Donny Cohen."

"How come you're always walkin around with that stupid camera around your neck?" she asked. "Sure isn't much interestin around here to take pictures of. I think you're just showin off."

"You're welcome," I said, pointing to the paper.

"Oh! Thank you from the bottom of mah hawt, suh. This po, weak suthun lady would have surely over-exerted hersef had she needed to pick it up on her own."

Her exaggerated accent and dismissive glare certainly didn't portend even a simple friendship.

"I dunno," I said. "It's just kind of fun. I'm no good but I get to be on the *Chatterbox*," our school newspaper, "so sometimes I can skip classes. What's your name?"

"You shittin me?"

Oy. Lame. Of course I already knew. Everyone knew her from newspaper pictures and articles about her father, Danville's most important minister, and his perfect Christian family. And from the four-color, full-page ads for his church, *New Creation Baptist–Danville's Happy Family Church,* always with "the fuckin picture," as she called it when I got to know her better.

In it, his large, square-jawed head, fronted by a handsome nose and developing jowls, was topped by slicked-back, groomed, black hair.

"Dyed." Clara sneered. "Not to mention that stupid, shiny, 'custom-tailored suit,' he always brags about."

A tightly knotted black tie was held by a custom gold, pearl-encrusted tie tack in the shape of a cross. His left hand across his ample stomach held a white, leather-bound Bible. His right arm snuggled across his wife's shoulder behind her neck. His face carried a respectful but imposing, almost stern, sort of smile.

Clara's attractive mom wore a conservative wool skirt that ended just below the knee and a white silk blouse with frills along the collar, accented by a string of pearls. Her makeup looked as painted-on as a Medieval portrait, heavy and dense. Held in place with about a can of hairspray, her hair was swept up in a classic beehive. It looked as hard and pointed as a Crusader's battering ram. She neither smiled nor frowned—more a neutral stare.

Clara was dressed in a wool, gray skirt, a high-necked, white blouse buttoned to the top, complemented by a closely-woven, multi-colored linen vest decorated with delicately-embroidered flowers. A sterling silver cross dangled from a thin silver chain around her neck.

"Only thing real, I mean, that I really care about, is the cross."

"Clara, Clara James," I finally said.

"Damn right, I knew you knew," she said, now with a bright smile–just as surprising as her language. "Now you wanna talk or you just gonna sit there shit-faced blushin?"

The Southern gentleman in me was shocked at her *chutzpa.* And smitten.

"So you're a Jew, aren't you?" she asked.

Please God, I thought, finally coming out of my shy fog. *Please, not another "Have you accepted Christ into your life?"*

How she knew? No surprise really, since we had our own picture in the paper—*Abe Cohen's Family Store, Fine Clothes from Our Family to Yours*—embarrassing, but at least not like the James's Second Coming. When Dad met Mom, it was love at first sight. His happy, sappy smile whenever he was around her shined through even in our black-and-white ad.

"Yes, I am."

"Guess it's my lucky day then," she smiled. " 'Cause after everything my asshole Daddy says, I've always wanted to get to know what a real fuckin Jew is like."

"I have two sets of clothes," she said a few days later, as we stood by her locker just before homeroom. "The vestal virgin ones, I wear from home," patting her frilly blouse, "and these," pulling out a short skirt and a low-cut top like treasures.

She wasn't a classic beauty. She still had bits of acne and too much eyeliner. But she was very cute. And her cleavage, as exposed as possible within the school regulations, long legs and blond hair were enough to make most guys' eyes pop out—mine definitely included.

"See how I'm not really smilin," Clara told me when she saw me looking at 'the picture' in the *Chatterbox*. "Daddy said, 'Let's all smile as if Christ has just arisen, put all the niggers back on plantations, and cleansed all the Jews.'" Her face tensed. "Oh Donny, that's so horrible. I shouldn't have told you."

"Doesn't surprise me. I've heard that stuff all my life—the South!"

"Shit, that's just terrible. He threatened to ground me forever if I didn't smile, but I tightened up my lips so any goddamned idiot could see it was fake."

I hadn't. But I said, "I see what you mean."

"And I think Mama hates him too. Says most men she's ever known aren't worth the ground to spit on."

"Why do you cuss so much?" I asked her a week after we'd met. "You cuss like a sailor. I mean, I'm a guy and..."

"Never, ever, ever around my folks. Not allowed," she answered. "Clara pure-white-virgin is what I'm supposed to be. I'd be crucified. But everywhere else, it's my freedom. My chance to show all these kids what bullshit they're all listenin to.

"And I just can't stand all these goddamned lily-white, gossipy, snot-nosed girls dyin to fuck around but too scared and intimidated by my father and his bullshit 'you'll go to hell' to do anything about it.

"And the guys are just as full of it. Two types. The church guys, actually buyin into tryin to live the celibate-till-married crap and jerkin off every night since they're so fuckin frustrated. And the football guys–their Susie-good-shoe church girlfriends drivin 'em crazy by not lettin 'em get any—scared of gettin a reputation. So then they ask me out, figurin since I talk that way and don't take any shit from 'em and it tantalizes 'em and they try to feel me up so they can brag about gettin some from the minister's wild daughter. And sometimes, I let 'em, to tell the truth, but never all the way. Just when they think they're gonna get it all, I send 'em on their way. Freaks 'em out. And they hate me for it and they tell everybody I'm a slut."

The next day, I watched her tear off a white envelope I'd secretly taped to her locker.

"Probably some shitty put-down from some guy," she said.

"Open it, you never know," I said with a smile.

At the end of a Valentine's Day card, after the *Be my,* I'd crossed out *Valentine,* and written in *Slut.*

She kissed me so hard I thought my big front teeth would break. Our opposite worlds clanged together like magnets.

CHAPTER THREE

A year later, about 3 p.m., hours before the fire, my folks had packed the family up in their brand-new 1965 Ford Country Squire station wagon and driven thirty miles south on Route 29, the two-lane blacktop to Greensboro, North Carolina, for my cousin's *Bar Mitzvah.*

I told them I was too sick to go. "Bad cold, Mom."

"You'll be sorry, honey," she said. "They'll have lots of your favorite, smoked whitefish."

I'd just turned nineteen. My entire family was going away for the weekend and I'd be alone in my bedroom, clean sheets and all, with my girlfriend. Whitefish?

Although, truth be told, it did give me a moment's pause—whitefish!

On the way, they would pass Ballou Park. The 150-acre city park was nicknamed Max's Park by my family, after my Great-Grandfather Max. He'd sold the land to the city after timbering it in the 1880s. He used the profits to open our family's clothing store.

As a small boy, I loved to swing there on the wooden plank seats suspended on fifteen-foot chains, pushed by Odessa Matthews. Christened Aunt O'dee by me at eighteen months, she was Mom's five-day-a-week, live-in Negro maid and my nanny for years. Her daughter May, five years older than me, often swung right beside me, and always higher.

In the mid-fifties, Dad steamed hot as his breakfast coffee after Elizabeth Gant, owner of the local paper, the *Danville Recorder*, successfully strong-armed the city council into taking down all those swings rather than, as she said in her weekly editorial, letting black kids "infect" them.

Clara snuck over after my folks left, telling her mother that she was going to the library to research a paper on the history of tobacco.

She'd never been to my house. I was still amazed that she'd be attracted to me, the big-nosed, pimply-faced Jew who ran around taking pictures at school with his hand-me-down camera.

She and I lay naked on a mattress on the black, heartwood-walnut floor of my second-story bedroom. I liked being right on top of that floor, caressing those gorgeous planks rather than suspended feet above them on a bed frame.

The black light on my ceiling made the day-glow numbers on the face of my clock—the base of a John Coltrane statue holding a tiny copper sax—shine weakly in the dark. It also brought to life the heart and "I love you, Clara" that I'd smeared on the ceiling with liquid detergent so that my mother couldn't see it in regular light.

Even in the dimness, my Selmer VI tenor sax, nestled in its stand on the other side of the mattress, gleamed like polished gold to me. I'd bought it with 700 dollars I'd earned beating nails for years at two-fifty an hour with Mr. E.

On the wall by the bed, posters of my jazz saints, Miles Davis and Trane, blessed us from above. Make me half as good as you guys, I prayed every night.

I shuffled my deck of cards and showed Clara the queen of hearts.

"Kiss it," I said.

"Kiss my ass. You drive me crazy with your fuckin card tricks."

"It's the only way an ugly guy like me can keep a girl as beautiful as you. Come on, just a little kiss. I love you."

Clara shook her head, the bells in her hair rattling along with her laugh, and kissed it.

"Now put it in the middle of the deck."

She did. I shuffled the deck.

"Now tap the deck."

"Oh Jesus," she said. She tapped.

I slammed the deck onto the floor, cards crashing and flying in all directions.

"Now roll over and feel your butt," I said.

She pulled the queen of hearts from between her cheeks.

"Holy fuckin ghost," she yelled.

I'd come to love hearing a minister's daughter cuss like that—in Christian.

She grabbed my head and started kissing my face until it must have looked like it was painted pink.

A truck with a loud, hole-punched muffler pulled up outside, then went silent. Clara's lips froze against my cheek.

"Damn," she said.

"What?"

"Daddy's goons. He sends 'em to follow me sometimes, just to make me think he always knows where I am and what I'm doin."

She rolled over and reached for the black and purple sheet that hung over my floor-to-ceiling window. We'd tie-dyed the sheet to replace the white crinoline drape my younger sister had made in sewing class from post-Civil War era petticoats. "It's so cute," Mom had insisted, as she inflicted it on my bedroom.

The truck door slammed.

Clara pulled back the sheet and peeked out.

"Hey, it's Mr. E," she said, looking across the street at his truck parked in front of the Reform Temple my family belonged to.

"He must've just blown the muffler," I said. "He wouldn't stand for driving around like that if he'd had any time to fix it."

They'd never met, but she recognized him from the pictures plastered on my wall—the two of us holding various carpentry tools and me always with a big, goofy grin—in front of finished jobs and of him and his wife at my *Bar Mitzvah*. And the picture he reluctantly let me take of him with his tool belt around his waist, holding my sax to his mouth.

"You is one strange fella," he'd said that day with a snicker, a pucker, and an awful bleet.

"Yeah," I said to Clara. "He's come back to lay on the last coat of shellac on the temple's pews. Takes twenty-four hours to dry. So they'll be ready before services tomorrow night."

Without putting on her bra or panties, Clara yanked on her skirt and light cotton blouse and ran barefoot down the stairs and through the foyer, slamming the heavy maple door I'd carved a year before with a scene of deer running through a tobacco field, rabbits scrambling out of their way, a farmer with a star of David on the front of his bib overalls firing at them with his shotgun. I'd not told my folks about the Jewish farmer part when I started the project—no one had ever known of a Jewish tobacco farmer and certainly not one who hunted—but they still bragged about my work to visitors. I stumbled into my pants and ran after her.

Mr. E was dressed as usual in a freshly-pressed, plaid cotton shirt and blue jeans, his Wolverine brand work boots always freshly polished to a shiny black.

"Dress with the same care as your work," he'd say. My messy fashion rebellion always annoyed him.

"You sound like my father," I said once in a rare pushback.

"I'll take that compliment. Can't see no problem with lookin clean and neat like him."

He pulled some tools from the truck, turned and walked toward the new gray-granite steps we'd recently replaced at the sixty-year-old temple, *Beth Sholom,* house of peace. Clara raced toward him.

"Hi, I'm Clara," she shouted as fast and loud as an out-of-breath fluttering Southern accent could manage, "and I've heard so much about you from Donny. You're living proof of the falsehood of my father's bullsh…" She slapped her hand across her mouth, stopping herself from cursing for the first time I'd ever seen. "…of my father's contemptuous hatefulness."

Mr. E cocked his head back, a smile mixed with a question mark written on his face.

"I'm tickled pink to meet you," she said, standing there starry-eyed, in full blush, like an awe-struck teenage girl meeting a rock 'n' roll idol.

"Well thank you kindly, Clara." He was opening his mouth to say more when I caught up, bare-chested and shoeless.

"Thought you was goin to Greensboro with your family," he said to me.

"I told Mom I was sick." I hoped he saw my pleading look.

He frowned.

"Watch out. Start that lyin and it gets to be a habit. Excuse me, miss," he said, as he took me aside. He put his big, calloused hand on the back of my neck. "You bein safe, boy? Don't 'spect you ready fer any little Donnys runnin 'round quite yet."

I slipped the corner of a Trojan packet out of my pocket.

"Don't tell, please," I begged.

As my face inflamed, his chiseled into a grin. He patted me on the shoulder and whispered, "Would've prob'bly done the same thing when I was yer age with such a pretty thing. Though bein a grown man and father, don't know if your daddy or momma or my wife would 'preciate me sayin such. I'll keep it to myself. Now go on, I got work to do."

"Nice to meet ya, young lady," he said, doffing his *86 Lumber Yard* cap.

"The pleasure is all mine," Clara said, with a slight curtsey, holding out her right hand to shake his. I was amazed—I'd never seen her act so daintily feminine.

For an awkward moment, they stood there, an adoring look on her face, her arm dangling straight out into the air, Mr. E looking down at it with a mildly befuddled expression.

I stood by the two of them, watching their slow-motion-handshake waltz, wondering what would happen next.

His eyes shifted to mine for an instant, then looked back at her, the corners of his lips raised in a Mona Lisa slight smile, if a black man, or any man, can have such. He cleared his throat, then put the palm of his right hand limply under hers and gently patted the top of it with his left.

"And mine as well, Miss Clara."

She threw her arms around his neck and hugged him before he could resist. His body went as rigid as a steel beam. His arms hung limp at his sides and his forehead jerked up into a mass of wrinkles. After an eternity, me holding my breath and nailed in place, Clara stepped back, her smile as bright as a summer day.

"Donny loves you so much, and now I do too."

His body still as a scarecrow, Mr. E's head swung side to side in a quick look up and down the street. Unlocking himself with a spasmed shake of his head and shoulders, he pulled a red-and-white-checkered handkerchief from his back pocket, wiped his forehead, then clenched it in his hand. His face relaxed into a soft smile, almost approaching a laugh. He whistled a long note.

"I can see why Donny-boy here cares so much about you too, Miss Clara. You break the mold—two peas in a pod."

I let out the breath I hadn't noticed I'd been holding.

Mr. E raised his hammer to his forehead in a salute. They both laughed. He turned away from us, waving his hand over his head, chuckling. He walked up the stairs, unlocked the temple door, and walked in.

He'd be in shackles the next time I saw him.

CHAPTER FOUR

A while later, lazing around again in bed, we heard his truck pull away. It was dusk, cooling, the humid air sweet with the fragrance of the flowers my mother had planted outside the window in the rectangular pine box she'd paid me to build.

I took a deep inhale and looked out at the temple. I saw, for the thousandth time, the three-foot-high, five-foot-wide, white marble lintel carved sixty years before with the words "*Beth Sholom,* House of Peace." The building was ten blocks away from the Orthodox synagogue, which housed the "authentic Jews," as their rabbi, Tichter, called them. He'd so indoctrinated the girls in his congregation that the only males they would touch or hug were their fathers. If I saw one at services or in public, girls I'd known and hugged all my life, they would extend and jiggle their arms in front of themselves as if hugging a big beach ball, careful to avoid touching me. Between them and my sisterly Reform female friends, Jewish sex expressed itself only in my imagination. Praying to my Jewish God had never worked, so thank you, Jesus, for Clara.

I hated Tichter's extreme brand of Judaism. What made a Jew "authentic" anyway? Didn't having the tip of my dick cut off at birth automatically qualify me?

But sitting in the hickory and cane rocker on our filigreed front porch, or just walking out the front door every day, I was filled with a cascade of mixed emotions and doubt about our own Reform Temple—where Moses's stern glare, from the fifteen-foot-high stained-glass window peered down from the temple's red-bricked parapet—and Judaism itself. Dad, through his only avocation other than golf, had labored at that window, by himself in our basement, for over a year.

"Why don't we sing at services?" I'd asked my Mom when I was a young boy, as we listened to the *goy,* non-Jewish, choir hired to sing our songs and prayers for us during services. Were we afraid of our own voices, or simply too lazy or embarrassed or proper to let ourselves open up and let the spirit course through our souls, like my black friends did at their church?

And why Moses, the seminal Jew, carrying the Ten Commandments, had left out an eleventh, "Love thy neighbor as thyself," didn't surprise me.

"You can fuck the non-Jewish girls," the unsaid and unwritten words had always been clear to me, "because they're trash, never to be married and sanctified." Even the *Torah* told men to go to the next village to mess around. Since Jews of that time often lived within geographically tight communities, the next village was usually not Jewish.

But I loved Clara, even if they said I shouldn't. Fuck them!

And I'd been told all my life that we Jews were special—God's children! If we were the loving people God had chosen to represent the pinnacle of his creation, why were we forever persecuted by people like Clara's father? And his mentor, Lynchburg's Jerry Falwell, who said we were the devil's seed, Christ's killers?

"What ya thinkin?" Clara asked as she jogged her fingers through my hair.

Her voice boomeranged me back to her.

I reached out beyond my bed through the torn window screen and picked one of the deep purple flowers, put it behind Clara's ear, kissed her on the lips, then ran my fingers from her neck to the base of her spine. Hate the Southern damp or not—it makes skin baby soft. I carefully massaged her calves, knees, the insides of her thighs, then her tummy, her ribs, and up to her breasts, waiting for the superficial muscles to relax, then probing judiciously, deeper, into the underlying areas of bunched up tension.

"Touching slow and gentle and deep is the way to a woman's heart and love," my childhood friend May, now, according to her, Danville's most expensive Negro lady-of-the-night, had instructed me years before. "If you don't rush the fuck, then it waltzes into lovemaking."

Clara purred.

"Saxfingers. That's what I should call you. Your hands play me like one of your songs."

She looked at me with the quietest of smiles, plucked another flower from the window box, and nestled the stem into my hair.

"Nicotiana. Been grown 'round here since the 1800s," she whispered. "Ornamental hybrid of the tobacco family."

In typical boy fashion, I'd never thought about what they were called, even though people planted them all over the city in deference to Danville's post-Civil War mantle of "The World's Biggest Tobacco Market."

"Redneck gold," I said.

I placed the record player's needle on Coltrane's ferocious rendition of "Body and Soul." We listened, cuddled up and cozy as two little puppies.

"Sounds like an angry rooster," Clara said.

"Cock-a-doodle-doo," I sang. "He's the king rooster. Nobody scratches the notes as fast and furious as him."

Thinking of scratching and clucking made me think of chickens. Which made me think of food. Which made me think of the smoked whitefish I was missing in Greensboro. I ran to the refrigerator. No whitefish. I opened a leftover jar of its bastard cousin, gefilte fish.

Years before, I'd watched in horror as my Russian immigrant grandmother, Bessie, wrestled out a live river carp she'd been soaking for two days in her bathtub filled with cold, salted water ("to pull out za dirty stuffs"), killing and slitting and scraping and slamming it to pieces, then soaking the mess again ("takes twice to get rid of za dirty stuffs"), then insulting carrots and onions by pulverizing and mushing them into the blend, then boiling and refrigerating it until it was a bland, pale, solid mash. I'd never understood why, but ever since Clara had first tried it, right after Passover, with horseradish, she'd developed a taste for it. Why Jews started eating this blasphemy in the first place should have been the fifth question.

Perhaps they'd picked up stranded carp that had plopped from the parted waters of the Red Sea when Moses led them from the Egyptian Pharaohs' pursuing chariots. Perhaps, being so famished and desperate for something, anything, to put on their tasteless *matzohs*, and being knifeless, they were forced to beat them into pate on the briny rocks of the opposite shore. Ever since, perhaps as some punishment by the god of carp, Jews have been forced to eat, and to pretend to like, this cruel debasement of an innocent fish at every one of their holiday meals. And perhaps, as my Jewish God's retribution for my getting into the heart and pants of a white-as-a-gardenia Christian girl, I was now cursed to accept that she adored the vile mix.

In any case, my mother never guessed the why of my sudden hunger for the stuff. She must have been happy that at least it was cheaper than whitefish.

I brought it back to the bedroom. We ate a bit off of each other's bellies.

"Hey," Clara said, digging a tiny pinch of Grandma's hot, homemade horseradish from her bellybutton and fearlessly, yet carefully, placing it between her legs. "If it does that to my tongue, what'll it do if I..."

Straightaway, I saw our night of romance turning into a visit to the emergency room. But her love for the condiment seemed to satisfy twice, heating her to desire.

I stood up and grabbed my sax.

"This one's for you," I said, putting Coleman Hawkins on the record player.

As I struggled to play along with "Sophisticated Lady," eyes closed, I was consumed by the rhythm of the jazz. I imagined Hawkins, or even someone as crazy as Ornette Coleman, might have considered the scene a disgusting insult to the name, if not the intent, of the ballad. But who was I to deny whatever inexplicable contentment it brought her by way of me–and gefilte fish?

After I forced myself through the first head of the song though, a flickering light started dancing across and bothering my shut eyelids. I stopped playing and opened my eyes to a soft ruddy glow slowly shimmering across Clara's cascaded blond hair.

She looked up at me from the bed. The skin on her face was almost translucent, the strange light exposing tiny pastel, bluish veins under her cheeks.

"Why'd you quit playin?" she asked, frowning, disappointed that I'd interrupted her gefilte frenzy. I stared down at her, the light now intensifying to a reddish Piedmont clay glow that licked her face, flushing it with a fiery radiance like those of the sinners our art class had studied in Hieronymus Bosch's hell.

I sniffed.

"Do you smell smoke?" I said.

She sniffed a few times then pulled back the curtain and looked across the street through the window.

"Holy shit, Donny, Jesus fuckin Christ, your temple's on fire!"

CHAPTER FIVE

I turned to the window and ripped away the curtain, Clara still shrieking.

Snake-tongued flames flicked in and out of the temple's high front corner window. Puffs of smoke seeped out around the edges.

I carefully placed my horn onto the mattress, zipped up my disappointment, ran down the stairs, and flew out the door and across the street.

Between looking up at the fire and the wan light of the crescent moon, I barely stopped short of a tall, thick man facing the inferno as he backed away from the heat. A pointy white sack covered his head.

"Fucking fantastic, ain't it, Sammy?" he hollered, hearing my footsteps behind him, as he turned toward me. Through the cutouts in his hood, I saw his eyes. Their rapturous glow drained in an instant to plain hate and fear as he realized that I wasn't his expected friend.

"Fuck!" he yelled as he jumped back.

I grabbed at him. He stank the rancid smell of working men who rarely take baths or use deodorant. I knew it well from the tobacco and mill workers who shopped at Dad's store. My hands slipped down his gritty, slick arms as he pushed me away. He kneed me in the balls, beat me down across the shoulders, shoved me onto the ground, and ran.

I heard a cracking noise from Dad's Moses window. From the ground, I looked at it, high up in the front of the temple. Smoke poured from Moses's ears.

I forced myself up and stood there, frozen—pictures flashing of my grandparents and uncles and aunts and cousins and friends walking under that window so many times for events and holidays.

As the flames shot from the glass, I shuddered at the thought that our 200-year-old *Torah* was being immolated, like the German Jews who'd hidden it during the Holocaust. It had been dug up after the war by survivors and brought overseas to our congregation. Its survival was a highly emotional metaphor, a "fuck you" to the Nazis—we Jews are still alive.

Still, I did nothing, watching the fire like a drive-in movie.

A part of me that I tried never to feel or admit fought off a cheer, almost a prayer, from rising from my gut: *Let the fucking place burn down to the ground.*

The twanging of metal and brick as it expanded and buckled reminded me of the ukulele Arthur Godfrey strummed and plucked on his popular TV variety show. He looked grandfatherly and told funny jokes. Why couldn't they burn down his Florida mansion—the one I'd heard about with the famous "No dogs or Jews" sign at the gates? Why did he hate Jews, me? *And why,* I thought, *did God fuck around so much with Jews in the first place?*

My muscles remained locked, voices screaming in my head, *Do something!*

"I'm gonna Jew you down today," men would say to me at Dad's store. I'd cringe inside, wearing the plastered smile Dad insisted I maintain. "A smile doesn't cost us anything, but a lost customer does," he'd say.

My face muscles twitched at the thought, a "fuck you, Dad," rearing up along with the instantaneous and ever-present self-hate and guilt.

I finally moved closer. Heat gusted out of the temple like a blast furnace, then belched a furious, whirling howl that matched my own internal maelstrom. Like flickering frames of a horror movie, pictures of Jews burning in ovens, screaming, flashed through my mind.

Like feuding brothers, two voices, Hated and Hateful, screamed inside me. One moaned at the flaming desecration and swore at the all the Jew-haters and the Klanner arsonist while the other roared thanks to him for burning down that symbol of constipated, hypocritical, spiritually bankrupt Jew-dom.

I watched the fire burning away the darkness, my body still paralyzed—except for my hands. As if ashamed by my immobility, they pumped open, then shut, then clenched into hard fists. The ache in my arms shoved the memory of a tattooed woman into my mind and shamed me out of my trifling litanies.

"Never forget the Holocaust, our devastation," the visiting lecturer with the thick German accent had shouted to our *Bar Mitzvah* group of twelve-year-olds as she yanked back the sleeve of her frilly white blouse to reveal the tattooed concentration camp numbers on her forearm. She was a small woman, under five feet tall, but the tattoo seemed enormous against her skinny arm.

"In Biblical times, the Egyptians, then the Romans, hated and killed us—then the Catholics in the Spanish Inquisition. Even after a thousand years in the Ottoman Empire, where the Jews were the highest of officials, we were eventually slaughtered.

My entire family was murdered in Germany, a country we Jews thought was the most civilized.

"I was the only survivor of my brothers, sister, mother, father and grandfather, and I only survived because we little ones figured out that the guards would not look in the cesspools behind the barracks. I can never forget how we stank and disgusted ourselves, with no clean water to bathe in when we climbed out. But still, we jumped into that filth day after day to avoid our death. I was only four." Tapping her tattoo, "We must always be on guard. Never assume you are safe. For Jews, it is not *if*, but always *when*!"

I'd taken her words to heart. Was it even right for me to feel happy, to have fun, to trust, when so many had died simply for being Jews? Here in the deep South, our hundred families were familiar with her warnings and her grief. Did singing and dancing insult the memory of the murdered innocents she'd imprinted on our imaginations? Our Christian choir and our rabbi's joyless sermons seemed to say so.

The face of Moses blew out in a ring of smoke. I shifted my weight from foot to foot, like the old men did when praying. Beads of sweat dripped salt into my eyes and partnered painfully with the tears. I wiped them away with my shirtsleeve.

Through my dazed fixity, from the corner of my eye, I saw Clara standing beside me.

But, "Fuck who you can't love and love who you can't fuck," ran through my mind like a bad song.

"Fuck them all," I screamed to her.

"What?" she screamed back.

I wobbled, dizzy from the smoke and heat and confusion. I puked onto the grass. It tasted of...gefilte fish...and hate: for the South, for hypocritical Judaism, for myself, and for having to sneak around my love for her.

"Shit, Donny," Clara shouted, "what're you gonna do? You gotta do something. You cain't just stand here pukin and swearin and starin."

I grabbed her hard by the arm, threw her to the ground and ripped off her panties. Some Southern-infected part of me laughed mean as I revenge-fucked Danville's Jew-hating Baptist preacher's own imagined vestal virgin under our burning temple, in some sort of perverse irony like the fiery crosses at their Klan rallies, while she sobbed.

That such a mad fantasy could pop out from my subconscious at that moment instantly convinced me that I must be as insane, as deranged as the part of the South that I hated—Ku Klux Kike.

I turned to her and said, "Better get out of here fast." She nodded her head, kissed me on the cheek, and ran.

Looking back at the inferno, I could almost see the copper ancestors' plaque, just inside the temple door, melting into oblivion. It was lit with the names of Great-Grandpa Max and my grandparents and relatives and people who had raised and loved me. I could almost hear their souls screaming, "Save us." No matter their faults, they were family. And no Klanner was going to enjoy a victory over their memory or over the destruction of the *Torah* our German cousins had fought so hard to preserve. Their voices in my head insisted that I could not be the one to let it go up in flames.

Above it all, the words of the real men of Judaism, the Israelis, who kicked ass against their enemies, echoed in my head, "Never again!"

My body jumped forward. If anyone was going to burn the fucking place down, it would be me, goddammit, not some potato-sack-headed Klanner.

I ran back to the house, called the fire department, and grabbed Dad's temple key. But I didn't even need it—the temple door was open.

"Strange," my mind's voice said, "Mr. E would never leave the place unlocked."

As I entered the foyer, the heat blew me back in a whoosh that knocked me down. I jumped up and grabbed a *tallit,* prayer shawl, hanging by the doorway, and wrapped it around my face. Smoke as thick and black as camp coffee poured around me when I stepped into the sanctuary. Even the Everlasting Light, always on above the ark, was enveloped. Coughing, feet burning, crouched low, I stumbled by rote through the dark cloud the fifty feet to the pulpit. Small flames erupted on each side of the aisle as the fire found Mr. E's shellac on successive sets of pews. I slid apart the wooden ark doors, the first time ever without saying the opening prayer, put my head in for a breath and yanked the *Torah* from its cradle—then staggered back outside.

CHAPTER SIX

"You all right, son?"

I'd passed out in the grass.

I looked up into the face of a sinewy, crouching black man. His head sprouted a flaming red, wild, untamed Afro, the curly strands shooting like sparks. He held my head in his hands with a worried look countered by a quirky smile, almost a laugh.

"Name's Ditto," he'd told me with a wry grin four months earlier, on his first visit to Dad's store. "All my family's mens fer four generations been called Red. Name started in slave times. Short fer Red Man. On 'count of our hair," pointing to his head. "So my legal's Redman the fourth. By the time I came 'round, though, with Grandaddy an Daddy all livin in the same house, shit, they got tired of three, now four, mens answerin ever-time somebody said, 'Hey, Red.' So they just called me Ditto. Been stuck with it ever since. Nice to meet ya," he'd said, hand outstretched.

I hadn't said a thing.

He wore bell-bottoms with beads sewn down the side, orange day-glow socks radiating out from shiny black tuxedo shoes. He was a head taller than me. A white cross was painted inside a pink heart on the front of his suede vest. When he turned to the sound of someone laughing behind him, the embroidered face of Jesus stared at me.

He must have noticed my head and eyes rising up and staring, mouth slack-jawed, at his gold-crowned front tooth with a cross cut out in the middle.

"Ain't nothin wrong with the tooth. I just likes the look. Now close that gawp-mouth full of them pearly whites of yers and help me find some fine bell-bottoms as these here is getting worn through."

"Nice to meet you, Ditto," I'd said. I shook his hand, my face flushed.

Red "Ditto" Combs looked to be about forty-five years old, six foot plus, skinny, maybe 160 pounds. I'd heard about him from complaining white customers but couldn't have imagined how he really looked until he walked into the store. He'd shown up in town about six months before. No one knew exactly where he'd come from or why or where he'd disappear. He walked all over town, hours a day, babbling and preaching the love of Christ for his fellow men and women. He'd walk up to anybody, black or white, reach out his long, slender arm and delicate hand, smile and say, "Howdy, hope all's well with ya. Jesus loves ya. A-men."

Most whites wrote him off as deranged, perhaps another mind-mangled war vet.

"Crazy nigger," they'd say, spitting their soggy tobacco sludge into a spittoon or out onto the street. "I'd kick his ass 'cept he's so fuckin nuts, he might go crazy on me."

White women clung a little tighter to their children or husbands when they saw him. Blacks would say, "That Ditto's as slick and polished as apples at the grocery store."

I'd heard that he sang like a man possessed in the choir at Danville's largest black church, ministered by our family friend Reverend Joseph Rampbell.

"Has a fine voice, but volume dynamics are not in his realm of understanding," Reverend Rampbell had told me.

He whistled, danced jigs to music only he could hear, and giggled, roared, or groaned for no obvious reason.

"Ain't no shame to bein strange to mens and womens, longs you normal with God," Ditto told me.

He'd snap pictures of any and everyone, black or white, with his little Kodak Brownie camera.

"Gonna send these pictures straight ta God fer his blessin," he'd say, shaking that camera up into the air like it was a direct line, "a lightnin bolt to heaven." Then he'd just walk away, humming some gospel tune.

I always wondered if it even had any film in it.

Whenever he met a youngster, he'd pull out a red-and-white-striped cinnamon stick. White mothers would quickly grab it away and toss it. Black-tainted. Crazy-infected. Negroes would laugh, shrug and say, "Ditto, you is a piece of work. Now, git on outta here." He'd just shrug, hand another cinnamon stick to the kid, smile, skip a little caper, then saunter off.

White men seemed to have an almost perverse respect for him. For his uniqueness. They couldn't set him into one of their tidy Negro type-cast containers, their neatly conceived categories of "niggerdom."

"Who knows whut that crazy nigger might do?" They'd shake their heads, exasperated, ashamed of their impotence. They couldn't back him down because he'd squish right out of their baiting and jeering and demands for servile respect with another full smile, "God loves ya, sir."

Every time some white guy complained about Ditto's latest encounter, I'd smile inside.

Ditto liked to whistle at a caked-up renowned white gal named Sylvia Campbell. At her church, the little Apostolic Christian Tabernacle, a few doors down from Clara's father's mammoth church, Sylvia always presented herself in full buxom glory—in her handmade push-up bra and low-cut elaborate dress, usually of a flowery motif. Her church had a disproportionately large percentage of single men, all just wanting a peek at her latest awe-inspiring mammary presentation. Even her fire-and-brimstone minister, Reverend Robert Marsh, another reputed Klan member, deferred to her.

" 'She delivers the men for me to try to save,' " Clara told me she heard him confide to her dad. "Probably jerks off in his study every Saturday night thinking of her while he's writin his Sunday sermon."

"You know Miss Sylvie?" he asked me when he suddenly appeared outside in front of our house days after the fire, after asking me how I was doing. "She 'bout the finest lookin white woman I ever seen. I swear, she gots the soul of a nigga gal," he laughed and slapped his thigh. "Got 'em, show 'em," he chuckled. "Make you pasty-faced, sex-sick, white boys come all over yerselves. Praise God." Without waiting for an answer, he sauntered off with a "woo-wee."

According to Clara, Ditto would show up in front of Sylvia's church every Sunday morning right before services, clicking away with his little camera.

"Yo, Miss Sylvie," he'd shout.

How he knew her name was a mystery. Blacks and whites went to separate churches, myself and a few others excepted, so he couldn't have ever met her in person.

"God bless the birds, the sky, the trees, an what you got, so bee-yu-tee-full! Hallelujah, praise the Lord," he'd sing-song as he clicked away. "You is God's highest art."

Every now and then, once she understood what was happening, she'd wave back to him, just barely, with the faintest of smiles.

"I get up early sometimes on Sundays just to go out and watch him," Clara told me. "He's so damn funny. It's almost like some kind of vaudeville act."

One Sunday, according to Clara, some of her dad's congregants, Jerry Joe Bursey and a few of his buddies, just couldn't stand what was happening right next to their church. Before services, dressed in their Sunday best, they ran over, ready to smash him, crazy or not. "Teach that crazy nigger a lesson."

Ditto grinned at them and started preaching. "Praise Jesus, boys, ain't she Eve from the garden? Yessuh, ain't nothin prettier than such a fine white woman. Hit me if ya likes, but I cain't help but thinkin ain't no nigga boozoms anywhere near as purdy. You all is lucky to be white boys cuz ain't no nigga ever gets no piece of pie like them cherries on two mounds of 'nilla ice cream. Woo-wee, you white boys is so lucky, yes, sir."

Jerry Joe and his friends couldn't deny or refute any of Ditto's pronouncements, his truths. They couldn't call him an "uppity nigger" because he was only telling them how great it was to be white—and how unfortunate he was to be black.

Ditto clicked their pictures, said, "God gonna bless you boys special when he sees these pictures," then just sashayed away, grinning, cursing "a nigger's bad luck," leaving the white boys regretting that they had wasted their time with him instead of just watching Sylvia.

"Crazy nigger," they all exhaled, sensing they'd been had, but not exactly knowing how.

"Can ya talk?" Ditto, squatting next to me, asked as I lay outside the burning temple. He gently lifted me to sitting.

"Uh, yeah," I said, coughing out a little smoke. I reached out, touching the *Torah* to make sure I'd really succeeded.

"What's that thang?" Ditto asked.

"*Torah,*" I answered automatically. "Jewish holy scroll. Old Testament. First five books of the Bible."

"You almost got yerself kilt fer God's words? Praise God an you too. Woo-wee! God bless ya," he said with an ecstatic bedazzling smile. "I seen that Klan man knock ya down, just as I was turnin the corner, comin home. Saw the whole danged thang. Man, he just tossed ya aside like you was light as a feather. Came over soon's he left. Would've jumped 'em myself 'cept I'm no fightin man. Lover, not fighter, like Jesus," suddenly laughing. "Not to mention what they'd do to my nigger ass fer catchin 'em. But I'll back ya up if ya need it, I'll back ya up."

How, in God's good name, I thought, *would or could he ever back me up?*

"Thanks, Ditto," I said.

Abruptly, he jerked his head up, tilted his ear. "Fire trucks comin. Better get my black ass outta here. You take care, ya hear?"

For a few moments, he looked deep into my eyes, running his hand through my hair with his fine, long fingers. He smiled, his eyes moist with concern. I felt weak, but soothed and peaceful. Somehow, beyond reason, I did feel protected. He pulled a cinnamon stick out of his pocket, handed it to me, and kissed me on the forehead.

"An now that we's friends and I'm yer protecter fer life, you can call me by my natural name, Red. Resurrected only fer my best friends."

"Uh, thanks, Dit…Red."

"It'll all be okay with ya, I promise. Jesus loves ya, a-men."

He rocketed upright, burst into a big laugh, jumped, kicked his heels on both sides, and strode away, twirling and waving—just as the fire trucks turned the corner onto the street.

I stood up, carefully caressing the *Torah.* The firemen arrived.

"That a baby?" one of them asked.

I lifted the cloth cover that dressed the *Torah,* exposing the white scrolls. He shrugged and ran inside.

Ten minutes later, I watched as they hauled a body out.

CHAPTER SEVEN

As the firemen mopped up and packed their trucks, grunting and cursing their smoke-sodden wetness, I stood in front of the smoldering building, haunted by the sight of the first dead body I'd ever seen. I still clutched the *Torah* tight to my chest, my only comfort, like some ecclesiastic teddy bear.

Fire Chief Homer Gilboy walked up to me. "You okay, boy?" His pale white face was strained but kind, creases all over. "What's that thing?"

"*Torah,* first five books of the Old Testament," I said in a robotic monotone, stuck in place again, staring at the smolder.

"You know this fella?" he asked me as he stopped the gurney and lifted the sheet. I nodded yes when I saw Mr. Albert Rippe, the oldest member of our congregation. His blackened face looked like some burnt zombie, the left side of his beard singed off, his left cheek and ear now charred bone, the eye exploded and sunk into a mushy mass in the socket. I threw up again. After the ambulance had taken his body away, I could almost hear his favorite saying, "Everybody wants to live long, but nobody wants to get old."

I knew that he would have gladly sacrificed his life to save the *Torah* in my arms. I also knew that I would have done the opposite had I only noticed him. In that moment, the *Torah* seemed almost profane. As if from someone else, from a place in myself that I'd never experienced, a deep, base moan rose from my gut.

Gilboy put his hand on my shoulder, "Sure you're okay? I'll be wantin to come talk to you after we finish cleanin up."

"I live across the street," I whispered, my lungs aching from the smoke. "Come over when you're ready. I'll leave the door open."

"That old man must've..." the fire chief said when he walked in about an hour later. He went silent and his face twisted into a startled question mark when he saw May, Aunt O'dee's daughter, sitting next to me on the couch, stroking my wet, smudge-stinking hair and face.

May knew my folks were out of town.

"Red called me," she'd said before I could even ask her how she knew about the fire.

The chief took a deep breath.

"The old man must've tried to get out," he said, still staring at May, "but only managed a few steps outta the back office. Smoke that thick..." Then he noticed I was weeping. He shrugged. "When the old wood floors ignited, pretty much the whole place went up. Can I ask you a few questions about what you saw?"

I looked up at him, incredulous. Who gives a shit, I wanted to scream at him. I let a man die. I buried my head in May's lap, crying even louder.

He took off his glasses and rubbed the sides of his nose.

"Though, guess him dyin and all, that ain't the point right this minute. Guess we can talk more another time. You can maybe help me figure out some details about how it got started and such. Get some sleep. G'night."

At the doorway, he looked back again. "Night, May. Sorry."

"Night, Homer," May said, still caressing my head.

I wasn't inclined at that moment to question their first-name familiarity, though it wasn't hard to guess.

CHAPTER EIGHT

The day after the fire, I stood beside the row of fifty-foot red oaks and giant magnolias that separated the Jewish section of Danville's cemetery from the Gentile side. The mourners had walked by my ancestors' headstones engraved with the Star of David, fresh swastikas spray-painted onto several of them. The sunny day failed to lighten me.

Jews bury their dead as soon as possible, often the day after death. There is no embalming or open casket—which is mandated to be a simple wooden crate with holes in the bottom so that the worms can do their diligence with minimal difficulty—"ashes to ashes, dust to dust."

"Our gladness at the saving of our holy *Torah,*" our temple's rabbi said at the Rippe family gravesite, looking at me with a sad smile, "is muted as we mourn the tragic passing of our beloved Albert Rippe."

Clara hid twenty feet away, peeking out from behind a big oak tree. Neither of our folks knew about our relationship.

Returning home, my smoke-drenched clothes still sat in a pile on the floor, reeking like an accusation. I hadn't let my mother wash them. The smell snapped me back to Mr. Rippe.

The thought that I might have rescued him kept breaking my mind into a scrabble of anger, guilt, and confusion. Might I have saved him had I not been so carnally besotted and then frozen in confusion? Might I have run into the temple sooner and noticed him before the smoke was so dense? What difference might those few extra minutes have made to him? I begged God again to forgive me for not saving him. I prayed that he hadn't suffered, that he'd passed out before being burned alive.

And Clara. When I'd first started telling Mr. E about her, he'd said, "Young love, Donny, is like green lumber—all juicy and fresh. But it takes careful attention and seasonin to keep it straight and good."

Until the fire, at least I was sure my relationship with Clara was straight and good—straight, in her case, being a relative term, but definitely good. Before, to me, making love with her had always felt more God-affirming than sitting in a "sacred" building or reading from the *Torah.* But now, the doing of it right before and even during the fire, while Mr. Rippe struggled to live, suddenly felt almost blasphemous. Watching the coffin being lowered into the dirt felt like an indictment.

As I cried, my parents tried to console me, "You couldn't have known, in the smoke."

Decades before, Mr. Rippe had gotten fed up with all the Orthodox synagogue's fanatic rules. "Bad as the Catholics," he'd said. He'd donated a large amount to help found the temple, "Where rules don't get between me and God." He'd been on the Board of Directors ever since. His extreme old age, baggy clothes, wild hair, and facial stubble—"I shave when I feel like it; age earns the right"—scared the little kids until he sent them away squealing and clutching shiny new dimes—big money in those days.

A Hebrew scholar, Mr. Rippe often loudly interrupted the Rabbi's *Torah* readings, correcting them, during services. A week after the fire, at the temple's unburned Sunday school annex, services would feel deafeningly empty to us without those familiar interruptions.

He'd always had his own key to the place and lived a block away so that he could walk over whenever he wished.

"I like to pray whenever I damn well feel like it, day or night. God doesn't wear a watch," he'd say when someone would suggest that he not enter the temple alone to pray at odd hours for fear that he'd forget to lock up or fall and get hurt. "I been here long enough to know how to lock the damned door," he'd reply with a grumpy smile. "I like how still and peaceful and full of God it is when I'm alone here, without a bunch of kids runnin around and makin a racket."

Sometimes he'd fall asleep right in front of the holy ark that held the *Torah.*

"Might be a strange place to snooze," he'd say to folks, "but for me it's like sittin by God's own fireplace—only place I sleep like a newborn."

Rabbi Tichter would have called this a vile sacrilege, though most in our congregation just thought of old man Rippe as kind of sweet and nutty. Since our temple and Tichter's synagogue were only a few blocks apart, Mr. Rippe and the rabbi would often cross paths walking to their respective services on a Saturday morning. Mr. Rippe had complained to Dad that Tichter, who failed to attend the funeral, would turn his head away and refuse to acknowledge or respond to his "Good Shabbas, Rabbi," greeting.

Often, after cradling the *Torah* like a baby in his frail arms, Mr. Rippe would put it back into the ark and go into the rabbi's office, adjacent to the pulpit, and doze off on the couch. He'd either wake up and go home, or the janitor would find him in the morning and send him along.

Save for this time, it cost him his life.

CHAPTER NINE

Two days later, Mr. E was hauled into jail.

"We are proud to announce that we have arrested the suspected perpetrata of the Jew-church fire," Chief of Police Eddie Baker, Jr., commonly known as "The Junior," told an assembled crowd including reporters from the *Danville Recorder* and the *Commercial Appeal,* the smaller county paper.

He sat triumphantly, his signature water moccasin boots—yellowish-golden snake leather with reddish-brown speckled scales—propped on his worn mahogany six-drawer desk piled high with metal baskets stuffed with papers.

I remembered how he'd brag when he'd come into our store to purchase uniforms for his officers or extra-large suits for himself, our store specialty.

"Kilt that snake mysef. A six foota. Bit off its head and had them boots made from its hide. One-of-a-kind, customized just fer me." No one had the temerity to ask him why he would be stupid enough to bite off the head of one of Virginia's most venomous snakes.

"Just hope the next snake he puts in his mouth doesn't kill him," Dad would say, laughing, every time The Junior left the store. "Wouldn't want to lose the uniform orders."

The Junior stood up and hooked his thumbs into a three-inch-wide black belt which struggled to hold up his massive belly. It'd been hand-tooled at the county's "retard workshop," as locals called it, to match the rose and five-pointed star designs on his holster that mirrored his badge. He heaved up his pants by grabbing onto its large, round, brass belt buckle crafted with the initials EBJ.

Our rabbi had been asked to show up at The Junior's office. Dad asked me to go with him to take pictures and to write an article for the *Chatterbox*. He always said it was good to educate the students about Jews and discrimination against us to encourage sympathy.

The Junior spit a dark brown clump into the brass spittoon by his chair, then reached into the back pocket of his blue uniform pants and pulled out a pouch of Red Man chaw. From his front pocket, he retrieved a tiny pearl-handled pocketknife, delicately carved a precise square from the plank and stuffed it into the back of his jaw between his cheek and gum.

"Mah father's little knife," he said, his face flushing with a slight tremor to fight back emotion. "Senior," pronounced Senia, as everyone had called his father during his own thirty-year stint as Danville's sheriff, "handed it to me on his deathbed. That old fart loved whit'len with this itty, bitty thang."

He picked up a small piece of wood from his desk and touched it with the pointed tip of the pocketknife. "Been carvin a little rabbit with it fer my new-born gran-baby—just like Senia would've done." He gently placed the rabbit and the knife on the desk.

I swear I saw a tear crop up in the corner of his eyes. He was bad, but like so many of his sort in the South's irony, there was still softness in his heart, at least for his own kind.

He cleared his throat, licked his lips, and swiped his shirt-sleeve across his eyes, then gave the tight-eyed look a tough man gives to ferret out and then intimidate anyone who might denigrate him for his moment of sentimentality.

"Outside the buildin," The Junior said, "we found a screwdriva. Carved into it were the initials, T an E, of this here nigra, Tommy Eldridge." He held up the mug shot taken of Mr. E at his arrest.

The words hit me like a sledgehammer. I knew Mr. E carved his initials into all of his tools. I even had a screwdriver he'd given me just like the one The Junior was holding. My mind went foggy, my legs wobbly. It was almost as if I was back in the fire. I thought I would faint.

"Now," he said, unlocking the topside drawer of his desk with one of the many keys dangling from his belt on a retractable key ring. He pulled out two clear plastic bags marked "Evidence."

"Right near the screwdriva with the T an E on it," holding up the bag with the screwdriver and pointing to the T and the E, "we also found this here cigarette butt," he said waving the second bag. "We also have a witness, a neighbor. Says she saw the suspect leavin the place just before the fire. Once we arrested the suspect, we found his fingerprints matched the ones on the screwdriva and on the butt. Puttin it all together, ain't much doubt we got the culprit."

He opened his mouth to continue but stopped himself as a loud train whistle sounded through a never-washed window facing the Southern Railroad's Craighead Street yard. With a look of disgust, freight cars on their way to Atlanta clanking below, he shook his head side to side and hollered, "If I should eva git mahself elected mayor, the first goddamned thing I'd do is move this goddamned office to the otha side of downtown."

"Amen to that," the *Recorder*'s reporter shouted back.

A fly buzzed by The Junior's head and landed on the wall. His thick-fingered wallop, surprisingly fast by anyone's standard, smashed it, adding to the gallery of broken wings and black-and-blood splatter on the gray, flaking wall. The ceiling fan shuddered against its loose screws.

"Anyhow, in regards to this accused nigra. In addition to everthing else, discovered inside the buildin, havin died from the smoke, was the body of ninety-four-year-old Mista Albert Rippe, former owner of Southeast Textile Mills. Since, under Virginia law, it don't matter none if the person settin the fire knew someone was inside or not, I am therefore, along with arson, chargin Tommy Eldridge with second degree murder, punishable with up to death."

It took me a minute to catch my breath, my heart beating like a tom-tom. Since the fire, I'd been sick with shame and regret over Mr. Rippe's death. But, now, Mr. E was added to the mix.

"He couldn't have done it," I shouted.

The whole crowd turned to me.

"I live right next door and saw the guy who did it. Mr. E," and then I caught myself, "Mr. Eldridge left way before the fire."

The Junior hesitated, scratched his head and looked hard at me.

"And who might you be, boy?"

"Donny Cohen, and I work with Mr. E and I saw the guy who did it."

The Junior heaved up his belly again.

"Wait a minute. You the boy who done all them carvins at your daddy's store down on Union Street?"

"Yes, sir. And I learned how to do it all from Mr. Eldridge."

The Junior chuckled.

"Well, now, I cain't rightly blame you for standin up for your friend. Gotta say he taught you dang well. But, boy, I got me as much evidence right here as plum pits in bear shit. When you got somethin that changes all that, then come an see me."

"But..." I said, when The Junior interrupted with, "Now, gentlemen, I got work to do and people to see."

As he ushered the audience out of the office, slapping backs and chatting, all 350 pounds of him acted so celebratory that his mottled neck swelled into a holiday crimson almost bursting his plastic collar button.

I pushed through to him, close, shaking and sweating and grabbed his arm.

"He'd never do anything like that. You can't just ignore me. I know what I saw, goddammit."

I never swore at adults, so cursing at him caught me as much by surprise as it did the crowd. The Junior jerked to a stop, turned and faced me. His face staring down into mine seemed as huge as one in a fairgrounds mirror.

"Ever curse at me again, boy, and I'll slap your face. Ever grab me again and that arm of yours won't attach to your body no more."

Turning back toward the *Recorder* reporter with a barely noticeable wink and strained smile he said, "We don't tolerate no hate towards our Jews here in Danville. I have vowed to pertect all our citizens and will continue to do that usin hard evidence."

I staggered out of The Junior's office. The rabbi uttered some calming words but I shook his arm off of my shoulder and ran.

"There are words for Southern law as applied to blacks—they don't include justice or fairness," Uncle Herman, my dad's brother and a lawyer, had always said about how black men were treated in the Southern criminal justice system. I'd always understood him intellectually, but now it was real.

Not to mention Southern jails. White men laughed about it, and blacks shook their heads with whistled groans.

"Bug- and vermin-infested food, random beatings from sadistic white guards, attack dogs, and minimal health and dental care are the norm," Uncle Herman had told our social studies class earlier in the year. Against the principal's wishes, our teacher, the school's designated liberal, had invited him to talk about the current civil rights movement and Danville's racist history.

Uncle Herman was one of the few lawyers who routinely represented indigent black defendants. "Broken teeth, arms, legs, torn flesh, and infections. Such poor sanitation," he sighed, "the filth and stink make you want to wear a gas mask."

Looking at the mostly indifferent faces of our all-white class, he added, "Battered and bloody, just as surely as was Jesus Christ when nailed to the cross." Seeing their shock, he said, "And even if they don't die, a lot of them end up with permanent damage if they make it out. Shells of their former selves."

Now, notwithstanding the seriousness of the charges themselves, I was terrified that the chances of such harm to Mr. E increased each day he was in jail. Because this Jewish boy loved that black carpenter as much if not more than those Southern Baptist kids claimed to love their sanctified white one.

CHAPTER TEN

My love for carpentry, and Mr. E, started when I was about twelve, seven years before the fire. I had a big itch to learn how to fix and build things.

My dad said, "Sorry, son, but I just never learned any of that stuff."

"We hire that out," Mom said. "Jews don't really do that kind of thing, Jesus excepted."

That's about the only way she and Mr. E were alike—they both thought their Jewish jokes were funny.

Finally, my pestering led Dad to ask Mr. E, the temple's handyman, if he would take me under his wing.

"Tommy, my son's driving me crazy. Would you mind?"

Mr. E frowned. He took a long pull on his cigarette. I could feel a tensed hump, sure rejection, in my shoulders.

"Of course, I'll pay you for teaching him," Dad finally added.

After what seemed like forever, and another suck on his cigarette and a smoky, slow exhale, Mr. E finally said, "Longs I can let him go if he don't listen and do what I say."

"Deal," I shouted, then blushed when both their heads swiveled to me.

"Deal," Dad said with a laugh. "Send me a bill, Tommy. Every week okay?"

"Yessir. But don't neither of ya expect miracles. I seen boys get all excited then lose steam after seein the hard work."

I put out my hand, shook Mr. E's and hugged Dad.

"Figured you'd lose interest and I'd be rid of ya soon enough," Mr. E told me later, after he realized I wouldn't give up.

Despite his patience, at first I was a klutz: squiggly lines, migrating butt angles, bloody fingers. But I was as determined as I was inept.

"Took me all my forty years to learn what I know," he told me early on, after I kept dropping tools and instantly forgetting his instructions in a nervous delirium. "So take yer time. Relax. There's plenty to learn, but also plenty of time to learn it."

He started by showing me proper hammering technique, the most basic of skills. But to me, "Use your whole arm, not just your wrist," was like ancient wisdom. I couldn't help but think about how the *Torah* taught Jews about what to eat, how to spend money, how to pray, how to dress, even how to have sex, and how often. Why not how to hammer a damn nail?

I inhaled Mr. E's teaching—the carpentry, plumbing, and even simple electrical wiring, though he wouldn't let me do that at first.

"Don't reckon you gettin 'lectracuted would sit too well with your daddy," he laughed.

Every day he'd teach me something new.

Back then, before so many power tools, a carpenter had many different types of handsaws.

"A saw's measured by teeth per inch, or TPI," Mr. E had explained on our first day together. "You call the name of the saw as one more than the number of TPI. Fer instance, it's called a seven-point saw if there's six TPI. Now, a crosscut saw is for going against the grain, a ripsaw for cutting with the grain. Panel, dovetail, gent, and tenon saws for fine, usually interior, joinery and finish work."

It was a whole new language, alive and useful, unlike the Hebrew we kids were forced to learn.

"If you wanna learn which to use when, and how to saw clean straight lines by hand, then you gotta stop that lazy young-fella mind most you boys is inflicted with," he said. "And to prevent waste and extra work, you got to be precise. Measure twice, cut once. Sounds so simple, but just 'cause it's simple, don't mean you throw it into the trash bin of obvious."

After a few months, as we sat around discussing the reasons for decisions and which tools we'd need for the next job, I jumped up.

"I'm speaking 'carpenter-ese'!" I shouted.

"Watch out," Mr. E had said. "Get too smart, soon you'll think you the *only* Jew ever could."

Patience and care felt like a celebration around Mr. E. And as he taught me to figure angles, it made the geometry I'd hated at school come alive and useful.

"Donny," Mr. E said one day, "I'm gonna show you how to make the corners of a foundation nice and square. You do it with triangles! It's called the 3,4,5 rule–carpenter's perfection. Don't ever fergit it. It's the Golden Rule of any good carpenter. Some ol Greek guy figured it out way back when.

"First, you nail the butt-ends of two two-by-six planks at what you think is a ninety-degree angle. Then you measure and mark three feet out on one of 'em and four feet on the other. Next, you measure across from one mark to the other and jiggle the boards till the marks are exactly five feet apart. When they are, you got a perfect square ninety degrees, where those two pieces meet. And yer on yer way to a house built just right."

When I'd told my ninth-grade math teacher about the amazing 3,4,5 rule the next day, his face lit up.

"Based on Pythagorean Theorem. Builds great minds and also great buildings," he said.

It was so beautiful in its simplicity that I jumped up and down and whooped the first time Mr. E and I used 3,4,5 to frame a house. It became as real and important to me as "eat your vegetables" was to Mom.

"3,4,5, boy," Mr. E smiled. "Pure evidence that it'll always make things work out right."

Much later, after his arrest, I found out that, other than carpentry, he wasn't always right on that point.

Soldering plumbing pipes was next. Melting lead was painstaking and dangerous. But there was an almost sensual satisfaction that came when that melted slag slid into the crack between two legs of copper tubing.

Toilet pride. The first time I installed one by myself, I beamed as high and bright as I had after finishing *leyning*, sing-reading, from the *Torah* in ancient Hebrew at my *Bar Mitzvah*. Most members of our small congregation would probably have reacted to such pleasure with, "That boy's a little odd."

Six months or so after I'd started working with him, Mr. E told my dad, "I won't be takin no more money from ya. He's a real hep to me now. I can tell him what to do and he can do it pretty much without me standin over him. I'll be payin him now myself. He's a good worker."

From childhood, I'd learned how to sell clothes from my Old Spice-cologned dad at his store. But I learned how to do real physical, manly things from Mr. E. His perfume was the sweet working-class scent of cigarette smoke and deodorant-free, man-work sweat.

He was the archetypal father figure most boys, at least as far as I could tell, yearned for: standing beside me on a project, bending down to patiently show me, over and over, how to do things right; how to make something amazing from almost nothing; how to fix stuff that made you feel like a hero. A father a boy would do anything for to get his, "Yeah, that's it, you got it...well done," with a pat on the back, maybe not even with a smile but just a quick forward thrust of his jaw and a nod of his head.

When he'd say, "Son, ya did a nice job," I'd get all woozy-warm and tingly inside.

One day he knighted me—and cursed himself. It was a little over a year after I'd started working for him. It was still six years before the fire, before he was accused, before he sat rotting in jail.

I wasn't sure that he cared about me like I did him until he actually showed up at my *Bar Mitzvah* party at the Holiday Inn, the fanciest place in town other than the Danville Country Club, which excluded Jews and Negroes.

Mr. E and Dottie, his wife, dressed in their Sunday church finery, walked into the lobby. Through the party room's plate glass partition, I recognized the dark brown, three-piece suit I'd fitted him for at Abe's—at the family discount, a rare offering from Dad. Mr. E held a long, bulky package wrapped in newspaper. The white desk manager, barely looking up, pointed and said, "Deliveries in the back."

"I'm not deliv'rin," Mr. E said, standing tall, stretching his six-foot frame high and imposing. "I'm a guest."

"Where's your invitation, boy?"

"Don't reckon as you asked nobody else fer one."

"Right here," said Mrs. E, pushing her husband aside and pulling the engraved white envelope out of her purse.

"Niggers still gotta go 'round through the back door," the manager said with a shrug. "Hey!" he shouted, as Mr. E grabbed his wife's hand and walked right in the front entrance.

Other than Reverend Rampbell, Danville's leading black minister and a close family friend, and his wife, Mr. E and Dottie were the only black faces at the party who weren't servers. Rev. Rampbell wore a custom-tailored suit as fine as anyone's there, versus our store's "good quality, practical, long-lasting" off-the-rack brand hanging on Mr. E.

"Somethin for ya," he said when I ran up to him.

I threw my arms around him in a big hug, the package poking between our bellies. We'd never hugged before. He was stiff as a board. I didn't care—*Bar Mitzvah* boy rights! He pulled away. His skin didn't flush like a white, but it did seem to glisten just a bit.

"Ain't much," he said, holding it out in his wide calloused hands, looking embarrassed at the table groaning with fancy, wrapped gifts.

"Come eat now, Donny," my mom yelled from the hors d'oeuvres table. "It's your favorite, whitefish!" holding out a plate piled high.

I ignored her and sat with Mr. and Mrs. E at their table. I ripped off the newspaper.

"A toolbox!" I said. "With my initials!"

He'd fashioned the three-foot-long, one-foot-wide, and one-foot-high box out of dry-cured lightweight pine planks. The corners were perfectly dovetailed. Black walnut triangles at each end reached above the box, connected by an inch-diameter mahogany dowel handle. On both sides, three-inch-long beaten copper plates were engraved with my initials. I pulled a wrapped package from inside the toolbox and shredded the paper to uncover the screwdriver and hammer he'd let me use since I started with him, each with TE, his initials, hand-carved on the handles.

"Been using 'em since I was yer age," he said. "Antiques," he chuckled.

"I can't take them. They're yours."

"Hush now," his wife said. "Just say thank you."

That's how she always was when I'd have lunch on a workday at their house—sweet, but never one for mushy sentiment.

"Got plenty more. Ain't no big thing," Mr. E said.

Between my loud whoops and Mom yelling "Whitefish, whitefish, come eat, Donny! Come eat," I'd attracted a staring crowd, hands holding bagels loaded with cream cheese, purple onion slices, and lox. For a second, I saw through their eyes—an uncomfortable-looking black couple sitting with a kid in a suit who was making a big fuss about a wooden box, a hammer, and a screwdriver.

Mishuganah, I could hear them thinking. But just as quickly, I forgot them. I caressed the deep-sheened, cherrywood handles, worn smooth as silk, tracing the T and E with my index finger. I pictured myself walking with Mr. E's new gift, full of my very own useful tools, right beside him.

"Thank you," I said, cradling them to my chest like sacred objects.

As the years passed, other guys my age fantasized about being Elvis and screwing tanned bikinied babes. I bathed in the sunshine of sawdust. By age sixteen, after four years of Mr. E's tutelage and three years before the fire, I was a skilled tradesman.

Mr. E had opened my world to things few Jewish people knew or cared about. Owning a store or collecting letters after their names was their measure of success while I had fallen in love with the smell of wood and the pleasure of tools.

Versus Dad's pleasure—standing around inside a store all day selling clothes.

"Helping a man find what makes him look his best, now that's what makes my day," he'd say.

He taught me well. The head salesclerk said, "We could make a preacher think he looked great in a clown suit."

But I could care less about ties or shoes or color matching. I hated it all, not to mention being stuck inside the fluorescent flickering, windowless dungeon, poisoned by mothball- and preservative-drenched, brain-cell-killing clothes all day—not even being able to tell if it had rained or been sunny outside. Compared to that, carpentry was spring-scented air, the whiffs of cedar or pine intoxicating.

Between his long hours at the store and his and Mom's golf, clubs, trips, and volunteering, they were consumed with their world, and I'd been left to find mine.

A couple of months before I started working with Mr. E, I called the state office of labor about Dad's insistence that we always be on our feet at the store. "Ten minutes rest for every four work hours standing on your feet," they told me. Dad was furious when I sat and told all the grown-up salesmen in his store that they had that right, too.

But I could stand and bang nails all day with Mr. E without even thinking of sitting down.

Repairing leaky faucets felt like meditation. Renovating an ugly basement became a testament to beauty. And I had muscles even under my fingernails. After a few years, I discovered something even better, a fineness as sublime as a Miles Davis trumpet solo.

"You like that delicate, slow work," Mr. E had noticed.

So he spent downtime teaching me about dovetails, biscuit joints, fine cutting and carving detail, using his scroll saws and jigsaws, planers and routers, gouges and chisels.

"Ya start with the big gouges to rough cut yer general patterns and shapes. Then ya git smaller an smaller, till yer barely takin out anything—almost just a speck of fineness."

He taught me how to carefully grind and hone the tools.

"This kind of carpentry works only as good as yer sharp edges."

What I could do with those sharp edges ignited my imagination like the sparks from his grinding wheel.

With money earned or birthday or Chanukah money, I'd run to Sears and Roebuck to buy their Craftsman lifetime-guaranteed gouge and chisel sets. Short butt chisels with beveled sides and straight edges for creating joints; carving chisels in-and-out channel gouges, skew, parting, paring, and V- or U-grooves for deep cuts, intricate designs and sculpting; L-shaped corner chisels to clean out square holes or for corners with ninety-degree angles, and more. In a while, I needed to build a special toolbox just for my carving tools and mallets.

"You git home now. Be with your famly. Go on, shoo," Mrs. E would scold when she'd hear me banging away some nights under the light of the single sixty-watt bulb hanging over her husband's dirt-floored workshop.

Three years before the fire, I'd become proficient enough to bring up the idea of carving designs into the six eight-by-eight-inch oak vertical support posts in Dad's store. "This is a clothing store, not a cathedral," Dad responded at first. I could appreciate his skepticism—but I had a vision of beauty that only I, and Mr. E, could see.

Six months later, he said, "All those people coming in doesn't hurt business at all." Word had spread about the store with the amazing carvings. Locals and out-of-towners came in to gape at and carefully touch the carved vines, fat angel faces, intricate varieties of crosses, Stars of David, and animals and floral designs, not to mention buy more clothes.

One summer day, a year and a half before the fire, Mr. E picked me up in his shiny red '57 Ford F100 pickup and took me to a gin-nosed tobacco magnate's heirloom mansion. He told him that he was leaving me there to repair some particularly delicate old Queen Anne trim.

"I got other things to do, so I'm droppin you off to do this job," he told me when I jumped into the front seat. "Take yer time and do it right 'cause this man's a German Lutheran. They sniff around like hound dogs, lookin for mistakes so they can take off from the bill."

Standing at the man's front door, the owner harrumphed, looking at my mismatched clothes and pimply face.

"Better than I am on that kinda stuff," Mr. E said respectfully, holding his cap in his hands down by his hips. "I'll do it, but it'll take more time and be no better. An keeps a nigger out of your house," he said with a wink to me.

The combed-across, blond-haired man raised his eyebrows, puffed his pinkish cheeks, shook his head, and flicked his hand for me to come in.

"Wonder who he'd have picked if he knew I was a Jew?" I asked Mr. E the next day.

"That's a damned fine question," he laughed.

Eventually, in our community, I earned the mantle of "the Jewish carpenter," often followed by "And it'll be the second coming if he shows up on time."

Not quite Jesus, but I did feel like the savior to many a frustrated Jewish housewife who had hassled, *hocked*, her husband for years to get things done around the house.

But Mr. E's arrest felt like toppling off a ladder.

CHAPTER ELEVEN

As I left The Junior's office after hearing his "evidence," everything exploded into a brutal reality. My consternation was suddenly more than my shame or guilt at my failure to save Mr. Rippe. Now, I realized that I might also be responsible for Mr. E's arrest.

Because, of course, I'd been there. My aching shoulder—from my confrontation with the real arsonist—was the first of two testaments to the untruth of The Junior's accusations.

I ran home as fast as I could, legs and lungs aching, barely able to breathe, a vein in my forehead pounding like a drumbeat—hoping, praying. I dove at my toolbox, the one Mr. E had made for me, clawing at the hand tools inside, tossing them out, scratching every inch—until I knew that the second testament absolutely disproved The Junior's screwdriver "fact," and I was definitely to blame for the mistake. Because, on the afternoon of the fire, hours before Clara came over, I'd helped Mr. E shellac the temple's pews. Fridays were half-days during my senior year, so I was free to work with him. As we'd walked out of the sanctuary, he'd grabbed my screwdriver from my toolbox to tighten a loose hinge on the sanctuary door.

"Once a door's been jerked on enough," he'd said, "the screw hole gets as big as a backstreet whore's. Starts workin its way out and that's why the door won't close proper. So ya stuff a couple toothpicks in it so's the screw has something to bite into agin. Makes it as tight as a scared virgin."

In the last few months, he'd told me I was old enough now, at nineteen, to hear how grown men talk. *He should hear Clara talk,* I thought.

"Yet and still," his eyes had shined on me as he took a drag on his Lucky Strike cigarette, "wouldn't do no good to tell yer folks I'm the one teachin ya such talk. I'd never frequent such women myself. But it's the way the old carpenters taught me to think, in pictures, so's to remember."

As usual, I thought he was brilliant. When he was finished, he put the flathead screwdriver back in my toolbox.

In the temple's front yard, walking behind him, I said, "You know about centrifugal force, Mr. E?"

I stood and swung the toolbox in big 360-degree whirligigs, swinging it in big circles over my head and back down a few times. "We studied it today in physics class." The shellac vapors must have made it seem more interesting to me than to him. "Amazing how nothing falls out."

Not even looking back, he said, "Quit foolin 'round and put that thing in the back of the truck so I can get home to early dinner." He flicked his cigarette butt behind himself into the grass by the temple's front door. "Gotta come back in a couple hours and put on the last coat."

I braked the box to a quick halt in mid-air. He didn't get grumpy often, but when he did, I knew to respond without hesitation. I raced after him before the toolbox even had a chance to settle at the bottom of its swing. Neither of us noticed the fallen screwdriver, the one he'd carved his T and E into, the one that he'd given me for my *Bar Mitzvah,* the one The Junior was so excited to have found.

CHAPTER TWELVE

At Mr. Eldridge's arraignment, a day after his arrest, ten in the morning, two beefy white deputies led him into Danville's courthouse. Its granite Greek revival columns, topped with marble filigrees and Latin quotes, suggested a respect for higher ideals of justice than ever were evidenced for most blacks who entered, whether accused, prosecuting, defending, or judging.

Mr. E's shoulders drooped at his sides, pulled down by thick, iron wrist shackles linked with a steel chain to a four-inch-wide leather waist girdle. Another chain attached the waist girdle to a set of manacles around both ankles. He was dressed in black-and-white striped prison pants and shirt, both too small, so that his muscular thighs and arms bulged out against the fabric. The deputies shoved him down by his shoulders onto a beaten-up pine bench in the waiting area. Reverend Rampbell, May, and I sat down with him. I'd cut school to be there.

"We're behind you, Deacon Eldridge," the Reverend said, his voice a deep rumbling even in hushed tones. "Anyone knowing you would laugh at this insanity."

"We love you, Thomas," May said, dabbing her eyes.

I sat there, dumbstruck.

Mrs. E was not there. "Told her to mind the house and get the kids to school," Mr. E said to May. "Told her I'll figure this thing out. No use them comin here and seein me like this," raising the rattling chains, then rubbing his bloodshot eyes, "and gettin even more upset. May, would ya mind checkin in on her?"

"Right now, Thomas," May answered. She stood up, patted and kissed the top of his head, and rushed out of the courthouse.

I wanted to squeeze his hand, to lean against him, to kiss his head too, to show him the love I'd show my own dad in such a situation. But I knew Mr. E would hate that show of affection.

The court clerk stuck his head out of the door, pointing to the deputies. "Bring the nigger in."

Hobbled by the chain connecting the two ankle cuffs, Mr. E stumbled and clanked, the heavy chain banging against the iron shackles. He slumped forward as one guard yanked him along, pulling hard against the portion of the chain wrapped around his wrists and waist.

Against this, Mr. E jerked back, rearranged himself, forcing his back stock-straight, and thrusting his shoulders erect. He slowed the pace with each firm placement of his feet.

"Git movin," the guard said, with a push.

Mr. E continued his slow, controlled walk.

"Dignified, even with all this," Reverend Rampbell said to me.

I shook my head in a yes right along with him.

In the courtroom, the guard pushed Mr. E down onto a squeaky, worn, red oak chair at the defendant's table.

Mr. E sat bolt upright, his normally mischievous eyes staring ahead with a fierce calmness.

I could barely breathe. Despite his brave countenance, I was afraid that my fear and confusion were an echo of his internal reality.

After reading the warrant, the judge looked down at Mr. E.

"Bail is $4,000. You got that, boy?"

"No, suh," Mr. E said.

"Well, then, since you ain't got the $4,000 bail, you will remain in the city jail until your trial next month." With a slam of his gavel, the judge walked out. It was that quick.

I ran to the door where the deputies were leading Mr. E out.

"They can't do this. I'll get you out, Mr. E. I'll get you out," I yelled, crying tears I wasn't ashamed of, reaching out to touch him. "It was my screwdriver, not yours."

"Fuckin nigger lover," one of the deputies said, pushing me away.

A large hand, Reverend Rampbell's, clamped over my mouth as I took a breath, ready to answer the insult.

"As Brother Martin tells us, 'Never show anger in the face of hatefulness,' " Reverend Rampbell had preached during his recent civil rights campaign meetings. "Calm dignity confuses and offends bigots much more effectively," he'd added with a guffaw, clapping to the laughter breaking out throughout the crowd.

"Calm yourself, son," he said now. "Harsh words will only inflame how they treat him once we're out of sight. "Let's go."

CHAPTER THIRTEEN

In France, I learned that their revolution's fight for individual dignity seemed to have progressed further than ours. Fine wine, French cigarettes, and pork sausage were close seconds.

Uncle Herman

I rushed to a phone booth and called Uncle Herman. It was my screwdriver, I kept thinking, and a lot of people saw him give it to me.

"Come on over," his long-time secretary, Mrs. Firestone, said. "He's always got time for you."

"How-do, Mr. Don," said Zeke, the old black elevator operator of the eight-story Masonic Temple office building, Danville's only "skyscraper," housing most of the city's lawyers and a lot of doctors and dentists. The place never failed to smack me into a sense of insignificance whenever I walked through its heavy bronze, cut glass doors and marble-floored, crystal-chandeliered entry hall.

Zeke opened the steel elevator cage. This was before elevators were self-operating. Walking in, hearing and feeling Zeke slam the gate shut, I thought of how Mr. E must've felt when they took him to his cell after his arrest—the door banging him into his hell.

"You okay, Mr. Don? Seem a little blue today. I'm gettin ready to come to yer daddy's store fer a new pair of shoes. Feets been botherin me somethin awful. Ain't seen you there lately."

I'd seen Zeke since I could remember, but never knew or asked his whole name.

"I've mostly been doing carpentry with Mr. Eldridge. Nothing personal, Zeke but it sure beats smelling dirty feet."

"I can see that is prob'bly God's own truth," he said with a hoot—until his brows and face wrinkled into worry. "Yer uncle gonna hep him? That why you so glum lookin?"

"I'm praying he will, Zeke."

"Me too, Mr. Don, me too."

He opened the elevator door to a sweltering hallway.

I started to walk away, then stopped and turned back to him.

"Zeke, I've known you all my life. What's your real name?"

"That's surely kindly of ya to ask, Mr. Don. Hardly never been asked, ever. It's Ezekial Hawthorne Harris."

Harris was a well-known, local, white family with strong Confederate credentials and unclaimed black descendants.

"Well, thank you for the ride. Would you like me to call you Mr. Harris or Ezekial from now on?"

"Shoot, Mr. Don, don't rightly matter to me after all these years."

His eyes lit up a bit, nonetheless.

"Ezekial would be nice," he said.

His toothless smile lifted my veil of misery for a moment. As the pick-up buzzer sounded, he closed the elevator gate, waved, turned the crank, and headed back down.

I looked down the hall. The humidity, heat-cracked linoleum floor, and blistered-plaster walls wilted me back to my desolate spirit. It reminded me of the soul of the South, so often fancy and made-up on the outside and a broken-down, sweaty mess on the inside.

I opened the door to Uncle Herman's cool, Persian rug-floored office. The air-conditioning, installed just months before and reviewed with oohs and ahs at the family inspection, raised goose bumps on my skin. After a lifetime of basting in the South, refrigerated air didn't quite equate to sex, but it sure came close.

"Hi, Donny," Mrs. Firestone said. "Isn't this cool air heavenly?"

Though she was always friendly and kind, my air-conditioned sensuality quickly evaporated as I looked at her teased and sprayed blue hair, powder-furrowed face, lips smeared over their edges with bright red lipstick, and billowing acrylic blouse, large with her low-hanging breasts. "Very nice," I said with a smile.

"Haven't seen you since the Christmas parade," she said.

Every year, all the cousins gathered at Uncle Herman s top floor window to watch it below on Main Street. Uncle Herman would drive along the parade route in his Citroën with American and French flags on wooden poles duct-taped to the side windows, fluttering above the roof.

"Not much of a car, mechanically," Uncle Herman had told us, "but it revives my memories of amazing times."

"He's waiting for you. Go on in."

I cracked open the door and peeked in. Uncle Herman leaned back, his wooden swivel chair creaking against its springs and his stocky body.

I took a breath as he flicked his hand to me through the ever-present smoke shroud around his head. Much as I hated cigarettes after watching Dad hack and cough and spit from his two-pack-a-day habit, I still always enjoyed that first whiff.

"So I think I know why you're here, nephew?" he said as I sat down on the other side of his family-famous, country French writing desk.

"Brought it home from Paris," he'd told us all a thousand times. "De Gaulle's senior staff gave it to me after the war." They also, according to Uncle Herman, still sent him a supply of *Gauloise* cigarettes every six months. "My war pension," he'd laugh. "The best cigarettes in the world. But don't tell Lorillard"—the giant tobacco conglomerate headquartered in Danville—"they're my biggest client."

Sitting around Grandma's big dinner table on Friday nights, Uncle Herman would regale us youngsters with his tales of life as a military intelligence agent for the OSS in occupied France. From that table in isolated Danville, we were all transported to the world of war heroes. He was also an encyclopedia of de Gaulle quotes.

I told Uncle Herman everything: Mr. E and my work on the pews, running out and saying hello to Mr. E, my initialed screw-driver, smelling the smoke, seeing the temple on fire, getting knocked down by the Klanner—everything except about being with Clara.

"So it's cut-and-dry that he's innocent, Uncle Herman."

He took a slow draw on his cigarette, closed his eyes, then opened them as he blew the smoke out in a measured exhale.

"I know it all appears that way to you, Donny. But The Junior claims he has hard proof against Tommy. You know, Donny, how the system works around here for a black man—guilty unless *absolutely* proven innocent. He is in deep trouble," he said, shaking his head.

"But I bumped into the guy who started it. And I dropped the screwdriver, the one that The Junior claims is Mr. E's."

"I know you like Tommy," he went on, tapping his Montblanc fountain pen on a legal pad. "I like Tommy, too. But how sure are you of your story? I mean, did you actually see this guy start the fire? Even if we could find out who he is, he could say that he was just taking a walk and happened to be around the temple when the flames started shooting out—or that you just made it all up to protect Tommy."

"Well, what about his Klan hood?"

"Really, Donny, how are you going to prove it wasn't just a stocking cap? And, in any case, how much does what you saw matter? In fact, seeing Mr. Eldridge there an hour before the fire is probably more incriminating than not having seen him at all. Add to that a white jury. Don't see it, Donny. Just don't see you being of much help in this one."

I could feel the blood gushing into my face. My stomach sling-shotted my lunch back up into my throat. My hope suddenly seemed as simple-minded as my certainty had been.

"But you know as well as me, Uncle Herman, that Mr. Eldridge would never do anything like this. You can't just let them convict him. It's just not right."

"It isn't that you're not right, son. I know Tommy would never do such a thing. Hell, he renovated this office." The walls were wrapped in deep green, velveteen fabric. Spotlighted behind his desk, in an elaborate, gilded frame, was a picture of General Charles de Gaulle, signed, "To Herman, my friend and fellow partisan. Vive la France!"

"I love the guy too. It's just that I don't think I or anybody else in this town can do much to help a black man especially when The Junior has such strong physical evidence—the cigarette butt and even a screwdriver with Tommy's initials carved in it. Not to mention the witness neighbor. And even more, when the alternative is to convict a Klanner, even if we could identify him, which in this town is pretty much impossible considering how they protect their own. Sorry, nephew. Let's not be naive here. This isn't a matter of fairness. This is what goes on here every day."

I sat there, stunned. This was Uncle Herman, champion of the downtrodden.

"I don't care what happens everyday, Uncle Herman. I only care about what's gonna happen with Mr. Eldridge. It was my screwdriver. It must have my fingerprints on it too. They'll destroy him, just like you described to us in class. I can't believe you won't do something. Why'd you become a lawyer if you didn't want to help people like him?"

"What's *gonna* happen is that he is probably *going* to be convicted and there's not much you or I can do about it."

Uncle Herman hated the sloppy Southern tendency of dropping "ing" or other letters from word endings. "It ingratiates you to ignorance," he'd say to us like we'd uttered a profanity.

"I'm as sorry as you are, Donny, but some things you've just got to accept."

"It's just not fair," I said. "If you won't help, I'll go find a lawyer who will," though I really had no idea who that might be. "C'mon, Uncle Herman, please help him. Isn't there a lawyer's version of the Hippocratic oath? Don't you have to do your best to bring about justice? How can you, as a Jew, let someone who's definitely not guilty be convicted without even lifting a finger?" I almost spat at him, even if he was right about the odds. "You're as much a hypocrite as they are."

I knew I was grabbing at air. I'd been the victim and perpetrator of Jewish guilt-trips all my life. Sometimes it worked. Now it had to work.

"You're just another money-grubbing lawyer," I said, my final guilt-stab.

He took another puff, held it, let it out in an even longer exhale and stared at me, elegant in his impeccably tailored suit, purchased on one of his yearly trips to Paris, one way too expensive to ever be sold at Dad's store. He brought his chair to upright and leaned toward me, his face reddening, jaw clenching tight, like my stomach.

"Donny, you know that I served in military intelligence during the war." He pointed at me, waving his permanently straight index finger, paralyzed from a shrapnel wound to the nerve, waving it up and down, his voice rising, a sort of jeer creeping onto his face. "I saw the concentration camps. I know what happens when good people do nothing in the face of villainy." Now he was almost hollering at me. "I've fought many a battle here in Danville just to try to do what's right. I know firsthand, goddammit," voice now at forte. "So don't you lecture me, young man!" slamming his palm on his desk. The stacks of papers jumped, and I did too.

"You have no idea how many times I've seen innocent Negroes sent to jail. It eats part of your soul. Remember Tulie Jones? Raymond and Eddie Harris? You think Tommy's the first? You think you're the only crusader?"

He pulled open the bottom drawer of his desk, yanked out a scrapbook, and slid it at me.

"Open it," he ordered.

I flipped through page after page of newspaper clippings, commendations, letters from mothers and fathers and inmates.

Below a picture of Martin Luther King and Ralph Abernathy: "There are not enough good words to thank you for your selfless work." It was signed, "Ralph Abernathy, Martin Luther King's right-hand man."

Written at the bottom of a picture of Uncle Herman standing alongside a big group with Thurgood Marshall at its front:

Dear Herman,

Without your help and the help of others like you, the integration of the armed forces and the passage of the 1957 Civil Rights Act could not have succeeded.

Respectfully,
Thurgood

Under a copy of the lyrics to "Only a Pawn in Their Game," Bob Dylan's lament about the assassination of civil rights activist Medgar Evers:

Hold this song close to your heart, because all of you lawyers were the strings on my guitar of hope for Medgar's mission.

—*Bob*

I looked up from the page, about to express my awe as my hand flipped to the next one. The rough tablet paper scotch-taped to the page scratched my fingers to attention. It was by far the simplest letter, shaming me the most. In primitive, almost crippled script, written in pencil, dated 1960, it said,

Dear Mista Herman,

My family an me wants ta thank ya frum tha bottum of our harts fer tryin so hard ta hep us save Tulie. We all knows he wud never harm no one. He was a gental soul. With no money an no hope fer none, you did yer best ta git him free. We'll never fergit you.

Yer frend,
Hazel Jones

Stapled to the letter was the newspaper account of Tulie's execution for the murder of white restaurateur "Hootie" Powell. Tulie had been his early-morning prep cook.

"Tulie said he saw Hootie's partner running out of the alley door just as he came in to work that morning," Uncle Herman said to me. "But the guy, a white man, timed it perfectly. When Tulie stepped in, his shoe stepped right into Hootie's pool of blood. Tulie's story didn't stand a chance."

Uncle Herman took another drag on his cigarette and sat back in his chair, shaking his head side to side.

"Uncle Herman," I said. "I never knew—all of these. Why didn't you tell us? You should be famous around here."

He laid his head back on his chair, closed his eyes, took another long drag, raised his head with a sighed exhale, and looked at me.

"Donny, I still have to make a living. And that means representing mostly white people and companies with money—Southern white people. Hanging a picture of de Gaulle impresses them. Hanging a picture of Thurgood or, God forbid, this," pointing to Mrs. Jones' letter, "Well, you get the idea." He sat up and turned a few pages and pointed to another scrap, "Hell, I've even defended Klan people."

"Why?" I asked, incredulous.

"I believe everyone has a right to a fair trial and counsel."

"Did you win?"

"Yes, but it was a fraud charge, not any Klan activity. That help earns latitude from those people in a strange sort of symbiotic way. The Jew lawyer helps them a little, and I get forgiven for helping the others as long as I keep a low profile on it. When it comes to working around the system, you slap it in their faces too much, and they'll slap back a lot harder. So you do it quietly and keep your mouth shut. And sometimes, what makes it the hardest is that your best friends, even your family, can be your worst enemies. It doesn't take but one proud, righteous blabbermouth, one strident admirer, to kill the ability to be effective."

"But what about Tulie? All the headlines."

"I made sure that the paper reported that I was forced to do it by the judge. The court has the right to force lawyers to represent indigents. That was my cover."

He slowly laid his half-finished cigarette onto the ashtray we boys always giggled over. The heavy bronze piece showed a very proper man with his arm behind the waist of a woman, both dressed in Victorian finery. Flipped over, the woman's dress was lifted by the man's hand as it grabbed her bare ass.

Uncle Herman took off his glasses and rubbed the bridge of his nose between his forefinger and thumb.

"Donny," he said with a weary stare, "It's hard to admit, but after a while, your tears dry up and you want to avoid the heartache. You want to turn away and pretend you don't notice."

He pointed his rigid finger at me again, his face contorting, darkening, but less in anger this time than in tired sadness.

"You have no idea the toll the South extracts from do-gooders," he said, his voice hardly above a weary whisper. "You want to live a normal life, to *be* normal, with laughs and fun, not looking over your shoulder at every shadow in this goddamned cesspool of hate."

Now, his tone was more gravelly and hurt, staring hard at me.

"Just take cases that pay well, like you accused me of, and forget all this fucking heroic idealism!"

He leaned back in his chair again, lit another cigarette, ignoring the other one.

Cursing was rare in our family. He'd never talked to me this way. It was a shock, even after Clara. I sat there, as stiff as his finger, looking down at the floor. My eyes itched.

"Sorry, Uncle Herman."

My chest heaved.

"He's…I…I love him as much as…" my eyes shifted to his, then away, then back again, scared at what I was about to say, "… as much as Dad." And I started crying.

"Jesus Christ, Donny..." He shook his head slowly, side to side. "Oy."

After a pained silence, he inhaled deeply, hefted himself up through his smoke cloud and walked around his desk. He put his hand under my chin, lifted it up, and looked at my watery eyes. He sighed with a weak smile, and then sighed even louder.

"I'm sorry, Uncle Herman. I'm sorry I said all those awful things to you. You're a good man. I'm so sorry." I was still bawling.

"Oy," he said again. He pulled out his handkerchief and handed it to me. I wiped away the tears and blew my nose. He waited until I composed myself.

With another full-chest sigh, "I'll see what I can do. I'll go see him and see what he has to say. But I can't promise you anything, so don't get your hopes all up. This is no fairy tale. There's no magic around here just because you *know* someone's innocent. Now get out of here."

"Thank you, Uncle Herman," I sniffled.

I stood up, turned and walked a few steps, glad, but ashamed too. I looked back from the doorway. I'd never really noticed the deep lines carved into his forehead and on either side of the top of his nose. His face seemed to droop into weary dark bags under his eyes as he waved me off. His stocky body sagged into his chair as if he weighed 500 pounds.

I'd been Sunday-schooled and preached at from the pulpit, the *bima*, that from Moses to Solomon, Judaism embraced the importance of resolving dispute through fairness and truth. "Justice, justice, shall thou pursue," the *Torah* said in Deuteronomy. Every Jew knew, after generations of pogroms and discrimination that being a Jewish lawyer wasn't just a profession—it was a mandate. Persecution could not be allowed to stand. It was part of their soul, their DNA.

That learning exploded into understanding as I watched Uncle Herman flop back onto his chair, lean with his elbows onto his desk, rub his knuckles hard against his forehead and eyes, his paralyzed finger a moving exclamation point, smoke curling up from the cigarettes half-crushed in the ashtray.

"You okay?" Ezekial asked me on the way back down to the lobby. I must have looked red-eyed and ashen. "Mister Herman gonna hep him?"

"Much as possible, Ezekial, which doesn't seem to be much at all."

"Yessa," he said with a sad whistle. "We'll all be prayin on it."

He patted me on the back as I stumbled out of the elevator.

CHAPTER FOURTEEN

A day later, a glorious, sunny, early fall day, May and I drove to the city farm jail to visit Mr. E. The entry road ran between two moss-covered, twelve-foot-high stone columns. A large sign, cobbled from three-inch-diameter tree limbs nailed together into letters, ran from column to column, "Hard work grows food and self-respect." It sent shivers down my Jewish soul.

Cool breezes blew a sweet-smelling breath from the southern pines and the dying leaves of maples and poplars and oaks. They were a balm to my queasy gut.

Cows chewed contentedly along the road winding through the farm's 150 acres of cut hay and orchards, ripe with reddening apples and grapes, the air fragrant with wild yellow and red honeysuckles. As kids, we'd tear off the bottom of the flowers and suck out the nectar, as sweet as the scent.

A several-acre patch of tobacco greeted us toward the end of the road. The suckers, shadowed bottom leaves, had already been plucked to allow more energy to ripen and intensify the yellowing top ones.

May stopped the car and pointed.

"See how they look like big, droopy, pointy ears?" May said. "When I was little, Mama and I would snuggle up at night by our woodstove and she would make up stories. Used to say we had to leave a few of the biggest leaves in our tobacco field so giants could come pick them when they lost their ears in some fairy-tale battle. Then, she'd tell us, the giants would breathe out a cool breath to sweeten the apples and peaches. Said that was their way of thanking us. And, I swear, Donny, we always did seem to have the best fruit even when others didn't."

A log-built, mud-grouted drying shed, topped by a corrugated, metal roof and chimney, sat alongside the field.

Identical sheds dotted small tobacco farms in the county around Danville. Inside them, on bare, hard-packed earth, farmers made fires of yellow pine logs, green and watery, letting it smolder for days in order to slowly dry the leaves, creating the famous flue-cured Virginia tobacco.

"The inmates here grow and cure and make their own rolling tobacco out of the plants here and then sell the rest in the commissary and to visitors. The superintendent's allowed to keep most of the profit from the sales of all this stuff, even all the food grown and used by the inmates here on city land," May said. "He told me all about it. His own little slave operation."

I no longer wondered how May knew such intimate details about important white men.

Just before the parking lot, fat, pink pigs and piglets grunted and rummaged through the garbage thrown to them from the kitchen.

"Bacon, ham, and sausage, too," May said with a turn of her head toward the oinks.

When we stopped, before getting out of the car, May put her hand on my arm.

"I'm hoping to death I won't break down, Donny."

It was a relief knowing I wasn't the only one with that prayer.

I opened the heavy, rusted, metal door. May put her handkerchief to her nose against the smell of ammonia rising from the mopped concrete floors. It was unable to completely overpower the stench of urine, backed-up toilets, fried food, the acrid-sweet smell of that morning's pancakes and syrup, and the sweat of unventilated underarms.

The guard looked May up one side and down the other without any pretense. Her carefully chosen, loose, low-cut blouse showed enough swelling cleavage to grab his attention.

"Can't hurt and might help," she'd told me when I picked her up. "Desire is my weapon around these cretins."

"You a relative?" the guard said to her when he finally moved his eyes up to her face.

"Yes," she bent a little lower to him and fluttered her eyes as his followed her chest back down. I couldn't help but take a peek myself.

"I'm his daughter, sir," she said with a slurry-sweet Southern accent.

There was a moment of silence.

"And you?" he said, eyes still glued to her torso, not even pretending to look at me. "You his lawyer?"

I'd worn my dark suit, white shirt, black tie and wing tips. I was only nineteen, baby-faced, barely ever needed to shave. But what other white man ever visited Negro inmates other than their lawyers?

I was tempted to say, "I'm his son." Instead, I said, "Yes, I'm visiting on behalf of his lawyer."

The guy shrugged. "Sign here," pointing to a line on the page of a long, khaki-colored ledger. "Lemme see the bag," he said, grabbing a brown paper bag I'd brought filled with snacks I knew Mr. E enjoyed. He took a quick look inside. "Okay, ya got twenty minutes. He's in the nigger section," pointing to a corridor marked "Coloreds."

We walked through a long hallway of cells. A third of the ceiling's fluorescent lights flickered and buzzed in harmony with the cloud of flies.

"Gimme some sugar, baby," one inmate said with fat kissy lips to May.

"Come on now and suck it, sister," another said, wanking his crotch.

"Howdy, Miss May," another man said with a respectful tone.

May stopped in front of his cell door. I recognized the man as a customer at our store. He had the same last name as a family of wealthy, white Austrian tobacco farmers who'd been in the area for a hundred years. He always smelled of alcohol.

"Why, Mr. Snedeker. What are you doing here?"

"Shit, uh, shucks, Miss May. You knows I gots a drinkin problem. They shut me up here once in a while when they finds me lyin outside somewhere. Don't never do no good," he said, shaking his head side to side. "But seems they think it might make me stop. Ya know, scare it outta me," he chuckled with a toothless grin.

"Well, Mr. Snedeker," May said with a smile, "I hope to see you at church again soon. I'm singing there next Sunday. You take care of yourself." The man extended his hand through the bars. May reached out and patted it. "I always love to see your smilin face out in the crowd."

His eyes went watery.

"Thank ya kindly, Miss May. You is as sweet as yer voice."

May looked at me, smiled, and walked the few more steps to the meeting room.

On the cracked, naked concrete floor, steel chairs with no cushions sat under metal tables pushed up against thick, six-foot-high glass partitions. Identical furniture mirrored the prisoner's side. Slabs of peeling white paint sprouted from the walls. An old ceiling fan with rusty bearings squealed just below another humming fluorescent light, washing us in a breezy mix of flickering, overheated putridity. I took a couple of deep breaths to push back my nausea.

Mr. E walked into the windowless room. His face was sunken, older. Even without the shackles, he seemed to drag his feet.

"How are you?" was all I could think to say after he'd dropped down onto his chair.

He looked at me like I was crazy.

"It was my screwdriver, the one you gave me," I blurted out. "I dropped it when I was swinging my tool bucket. And I wrestled with the guy who lit the fire. They won't listen to me, Mr. E. They don't care. They think I'm lying because I love you. Oh God, it's my fault. I really screwed up. I'm so sorry," and I started weeping. "I'm so sorry. I'm so sorry."

When I looked up, Mr. E's face seemed to have returned to that of a caring parent.

"It's okay, son. We'll get through this."

He patted the glass partition above my face.

"We're all praying for you," May said, pulling her white silk hanky from her sleeve and dabbing at her eyes.

"I know, honey," Mr. E said, touching the tips of her fingers through the four-inch space between the tabletop and the glass wall. "The Reverend visited yesterday. Said he was raisin all kinds of heck 'bout all this. Said things would work out. Tried to act all confident. But, truth be told, May, he weren't very convincin."

"Be strong," May said. "We're going to figure this out, come hell or high water. Damn," she said as she started crying into both hands.

Mr. E shuffled in his chair, cocking his head, his faint smile showing more concern about consoling her than about receiving her compassion.

"Sorry, Thomas. I swore I wouldn't cry in front of you."

In man-time, it seemed forever before she stopped, blew her nose, shook her head, and raised her eyes to his. Pushing her fingers harder against his, her chest rising up with a big breath, eyes boring into his, she said, "If it's the last thing I do, Thomas, we're going to get you free, whatever it takes."

I had no confidence in May's words or in any of my assurances. They sounded no different than old slave songs about gaining freedom.

We all sat there in silence, then answered his questions about how his family was doing. May told him that a collection had started at their church to help out. Then silence again.

Finally, "Has Uncle Herman talked to you?" I asked.

"Yes, yes, he has, Donny. Called me here this mornin. Said you almost took a hammer to him. Said he's comin to talk to me tomorrow." He closed his eyes for a moment, took a breath, then opened them, the bloodshot whites shining with moisture. "Said my chances were in sad shape. I 'preciate you tryin to help, though," he said with an exhausted smile. "You a good boy. I 'preciate it."

"Yeah, me and Jesus," I said. I always winced inside after I'd try to be funny with these stupid Jesus jokes.

Mr. E closed his eyes again and took another big breath as his head slumped. He raised it up, then sniggered with a forced grin, "Bet he told better jokes than you."

"Amen to that," May forced a laugh back.

Grabbing my bag, May said, "We brought you some Baby Ruths, some hoop cheese, some hard sausage, and some of those saltines Dotty said you liked. Will they let you take them to your cell?"

"Sure hope so. Food here's no better than pig-slop."

"Time's up," the guard said right behind Mr. E. "Let's go," tugging at his shoulder.

"For Christ's sake, we've only been here a few minutes. You said twenty," I shouted at him.

"Been twenty plus a few. Talk back at me like that agin, son, and I'll make sure you won't be comin back even fer that much."

I wanted to say, "Fuck you." I wanted to hug Mr. E. I wanted to tell him it would be all right. I wanted him strong, not pathetic and battered. My heart beat against my chest like a jackhammer.

I must have looked like a raving maniac, because as I opened my mouth to talk back to the guard, May raised a "shhh" finger to her mouth, with the stern look of an older sister. I slumped into my chair.

Mr. E stood up and walked to the exit door. He turned to us and lifted his hand in a weak wave, his face as broken down as the inside of the jail and as miserable as our spirits.

I stared at the rusted, peeling door, imagining Mr. E on the other side, crammed into a stinking cell. I sat there, sweat-stuck to my seat, fists clenched, dead-weighted down into the hard metal chair. *I'd let one man die,* I thought. And now another was expiring, in spirit if not in body right in front of me. Mr. E's pitiful wave played like a movie again and again across my mind.

"Let's go, Donny," May said. I hardly heard her. She tugged at my arm. I could smell her perfume as she feathered a finger down the side of my face. It was such a contrast to the rough stink of the place that it made me cry again.

"Let's go," she said again. I looked up at her, standing above me. She wrapped her arms around and pulled my head to her waist while I heaved out my tears. She ran her hand slowly back and forth through my hair.

"Come on, Donny. We've just started."

CHAPTER FIFTEEN

As we drove back, Mr. E's slumped body, his fractured face looking back at me, his feeble wave, all reeled in my mind, frame by frame, over and over. How could I have been so careless, so goddamned stupid, as to not notice the fallen screwdriver?

May dropped me off downtown at Dad's store.

I hopped onto my bike. Struggling up Danville's steep, ten-block Main Street, I knew Uncle Herman was right. As much as I appreciated his help, I hated his truths even more. This was no fairy tale. There was no magic. I was just a stupid, idealistic, do-gooder teenager. I was sure that Mr. E was doomed.

I pedaled with a fury, my head spinning as fast as the pedals. As usual, my face was wet with tears.

Until a voice, a calm voice, whispered in my ear, *The card, up your sleeve.*

I gasped, like Clara's gasp when she pulled the queen of hearts stuck between the cheeks of her ass. Like the gasps of the little neighborhood kids I'd charged three cents each to watch my magic card tricks in our basement when I was ten—the magic I'd studied and practiced from my *Harry Houdini Magic Card Tricks* book.

"Houdini was a rabbi's son!" my grandfather said when he presented me with his signed copy, like a treasure, for my eighth birthday. Grandpa and I spent hours together, working on tricks from his own deck. The hours felt like Houdini himself was watching us, blessing us.

"Presenting Houdinala," Grandpa would say, grinning, arms across his big belly, on the nights I entertained the family around the Friday night dinner table.

But the gasp of this magic was worth more than any amount of money or praise. This trick could save Mr. E's life.

I jammed on the brakes, jumped off my bike, and tossed it hard against a big pin oak. Acorns rained on my head. I threw a handful in the air. My mind slipped out of its straitjacket. I screamed, "Yes, goddammit, yes!"

I remembered one of Uncle Herman's favorite de Gaulle quotes: "Faced with crisis, the man of character falls back on himself. He imposes his own stamp of action, takes responsibility for it, makes it his own."

Miles Davis might have simply said, "Finds his own groove and runs it out."

"God is a sneaky magician," Reverend Rampbell liked to say.

My mind fell back on my new card. When it had appeared, I'd figured that it held no useful magic, a fool's lump under my mattress. Until this instant. This card had the face of Reverend Jimmy James, Clara's dad, who would never, in his wildest imagination, think of helping a black man.

And in the time-tested Jewish tradition of being forced to find opportunity in impossible circumstance—like Moses parting the waters, Israelis making the desert bloom, my great-grandfather creating a successful business in the middle of Klan central—I was instantly ready to perform the trick, to impose my stamp of action, to play my groove.

The magic card had slipped into my sleeve two weeks before the temple burned. At the time, I thought that it was useless, even cursed. Ultimately, though, I didn't care if magic or luck had turned it into a blessing. I just said, *Thank you, God.*

I'd casually mentioned to Clara that I'd like to see the inside of her father's church, with its renowned glass-domed sanctuary. It had always been a spectacular sight even in a town with the most churches per capita of any in America. I'd always wondered, as a carpenter, how the outside translated to the inside. She shoved the key at me.

"You don't have the fuckin balls."

Not that I had to prove my manhood to her anymore, but still... In any case, I was as curious as I was scared senseless.

"Daddy gives everybody Wednesday afternoons off so it'll be empty. Anyway, nobody'll be there and I guarantee you'll be the first Jew ever to set foot there—and the last if he catches you." She laughed.

I didn't.

I asked Dad if he'd ever been in Reverend James's church.

"It's a Jew-free zone," he half laughed. "Never been invited and never expect to be."

Mr. E said, "Those folks hang coloreds on trees and a Jew on the cross. The Negro gits forgotten. The Jew gits famous." Then he laughed.

I'd brought my camera to prove my bravery to Clara. She'd instructed me to go in through the alley instead of the Greek-columned front entrance. A mongrel was taking canine communion at the garbage cans. I kicked at it when it bared its teeth at me and growled, then quietly turned the key in the door. My heart clanked against my eardrums like a gospel stomp. I entered a wide, colonnaded hallway that encircled the interior, according to Clara's hand-drawn map. Every four feet, faux marble columns arose from the heart-oak floors.

The hall widened to a real marble-floored vestibule about forty-by-forty. Doors, inlaid with rosewood crosses, led to the main sanctuary. They were high enough for a giant to step through. In fact, straddling either side and above them stood a thirty-five-foot-high, papier-mâché touchdown Jesus dressed in a football uniform, a leather ball held to heaven in one cocked hand.

"Fucking cheerleaders seduced the shop guys to make it for them," Clara had told me.

Above his raised arms was a temporary sign: "GO REBELS!"

Robert E. Lee, our all-white high school, was playing in the state championship two days later. I stepped through the door between Jesus's legs.

Inside, my underarm BO fused with the smell of a thousand prayer books and the dirt of thousands of shoes on shag carpeting. If my big nose could have left without me, it would have stampeded out then and there.

I snapped a few pictures of the forty-five-foot-high silver cross. At least there was no Jew hanging from it like the Catholics seemed to enjoy. Flanking its left side was a thirty-foot-high Confederate flag, its Virginia cousin to the right. All were gloriously illuminated by a perfectly calibrated shaft of natural light, bleeding dazzling white through the sixty-foot-high, crystal glass dome in the middle of the ceiling, shining down like heaven's own beacon. It felt so peaceful and balanced that I wondered if the architect had practiced what Mr. E called "the Golden ratio," cousin to 3,4,5.

"Started way back with those Greeks," Mr. E once told me. "Ain't somethin a normal black man, nor even white, knows 'bout. All 'bout balancin angles and light and space in a buildin so's you just feel good bein in it without even knowin why. May Matthews showed me a bunch of those kind of buildins in one of those books she's so crazy 'bout. Made me wanna travel to places and see 'em fer real, though the wife would be too scared fer that kind of foreign travel—not to mention the cost—and I ain't far behind in the scared department."

I hung there, riveted. Revile him or not, Clara's father knew how to wow a crowd—and to hire an architect.

Hardly noticeable at first, a sound, familiar and growing louder, grabbed me from my stupor. I tried to deny what my imagination shouted to my mind. But curiosity, or just simple nosiness, called me to it. I crept in its direction.

Moans. They seemed to be coming from a window that looked down from high above the elevated pulpit in the rear of the room.

I tiptoed past an ocean of pews, up onto the dais. At the rear, twenty feet behind the lectern, I saw a small, rounded, mahogany door. An easy twist on its square, brass knob opened onto a landing, which led to eight, dark brown, worn, carpeted steps. My eyes, still somewhat blinded by the light, strained through the sudden gloom. I saw, "He Has Arisen," ornately carved in huge letters across the top of a heavy dogwood door at the top of the stairs. I couldn't help but think that Mr. E and I would have done a better job. A two-foot-wide brass plate below "He Has Arisen," announced "Office of the Minister."

I took off my shoes and jumped a silent dancer's leap to the fourth stair.

Nailed to the middle of the door, a neatly printed rosewood plaque read, "Door never locked to the righteous."

I assumed it was locked.

With another small leap to the sixth step, I landed eye level to a big, old-fashioned key sticking out below the cut glass doorknob.

Now the moans were thick, hard grunts, skin slapping like applause. I bent to the door. Soft as angel wings, slow as a Sunday sermon, I pulled the long key from the open-mouthed keyhole.

The whomping stopped.

"Did you hear something?" A man's voice.

Silence.

"Nah, fuckin mice." Another man's voice.

Whomp.

I held my pee in, but my breath dribbled to the floor.

I peeked through the keyhole.

It hardly took another moment for me to imagine how these two, how this impossible connection, could have happened.

I guessed they'd met at Max's Park. For years, lovers had found privacy in the lush undergrowth and forest of large oak, weeping willow, walnut, pecan, magnolia, and poplar trees that had grown since Great-Grandpa Max had timbered it. The hidden crannies, crevices, and corners of the park provided refuge. With the packed, multi-generational houses of the post-World War II city, privacy was hard to find. Clara and I had often enjoyed its verdant security.

One section of the park had, by word of mouth and action, become the domain of the homosexual crowd. "Perv Pasture," it was called by the teenage boys who took pleasure in random drunken attacks during weekend bouts of small-town boredom.

What must have been lonely, desperate gay men would hide in the darkness searching for another. One heard only the muffled sounds of grunting and the whumping of bodies against one another, of soft moans.

It never hurt the police department to occasionally wage a queer bust. Big headlines.

Out of fear of these inevitable raids and their ruinous potential, particularly for men of high standing in the community, personal relationships must have developed so that they could meet in less public places, such as where I now stood.

Through the keyhole, I saw in profile Rabbi Mordechai Tichter being fucked in the ass by Reverend Jimmy James, Clara's father. The three-foot cross to the right of his desk bobbed in and out of view as James's heft jerked forward in front of it, illuminated perfectly by a well-placed window's shaft of light, then re-cocked for another thrust into Tichter, lying prone, splayed across the desktop. The sun shined right into their faces. I didn't know if I would throw up or laugh. Then the sad face of Rabbi Tichter's wife hurdled into my mind.

I shivered, sweating.

My Dad had always preached that a good businessman jumps on opportunity. A photographer is no different. Automatic.

What would Clara do? I thought. *At least if it weren't her own father.*

I noticed what looked like a vestment hanging on a hook by the door. I grabbed it. It felt like silk, with a faint smoky smell. It took me a moment to understand. No cheap potato or Martha White flour sack for the Reverend. I slipped the hood over my head and arranged the eyeholes.

All of a sudden, a commotion, heavy shoes hitting the floor. My heart knocked against my ribs as if that quarterback Jesus had heaved his football full speed at me. I held my breath until it felt like my eyes would pop out. I prayed that my exhale wasn't as loud as the shuffling sounds on the other side of the door. My mind jumped down the stairs, but my feet, dead-weight glued to the floor, failed to obey.

The door didn't open. I refilled my lungs and put my eye back to the keyhole. Now Tichter was the fucker, on top.

I checked my aperture setting, shook myself steady, and took another breath. My Old Spice deodorant, a comforting familiarity, fought against the fear stench soaking my pits. Holding my camera with one hand, I slammed the door open with the other and fired the shutter. *Click.* Their heads turned in unison, frozen. Deer in headlights. One-thousand-one to advance the film winder. *Fire.* Two pictures before they thawed. I grabbed my shoes and was gone before they could stuff their erections into their pants without zipping their dicks.

Running all the way home, two miles, I kept thinking, "What the hell have I just done?" I was moving so fast that I stumbled right in front of my house, hands scraping across the concrete sidewalk like a facedown slide on a sandpaper home plate.

As usual, no one was home, Mom off to one of her endless charity meetings or bridge games, Dad at work, and my brother and sister attending some club or sports activity.

Neck outstretched, Fluffy, our pet duck, ran to me as he did everyday when I returned home. He'd lay there until I patted and soothed his feathers, then quack contentedly and follow me to the doorway. For once, I ignored him. He followed me toward the front door, quacking angrily.

I ran inside and slammed my bedroom door shut. Leaning against the cool, pinewood paneling, panting, eyes shut, I yanked the hood off. As I'd run from the church, I'd forgotten I had it on.

I looked down at my bloodied hands. My whole body twitched from the pain and oozy blisters bubbling up. I wiped my palms against the hood. With nauseous tremors, I dug out a few pebbles from my fingers and struggled against shaking, grimy, slippery, blood-wet hands to roll the film to the end. I grabbed a tin film canister off of my dresser, stuck the film in it, and screwed on the lid, then stuffed it underneath my mattress and collapsed.

"What the hell have I done?" I kept thinking.

Safe for the moment, I started to doze, more a faint. A picture popped into my head, an understanding, finally. Something that had been eating at me since I was fourteen—when Rabbi Tichter's wife, Nadya, had seduced me.

CHAPTER SIXTEEN

I'd always thought that most preachers were creepy, and Clara's life only reinforced that opinion. So it wasn't much of a leap to believe in her father's perversion. In its own twisted way, it almost seemed as Southern as a mint julep. Rumors of all sorts of dalliances and deviances flowed through small Southern towns: farmboy bestiality, black-white attraction, "call John at xxxx for a good dick-sucking" written on bathroom stalls, tales of girls that "did it," and the whispers about charismatic preachers and the women they preyed on.

But a homosexual Orthodox rabbi? And married? With a Klan preacher lover? The thought would have been impossible to imagine had I not been part of a shameful secret. I'd always assumed Jews were somehow above it all, my own tidal waves of lust notwithstanding. Now, it started to make awful sense. I thought back to when I was twelve.

"Sit down and start reading your *parsha*," my *Torah* portion, Rabbi Mordechai Tichter had commanded me.

"In spite of your father's desertion to the blasphemous Reform Temple, I have agreed to teach you as a favor to your grandfather so that you will not become another *goy* Jew," he said, stroking his gray hedge of untamed beard.

I was just beginning my *Bar Mitzvah* studies. It was about seven years before the temple fire. I'd just started working for Mr. E. While Mr. E eventually embraced me, Tichter seemed only to want to disgrace me. Dad had left the Orthodox congregation years before.

"Keep me or keep kosher," my mother had insisted when he asked her to marry him. Grandpa forgave him after he agreed that my brother and I would be tutored by and have our *Bar Mitzvahs* at the Orthodox synagogue.

"These Reform are not real Jews," Rabbi Tichter announced, when he arrived with his new bride in the late '50s. He said this to my grandfather, a founder of the Orthodox congregation and its president for fifteen years. I heard it all the first time Grandpa invited Tichter to our regular Friday night family *Shabbas* dinner.

"They betray the covenants by working on the Sabbath, by not keeping kosher, by allowing their women to dress shamelessly, displaying their breasts and using makeup like whores, by not praying daily, and by failing to follow faithfully the unbendable Jewish laws and rules of daily living. They are heretics and should be condemned. Excommunicated! And their profane rabbi should be shunned by our followers. I will not sit at the same table with him, and neither should you or our members. It defiles all of us to even associate with these infidels."

Grandpa replied, "My son, his family, and his congregation are welcome here. I love them. Reform, Orthodox… these are all my family and friends. We don't need a schism. We've all grown up together here in this Southern diaspora. Only one hundred Jewish families. We hired you because of your passion for Judaism. You're young. Please don't confuse yourself, don't turn that passion into poison. Here in the deep South, all of us, the Reform, too, have made our choices for survival's sake, out of necessity, so that we can make a living and find a Jewish wife and get along with the Gentiles."

Rabbi Tichter replied, "No life is worth living and no wife is worth having if she is not strictly observant."

He and Tichter never got along after that, but the Orthodox congregation was so thankful to have found a rabbi willing to live in the small, Southern town that they wouldn't fire him.

After my first few lessons with Tichter, I begged Grandpa at *Shabbas* dinner to let me prepare with Rabbi Gross, our itinerant hippie rabbi, instead.

"I see why people hate Jews!" I screamed and cried.

Dad's face turned so red I thought he was going to slap me.

"Donala," Grandpa Abe pleaded, patting me on the head. "Both communities will come to your *Bar Mitzvah*. It might help create peace between them. You will be the antidote to this rabbi's venom."

"More like the sacrificial lamb."

"Hush now," he said, his face approaching the color of Dad's. "You're almost a man. And some things a man must do for the greater good. End of discussion!"

When I'd go to Rabbi Tichter's house for those lessons, his wife Nadya, the *Rebbitzen*, was always nice to me. She'd wave, smile, and leave homemade chocolate chip cookies. She seemed as fresh and sweet as her cookies.

"I was raised in a classic Orthodox Brooklyn *schtetl*," a strictly Jewish neighborhood, she told my *Bar Mitzvah* class one day at their parsonage beside the *shul*. We had spare time because her husband was late for our group lesson.

Though dressed plainly and with little makeup, she was nevertheless an attractive, full-figured woman in her early twenties. Out of all the *Bar Mitzvah* class, I liked to think I was her favorite.

When she leaned over our table to deliver a plate of baked goodies and glasses of milk, wearing her loose, Israeli-style, cotton blouse, we boys would crane our necks to peek at her marble white breasts and snicker to one another.

"Some moderns complain that Orthodox women are limited to only serving men and the community as wives and mothers and for continuing the religious traditions in the home," she told us that day. "But my sisters and I studied all sorts of things. Around the dinner table, all of us—boys, girls, family, and guests—always discussed important secular issues and business ideas. And, of course, debated Biblical interpretations and other things that mattered, all wrapped in a synagogue-centered community. I loved it."

She'd look around as if to make sure no one else was listening. "And I don't see why girls can't read directly from the *Torah*—can't be a *Bat Mitzvah*. It's tradition, yes. But it's not Jewish law. Men have stolen our right to read the *Torah* from us."

We nodded our heads with vigor. As long as she kept bending over at the right angle, raising our hopes for the nipple jackpot, and giving us cookies, we didn't really care.

Just as she finished speaking, we heard the doorknob turn. Her skin flushed with what I eventually realized was plain fear. She put her finger to her mouth. "Shhh," she whispered. "He's coming."

Two years later, a year after my *Bar Mitzvah* and five years before the fire, I was again sent to the Tichter's little house, this time to deliver a suit. Just turned fourteen, with a newly minted driver's license, I'd become the store's designated delivery *schlepper*.

"The Rabbi is teaching in the next town for the rest of the day," the *Rebbetzin* said. "Please come in, Donala, for tea and cookies."

Because she was in her own home, her long, shiny, straight, black hair was uncovered—not hidden with the customary wigs she always wore at our classes and in public. It made me realize that she was much younger than her husband. Her husband's congregation, at his behest, demanded that the women wear wigs or scarves completely covering their hair everywhere except in the private company of their husbands and kids.

But after only three years of marriage, she looked very different from my Bar Mitzvah days; now, worry lines creased her brow. Her rosy-cheeked radiance had disappeared, eyes sallow and sunken and fearful like those of a beaten dog.

Though ill at ease—what does a fourteen-year-old boy talk about with the Orthodox rabbi's wife—I knew it would be impolite to refuse her kind offer of tea and cookies.

"But could I have milk instead of tea, please?"

"Yes, yes, of course."

A scratchy recording of a female singing in Yiddish was playing on her record player. It was mixed with weird-sounding clarinets and tambourines and stringed instruments—"It's a *klezmer* band," she said. I thought it sounded awful.

She led me to the kitchen, nodding for me to sit. Four blue-speckled, vinyl, straight-back chairs were arranged around a lighter blue plastic-topped, steel-rimmed table, the four chrome legs splayed out spiderlike.

I felt a tension in the air, like we were both holding our breaths. I certainly was.

She carefully poured the milk, placed the plate of cookies in front of me, sat down on the chair beside mine, and took a deep breath. She closed her eyes, ironed her skirt smooth with both hands, sighed, then stared at me. Her eyes seemed to shine with a sort of glaze.

"Ours was an arranged marriage," she said out of the blue. " 'You are marrying a *rebbe*,' the whole family, young and old, purred. 'Oh, you lucky girl! God has blessed you.' "

"Oh," I said, taking the first bite of my cookie.

"My family felt honored. I was happy to get married."

I nodded and licked my milk mustache.

"But I am not happy. How can you live down here in this little Southern town, Donala, and not go insane?"

"Well, I've just been here all my life," I answered after taking another bite of a cookie and then realizing by her silent stare that she expected an answer. "But I know what you mean. Every class stands, no matter what the teacher is saying, when the band practices 'Dixie.' "

Don't talk with your mouth full, I could hear my mother saying.

It seemed the *Rebbetzin* hardly noticed that I'd spoken. Her eyes darted around as if she was being bothered by bugs flying around her head. She even swatted her hands at them once or twice, though I didn't see any.

" 'We must help these desperate Jews,' my husband insisted when he was offered the position here," she said. "He said, 'They are forced to live amongst the heathens. They have begged me to move to the South. Their spiritual lives are desolate. It is breaking my heart, Nadya, for us to have to leave our rich New York community.' He almost cried to me. 'But sometimes, Nadya dear, we must sacrifice our own comfort and convenience to bring God's words to the less fortunate. Nadya, God has called on us. It is our duty, our destiny.' I felt so unworthy, Donala, so spoiled and so thankful to be married to such a virtuous man.

"But these Southern people are so strange to me. They worship pork barbecue. I can barely understand their mumbling speech. When I speak, they keep saying, 'Come agin?' " she said, failing miserably to imitate the local drawl.

"In New York, our community spoke English in public, Yiddish amongst ourselves, and Hebrew in synagogue—so I know I have an unusual accent. But, do I sound that strange to you, Donala?"

She was beginning to *look* strange at that moment—again staring past me as she spoke, eyes watery, swatting again above her head.

"Wayyull, it shorely ain't like we talk round heeya," I said. I thought she would laugh at my exaggerated accent. But she only grimaced.

"I have no culture, no friends, no family, and no love."

She clenched her hands into fists, rubbing one against the other, round and round.

"People here say we are 'Christ-killers' and some have even spit at me. Oh Donala, it is killing me. My spirit is dying."

I grabbed two more cookies and gulped the milk.

"But I would be able to continue my existence, with God's help, amen, even with this type of desolation if only my husband had the intention to bestow upon me as his wife, bound to him for life, the love and affection, which my family, God bless them, always informed me the bonds of a marriage would contain."

I was feeling jittery. Her English sounded even more stilted and drawn-out than usual.

"Almost from the start, he ordered me around as a master does a slave. He has never said 'I love you.' My dream has become a nightmare. But as you know, in the Orthodox world, divorce for these reasons is not an option."

I didn't know.

"I'm really sorry," I said.

I started to stand. I wanted to run.

"Thank you for the cookies," I was about to say, but her hand on my shoulder pressed me back onto the chair. I clutched at another cookie.

"He touches me only on *Shabbas.* After we were first introduced, the first time we were ever alone, he told me very seriously, 'The Bible says that it is a man's duty to be intimate with his wife on *Shabbas.'* I thought he was making sure that I knew that he cared about his holy duties to his wife, based on the *Torah*—a Jewish man's duty to please his wife. He seemed so sweet, like a shy little boy, even though he was twenty years older than me. But there was no affection. His touch is cold. On Saturday morning, he says only, 'It is time to copulate.' I feel more like a bag than a woman. And when he is done, in a minute… or less," as a tear shimmied down her cheek, "he rushes out to study or leave."

I gaped at her, flinging my hand to the remaining cookie, guzzling the last of the milk.

"More milk?" she poured from the glass pitcher before I could answer, splashing half of it over the top of my glass. She walked barefoot over to the counter, tossed more cookies on the plate, dropped it wobbling onto the table, then plopped down.

"He tells me I am lucky to have him, especially since I have not given him children.

" 'Who wants a barren woman?' he sneers at me," her eyes rolling up again toward the ceiling, her eyelids fluttering like a moth's wings.

My leg started bouncing like my old pogo stick. I wanted to jump on it and bounce right out of there.

"The women will say that it must be my fault for not inflaming his passions. Oh, Donala," turning her head to me, "I must be evil to have been cursed this way. I miss my family and real love."

My face itched, hot and frozen. Her hands were shaking, tears falling. I felt helpless and sad and lost. So, as my Mom or Dad would do for me, I reached over to her and patted her arm.

In an instant, her chair scraped against the hard linoleum floor, its metal leg clanging against the table leg between us. She yanked the chair in a clean lift over it to face mine, our knees now touching. Her hand shot to mine, pulling and caressing it to her teary face.

"Oy, oy, oy. Why, why, why?" she kept repeating.

"I'm...I'm really sorry," I said, as a cockroach scurried across the floor.

She stomped it and squeezed my hand tighter. She lifted it to her lips, kissed my knuckles gently, laid her wet cheek on them, and closed her eyes.

"You are so wonderful to talk to," she said.

I'd said practically nothing, especially since my mouth had been stuffed with cookies.

My hand vise-gripped, I sat stone-cold still. Her other hand seemed to float to my head. Her fingers hesitated, then waltzed around my scalp in a rhythmic kind of massage, tenderly grabbing and pulling and shaking my hair close to the scalp, back and forth.

She sighed deeply again, her bloodshot eyes swimming through pools of tears toward mine, the corners of her lips in a strange kind of crooked smile.

I felt dizzy. My head swayed backward, then side to side as she stroked it. My eyelids felt heavy.

She leaned closer, her breath scented with *matzoh* ball soup. I could see the pot on the stove. I loved *matzoh* ball soup. I felt as warm inside as when I ate the stuff. She steadied my chin in the cup of her right hand. Her other slithered across my head from the top to the back. She pulled me toward her face and kissed my forehead, then my cheek, her warm tears lubricating the glide of our skin.

With a startle, she drew her head back, staring through me, ropey lines cinching on her forehead, her eyes blinking like a shorting light.

"Why, why, why?" she kept saying.

Only my jaw moved, a ventriloquist's dummy, without words.

Her index finger, clean, with no nail polish, floated across my lips and onto my lower teeth. I didn't know whether to bite it, lick it, suck it, or try to say something sympathetic with a finger in my mouth. Then, ever so slowly and lightly, her face relaxing, uncoiling, her finger on my cheek, she looked into my eyes and kissed my mouth.

"Oh God, oh God, oh God," she murmured.

The combination of her chicken-souped breath and her kiss sent warm shivers down my spine.

"What is my life? What have I done to deserve this? Where is my God?" She kissed me again. Then again.

I didn't resist. Her tongue dog-licked the inside of my cheeks, my tongue, my teeth, pushing.

I pulled my head back to take a breath. She was so beautiful now. I felt insane, flooded, heavy, delirious, and...pretty damn GREAT.

Except for the fleeting instant it took me to recognize, then ignore, the same scorching, vacant eyes as the woman we called "Crazy Lady." She would storm into our store on Saturdays, her hair disheveled, wearing a tattered, dirty, floral dress, ripped sweater, and workman's boots without shoelaces, front teeth missing, fiercely shouting, "Ya gots any money fer me?" Her desperate, empty look somehow rendered us helpless to deny her our pocket change.

"Oh, Donala, you are so sweet," the *Rebbetzin* said as she pulled my head to her chest, "and my heart is broken."

Her heart was bongo-beating and mine doubled hers.

Slowly, her hand undid the top button of her blouse and then the one below it. She placed my limp hand under her bra. I felt my first non-mother breast, big and full and heaving. She jammed my hand against her hard nipple, rubbing it, roughing it. I was floating, feverish, scared...though not enough to say stop. Her kisses assaulted me. We groaned.

In that instant, I could hear my, "your-mother-was-my-first-and-only-love," Dad sitting on one shoulder saying, "This isn't right." On the other, I could hear my buddies screaming, "Jesus Christ, wow!" At that thought, a small grin escaped.

She noticed. "You look strange," she said.

Me? I thought. *Look who's talking.*

"Are you not liking this?" she said, pulling away, popcorn-eyed.

I was about to explain when she slid from her chair onto my leg, straddling it, then slowly moving her hips forward, back, forward, back. Faster, faster, her head and neck swooshing up and back, lips pursing with each thrust, pushing straight-armed against my chest, then pulling back with her hands around the back of my neck, eyes closed.

I sat there doing nothing in return, her movements like shock waves of crazy pleasure and confusion. I knew she must be crazy, but I was fourteen—it felt like a dream, the one most fourteen-year-old boys imagined, only this was real. I wanted it.

She shoved my hand between her legs, up past her white support stockings, the kind that old and devout women wore, past the garter belt clips until I felt the soft flesh of her upper inner thighs. Her panties were so wet I thought she had peed. I didn't know anything about women. Did they pee before sex? I wished I could look it up in a book.

Moving up and down, side to side, sliding on my leg on a wave of warm woman wet, she pushed the fingers of my hand into her vagina.

"God forgive me," she cried. "I have become insane."

I thought that was definitely the truth. But from some place beyond my dick that young boys are never given enough credit for, I answered, "God loves you."

And, at that moment, so did I—at least the part of a fourteen-year-old that sends emotions from the crotch to the heart.

Then she stopped.

"I cannot let you have sex with me."

"Uh…what?" I said. *If this wasn't sex,* I thought, *what was it?* And, assuming it was, was this the way it started and ended with an older woman?

"You cannot make love to me. My upbringing," she panted, "will not let me violate my marriage vows with fornication, no matter what. The *Torah* forbids fornication."

I didn't know what to do with my hand.

Her eyes rolled high into her head. Frown lines deepened between them. She seemed to be thinking. Then they returned to me with a piercing stare.

"But that is all that is explicitly forbidden."

Two days later, she called the store and ordered a shirt. When I arrived, she handed me a salami, about eight inches long, and said, "Try this."

"I'm not really hungry," I said.

"No…put it in me."

"Is it OK?" I said, thinking of the hygienic as well as the anatomical safety of putting a salami up a woman's vagina.

"Of course, it is," she replied academically. "It is Hebrew National, completely kosher."

I learned what I assume lesbians know by instinct, that great sex can be had without a dick. I also learned that one can do a lot with salami.

"Deeper, more, deeper," she insisted, shouting out to me in her desperate frenzy. I was scared that I would hurt her, not to mention scared in and of itself. But she pushed against it and jammed my hand to make it go as deep as it could. I never imagined that an entire salami would fit into a woman.

"Life is not just," she sighed afterward, "but God provides. I had never had an orgasm before today. My husband never cared."

But I did, even if the whole thing felt wrong. To feel her, us, shake at those moments—whether due to salami or my hands or my leg against her genitals, she kissing me and putting my penis in her mouth or rubbing it with her hand and saying how wonderful I was—was the most thrilling thing I had ever known. So overwhelmingly wonderful that it was easy for me to ignore her crazy eyes, her fly-swatting at unseen insects and her, "Oh God, how can I be doing this?"

"I have to have you inside of me, one way or another," she insisted a few weeks later, our third time together, her husband gone as usual. She bunched her faded sack dress above her sumptuous porcelain butt, then pulled it up and off of her broad shoulders and head. Her dark black, shiny hair cascaded down to her lower back. She had no underwear on.

"But, I thought fornication was…"

"Please, my Donala, just try it. It is not fornication," she interrupted, pointing.

Since puberty, in my non-stop wet dreams, I thought I'd imagined doing about everything a fourteen-year-old boy could do with a female. But I'd never thought of "it." I had no idea what to do.

"I have been preparing myself," she said, holding up a fat kosher hot dog. "Carnegie Deli brand, shipped straight from New York City by my mother," she said with a strange sort of pride and a crooked smile. "They are my favorite. Do you like them, Donala?"

A picture of Mom's Sunday lunches popped into my mind. "Yeah, I always eat two."

She lowered herself onto the floor, on all fours, her butt shining, slathered with mayonnaise ("Hellmann's—the others are not kosher," she told me earnestly later), awaiting me. Her alabaster cheeks with the hint of her labia peeking out below, like a pink maple leaf against an early fall snow, was so strangely alluring and exciting that I felt dizzy.

"Oy oy oy," she almost sang as we lay together afterward. "I loved you inside me, finally." She smiled, kissing me all over. "I feel split in half."

I hoped that was good.

"It was a reminder all day long of the pleasure and love that you give me," she said at our next rendezvous.

"Oy, oy, oyyyyyyyyy veeeeeeey!" Nadya would scream when she orgasmed. Four years later, Clara would scream, "Jesus, oh Jesus, oh Jee-suussss Chriiiiist," when she came.

"Even though we both know this is not a real relationship," Nadya said the fourth time we made love, "we have a very special bond, my sweet *boychik*."

In post-coital bliss, we talked about our lives like best friends.

"Do you have a girlfriend in your school?" she'd tease me. Then, "The Davises, members for twenty-five years, have just left the congregation after my husband accused them at the board meeting of eating *traif*," non-kosher, "in restaurants."

Since our lovemaking had started, her worried, beaten look had transformed into the sweetness I remembered from my *Bar Mitzvah* days. The color had returned to her cheeks. She seemed almost happy.

Except that she would still cry at times, and sometimes still swat at those imaginary flies. "I am such a sinner," she'd moan while I lay beside her, trying to think of soothing words, knowing that she was right and what we were doing was wrong. "I live in a world of guilt and self-hate," she'd cry. "Though I make salami and hot dogs and Hellmann's seem funny and carefree, it is really my feeble attempts to make light of what we do, of the sin I have embraced, of the wretchedness I have woven you into like a spider spinning a web for her prey."

I had trouble knowing, even while making love, if her tears were of joy or despair. But neither of us could stop ourselves. "I am desperate," she'd say, "to feel human love, to be more than a religious theory."

I appreciated her pain and struggle as much as a young boy could. But my empathy was a transient itch when thrown against her grabbing, frantic need and my own lust. I was a willing victim of her desperation.

Nadya always took extra time after I'd arrive checking and rechecking the lock to the door of her house, "in case *they* come after us."

"Who?" I'd ask.

"The ones who leave the terrible notes about killing Jews."

I would hear her clicking the deadbolt and shaking the door each time as I left. She'd told me her husband kept a gun.

"He says the Jews in Nazi Germany who let themselves be exterminated were fools."

It was one of the few thoughts that he and Reb Gross agreed upon, though Reb Gross would never call the victims fools.

On my fifth trip to her house, the door was ajar.

"Anyone home?" I shouted. No answer.

Looking around, I saw that the alley door, the back door to the synagogue's sanctuary, was wide open. I walked the ten feet to the door, frozen gravel crunching under my leather-soled shoes, glad to be wearing my wool overcoat.

"Hello," I called as I stuck my head through the open door. It felt as cold as the outside. To save money, the synagogue's heat was always turned off on the many days the rabbi was out of town visiting small Jewish enclaves too poor or underpopulated to afford their own rabbi.

I heard sobbing. No lights.

"Nadya?" I called.

I strained to see through the dim, dusty light, filtered through grime-coated, stained-glass windows. The familiar smell of moldy carpet insulted my nostrils. I stepped inside, tripping on a rip in the carpet. The room was as familiar as my own house. But today, somehow, its high-ceilinged gloom was so dense that I staggered like a blind man, my hands outstretched to avoid the chairs and tables.

I stumbled up the two pulpit steps onto the flat expanse of the *bema*. I walked, step by step, another five or so feet until my foot caught on a lump, sending me sprawling onto the floor.

"I am invisible to my husband and to God. They have abandoned me," the lump moaned through the darkness. "I have violated the holy covenants of marriage."

I sat up, hands searching, until they found Nadya's bare feet. Like a spring-loaded hinge, she jolted upright to sitting, throwing her arms around me. The two sides of the *Torah* scroll she'd been clutching to her naked breasts—each three feet high and as thick as rolled beach towels—fell to the floor on either side of her thighs.

"We pray through it but are banned from reading from it," she whispered. Her breath felt hot against my ear. "Why does God hate women?" Her hands scratched in the air down toward the parchment between the scrolls. "Why has he left me in darkness?"

Then the unique blackness dawned on me.

"You blew out the *Ner Tamid*?" The Everlasting Light, a scrupulously filled oil lamp hung above the *Torah* ark, was never extinguished as a symbol of God's eternal presence in our lives.

"Oh Nadya," I said. "What have you done?"

Her head snapped up. I saw her "Crazy Lady" eyes as mine adjusted.

"Donala? My savior? You have returned to me?"

"Christ, Nadya. Are you ok?"

I thought to myself, *What a stupid question.* Not to mention invoking Jesus while crouching in a synagogue with a naked rabbi's wife.

"Read, read it to me," she said. "Read, Donala, read God's words," touching her index finger to the hand-lettered Hebrew characters on the ancient scroll next to her left leg, leaving a fingerprint-sized oil stain on the goatskin page. "Tell me, tell me why women are cursed. Why can I not know God's own words? God has left us in darkness. Read to me, Donala."

I wanted to leave. I wanted cookies and milk. Nadya was shivering.

"Oh Nadya," I said, putting my cheek to hers. Her shoulder shuddered at the touch of the cold silk lining as I draped my overcoat around her bare back.

I forced myself to stand and walked behind her. With my arms on either side of her waist, I reached down to the floor, grabbed the ends of the wooden scroll shafts. But the twenty-pound scrolls slipped out of my sweaty hands, falling to the floor again, the section across her legs ripping slightly, pinning down her knees. Nadya sat frozen. Pushing from the balls of my feet to straighten my bent knees, I lifted the two rolled columns vertically above her head, fighting to keep from further tearing them. Finally, I laid them on the cloth-covered reading table at the front of the pulpit, just in front of us and the ark.

I hoisted her up and buttoned the coat, pulling it around her chest and waist and legs.

"Let's get out of here," I said.

She didn't move. She only moaned louder, "Why, Donala? Why am I forbidden to speak to God?"

No matter my tugging, she seemed cemented to the floor.

I was desperate to do something. Anything. How would I ever explain any of this if I had to call an ambulance, or Dad, or Grandpa, or if her husband returned?

"Let's read the words," I said, banging my hand onto the scrolls. "Let's read from the *Torah* together. Let's make you a *Bat Mitzvah*."

Her head tilted like a child struck.

"Women are never allowed. We are cursed."

"Nadya!" I shouted, hoping it would snap her back into herself. "That's tradition, not law. Like you told my *Bar Mitzvah* class."

Her eyelids blinked willy-nilly, like a short-circuiting neon sign, then snapped wide open.

"Can we read now?" she asked, suddenly sounding almost academic, normal.

"What part?" I asked.

"It does not matter. God will show us."

I tightened the scroll ends until the section between them was flat. I reached under the table for the candles and matches that were used for the *Shabbas* blessings every Friday night. I scratched the match against the bottom of the table. The light erupted onto her face. It looked like the face of a stranger.

We said the required prayer before reading from the *Torah*.

"Donala, the letters are dancing on the page."

"Read them," I barked.

"Ah –may – ay – ay – ayn," she sang haltingly, the amen said before the start and after the blessings at the end of any reading of the *Torah*. Her voice quivered, reed-thin. As she continued, it rose and fell, her tears splashing on the parchment. A cold breeze from the open door flickered the candlelight dark, then bright against her face and stumbling efforts.

She read five paragraphs, a traditional number, then stopped. It took only a few minutes.

"Did I read well, Donala?" she asked, sounding as innocent as a thirteen-year-old girl.

"Yes, Nadya, perfect. You have done your *mitzvah.* Now sing the prayer after the reading and amen. With one last burst of enthusiasm, she sang.

"I have read from the *Torah,*" she exhaled. "I am a *Bat Mitzvah.* I have talked to God."

"Yes, yes, you are, Nadya. You did a great job. God is pleased."

It was the first time a woman had, or probably would ever, read from the *Torah* in the many decades of the *shul.*

"Now, let's go home," I said. I put her arm around my shoulder, holding her hand in mine as I put my other arm around her limp waist. I leaned her down, like a puppet on a string, so that I could pick up her clothes, then shuffled and dragged her past the door. We were soaked in sweat, yet shivering. Just outside, she braked. Her head darted back and forth around the alley, eyes again speed-blinking.

"What if God strikes me down? Or if my husband discovers my blasphemy? Or if they are waiting to hurt us?"

Before I could say a word, she mumbled, "I am so tired," her eyes drooping shut.

We stumbled into her house and then to her bedroom. I sat her on her bed. She didn't move, sitting upright, her eyes closed. I found her nightgown, tugged my overcoat off of her, pulled the nightgown over her shoulders, slipped her under the covers, and lay down on the bedspread beside her. She fell into an instant snore. I kissed her forehead and locked the door as I left, then locked the synagogue door, and threw up in the alley.

Nadya called a few days later, a Wednesday. I skipped school during lunch break. I was scared to see her and scared not to. She opened the alley door, took one step out, put her left hand flat against the front of my shoulder and her right over my lips. Her eyes were sunken, her hair wrapped in a black scarf, the old lady stockings visible below her ankle length wool skirt. She looked straight at me with a clear, no longer crazy, sad smile.

"You have been a healing for me, Donala, because I have been wounded in so many ways for so long," she sighed. "Your care and affection have pierced more than my body, but it cannot continue. It is unfair to you, so young, and not right by me. I am a despicable horror, nothing more than a whore no matter my supposed justifications. I hope I have not hurt you. I am sorry."

"But…" I started to protest.

"Shhhh…" the tips of her fingers braced around my lips. She kissed my forehead, turned around, and disappeared into the doorway, looking back with a last weak wave.

"Does he know…" I tried, but the door closed and the lock clicked. I saw her silhouette through the curtained window, arms floating to her face as she turned away.

"Dixie" wafted across the river from the high school marching band's practice field.

My feet were bricks. I went home, locked the door to my room and stared at the ceiling. For the next two days at school, my best Jewish buddy, Ben, called me "the wandering zombie-Jew," though he never guessed the why of it.

I knew the affair had been a blasphemy, and I knew that Nadya was a hundred percent correct in ending it and that I hadn't had the guts to do it myself. Yet, I had to admit that it was wonderful in spite of its and her insanity. Perverse though it was, Nadya had shared with me the God-given joy and love a woman can share with a man and vice versa. In spite of whatever condemnations grown-ups, and even my own young forming ethics, might have rendered, I felt deep love for her and was grateful within my shame.

Five months later, she and Reb Tichter attended my grandparents' weekly family *Shabbas* dinner. As I peeked sideways to the end of the table, she looked like a plum gone to prune. She'd lost so much weight that between her saggy skin, vacant eyes, and pasty skin, she looked like a walking zombie. She barely even acknowledged me, or anyone else.

Her husband, slurring from Grandma's homemade wine, stood up. "I have a funny joke to tell," he said.

"A sixty-ish widow lays on her towel at the beach," he boomed. "A similarly-aged man places his chair nearby. Catching him looking at her, she gestures to him to come sit by her. 'Are you married?' she asks. 'No,' he shakes his head. 'My sweet wife died of cancer three years ago.' 'Oh, my husband too,' she says, shaking her head. 'Are you lonely?' she asks. 'Oh, terribly,' he replies. 'Only my dog and I now.' 'Oh, and do you like pussycats?' she asks. With that, the man yanks off his swimsuit, tugs hers off, and copulates with the woman.

'That was wonderful,' she says. 'How did you know that was exactly what I wanted?'

'How did you know my last name was Katz?' he answered."

Roaring with laughter, the Rabbi took another drink of his wine and sat down.

How could this man, one who claimed to represent God's love, treat Nadya like he did and still live with himself? I wanted to shoot him, like Marshal Dillon did to bad guys in the TV show "Gunsmoke." My six-year-old sister's eyes darted question marks at the still-quiet crowd, heads slightly bowed, staring at their fascinating lap crumbs.

Rabbi Tichter reached for more wine.

Grandpa, beet-faced, started to stand, napkin bunched tightly in his fist. Grandma gave him the *sit down* look, cleared her throat, shifted in her chair at the far end of the table, and rang the bell hard for the maid.

"Desert anyvon?" she asked, slightly shaking her head side to side at Grandpa, who sat back down.

The maid, Aida, walked in with the sterling silver tray Grandma had brought when she'd fled the Russian Revolution. It was laden with Nadya's homemade cookies and pastries.

Nadya sprang up from her chair. "Let me do that, please," she said, yanking the platter from Aida's hands. She walked around the table mechanically delivering her desserts.

"Would you like some cookies?" she asked blankly when she finally reached me, as if I were simply any other fourteen-year-old boy at his Grandmother's table.

I stiffened. I wanted to talk to her, to feel her hand.

"Yes, please," was all I could manage.

She plunked down some cookies and walked away, dull and dead-eyed.

Neither she nor her wretched husband had any inkling of how our lives would collide into Mr. E's five years later.

CHAPTER SEVENTEEN

The day after my picture-taking adventure at Clara's father's church, Clara rushed over to me in the hall at school, a naughty co-conspirator's smile lighting up her face.

"How was it?" she asked, seconds before first period. I'd come to school late, trying to avoid her.

"Oh, it was okay," I sputtered. "Ran out. Too spooky. Heard noises."

"Prob'ly mice. Daddy says they're runnin all over the place. But what'd you think of the place?"

"Nice place," I said. "God would be proud of his son."

"Very funny," she answered. She cocked her head, her face somewhere between a grimace and a smile. "No, really, how was it?"

"Gotta go. Late for class," I said, as I ran into the classroom. I was so nervous and agitated from what I'd seen that I couldn't calm myself enough to even lie well.

For days afterward, she bugged me to tell her more about what I thought of the place and how I felt being in there. But every time she asked, all I could think about was her father and the rabbi—and what recklessness had pushed me to barge in and take their picture.

What good could telling her then have possibly done? The fire hadn't happened yet. Mr. Rippe hadn't died yet. Mr. E hadn't been arrested yet. I couldn't see any positives in saying, "Oh, by the way, Clara, your dad is a homosexual butt-fucking hypocritical adulterer, with a rabbi no less."

No. Leave the useless pictures under the mattress, try to forget about it all, and start whatever lies or diversions I could to get her off my back.

And so I tried to act as if it was no big deal, making jokes about her father's Taj Mahal church or changing the subject, hoping she'd also just forget about it. Soon, she did. But I remembered Mr. E saying how once you start lying, it's hard to stop.

And I couldn't. And it showed. For the two weeks preceding the fire, my lies were all about her father's heinousness. I could never figure out why telling her would solve anything or help her with her life. And it ate at me as certainly as a parasite slowly devouring my soul, and our relationship.

But now, since the fire and my revelation about what to do with the pictures, I was even more stricken.

"What's wrong, Donny? You're so tense," she'd say. "You're holding something back from me, ever since the fire."

It was almost a relief that she thought my growing obtuseness and distance was *only* about the fire.

She tried to counsel me, to sympathize and empathize, to open me up. She tried seducing me. She cried and begged.

We went to our cemetery redoubt, leaning against one of the rebel mausoleums.

"Are you seein somebody else?" she said. "Do you not like me anymore? Did I say somethin or do somethin wrong? Is it cause I'm Christian? Is it about the fire?"

"It's all so fucked up. I'm in a deep hole of existential angst," I answered, trying to swat away her concerns.

"And what the hell is that supposed to mean?"

Our philosophy class had just studied Sartre's *Existentialism and Human Emotions.* His ideas felt like boxing gloves to dodge and deflect and beat back her fury, to hide what I knew about her dad.

"Sartre said that, 'Existence precedes Essence.' It means that I have to figure out what I'm supposed to do with the fact that while I was merrily fucking your brains out, Mr. Rippe was burning to toast and now Mr. E's sitting in jail for it. It means I have no fucking idea how to make up for killing Mr. Rippe. Or how to get Mr. E out of this mess."

"Thank you for the lecture, jerkoff. Is that it? You don't think I'm deep enough to go there with you? You think all our relationship is based on is 'merrily fucking'? Well, shame on you, Donny. Shame. Fuck you and your holier-than-thou attitude and whatever it is that's stuck up your ass."

Some mean part of me wanted to answer, "Ha, you should know what's been sticking up your Dad's ass."

She stormed away, fists clenched.

My head ached. I slumped onto the ground. My nerves felt as crinkled and cracked as the dead leaves. Lying there, the comfort of the coffins below me suddenly seemed very appealing.

An old quote friends and I would say in the seventh grade popped into my head, "Do you have the audacity to insinuate that my veracity is prevaricated?" I chuckled in disgust. If my prevarications, feints, and lies to Clara were nails, there would have been enough to hammer a shame mansion.

I drifted into a nap, my escape ever since childhood when my mother hooked up a hammock under our old oak tree every afternoon.

In a dream, I saw the neck of a black man I first thought to be Mr. E standing with his back to me in front of a house under construction. He turned to me. I recognized his face from my philosophy textbook. Jean-Paul Sartre, but with black skin, in overalls.

"Think hard about a problem," he said with Mr. E's voice but with a hard French accent. "Look at it from all za angles—in your mind and on za site. Then make za call, construct your reality and move forward without further hesitation. Along za way, as things are getting built, you might encounter za necessity for other changes. Do not worry about mistakes. To become a man of fluid essence, you must embrace flexibility."

Mr. E walked out from behind him, white-skinned, in the three- piece tweed suit and black-rimmed glasses that Sartre wore in the textbook picture. "That's all you can expect from any man," he said to Sartre, shaking his hand. Then he lifted a gold soprano sax to his mouth and played Coltrane's seventeen-minute version of "My Favorite Things."

I awoke to a dusky pink sky, disappointed that it was only a dream, but whistling the tune as I walked home, trying to make sense of the message.

"Hi," I said to Clara the next day in class, trying to sound upbeat.

She wouldn't look at or talk to me.

My hands A-framed in front of my mouth.

"Clara, I…"

She raised her hand.

"Mrs. Hatcher, may I go to the bathroom? I'm feeling nauseous," she said to the teacher.

I ached to touch her and tell her everything. I wanted to let her know that her father was even worse than she thought. I wanted a partner in my plans. I wanted to crawl inside her, to relax in her warm juice. I wanted her energy and passion and love—to give me strength. I wanted to trust her and I wanted to let her know that she was as important to me as anyone in the world. I wanted her to laugh and cry again with me.

Almost two years before, when I'd first fallen for Clara, my friend May had said, "You've got to turn that new girlfriend of yours on to my Billie Holiday records," after I'd told her how strange and bluesy Clara was. I'd excitedly told May that a Jew had written one of Billie's best tunes, "Strange Trees," about the price the South exacted on blacks. May loved the tune.

"You Jew folks sure are surprisin and amazin," she'd said with a kiss to my cheek.

And, as usual, May was right about Clara.

"That Billie Holiday is my lifeline to reality," Clara told me after she'd listened to May's collection non-stop for days. "Even my mother says she 'hits a nerve.' But we have to hide the records and play 'em when my shithead father is away."

Now Clara's and May's favorite Billie song kept looping through my mind,

If my heart could only talk,
Dreams would all come true.
'Neath the starlight I would walk,
Hand in hand with you.
I would have to seek your lips,
Thrill to your fingertips.
If my heart could only talk.

Yet as Clara walked out, I knew Sartre and Mr. E were right. I had to create my own destiny, without her, if I was going to free Mr. E.

I kept telling myself that I'd caused enough damage and sadness. I couldn't bear inflicting more pain and suffering on another soul, especially Clara. But I knew that was mostly a lie—that I was about to become just another hypocrite.

Because I had to admit that I was excited, after all the abuse Tichter had inflicted on me and on his wife, and Clara's father on her, to hurt and humiliate them. Excited to be cruel to those two men, to "burn" down their wicked houses. They were *schmucks,* but as related to Mr. E, they were innocent. I had to admit that, ethically, it wasn't fair to either of them. I understood that, as a Jew, what I was about to do might even be what my hippie rabbi friend, Rabbi Gross, would call an *avaira,* a sin.

And another truth, sadder for me—I was afraid that Clara's reaction to my telling her about her father, the same unpredictable, fervent kind of reaction I loved her for otherwise, might somehow jeopardize the impact of what I was about to do to him in the name of Mr. E's salvation. What if she, with the best of intentions, confronted him with my information?

I remembered Uncle Herman's warning about how friends could be your worst enemies when it comes to subverting the system.

Mr. E, Sartre, and de Gaulle taught me that I had to be personally responsible for my own destiny. The power over Clara's father was in his fear of the secret. If losing Clara was the cost of freeing Mr. E, it was a price I was willing, or at least resigned, to pay. Because the pictures of Reverend James's tryst, in that tin can under my bed, were the magic cards to saving Mr. E.

Perhaps I was justified, in some karmic sort of balancing act, in using the pictures to force Tichter and Clara's father to help save Mr. E. If it worked, I'd only have made them sweat and fret like they'd done to so many others. No real harm.

But even in my absolute determination and willingness, my fear of failing and of simultaneously losing Clara was as deep as my certainty.

"Flimsy foundations always make shaky houses," Mr. E would say when I first started working with him, when my sawing and hammering were as weak and wiggly as a young boy on his first date. “Clarity of mind and action,” he’d pound into me. “Always ask yerself where your hands and feet are before any cut is made or lumber is impaled.”

Mr. E was no longer around to review my calculations or to protect my safety, to make sure my magic cards weren’t simply a house of cards. I thought hard about where I stood. I had to make sure my plan was as finely measured and executed as any project we ever attempted. Mr. E’s desperate circumstance was my chop-saw of necessity.

But I hoped and prayed that someone else, a grown-up not bound by Uncle Herman’s legalities, would help me, would even make the cut for me.

CHAPTER EIGHTEEN

A grown-up. Not bound by Uncle Herman's legalities—the thought kept echoing through my mind.

I went to see Reverend Joseph Rampbell.

At his Sunday sermons, which I loved to go to, he often quoted Saint James, " 'But be ye doers of the word, and not hearers only.' "

Now, I was taking him at his word.

In 1944, Joseph Rampbell received the Purple Heart for wounds received during ferocious, successful fighting in northeastern Italy against Field Marshall Albert Kesselring's tough 14th Division. It sat framed by his office desk, inspiring his son, Moses, and me to imagine his daring past.

The Reverend was six feet, two inches tall, 225, broad-shouldered, and muscular. He'd been a lieutenant in the "Buffalo Soldiers," a name coined in the 1860s by Indians who thought that black soldiers, with their dark skin and curly hair, resembled buffaloes. The black division of the 370th Regimental Combat Team of the US Army 92nd Infantry Division was reactivated in

1942. His was the only black division that saw combat in World War II.

Despite our enthusiastic childhood pleas, he only talked about his soldiering days once, on a fine, breezy spring day, when I was eleven, playing with his son, Moses, at their house.

"It was awful," he told us. "Goddamned Germans," he said, our faces in open-mouthed shock from never having heard cursing purse his lips. "They locked folks inside wooden buildings and set them on fire. Whole Italian villages burnt to a crisp. At first, it took awhile to realize what we were looking at—melted people. Any survivors who'd managed to hide looked like rag dolls—vacant-eyed human scarecrows—even worse than the most woeful Southern dirt-poor niggers I'd ever seen. Those poor survivors begged for food, clutching at us like we were Jesus himself come for deliverance. Oh gracious, the mud and stink. First place we came across like that, we got to on one fine, misty April day, spring flowers busting out, birds singing, the perfumed air all of a sudden mixed with the smell of fresh-roasted human meat. We grown men, hardened already by war, puked up our guts and cried like teenage girls at the sight of it all. It messed up our minds. Filled us all with hate.

"After that, you couldn't stop us. Inch by inch, up hills and mountainsides, the Nazis shooting down at us, we pushed them out. Got to where I enjoyed the killing. Got to where I wanted to find their wounded begging for mercy, showing us pictures of their families to get us to spare them just so I could feel my bayonet sink into their flesh and dreams.

"Messed me up real badly for a long while, boys. Tore up my soul to where I felt like I was as big a monster as they were."

He stopped himself with a far-away stare.

"I'd been so proud when I first walked off the troop boat ramp, when we arrived in Italy and saw those happy, clapping Negro men, proud of me for showing them that we could stand

and fight and kill, rather than simply do the cooking and cleaning work.

"But after the war, back home in the South, everything went back to normal. It was bad enough before for Negroes, but now I was full of hate at seein our people still doing grunt work and getting beaten and killed by white Americans instead of by white German ones."

Moses and I were glued to our chairs, silent, hardly breathing. My boyish soldier hero fantasies, inspired a year before by Moses's discovery of his dad's old army uniform, side gun, and rifle in their attic, were now reduced to this giant of a man dabbing his eyes with his white shirtsleeve and Moses and I trembling and distraught.

Reverend Rampbell looked back at our wide-eyed, blood-drained faces, stricken that perhaps he'd injured us, torn up our innocence, with his horrid secrets.

"That's enough," he'd said, flicking his hand with finality at us. "You boys go out and play."

I looked back at him as we left. His entire being seemed to have sagged and shrunk. Not until years later, in Uncle Herman's office, did I remember that look, the look of a man beaten down by the burden of hard memory.

Minister of Calvary Baptist Church, the largest black church in the area, he'd known me since he stuck Moses, my age, in the crib with me at Dad's store while he shopped. Over the years, Moses and I hung out together when my family, usually the only white people there, went to his dad's church socials. The Reverend always joked around and threw footballs with us. I felt comfortable around him. He had an affinity for Jews, for Uncle Herman, ever since his Civil Rights days.

"Hell," he said once, "in the early days, Jews were second in number to Negroes marching."

He'd learned Hebrew from his best pal, Danville's hippie rabbi, Reb Gross, so he could translate the Old Testament directly. Together, they connected the dots to the gospel songs, like "Go Down Moses" and "Run, Mary, Run," which recast the Biblical slavery stories of the Jews to those sung by black slaves. Hearing them made me proud that Jews, I, had some shared experience that had been helpful. It made me feel connected to my Negro friends' suffering and proud of my family's attitudes.

I stood outside Reverend Rampbell's church. As I walked up the sidewalk, Red popped out from behind a bush and waved with both hands like a hallelujah over his head.

"Well, if it ain't Mr. Don, savior of holy books," he said, laughing and waving. "Jumpin inta any more fires lately?"

Before I could answer, he was half way down the block, clicking his heels and tossing striped candy canes to the little nit-haired black kids running after him.

"Cheaper than the cinnamon ones," he told me the next time I bumped into him at an always-unexpected place and time.

I walked into the church and knocked on the Reverend's office door, closing it as I entered. The worn wood floor, peeling paint, and old furniture was a stark contrast to Clara's dad's palace.

"What we lack in fancy, we make up in spirit," Reverend Rampbell always said.

I must have looked ashen, because he said, with a laugh, "Donny-boy, you okay? You look about as bad as an angel who's lost his wings."

"Rev'rend Rampbell, sir," I said. "Can you please not tell anybody what I'm about to tell you? Will you swear?"

He squinted his eyes.

"A teenager asking a minister to swear. That's rich, Donny. And on whose name? We doing this Jewish or my way?" He chuckled.

"Could you please close the window too, so that nobody can hear us if they walk by?" I asked, even though the breeze blowing through it felt so cool against my heat and nerve-soaked white shirt.

He laughed again. "You're sweating already, son, and now you want me to stain my good shirt, too." Then he stopped. "Is it that bad?"

When I failed to laugh or change my glum expression, he stood and closed the window.

I started telling him about my visit to Clara's dad's church and the fire, all of it except for the pictures, including the Clara part—the part I hadn't told Uncle Herman about.

"You're making whoopee with Rev'rend James's daughter!" he said, coughing Coca-Cola on his clean shirt. "Oh my, that really is rich, very rich."

Then I told him about the pictures.

His eyebrows floated upward like they were going to fly over his head.

"Even blind squirrels sometimes stumble upon an acorn," he said. Then he mumbled to the ceiling, "*Mentula culus.*"

"What?" I said.

"Latin, ass screwing."

He was quiet for a moment.

"Must have been about the ugliest thing you ever saw," breaking into a roaring laugh that he couldn't seem to stop. "Oh my, my, my," he finally said, still chuckling, as he pulled a handkerchief out of his front pocket, leaned back in his chair and mopped away the tears.

I sat there, miserable.

He closed his eyes and chuckled again, then looked back at me.

"Still not laughing, Donny-boy? So I guess there is more here. Tell me then, son, what this has to do with anything other than some terrible, immoral, wonderful gossip, some *Loshun hora*?"

I was impressed. Latin and Hebrew, one right after the other.

"It has to do with getting Mr. Eldridge freed. It's my plan to get him released. You're my 'Oy Oy Seven.' " I failed at a convincing laugh.

"Come again?"

"Like Reb Gross would say. You know, James Bond. I want you to fix the situation like Double-O-Seven would."

"Oh, got it. Double-O-Negro," he laughed again. "So what do you propose I do?"

"Well, I talked to Uncle Herman. He thinks Mr. E doesn't have a chance, based on The Junior's evidence. So my idea is for you to just talk to The Junior to get Mr. E released. Tell him no deacon in your church would ever do something like this, especially Mr. E."

Deacon was an honorary title of respect, earned in recognition of years of spiritual and community work. They were the lay backbone of each church's poor community.

Without hesitating, Reverend Rampbell said, "First of all, my friend, most whites are basically unaware of these men's deep, spiritual connections and responsibilities. They've never even thought about the kind of lives black people live outside of white society. They're simply Tommy or Frank, regardless of their age. No *Deacon* Eldridge. Negroes are invisible except as hired labor."

A smirk raced across Rev. Rampbell's face.

"No, Donny, deacon carries no weight out there."

I expected this rejection.

"Okay, I guess I figured that, so here's a better idea. It's so simple," I said, praying inside to any available god. "You just meet with Reverend James and convince *him*, based on my pictures, to talk The Junior into letting Mr. E go."

Reverend Rampbell's face seesawed between a smile and a sneer.

"Old fashioned blackmail. Using that acorn you stumbled upon. I like it. He'd do it to me in a heartbeat. But, my young friend, you're mistaken about the 'just meet' part. If I called Reverend James to get together, I could hear him loud as a carnival barker, 'And why would I meet with yo' nigger ass?' Though I must admit," Rev. Rampbell said, with a rapturous look upward, "after all these years of abuse and degradation by that evil man, it would be a beautiful moment. For once, the black man would have the goods on that perverted white devil.

Reverend Rampbell continued staring up at the ceiling for a full thirty seconds, grinning like a fox in a chicken coop.

"Whew," he said, looking back at my sad face, as his converted from happy into a furrowed brow. "You're right about one thing. This isn't something to cure within the public legal structure. This is going to take a different kind of plan.

"I know The Junior wants to run for mayor and maybe even the legislature. He likes the crowds, the fame, and the feeling that a big, ugly man gets when he can impress good-looking women. He's only been police chief for two years and hasn't had a big case before. He's not dumb. Maybe he's figuring he can get the hate vote by the simple act of convicting a black man. Maybe even the Jewish vote for supposedly finding the arsonist. And wouldn't he just love to do it without owing anything to Jimmy James. Rumor has it that the two of them don't care for one another. So I don't think Jimmy James would be much help."

He shook his head with the same gloomy countenance I'd seen from Uncle Herman.

Although a savvy politician, Reverend Rampbell was a good man. He was renowned for his uncanny ability to take advantage of opportunities to advance the Negro cause—and a little of his own alongside it. He secured funding for jobs, early childhood learning, food programs, and birth control.

He'd preach, "Without birth control, we'll produce unwanted, fatherless children. Without sufficient prenatal care, they will be damaged. Without adequate nutrition, a child can't grow and learn. They and their mothers will be stranded in poverty and ignorance. Without jobs, Negros can never have dignity. And without education, black people can never rise above poverty to take their rightful place in the halls of power in America."

During the early days of the Civil Rights movement, Reverend Rampbell organized a boycott of the white businesses in Danville. My dad's store and a Jewish-owned women's store were spared. They were the only white businessmen in town to hire black sales help up front, rather than just as stock clerks or janitors. When Dad hired his first black sales clerk, many long-time white customers refused to let Nat, Nathan Wimbush, help them.

"Ain't no nigger waitin on me," they'd huff at him, either leaving in disgust or seeking out a white salesman. But Dad persevered in the name of rightness, even at the expense of lost business.

One day Reverend Rampbell came to Dad and asked to speak to him in the back. The Reverend told Pop that he would guarantee him all the black business in town if he would fire all of his white help and hire all black help. Pop didn't hesitate.

"Do you believe in the Golden Rule, Joseph?" Dad asked.

"Course I do."

"Then," Pop said, "if I help your people by mistreating the whites, isn't that just as bad as what the other white merchants are doing to your people—all because of their skin color?"

"Well, my, my," the Reverend said, flashing his big, disarming smile, sticking out his hand and shaking Pop's. "Thanks for setting me straight. I guess we all get a little carried away at times, trying to get this right."

"No, sorry, Donny-boy, but I can't accomplish your plan," the Reverend finally said in his Negro, college-trained, accent-less baritone.

Sweat was beading his forehead and staining his shirt.

"Man, wish I had some of that air conditioning," he said, swishing a wide paper fan with a picture of a black Mary holding a dark infant Jesus. "No, it's got to come from a white man. Reverend James would just see me as a nigger in the woodpile. Even should I win this battle with those pictures, he would surely see to it that my church and community suffer for it in the future."

"What about mine?"

"No, he can't mess with the Jews too much because they have the money and power. But blacks are too poor. He would definitely try to get back at me or some other poor black man as revenge. No, son, can't do it. Just wouldn't work."

The tornado of his logic was blowing down my house of cards.

But as I sat there in his office, defeated, his face suddenly broke into a sly smile, eyes as bright as searchlights.

"Maybe there is another way. Maybe we can get a different, equally unlikely, white man to help Tommy."

The reverend opened his window, shook his head up and down with the smile of a satisfying breeze and a satisfied memory and said, "The May Way."

Reverend Rampbell's idea revolved around his own dynamic male ferocity and charisma. It virtually mandated, like a mosquito to blood, a binding female force beyond one wife's ability, or will. It revolved around his need to "re-spark," as he put it, with the fresh energy of an exuberant female "re-charger."

"My batteries," he called those women. His Godly incantations, blemish-free russet skin, decorated by a one-inch war scar—"bayonet, hand-to-hand combat"—running diagonally over his right eye, his big, fluorescent white teeth and steely physique attracted them like a magnet.

"But only one at a time," he'd told Reb Gross.

"I trust in his love," the reverend's wife was heard to say. "Longs it don't hurt nobody and it's quiet, it don't 'mount to much of anything. A man fuelin this community like he does, I know can need more than one woman to fill his gas tank."

Which was pretty much the prevailing attitude of his community.

"He puts zo much fire, positivity, daring and hope into za community that occasional peccadilloes are like a fly on a bull's neck—nothing important," Reb Gross told me. "Vithout him, and men like him in other Negro communities, black people fall into depression, resignation, and hopelessness at za impossibility of zeir status and situation in za South."

"The May Way," was all about our friend May. In addition to her "professional life," she was the lead singer in Reverend Rampbell's gospel choir. But May was much more than that.

CHAPTER NINETEEN

I was much closer to May, than anyone, including Reverend Rampbell or my folks, knew.

"Strange grows normal in the South," she always said. And her life transformation was about as strange as it could get.

Any idiot in the *shmata* trade would have yawned at what I had awakened in the mind of Maybelline Matthews, three years before the temple fire, after she'd announced to me her intention of becoming a madam.

"Sell a hat for ten dollars with a profit of five dollars in about half an hour," I'd told her, "or sell a suit for a hundred dollars, for a fifty-dollar profit in the same half hour." Not rocket science, but to her, it was a revelation.

Even at almost sixteen, having sold clothes to adults since childhood at Dad's store, I was as expert at sales sense as a karate master was at breaking boards. With the added benefit of junior high debate club, I could connect logic dots like pearls on a necklace.

"What you mean 'xactly?" May asked me down in her room in our basement.

"What exactly do you mean by that?" I corrected her since she'd asked me to teach her to 'tawk raht' after she moved in with my family when I'd just turned fifteen. I started hanging out in her room after school like a slobbering puppy. It was the last month of my eighth-grade school year.

"Yes," she replied impatiently, "What do you mean by that?"

"Well, you can keep on getting poor black men to pay you a day's wage, maybe eight dollars a trick, or you could get middle-class, probably white, guys to pay twenty-five dollars. It's the same product, just at a higher price."

I felt pretty sophisticated saying "trick," as if I knew all about prostitution, which was indirectly true from years hearing whispers, snickers, and stories from men in Dad's store.

"And even better," I said. "You could even charge one hundred dollars. Dad always says, 'Before you can be a successful salesman,' "—and then I slipped a look at May—"or successful at any trade, 'you have to understand how to convince the customer that it's worth it.' "

"Seems that ain't never been no problem, what with men wantin what I got ever since I become a woman."

I shook my head in desirous understanding.

"Became," I said. "Look, every man wears a suit. But what is a suit? You might say it's just fabric sewn together that covers a man's body. So, in some ways, all suits are the same. But some men pay twenty-five dollars for a suit and others one hundred. Why?"

"Yeah, why?" she asked.

I parroted Dad's incessant preaching, " 'The only difference is in the perceived value of the suit and in the man's desire and ability to pay for it. If he can afford to pay more, he'll do it because of his appreciation of the quality of the fabric, how it was tailored, and his pride in wearing a suit brand known for the highest quality, the perfect suit. A suit that few guys can afford and a lot of others will covet. In your case, May, you're the material made by God. So do you want to turn yourself into an eight-dollar, a twenty-five-dollar, or a hundred-dollar suit?"

"You preachin to the choir, honey-chile," she sang.

"You certainly have a good point there," I made her repeat.

May was quiet.

"May, are you listening?"

"Course, I'm list'nin, fool. What you think I'm doin? I'm list'nin so hard I gotta stop and let it all sink in. It's like a good, cool rain on a hot, muggy day."

"Well, like I said, you're already the fine material. But you need the rest, the fine tailoring, so to speak, that is education and the refining of your speech if you want to get all that money from the rich guys. And maybe even more important, you need a reputation for integrity. Once they trust and respect you for more than simple sex, once they know you'll keep their reputations safe, they'll come back like cats to cream."

I knew because Great-Grandpa Max's, then Grandpa's, and now Dad's store, had prospered due to the trust and respect they had fostered between the customers and our family over the years.

Most tobacco farmers came into town only a few times a year. With a population of fifty thousand, Danville was their New York City. After selling their crop, it was party time in the big city. They'd sometimes get drunk and lose their crop check, virtually all of what they made for the entire year. A stolen check could easily be cashed by anyone at any bank since there were few formal forms of identification back then. Or their once-a-year wad of cash could be pick-pocketed at a bar. Knowing this, many would leave most of their earnings with Grandpa or Dad until they sobered up. Coming to our store was about more than just buying and selling.

"Pretty much the same with your business, May, if you want them back time and again. It becomes like a family affair.

"Otherwise," I kept on, "you're just another good-looking, cheap, black whore and on to the next one." I hesitated. "May, I didn't mean to call you a cheap whore."

"What I was, but ain't what I wanna be. Just like you sayin. God made me tha cloth, up ta me to make use of it."

"You want white men to wish they were black so that they could have you, you know, marry you."

"Marry me? No white man's never gonna do that 'round here."

"Yeah, that's what I mean. That's sort of the best part. Because you become unobtainable to them. They can never have you in public, or own you, or show you off, as much as they hurt to. But you'll let them 'own' you in private. Custom. A suit so fine that they can only wear it in the most rarified of circumstances."

"I'm so excited, if I was white, mah face'd be burnin red as a rose," May said.

I felt like the black Langston High School drum major blowing his whistle in front of his marching band at the Christmas parade, kicking, prancing, and high-stepping down Main Street in his white top-hat and tails, twirling his baton.

I was so pleased with my eloquence that I felt like a real grown-up.

"Mah heart's as jitt'ry as a girl's first kiss," May said. "You evah sell them kinda suits at yo daddy's sto?"

"I could if we carried them. But Dad always tells us how much richer his best friend Murray is because he only sells exclusive brands in his high-class women's store. I'm stuck selling the cheaper suits to the working class. But I could if we had them, just like you can."

"Well, shit, Donny, you right 'bout what you sayin."

"I can appreciate what you've said," I corrected her.

"Yeah," May said. "What I meant."

She'd been crowned Miss Black South Central Virginia at age sixteen. At the talent finals, her Afro looked like a zig-zagged black halo explosion around her head and face. The tops of her breasts, pressed tight together in her white, sequined evening dress, swelled up and glistened like dark grape Jell-O.

May brought down the house with her variation on Odetta's gospel version of "Oh Freedom."

Oh, oh freedom over me.
And before I be a slave,
I'll be buried in my grave,
And go home to my Lord and be free.

When she sang "No more tommin," a reference to the black man's compliant kowtowing to whites, the crowd rose, howling and screaming, hands raised in unison. As she wailed from deep in her belly, her clear, fulsome tenor as spectacular as her face, even the judges stood up, clapping and shaking, teeth big and white in smiling jubilation.

"My folks couldn't afford the entry, travel, and outfit costs of those competitions, so I was sponsored by Reverend Rampbell's church," she'd told me.

May also sang lead in the Reverend's fifty-member mixed gospel choir, The Soul Rollers. For three years in a row, they'd won the Virginia Black Baptist Convention of America's annual gospel competition in Norfolk.

May's dad, Robert, had been a hard-working, poor tobacco farmer, lucky to own land passed down to him since Reconstruction. Until I was about eight, Robert would often drop by our house when May's mother was babysitting my sister and me, with May on Tuesday afternoons when Mom was at the beauty parlor, or Thursdays, when she played bridge. Once May and I were old enough, he and May's mom would sneak away for some "comfort time," leaving May to look after me.

Aunt O'dee died in a car accident the summer after May's junior year in high school. Robert was left a quadriplegic.

"I dropped out of school after Mama died so's I could take care of Daddy at home," May told me right after she moved in with us. "I stayed with him for four years—till he died, just after I turned twenty-one. I didn't have no relatives around and no money. I know'd you and yer folks since I was a little girl. Remember you and me swingin in the park and me helping mamma when you was little?"

"Yeah," I said.

"Well, they was always so nice that I asked your mama if she would take me in as a live-in maid. So I could finish mah last year of high school in town. I knew I wouldn't have to shuck and jive fer yer folks."

Just shy of fifteen, three years before I met Clara, I was infatuated the instant she moved in. She was the black Snow White.

May would help Mom around the house, baby sit my six-year-old sister, Lisa, and participate like a member of the family. She'd even eat at the table with us, something very unusual in Southern white homes, even Jewish ones. She was like an older cousin.

Her basement room was plain, but private and quiet, the hum of the furnace notwithstanding. The bathroom thrilled her, even though she had to pass through Dad's cluttered stained-glass workroom to get there.

"Ain't never had indoor plummin—and hot water longs I like, right outta the faucet. And cool air all summer long. Like a palace."

In her room, she listened to WILY, the black radio station started by our Jewish neighbor, on the old, fake-wood, plastic desktop AM radio that Mom, who never threw anything away, had dumped in her room.

Soon after she moved in, I started hanging out there after school. One afternoon, May asked me, "You wanna learn 'bout soul music? 'Cause if you do, I am the soul pro-fes-sor."

"Sure."

"Soul music's kinda like gospel, but without the Jesus part. Coloreds ran up north to Chicago after the Civil War and made church music into city-slick. Added some funk from your hips and a little rhythm and blues and told stories 'bout life and love sickness. Ray Charles really got it goin mainstream. You ever listened to him on Willy, Donny?"

"No," I shrugged. "I've only heard WDVA and I hate it," I said. It was Danville's white radio station. "All they play is that Live Old Opry hick stuff."

I could picture the rotten-toothed, Bible-thumping redneck stars my Russian immigrant Grandma Bessie inexplicably loved to watch on television Saturday nights, when it was my turn to spend the night at her house, ever since Grandpa died. I think the pressure of dealing with Rabbi Tichter hastened his passing. Being surrounded by yokels every day was enough for me without having to suffer their syrupy love and poor-me songs moaning on the radio. On the other hand, I'd never even considered listening to Willy either.

"Well, anyway," May said, "Ray kinda started it all with *I Got a Woman* in '54. But Nina Simone, now she's my favorite. The High Priestess of Soul, they call her. Could sing low as a man, then shoot up into tenor and even alto. Make you cry one second then feel happy as a princess the next. So romantic, ya do the two-step to her songs and you could fall spot in love with whoever you was dancin with. Mah voice is most like hers, different from Etta James's *At Last,* in '61. Now, she sings in the high ranges. Man, that woman makes ya want love so bad ya could almost explode."

I learned about Mahalia Jackson, Ruth Brown, known as Miss Rhythm, Solomon Burke, Little Richard, Fats Domino, all the way back to their precursors, Reverend Julius Cheeks and Jesse Whittaker of the Pilgrim Travelers and Sam Cooke's Soul Stirrers.

May's most prized possessions were a small, square record player with a pop-off lid and a huge stack of 45s and 78s from the twenties to the early sixties that she carried in a big, old, scuffed-up brown leather suitcase. They were all carefully wrapped, some in their original covers and others in jackets handmade out of discarded newspapers and grocery bags, labeled with her crude printing.

"The one thing I'd spend my peach-pickin money from the farm on," she said. "And soon's neighbors and people from church knew I loved all that music, even the old stuff, they'd give it to me instead of throwin 'em out.

"Now take Jackie Wilson's "Lonely Teardrops." Shit, Donny, almost makes me pee in mah pants. That man started down there," pointing to my crotch, "took it to your heart and then made ya cry."

"Wanna dance?" she asked one day about nine months after she'd moved in. "You never danced befo?" she said, stunned, when I said I didn't know how.

I told her about the tattooed Holocaust woman and honoring the memory of the six million dead by not dancing or singing or acting too happy.

"You think they'd feel better with you sad and feeble, or with you joyous and happy?"

"That's what Reb Gross says."

"You mean that crazy-lookin old white guy hangs out with Rev'rend Rampbell?"

"He's not crazy! That's what my folks say too! He's a real holy man. He's my friend!"

"Sorry," she said. "No harm meant. Sure cain't dance though."

But May and I danced.

"We'll start with a slow tune, "Only You," by the Platters, jus to loosen ya up a little. You'll learn fast."

She leaned tight against me.

"Come on baby, put those arms 'round me. Let me feel some *pulse*."

The first time, stiff all over, I mainly felt only one pulse. I blushed like a schoolgirl.

"Nothin to worry 'bout, honey. Not to be braggadocios, but I'd be more worried if you didn't get that way with a girl like me pulling you up so close," she said, the warmth of her breath dizzying me. "Shows you a man like any other."

Her smile relaxed most of me.

Pretty soon, we moved on to fast dancing the Shag in that little basement room, the sound of the furnace like a privacy curtain from Mom upstairs—to "Sixty Minute Man" by the Dominoes, "Fat Boy" by Billy Stewart, "Think a Little Sugar" by Barbara Lewis or to whatever else tickled her fancy.

"Now, don't move your chest and hips hardly at all, 'cept your arms directin and your legs and feet movin and gyratin. You gotta control the woman. She gotta keep her arms strong 'gainst you, not floppy, but you gotta push and pull back and make her move the way you want. Make a woman hot knowin you in charge, slidin all 'round her and makin her look so good."

It took me a while to feel the pulse all over. But after a couple of weeks, something other than simple lust started stirring in me, our arms and legs and bodies Mix-mastering into a swirling, rising, falling, splashing, crashing razzle of movement.

We danced so hard that we'd flop onto the floor, hot-breathed, sweating, giggling. Her deodorant-free scent smelled even better than Uncle Herman's cigarettes or Dad's *Old Spice.* With her laughing and showing me new steps, I learned to control and twirl and whirl her like a matador, until I got the ultimate compliment.

"You got the moves of a soul man now, Donny," she told me one night after a Reverend Rampbell social, when they'd spin records and let people dance in the church basement.

"Ver did you learn zat, Donala?" Reb Gross asked, failing utterly to spin Dottie Eldridge, as Mr E, contentedly puffing his cigarette, guffawed.

"Learned it from me," May beamed.

"Vell zen, you is a good teacher."

"Why, thank you kindly, Rabbi."

After one particularly wild dance, to Jimmy McGriff's "I've Got a Woman, one of her friends walked up to us and said, "He don't dance like no white boy I ever seen."

"You *is* a piece of work, Donny," Mrs. E agreed.

"Can't walk on water, like your cousin, but then I bet he couldn't dance good as you neither," Mr. E said.

Reb Gross slapped him on the shoulder and they both laughed their heads off.

As her songs and stories worked their way into me, I began to hear and see the world through her eyes; to feel another kind of pulse, a world full of yearning, sorrow, poverty, and hate for Negroes, with little chance of escape or of fulfillment except for moments in their churches and in their music. Especially for an uneducated Negro woman.

"I ain't settlin fer the life of most black folk," May said to me right after she moved in, ironing by the old floor lamp with the lampshade I'd made in Cub Scouts, the white plastic lanyard ribbon looped along the bottom rim. "Bein a farmer's wife or maid jest ain't no way fer me. Cain't do it. Won't, should say. I wanna be educated, like you high-falutin white folk. Talkin to you and bein here with your famly is showin me tha way. So, just cause you a rich white boy, don't make no 'sumptions that I'm low-class nor dirty nor don't know good from bad. I'm ignerant, but I ain't stupid. So tell me," she'd insisted, "when I'se sayin thangs wrong."

That's when I started correcting her speech.

She started reading all of our books. At dinners, we'd listen to her *Encyclopedia Britannica* or *Funk and Wagnall's* discoveries in alphabetical order—a few days of A's, then on to the next letters.

"That girl flits around subjects like bees on flowers," Mom whispered to me a few months after May moved in. "She never stops."

"Ahm gonna suck whatever I can from you," she said. I could only hope.

At the city's library, the librarian, Miss Lange, picked books on the subjects May asked about. She'd hand them to her out the back door, since Negroes weren't allowed in the building, the renovated mansion of Civil War tobacco magnate Harry Sutherlin, where Jefferson Davis spent his last days as President of the Confederacy, earning Danville's claim to fame as "The Last Capital of the Confederacy."

"You're reading Sigmund Freud?" I asked her, someone most of us Jewish kids had heard of, but only because of the words "sex," "ego," and "guilty conscience."

"Miz Lange told me to try it when I asked her fer books 'bout how mens thinks."

One day she showed me a book about the National Parks. She couldn't get over the scenes from Yellowstone.

"Gotta learn 'bout this whole big country. Git mah head outta this little town."

She flooded everybody in the family with questions.

"You are a black rose blooming," I said one day after she peppered me with question after question after I'd told her about my chemistry class. "And we're the gardeners."

"Leastwise, the cowshit," she said, poking me in the ribs.

About eight months after she moved in, I was down in her room. I'd just turned sixteen. Mom had gone to the beauty parlor. My sister was at a friend's house. The radio was playing the Miracles' "You've Really Got a Hold on Me," the heat smell of May's ironing a comforting perfume.

She smelled starch-fresh and laughed at my stupid teenage boy jokes. She made me feel smart, her curiosity a sponge to facts and ideas that I took for granted. I loved looking at her. And, for some reason, seeing her unshaved underarm hair was tantalizing. Around her, it was hard to concentrate.

I told about my seduction by Nadya, Rabbi Tichter's wife, when I was fourteen.

"You braggin mostly," she said, "but yer face says they's a blister still on yer heart. Does all Jews do that," she asked, eyes big as full moons, like a Klan cartoon, against her slate black face, "with the minister's wife?"

"They're called rabbis and she's the Rebbetzin."

I could hardly look at her. I felt ashamed to have even mentioned it.

"And no, it's not normal for a Jewish boy ever to do such a thing. And truth be told May, she kinda went crazy and I'm kind of ashamed that I couldn't stop myself from doing it with her more than once."

"Well, Donny, you don't need to brag or be 'shamed none to impress me. Ah'm already crazy 'bout you. You the dancinest, sexiest white boy I ever seen. You this colored girl's one and only little Jewboy, too."

"Don't call me that. I hate it. 'Jew you down,' 'Jewnited states,' 'What d'jew been doin today'..."

"Whoa, baby, take it easy. You don't need to tell me 'bout that sorta crap. Us folk can call one 'nother 'nigger' in private, jest 'tween us, but otherwise..." she paused, shaking her head side to side.

"OK, but for Christ's sake, May, if you're going to say it, it's 'you are,' or 'you're my Jewboy,' not 'you mah Jewboy!' "

As the Impressions sang "It's All Right," she put the iron, still steaming, onto its pedestal and turned away from the board. She pulled me hard to her, like we were going to dance slow, put her hand on my crotch and said, "Well, then, if you are *my* Jewboy," drawing out the words—my...Jew...boy—"then I want to see what it is that the Reb...the Rebitt...that lady got to see."

Her breath was a breeze of licorice from the sassafras roots she sucked on from her farm. I couldn't believe she was serious. She was way out of my league. I mean, this was Miss Black South Central Virginia.

"Yeah, right." I tried to be cool, dismissive, though I heard James Brown singing, *Please, Please, Please* in my head.

"I only say what I mean," she said as she squeezed me, already inflated like a blow-up toy.

At first, I was so surprised and nervous that I started shaking like a cold dog.

"Shuh, sugah," she cooed to me, talking softly, rubbing my shoulders until I calmed down. She kissed my neck and swirled her tongue in my ear. "Donny, I like the way you walk, the way you talk, and the color of yo hair. It's so soft, like silk," she whispered, running her fingers through my longish, Indian-black, straight hair. "I ain't never felt such soft hair."

"I haven't ever..." I said.

"Shut up now," she said. "You sho' this okay?"

"Are you kidding?" I said.

"Not freakin out, are you?" she asked, kneeling down as she unzipped my pants, dug out the brain of a teenage boy, and sucked on me like a millionaire on a fifty-dollar cigar. I was so hot I could've blown smoke. My legs were as weak as a swooning Southern belle. I didn't know if I would faint or come first. Then I gushed into her mouth like a hard-shaken Coke.

Once she caught her breath, she said, "You like that Old Faithful geyser"—pronouncing it *geezer*—"I seen in that book, only faster," she laughed. "And shorter."

My other brain cruised full speed out in space.

"*Guy-sir*," I heard myself mutter.

"That smart mind of yours never stops, do it? Well, come on boy, let's take off them clothes."

Her Goddess-sweet voice sang along with the Supremes' *Baby Love,* as she pulled her pink rayon, lace-edged panties down off of her feet and then unbuttoned her starched white uniform.

I'd never, and have never since, seen such a perfect female body. Rebbetzin Nadya's was goose down, pillow-fluffy, the Pillsbury Dough Girl, her youth the only excuse for any tone at all. Nadya's breasts hung awesome heavy, one slightly larger than the other, the nipples shoe-polish red against her never-seen-sunlight, kosher butter, white skin.

But May's body was tight. Her mid-sized, thick-skinned breasts stood out from her chest like the ones in the pictures of a Nubian goddess. Like the ones on the black velvet paintings in Mr. Samuel Ingram's, Sam's, barbershop when I *schlepped* clothes there for his gospel choir. I'd always fantasized seeing one of them in the flesh—"so fine," as Sam would laugh when he caught me peeking.

Her thighs and arms were firm and farm-strong, without a trace of fat. Her belly was just slightly rounded with an outie belly button leading to soft, billowing pubic hair, which I thought must be unusual for a black woman.

She laid down on the bedspread she'd put on the tattered carpet remnant that my folks had saved when they installed the new white living room plush upstairs.

"Lick my honey pot," she commanded softly after I lay beside her. Her left hand caressed the back of my head with just enough force to move it. I wondered—a white boy, crazy thought, for just a fraction of a second—if she would taste like fudge. She adjusted herself at just the right angle. "Now, jist, uh just, lick my little button there," she said as she pulled the dark skin away from her deep pink clitoris with her right hand, lifting her head to see me, guiding my tongue, lifting her leg slightly so that I felt the juice from the inside of her thigh against my right cheek. As my tongue touched her, her body quivered. She let out a soft groan, her left knee raising and opening, shaking a little bit.

"You okay, May?"

"Oh yes, Donny, so all right, so fine," she purred, moving her hips slowly against me, adjusting the pressure with her hand against my head. "You're doin it just right. That other woman taught you this part real good...well," she sighed.

Licking her was like eating melon with a hint of salt. She had a slight smell of the yellow pine she'd told me she used for her woodstove when she went back to her little farmhouse on the weekends. She'd never let me drive her there. "I go there by myself to feel my folks' spirit and to keep the place from going to ruin, so's I can sell it someday."

I could almost hear Nadya guiding me, "Make circles, easy now, now harder, up and down, side to side, now suck on my lips," until May tensed and released in a spasm of *ummms* and *ahhhs.*

"You've been teaching me how to talk and think right," she said as she pulled me up to her side. "So now I'm gonna…going to…teach you how to love a woman the right way. In the proper part—something that rabbi's wife, bless her heart, couldn't do."

She rolled me onto my back, then settled onto my erection, downy and warm and slow like a queen hen onto her egg, careful not to break it.

I started crying.

"I'm sorry for crying," I said to May.

She leaned down over my chest. Her pink nipples, standing inside dark brown, silver-dollar-sized areolas, swam across my gloomy face. Her skin glistened with a deep brilliant, eggplant-purplish sheen. Her pillow-lipped kisses soothed my weepy cheeks like Calamine lotion on poison ivy.

"You ain't old enough yet for a well of sadness, but seems you got a bathtub full from what that rabbi lady and you did."

Cupping my dripping face, her pink-palmed hands warmed that water. As I exhaled, a clot of sorrow seemed to inch up from the bottom of my diaphragm and out my nostrils. I felt like the virginal soldier in the movies as May, the nurse, wrapped healing dressings around my still-tender wounds.

"Her husband's a mean jerk," I said, my chest ricocheting off every sob. "And I was just a stupid kid." I couldn't stop crying. Eyes wide, face like a crumpled peach, I stared up at May, mortified that I was blowing the chance of a lifetime. "I shouldn't have done it with her."

"I don't know how you see it in your Jew way," May said softly, "but I see it from Jesus's. You was just a boilin hot boy and she took advantage. Yet and still, you gotta forgive yourself and that poor woman."

She reached over behind herself to turn down the radio, then started slowly singing, quiet enough for only me to hear,

Sometimes I feel discouraged and think my work's in vain,
But then the Holy Spirit revives my soul again,
There is a balm in Gilead to make the wounded whole,
There is a balm in Gilead to heal the sin sick soul.

From her mouth, down her chest and guts, straight through her vagina, her voice vibrated through me like a perfect note on a tuning fork.

She moved on me with the calm gracefulness of a master gardener, dancing carefully confident amongst her flowers, making sure not to hurt any of the delicate parts. As she hummed, my heart seemed to relax, retuned. Versus Nadya's furious desperation.

"This feels so different," I said.

"It's cause I'm a free woman." She reached over, turned off the radio and put on a record.

"Open your eyes and look at me, darlin," she said as I started to drift away. Her eyes blazed against the moist darkness of her face. The rhythmic cadence of her undulations, swaying her pelvis like rocking a baby, to Otis Redding's "These Arms of Mine, kept sending me nodding into a foggy bliss.

She guided me like I was blind, conducted our movements like a maestro. She could tell when I was losing it, about to climax. "Breathe deep," she instructed. "Take it slow, sugar," seeming to know just when to back off, slowing down, and massaging my shoulders and neck so I would relax.

Finally, she stopped being the teacher and started moaning and growling and riding me hard until we were storming through each other like thunder bolts on a summer's day.

I couldn't stop a groan erupting from the back of my throat, something I'd always controlled, silent as a stone when I'd been with Nadya. May gently slipped her hand over my mouth before she arched up as if she could feel my stream slap against her insides while the peristalsis of her vagina milked and inhaled me. And I was lost and melted into the heat of her juice until I felt like I would disappear right into her.

I floated in a cloud of pleasure and love beyond anything I'd ever known.

After forever, she rolled to my side and we lay there on our backs, no talk, legs spread apart, the little black metal fan beside her ironing table humming, the air tingling our wet places.

"Now you know," she whispered with a kiss, "how to make a woman feel whole good, to satisfy her like a man is 'sposed to, in the right places."

I thought I'd known before.

As we put on our clothes, she stood before me, ran her hand through my hair once more and kissed me on the cheek.

"You know, Donny, just as much as me, we could never really be together—just the way it is. So I have to tell you, we won't be screwin 'round no more. I had to let you do it with me once to teach you how it's done right and for you to see how much I do love you."

My face fell like stone to the floor. "Stay, Just a Little Bit Longer," by Maurice Williams and the Zodiacs, raced into my mind. I wanted to feel that hundred-dollar suit against my skin again and again.

"Not ever?"

"Jesus bless you, you know child, I'm not leavin you though, like that other woman. It's just you were so hungry for me and nervous and sad and you needed healin. And so's maybe now you can relax a little more 'round me since you got what you wanted so much. And so did I, I guess.

"Now it's time for you to move on in life with girls your own kind and age. Just like it's time for me to grow in mah own way. But now, we'll be friends, good friends, if you'll let us. I need a friend who ain't just lookin to git inta mah pants. A real friend. Somebody I kin trust with mah secrets, mah plans, even mah life."

My throat and arms and chest and legs felt as tight as a white Protestant at a black gospel revival.

"Can you let your heart want me from now on as much as your beautiful privates did before?" she said with the nurse's sisterly stare.

"Gilead's balm," I forced myself to say.

"Yeah, honey."

"But, never again? You're the best, May. I want to do it with you again. I'm in love with you. You're breaking my heart," which felt physically true—my chest ached and I felt like crying again.

"Honey, just couldn't never be good. Yo mama and papa would kill me from just this one time. You gotta let it be and just be my best friend."

"Shit," I said before I could stop myself. "It's not fair. Where'd you learn all that anyway?" I said, another tear sneaking out.

"Been practicin."

"Practicing? You mean you've screwed around that much? I thought you were a church girl."

"After the accident, what with Mama dead and Daddy crippled, we had nothin, nothin at all. That's when I started doin it, Donny.

"Men'd always been askin me, showin me money, even in the choir. But after the accident, I couldn't leave Daddy alone even for an hour. So I started sayin yes. Even with some of Daddy's friends. They'd come in the back door and I'd try to sneak 'em to the back bedroom. I think Daddy knew. But it shore was better than letting him rot and die in some craphole place they stick poor, sick old niggers in. And it sure beat workin all day as a maid, makin less than I could in half an hour right there at home.

"Worth it. Worth it in spades. Not to mention not havin to "yessum" and "yessuh" all day long. But I knew that 'venshully... eventually...once he passed, that I had to git...get... educated if I wanted to be more.

"So I made a plan."

"What kind of plan?" I said.

That's when she told me about her plan to become a madam and started asking me questions about how business works. And when I started telling her about the hundred-dollar suits. And when she started practicing to "tawk real good," and suck learning like a vacuum.

From then on, we talked with each other about the most intimate details of our lives—she the big sister to my stripling travails, me her closest confidant.

Once she graduated high school, she sold the family farm. It fetched enough for her to buy and renovate a run-down house in one of the nicer black neighborhoods, run-down itself by white standards.

I helped Mr. E renovate it into a cozy jewel.

I'd ride my bike down her scrub oak-lined street. Its barely one-and-a-half laned, gutterless, splattered tar-and-gravel potholed route took me past porches full of rocking chairs and kids no bigger than minutes playing stickball, her neighbors waving to the only white boy they ever saw around there, many knowing me from Abe's. I felt lucky and full and rich.

When Mr. E and I had finished, she turned on the red light. Even then, she would call me every few days, telling me all sorts of stories and details.

"You know enough about me to ruin my life and a lot of others," she said one day after her business had quickly skyrocketed.

"But I've got to have someone to talk to. And you, my lovely Jewboy, are the lucky one."

Sometimes I almost wanted her to quit telling me so much. The difference between love and sex and power and business began to blur in my boyish mind. But mainly, I felt honored.

In poor, black, small-town society, it didn't matter much what you did, since so many had menial jobs, but how you lived in the community. Other than a few righteous-loud ladies, few at May's church held her vocational choice against her. Mostly, they appreciated her tithing and, perhaps even more, loved her singing.

When she sang, with the men and women of the choir behind her, the church felt like it was vibrating, pulsing through delirious ears to hard-beating hearts to swaying pelvises and out through dancing, jumping feet. People, men and women, shouted and swooned. It was not unusual for folks to pass out from what Asian Indians would call the Kundalini, or serpent energy, something Reb Gross had told me about.

"Za primal energy runs back from za throbbing floor through zeir feet to zeir loins, through zeir hearts up to and out of zeir heads. If zey didn't pass out, zeir head might pop off," he giggled.

As May and the choir turned up the spirit flame, Reb Gross, Reverend Rampbell, and I would often stand together, clapping and moving with the rest of the congregation.

"Ours isn't the perfect-posture white church choir," said Reverend Rampbell, "praise and thank God for that! Those white choirs aren't bad technically. But compared to May and my singers, it's like a dick in a cast, capable of movement, but highly constricted."

We all cracked up.

Rabbi Gross danced, his *mateh,* a big stick he carried everywhere, banging and swirling through the air, his *payas,* a braid by his ears, and beard flying like a dervish, his dreadful voice and impossible clunky rhythm making the folks and me laugh and rejoice along with him. We were two small vanilla scoops in a sea of hot fudge Sundays. Many times, he and I rekindled our Jewish souls together under Jesus's black banner and the spell of May's amazing grace.

None of us had any idea of the song she would have to sing to try to save Mr. Eldridge.

CHAPTER TWENTY

"Donny-boy, I've made an appointment for tomorrow to visit Maybelline about the situation with Deacon Eldridge," Reverend Rampbell told me over the phone the day after my visit to his office. "She knows The Junior well and has confided to me in the past of the weak spot he has for her. But you know that she has her own mind. She does not like to be told what to do or how to do it. Nevertheless, I think I can convince her to help."

As he spoke, I realized that I'd never heard him sound so formal with me. As great as he was, this seemed like a gun he was reluctant to shoot.

It reminded me of another of his favorite sayings, "For the Negro in the South, disappointment is often considered a victory. It still leaves open the window of hope, compared to utter failure, too often the norm."

I could feel my disappointment, but I still hoped.

"Christ moves through the two of us," May told me he'd said to her when she was twenty two. "You're my one-and-only recharge battery. The love you give me shines through me like a ray of sunshine throughout this community. You are the fuel for my fire."

He was the only one, other than me, once, that she graced for free, often.

"He's the 250-dollar spirit suit," she told me over the next few years. "Besides, even I need the real love of a good man, like any other woman. And he's the best one I've ever known. I do love that man in the deepest part of my soul. The body is an extra blessing."

She left our house after one year, almost four years before the temple fire. In short order, she'd become Danville's most expensive lady of the night, at least according to her.

"Donny, I'm making as much in two weeks as a full-time, live-in maid would make in a year."

She'd continued to educate herself through correspondence courses, speech coaching, and voracious reading. In due course, she traveled to Europe, having become enamored of Shakespeare, Mozart, and the European masters.

"Those stories and art books I got from the library brought me closer to God," she said. "Only His spirit could inspire such beauty."

She and I had remained as close as we'd been that day down in her basement room, at least in the heart area. I loved the sound of her voice and never tired of the details of her expanding life. Her stories were better than gossip, a real Southern-style odyssey.

"We really are like sister and brother, Donny. I can talk and you truly listen. There's nobody else I trust like you."

As her business evolved, she insisted, "My clients address me as Miss Matthews, and I require that they be extremely clean, mannerly, and not have any reputation for mistreating black people more than normal."

Occasionally she'd blow a fuse, ranting about some real or imagined slight at church from the righteous-louds, or on the street.

"Some may condemn me as a sinner. Hard for me, but I try not to judge them back. I have to believe God made men want me the way they do and gave me the ability to satisfy them the way I do, so I could raise myself above the yoke most black women around here are fated to bear. Ten percent of my money goes straight to the church, and more for the poor, on my own. I sing the best and holiest I can for the faithful, and I work my ass off to educate myself and be an example of what a colored woman can achieve even here in this hard, clay, hole-in-the-wall God stuck us in."

I knew not to say anything more than, "Amen."

May confirmed that, "The Junior wants me as much as a fox wants a hen."

For two years, once he knew about her, she'd handcuffed both his threats to close her business and his desire for her. She would not bed him.

"You are too unrefined," she'd say to him.

"I'll bust yo little operation," he'd threaten.

She'd say demurely, "Chief Junior, baby, you do that and you'll *never* have a chance with me. You keep improving yourself, honey," she'd lie, with a flutter of her eyelashes, "and one day you may be refined enough for me."

"He was insulted," she told me, "but I knew he was too hot for me to make too much of a stink. And, it also doesn't hurt that some of Danville's leading white citizens are my clients and we have a kind of unique love that shelters me from him. Some politicians even come all the way from Richmond. Remember how you used to tell me how important it was to not just satisfy their body, but also their soul. Well, I guess I do a pretty good job of that too."

May called me after Reverend Rampbell's "appointment" with her.

"Awful thing just happened, Donny." May's voice was as taut as the catgut strings on my tennis racket. "I was just with the Reverend."

"Oh." I tried to sound surprised.

" 'May, honey,' he said to me, in that imperious kind of voice he uses in church, 'There is a job that needs doing. And only you can do it. Usually, I try to save folks' souls, but today we need to save a man's life. The Lord has called on you to help save Deacon Eldridge.'

"I'd never seen him so nervous," she told me. "He was in a fretful sweat, even with us naked and my air conditioner going full blast.

" 'So honey,' he said, 'I, we, this community, needs you to do what only you can do. Nobody else can do it and it is for God's own sweet grace.'

"Donny, for a man used to speaking his mind to hundreds of people, it seemed he could hardly bring himself to say whatever he had to say out loud to *just* me.

"He said, 'You know, May, I'd only ask you if I couldn't see any other way. I am as blind at this time as a man with no eyes to any other solution. We, Deacon Eldridge that is, needs you to let The Junior have his way with you in exchange for the Deacon's freedom.'

"Lying there next to the only grown man I've ever loved, Donny, his words felt like a spike to my heart. I didn't utter a word. So he said, 'May, May honey, you all right?'

"I just lay there like a log, still not saying a word. Finally, I couldn't hold myself back, 'Goddamn you, Joseph. You think you can trade me like a cow? I may be a sinner to some, but I am not a slut. And I am not your private commodity to be passed around like a possession at your convenience. Don't you make the mistake of believing that just because of the way I earn a living, *earn it*, that you have the liberty to make any other assumptions about me.'

" 'But May,' he said, 'that's the way things are done around here. You can help get Tommy free, and no one is hurt.'

"That's when my knee kicked his manhood half way to his heart, Donny. His eyes rolled up to white.

'Well, I guess then, Joseph, that you consider me no one. Because if you think that it won't hurt me to let that stinking, Negro-hating, nasty man violate me, that it won't desecrate *me*, then I have to reconsider who I am lying next to right now. And to your heartless insult, add one just as brainless—the assumption that if I did do what you are so callously asking, that The Junior would really set the Deacon free.'

" 'You've got a point there, sister,' he said back to me, rubbing himself between his legs, wincing. 'But it's just once, May, honey, just once. Never again, just once,' he said.

"That's when I jumped up, Donny, and grabbed whatever was handy, which unfortunately turned out to be my expensive antique statue of the Virgin Mary that I bought in Italy. I threw it at him and it broke all to pieces right on the wall when he ducked his head."

I could tell she was crying now.

" 'You know good and well, Rev'rend Dim Wit,' I said, 'that The Junior would say anything to get into my pants, but once done, why would he deliver? After all, really, I'm still only a powerless nigger whore to him. And I'm beginning to think that you might hold a share of that opinion about me also.' "

" 'No, May, no...'

" 'We gonna get this agreement in writing, that what you think, Reverend Black-ass? And get it notarized? Gonna take it to a judge and make it legally binding?'

" 'Well, no, but, but...'

"Donny, for the first time in my life, he was speechless. He just scooted out of bed and stood there like a scolded schoolboy, rubbing his hands around and around down in front of himself from where I kicked him, his head shaking back and forth and sunk down onto his chest."

" 'And what if once isn't enough?' I said, screaming so hard I scared myself. 'You think The Junior's going to get honorable all of a sudden? Once he knows that I want something from him, he'll have me right where he wants me. You show me the guarantee, mister,' and I waved my finger in his face, 'and I'll be happy to help, but until then, you can forget we ever even had this little chat. Now please remove yourself before I throw up.'

" 'Hard to argue with you, May,' he said. 'Just an idea, a bad one. So sorry, May, no disrespect meant.'

"Then he threw on his clothes and grabbed his coat and hat and ran out like a scared rabbit. As he was leaving," May told me with a sad-angry chuckle, "I could tell he was afraid he had forever lost his re-charge rights. And, truth be told, Donny, he might have."

Reverend Rampbell called me that night. He had no idea I'd already heard it all from May.

"Thought I could convince her to help, Donny-boy, you know, doing what she does, with The Junior, but I couldn't. She said how could she trust he'd let Tommy go. We'll have to figure another way. I'll continue to think on it too. So sorry."

My James Bond had shot blanks.

Mr. Eldridge's approaching storm was bearing down on him, and me. My brilliant idea, the grown-up option, had missed the target by a mile. And the "magic cards" were still hiding under my mattress, useless. It was decision time, again.

CHAPTER TWENTY-ONE

Clara's black eye made the decision for me. She hid the bruises pretty well, but I could see them through her thick makeup. She walked up to me after class, grabbed my hand, and pulled me outside.

It was two days after Reverend Rampbell's fiasco with May and a week after Clara had stormed away and stopped talking to me.

"I told Daddy about you and me and seein Mr. Eldridge outside the temple before the fire and the arsonist guy," she said, whimpering like a kicked puppy. I could count on her to rant, swear, complain—but never whimper. "I figured I had to help, even though you've been a total fuckin jerk. I had to try.

" 'You tellin me you was at that Jew's house?' Daddy kept asking me. I told him your parents weren't there. I said, 'Daddy that's why I want you to go with me to tell The Junior, 'cause Donny said he wrestled the man who lit the fire. And by the time I got outside, I saw him runnin down the street too. We've got to help free an innocent man.' That's when he hit me."

" 'You goddamned slut,' he said. 'Alone with a boy. A fuckin Jew no less. Lettin him put his filthy hands on you. Do you realize what news of this could do to my reputation? Our reputation? Them Jews are nothing but perverts and nigger lovers and…oh mah God. I'll be the laughin-stock of the whole town.' "

As Clara sobbed, her cake makeup became an oozing mudslide.

"You told him my name?" I said.

"Fuck you, too," she said, pushing hard against my chest with both hands.

"Sorry, sorry," I said, pulling her back.

"I feel so stupid. Lettin my guard down around that prick. Some stupid little girl part of me figured he might care about the truth. And helpin. I'm such an asshole. 'You don't tell nobody,' he yelled at me. 'Nobody, ya hear.' Then he hit me again, right in the same place. It hurt worse the second time," she said, fighting to keep from crying. "Bastard. Then he screamed at me, 'What kind of white trash whore have you become?' "

I held her tight. I felt helpless, heartsick, which seemed to be more and more the norm. But, mostly, I was pissed. Pissed at her for being so naive. Pissed at her father for hurting her. Pissed at myself for my failed attempts with Uncle Herman and Reverend Rampbell.

Regardless, I was sure of one thing. Had I told her about the pictures, it seemed certain now that she would have said something about them to her father in the heat of anger. Not telling her about them was the absolute right decision.

"You're braver than me," I said. "I haven't done anything." That stopped the crying. She eased away.

"He said I can't see you anymore. Grounded. Said he or one of his assholes will take me to school in the morning and pick me up after. Do my homework in his office." Her chest collapsed in another whimper.

If "hell hath no fury like a woman scorned," then a close second is the fury of a beaten girl's Southern boyfriend.

Jew-hate was one thing, but this was Clara. Nadya had been a young boy's sick, erotic fantasy. May had taught me the right way to move with a female and about deep friendship. Now, with Clara, I was beginning to understand being in love. Until her, I guess I'd thought that having sex qualified me to call myself a man. But now I knew that standing up as a man meant more than the action of my penis.

Any moral dilemmas about blackmailing Reverend James were gone, fractured like my heart by Clara's tears. His fist against Clara's face, the purple and yellow angers shouting at me from her eye, bought my license.

Still, I could imagine Reb Gross's voice, "Are you crazy, *meshuggah*? Zat man is dangerous and you're only a kid anyvay. Not to mention zat zis is blackmail. I cannot condone this, Donala," he'd say.

But my mind kept repeating his teachings from Hillel, "If I am not for myself, who will be for me? And if I am only for myself, what am I. And if not now, when?"

That's why I didn't tell him.

I felt as alone as a black man at a Klan lynching.

Back home that night, in a fit, I wrote:

Dear Reverend James,

I have some pictures in my possession that I imagine you would not want made public. Please meet me at 4 p.m. on Tuesday at the old rock quarry lake.

Sincerely,

Someone in need.

My courage and bravado slid away as fast as my feet ran away from his church's front door, where I'd tacked the letter that night, the envelope marked "Reverend James, absolutely personal."

I called Reverend Rampbell and told him what I'd done, and was going to do.

"I can't believe I did it," I said. "I'm really scared. Her dad might kill me."

Reverend Rampbell's voice was calm. "Oh my, Donny-boy. You surely have taken the leap. Okay, let's calm down and try to figure this out. Give me a second."

The few seconds of silence felt like an eternity.

"You must tell Clara's dad that we all have secrets and we are all sinners in our own ways, though how I would love to roast that awful pervert myself. Lots of rumors and innuendos are always floating around about that man, but nobody's ever been able to hang anything on him. Sly as a fox," he said, almost admiringly. "You tell him that all you want is to get the charges against Deacon Eldridge dropped and to identify the real culprit and to get the arsonist charged and punished in the name of justice and to preserve the good relations between the Jewish and black communities. And tell him that since you suspect he has connections with the Klan and The Junior, he was the only person who you figured could be of help in this situation. In return, you tell him that he will get the negatives and all prints. And make sure you tell him that they are all being held in a sealed envelope by a person of impeccable character, who has not seen them and who will release them should anything at all happen to you. Can't be too careful with a man like that."

Tuesday came both too fast and too slow. In either case, I was a nervous wreck. I dressed in a white shirt and tie and my best brown penny loafers.

To get to the rock quarry, I drove past the area's only porno drive-in, *The South,* just over the border in North Carolina, then turned east and drove about a mile to the end of a rutted dirt road. Despite the warm autumn breeze, I was quaking like the rusty poplar leaves on either side of it. I looked for Clara's father's car, almost hoping that I'd find myself alone, then instantly hated myself for my lack of courage.

The parking area, high above the lake and big enough for about thirty cars, was scraped and potholed by countless drunken teenagers' wheelies and tire spinnings. I stopped the car by an island of couples-in-love carved poplar trees. Before opening the door, I pulled out the notes I'd written down of Reverend Rampbell's most crucial points, just like Mr. Horwith had taught us in debate class. I took a second to re-read them. My heart rattled against my chest like my musician friend Washboard Charlie's thimble-covered fingers against his metal instrument. My shirt stuck to my skin.

"Baruch hashem, baruch hashem," please God, I said. Then, *"Yasher koach,"* courage, Reverend Rampbell's favorite Hebrew expression.

Walking twenty feet, I peered over the edge of the abandoned gravel quarry's forty-foot, vertical walls. At the bottom of the steep, rock-strewn, bulldozer road, right by the deep, spring-fed lake, I spotted Clara's father's red Mercedes with its famous custom license plate holder, "Relax, Christ is my driver." I wished he'd brought his driver.

I remembered that my note had said to meet me at the quarry lake. I hadn't imagined that he would take the words literally to mean right by the lake where black kids swam in the summer. It was so clear that I could see thousands of submerged, worn-out tires sentenced to their watery grave by Tim's Tire Town.

Only months before, noting Tim's desecration, Reverend Rampbell had managed to get a bond passed to build Danville's first outdoor public pool. But, the Mayor was quoted in the paper, "The bid came in twenty thousand over the approved half-million-dollar bond amount. Spending more would be fiscally irresponsible. We've done enough for *them* already. They can swim inside at the Y on Tuesdays and Thursdays, like they always have, right before it's disinfected."

Walking down the road, *Wade in the Water,* one of May's favorite spirituals, swam through my head. About escaping slaves avoiding the bloodhounds by taking to the water:

Jordan's water is chilly and cold.
God's gonna trouble the water.
It chills the body, but not the soul.
God's gonna trouble the water.

Except that I was strolling right up to the bloodhound. Still, I prayed God would trouble Reverend James to help me.

"Bravery is not za absence of fear," Reb Gross would often say to me. "It is doing vat it takes despite one's fear." *Yasher koach.*

As I walked down, Clara's father looked up, shading his eyes with fingers that seemed as large and liquor-swollen as those fat kosher hot dogs Nadya had enjoyed so much. When I realized that he'd seen me, my heart started pounding so fast and furious that I thought I'd drop dead on the spot.

He was sitting on a gray, granite boulder, kicking his feet into the air and then back against the boulder with his black wing-tips. He looked like a tall, puffy, coiffed Buddha in a three-piece suit, with thighs grown too fat to allow him to cross his legs. That part of him never showed in "the fuckin picture." Still, I could see how his handsome, square jawed face, not to mention his height, would translate into a charismatic asset. Being average-looking myself, I'd seen how good-looking faces gave most an instant advantage. It always pissed me off, though I was as guilty as anyone of wanting to have, or at least have the attention of, those kinds of faces.

Since I'd had his Klan hood on when I took the pictures, he couldn't have had any idea of who I would be or what section of his ass I wanted. But I was betting he was ready to give it up for a reasonable price.

In any case, in the ten minutes it took for me to walk down to him, the Reverend was a nervous, sweating, rock-kicking mess, *on schpielkas.*

As I walked and looked down at the man Clara and I hated and feared, a picture reeled in my mind—laying naked with Clara, a few weeks after we'd met, on a blanket, hidden between two big, dark gray, rebel-flag-topped granite mausoleums at the Robert E. Lee Federal Civil War Cemetery, where they played Dixie each morning instead of the national anthem.

"Wanna hear one of my daddy's bullshit sermon tapes?" she'd asked. "Sells them to idiots all over the place."

"Sure," I said.

I was in love—beside the smartest, softest, toughest girl I'd ever known. And she actually liked me too. For that moment, nothing else could touch or hurt either of us.

She plucked a wild scallion and stuck it in the space between my two front teeth, then worked her mouth down it until her lips touched mine.

"Says the world started ten thousand years ago and that humans and dinosaurs lived together."

Looking up at the pastel sky, songbirds singing around us, her leg draped across mine, Clara hit the play button on her portable cassette player—out blared her father's mellifluous baritone.

"Folks, Jews are takin over the world with their communist, homosexual allies. The Jew-nited States of America will be fully niggerized by the miscegenation encouraged and practiced by the Jews. They are the natural enemy of our Aryan race.

"As brother Reverend Richard Butler, says, 'The Jew is like a destroying virus that attacks our racial body to destroy the Aryan culture and the purity of our race.' They are the Christ-killers, brethren, who will burn in eternal damnation in hell. But don't you worry folks, 'cause as it says in John 1.11, 'Those that deny that Jesus came in the flesh are deceivers and the antichrist.' When the Rapture starts, as stated in Revelation 16:16, then the Jew, the Catholic, and the nigger will be vanquished from this earth."

Even after a lifetime hearing this kind of stuff, I still had to force myself to choke off the blood rush to my head and the prickly current running up my spine that coursed somewhere inside every Jew I knew—that we had all, consciously or otherwise, learned to stifle so that life could be full, or at least bearable. Still, my face drained as white as a hung corpse.

She kissed it fast and hard.

"Fuck him, my sweet Jewboy. I love my kosher meat," she laughed. "And I get it for free—vut a deal," she said in a miserable attempt at an East European accent, jumping back on my slowly slumping erection.

"Fuck you too, cracker."

"But don't forget," breathing hard against each thrust, "that-you-get-to-fuck-the-preacher's-daughter. So-I'd-say-we're-even."

Afterward, she told me, "I memorized the whole damn New Testament and most of the old one too. And that's when I started to realize how full of shit he is."

"You memorized the whole thing?"

"He forced me to at first, but one night Jesus spoke to me in a dream. He was standin there pattin the heads of all sorts of kids, all sorts of colors, sayin to me that God loves all his children. Not like Daddy says, calls colored people 'monkeys' and says we should send 'em back to the jungle.

"And I started thinkin about the coloreds I saw 'round town. They mostly seemed to be all right. Figured if Daddy was lyin about some, I wanted to know how deep it went. Then I got really pissed. How could God hate anybody just 'cause of the color of their skin. You shoulda seen the look on his buddies' faces when I mentioned one day that their golf tees were invented by a black man. Scumbags.

"Plus, he acts so holy in church, but he treats Mom and me like crap at home."

"Wow, no wonder you always seemed so angry before I got to know you," I said.

Clara stared at me, kissed me softly, delicately, more a brush of her lips against my cheek, then ran her hand down my face and rested it over my heart.

"Man, bein close to a Jew, to you, Donny, lets me know I'm not crazy."

When I was within spitting distance, her father slid off the boulder. A red silk tie with three parallel vertical lines of tiny, evenly-spaced, embroidered gold crosses hung down from his doughy neck. I could smell the Vitalis in his hair, the same kind Dad used. As I started telling him about the pictures, the vein that crossed his gibbous nose seemed to throb and grow into a red and blue spider-web.

"Rudolph the red-nosed, child abusing, hypocritical, homosexual adulterer," popped into my head right before my heart jumped there.

"So you the son-a-bitch that snucked up on us! How dare you bust into my church, you bastard. You don't know who or whut you messin with here, boy. What's yo name?"

"Donny Cohen." I was surprised I could even speak.

His face puffed up as big and fast as a helium balloon.

"You the kike slime that's been fuckin my daughter, too!"

He grabbed my collar so fast I thought I'd topple over face first. Hauling his other fist back like the string of a bow, he said, "I should beat the crap out of you right here and now."

Beyond his boozed mask of age and fat, I could see Clara's face in his. I couldn't fathom how a father, a minister no less, could beat that beautiful face. The image of her tortured eye and of his fist against it flashed across my mind. It made me brave while I watched his mind seesawing between rage and fear—just like mine.

"Like you did her, you prick," I blurted out.

He looked hard at me—perhaps as surprised by my response as I definitely was. He pushed me away, sagging against the boulder, his shoulders drooping like tree branches loaded with the burden of a heavy snow.

As it turned out, I didn't even need to tell him much about the pictures.

"My only interest, Reverend James," I said, dying to pull out my note cards, "is in getting your help with getting the charges against Mr. Eldridge dropped and getting the real arsonist convicted. Then you'll be getting everything back."

Getting...getting... getting, I thought to myself. I could see Mr. Horwith shaking his head in disgust.

Reverend James's hand rammed inside his coat pocket, grabbing.

In the blink of an eye, I imagined the headline: *Son of Local Jewish Merchant Found Shot Dead at Abandoned Quarry.* Instead, he snatched out a sterling silver flask, unscrewed the cap with a fury and fired it hard to his mouth. He took another chug and sat silent, staring daggers at me. I could see how, between his bloated, yet manly, good looks and charismatic power, he could slice anyone's will to shreds.

The fragrant vapors reached out to me. I wished for, craved, a taste of that tranquilizer myself.

Finally, shaking himself straight, like a hosed dog, "I am always interested in heppin our black brethren as Christ would have done. And I certainly do not wish to see an innocent man convicted of any crime."

Jimmy James, like his daughter, was smart. He knew a good deal when he saw one, and this was about as good as he could get, all things considered.

"But how do I know you'll give me all them pitchas?"

I tried to answer nonchalantly, despite my guts wrenching bolt tight.

"You know, sir, that my family has been here since the late 1800s. My dad runs *Abe Cohen's* and we've built a reputation based on honesty and honor—even if we are Jews." I figured I'd preempt that response.

He raised his eyebrows.

"All I want is for you to find who did it and then go to The Junior. He'll have to drop the charges against Mr. Eldridge and file against the real arsonist."

"That could be tough," he said. "Why would the perpetrata, if he *is* one of ours, tell me?"

"That's for you to figure out, sir. I just know that I saw a guy with a hood on do it."

I thought my voice sounded as high as a quivering banjo string.

"And with my testimony and yours, we could get him convicted. No jury here in Danville would believe me alone, but with you up there too, they would."

"What 'bout the otha, uh, person in the pitcha?" he asked, tugging at his collar like at a hangman's noose. He wasn't looking at me, more staring into the sky, as if having a discussion with himself. Before I could construct an answer, he took another slug of whiskey. He held his flask out to me in a strange kind of Southern graciousness that somehow seemed normal. "Guess there's no reason for him to talk 'bout it."

I grabbed the flask, hoping he wouldn't notice my shaking hand, took a sip of the whiskey and handed it back to him with a sincere, "Thanks." Going down, it felt like an internal massage.

I didn't blame Reverend James for hating me. At least he could have had an opponent of some bearing and prominence in the community rather than a high school kid. Not to mention that I was having sex with his daughter. And a Jew.

"Reverend James, our families have been here a long time and I'm just trying to do the right thing."

"Oh, like sneakin up on me at mah own damn church an shootin them goddamn pitchas!"

"Vell, as Reb Gross would say," I said, feeling the whiskey and trying to lighten things a little, "success izn't having everyzing in your life easy. Success is figuring out how to handle vut comes your vay. Who knows ven opportunity or catastrophe vill strike?"

I immediately regretted it.

"Yeah? Well, fuck that crazy ole bastard and you, too. Now let's git down to bidness. Why you care so much 'bout that nigger anyhow?" he asked. "That's the problem with you Jews. You cain't help but being nigger lovers, can ya? You suck 'em dry sellin 'em stuff, then cry with 'em fer civil rights, then go pray in your own pure white temple and then go home, just like us, and live the good life."

There was some truth there.

"Whatever you do, marry a Jew," the adults always said to us, conveniently hiding their own racism. We had to love blacks as ourselves because they were our kin in suffering, unless we fell in love with one.

"But Reverend James," I said, "that has nothing to do with our mission to save Mr. Eldridge. I just need your help in getting him free."

"Ah'll hep you..." he said, taking a last drink. He reached the flask out to me again.

I wanted to drain it. "No thanks."

"You fucking kikes even drink like pussies."

Something I'd always been proud of.

He swiped his sleeve across the dribble of spit slipping from the corner of his mouth. His fingers poked me in the chest, his face inches from mine, the silver cross embedded in the ruby of his knuckle-sized, diamond-encrusted gold ring reflecting the sun.

"But this has nuthin to do with any fuckin mission of mine 'cep to save my own white ass." His cratered, mumpy cheeks, cauliflowered nose, and face shined like wet sunburn.

We stared hard-eyed at each other. I prayed for strength.

"I can live with that," I said. He started to move. "But one more thing."

He slumped back against the rock.

"Whut, goddammit?"

Thinking of Clara whimpering—Miss Tough, whimpering—I forced myself to answer.

"You'll never hit Clara again and you'll let her see me or I swear I'll send those pictures everywhere I can think of no matter what happens to Mr. Eldridge."

Inside my bluff, I thought I must have sounded like a shrieking teenage girl.

"You do that and I'll kill you."

I was afraid I'd melt right there in front of him. But Clara's black eye shouted at me again.

"If anything happens to me, I've arranged to have several sealed envelopes with the pictures inside, unopened as of yet, sent to every newspaper in the county. Now do we have a deal?"

He glared at me.

"Now I see. Fucking my daughter's even more important than savin that nigger, ain't it?"

"Fuck you," someone with my name and my body blurted out.

"Fuck you, Jewboy."

"Do we have a deal?" I said, sweat pouring down my face, but his too.

He stood up and kicked some dirt at me.

"Deal," he said. He climbed into his car, gunned the engine, stomped on the gas, and sprayed me with dirt as he fishtailed away.

I stood there watching him snake up the narrow road until he was out of sight. In the silence, my whole body shaking and drenched, I wondered what I had unleashed.

CHAPTER TWENTY-TWO

I trudged back up the steep road, more exhausted than elated. I drove to a pay phone by the five-dollar-a-night Economy Lodge Motel, just inside the Virginia border, where Clara and I had gone one night instead of the Fall Tobacco Festival Dance at school. I put in a nickel and dialed.

"Hello," Tichter answered.

"Rabbi, this is Donny Cohen. I need to meet with you in private."

"Your *Bar Mitzvah*, which was barely adequate, I must say, is long over. Why would I want to see you?"

"I need your help saving Mr. Eldridge from going to jail."

Mr. Eldridge was the handyman at Tichter's synagogue as well as my Reform Temple.

"We Jews have enough trouble here without getting involved in that," the Rabbi replied. "Besides, I wish that *shvatza* had succeeded in burning down that blasphemous excuse you call a Jewish place of worship."

That was all I needed to hear. Actually, I didn't need to hear anything. It was more a struggle to not enjoy this too much. Tichter calling Mr. E a 'shvatza', Yiddish code for "nigger," though most Jews would deny it. And I could still picture Nadya's misery at Grandma and Grandpa's dinner after her husband told his disgusting joke, not to mention the misery of her life in general.

"Rabbi, I hate to do this, but I have a photo you might be interested in."

Silence.

"When?" he finally said.

"I can be at the *shul* in fifteen minutes."

"You disgust me," he said as the phone slammed down.

That was it. I'd shot my second bullet of the day. I didn't feel like a Double-O-Seven hero or even much of a grown-up. I felt like a scared senseless boy up to his ass in muck. But I needed Tichter to help Mr. E's family.

"How dare you threaten me?" he barked as we sat in his study. "Give me that picture you *mumzer*, creep."

His eyes threw the same well-practiced daggers that must have sliced the frightened hearts of his flock into submission. I was scared, though compared to Reverend James's menacing violence, Tichter's threatening gaze fell flat as *matzoh* in my oven of fear.

"I'm not twelve anymore, Rabbi, and you can't intimidate me anymore. But I'm not interested in doing anything to embarrass or hurt you, sir." I hoped that giving him the respect of calling him sir might take the intensity down a notch or two. "But I need your help to free Mr. Eldridge."

"And you propose to do that by coming to this holy place to blackmail me?"

"All I want you to do is to organize your congregation to start a campaign to free Mr. Eldridge. The Jews here have enough power to maybe make The Junior think twice before proceeding with this case. And besides, isn't it our moral duty as Jews to try to repair wrongs and to stand against injustice—*tikkun olam*?"

"You dare speak of morality to me."

Pot calling the kettle black, I thought to myself.

"Please, Rabbi, please just help. I don't want to give you any trouble, but I have no choice. Reverend James is doing most of the work."

"Yes, he loves Negroes. I am sure he is happy to help." The hatred in his stare was like the face of the devil, with whiskers. He stood up, hands pushing hard against the top of his desk. "You are despicable."

In a way, he was right. But I remembered Nadya crying that first day, years before. "When my husband penetrates me…" she'd sobbed "…I feel more like a bag than a woman," not to mention the life, the misery, he had inflicted on her. Now my disgust didn't care about her husband's anger—my conscience simply shrugged.

"I can see how you might hate me, sir, but I'm more concerned right now about Mr. Eldridge. He's like a father to me. He taught me how to be a man and a carpenter."

"Yes, you are Jesus Christ himself."

"Fuck you, you pervert," I made myself not say. Thinking of Mr. Eldridge in jail calmed me, hardened my resolve. "Whether either of us like it, I need your help. Mr. Eldridge needs your help, and I don't think you would care or help if I didn't have something to force you."

Tichter raised his furry eyebrows.

"Mr. Eldridge's family is desperate for money to help them survive until he's freed. Everybody in your congregation knows him and might want to donate to help his family.

"And what if they don't, since *they* are not being forced?"

"If they don't raise enough, you can make up the difference yourself."

"How much do you want? How much extortion?"

"I figure their mortgage is about sixty-five dollars a month. Food is another fifty dollars. Utilities are fifteen dollars. Then if we add on miscellaneous stuff, I'd guess that two hundred dollars a month will cover them. They're already getting behind. So maybe three months' worth plus another two hundred. Eight hundred dollars total. If we can get him out sooner, then they can use the extra money to get back on their feet, maybe even pay Uncle Herman some."

"Blackmail *tzedakah,* charity," Tichter sneered.

I looked at him with a blank expression. "I need it in two days."

Again with the eyebrows.

"And you will destroy those pictures?" His voice, trying to hide his pleading, squeezed the words out like air forced from the pinched neck of a balloon.

"Yes. On my family's honor. Once Mr. Eldridge is free."

"I'll have it. Now get out."

"And one more thing, please. I'd like your wife, as representative of your congregation, to deliver it to Miz Eldridge with me and to accompany her to visit her husband in jail and in court. I think the guards and justice system will be more respectful if a white woman, a minister's wife, goes with her."

"She will not be part of this wicked spectacle."

"Let's let her decide," I said without blinking.

He glowered at me, yanking on his beard, small pubic-like strands of gray and black hair floating down to his desk.

"Please have her bring the money when I come to pick her up."

That was the last time we ever spoke. I picked up Nadya and the money in front of the synagogue two days later.

"Why is he letting me do this?" Nadya asked me in the car.

At nineteen, five years since our affair, I'd gained some maturity. We looked at one another with fragile, china-doll smiles. Our time together seemed like a perverse fairy tale.

"I asked him and he agreed. I told him Miz Eldridge would be more comfortable if you came along."

She cocked her head and narrowed her eyes.

"Still, it is somewhat strange to me." She looked out the window in silence. "Anyhow, Donala, it's good to see you. You look good."

"Thanks, so do you," I said, though we both knew it was a lie. After all the years, she looked even sadder than I remembered. Crushed, like a prisoner resigned to her fate. Cruelty hadn't taken a vacation.

We drove in silence.

But like an unforgettable perfume, something about her smelled familiar.

"Do you want one?" she asked, pointing to a brown paper bag on her lap.

I pulled the car to the side of the road in the heart of "niggertown," in front of Belle's Diner, famous for the best breaded, fried liver, okra, and gravy-mashed potatoes in town, black or white. I turned to her.

Nadya raised both hands to me, the butter stains from the chocolate chip cookies melting through the napkin resting in her palms, a sparkle escaping her gloomy eyes.

"Fresh out of the oven," she said. "Would you like one?"

I laughed, and so did she.

"Yes, please." We looked at one another. No crazy eyes. A tear shimmied down her cheek.

"Forgive me, Donala, for all that I did to you."

"We both did it," I said.

"Friends?" she said.

"Always," I answered as we each munched a cookie.

CHAPTER TWENTY-THREE

"I can't take this, Donny," Dottie Eldridge said, touching a Kleenex to her face. She tried to push the envelope back across the shiny mahogany, hand-carved, claw-foot dinner table her husband and I had made in his workshop. It was as fine and delicate as the European-styled furniture my family bought, at the family discount of course, from our relatives' high-end store in High Point, North Carolina.

Learning to turn wood for that table or gouging intricate details with chisels was harder than any framing, electrical or plumbing I'd challenged myself to learn.

"Another piece for the fireplace, Donny-boy. Try agin," Mr. E would laugh as I struggled to form wood on the lathe or chipped off an edge with a gouge. "Watch that bad language, young man, or I'll have to take a switch to ya," he'd say, he and his little boys laughing harder and harder the more I cussed.

I'd eaten many a home-cooked meal on that table through the years, when Mr. Eldridge and I would come home for lunch or dinner during a job.

But now, Nadya, Miz E and I sat arthritically in the front room of their little frame house, Dottie Eldridge's bright, hand-embroidered, floral curtains fluttering in the breeze against our gloom.

Nadya reached toward the window trim.

"Mr. E and I carved every leaf and flower on those vines," I said. "Ten different varieties, all Virginia natives."

"Can I touch it?" Nadya asked.

"Of course," Miz E said. She smiled at me. "Yes, you did. But this house is such a mess," she said, shaking her head, looking around.

The house was spotless, as usual.

We all sat there, fidgeting.

"Miz Eldridge," I said, swallowing a sob, taking a breath, forcing out more words. "I love Mr. E like a second father."

Nadya reached over and patted my shoulder.

"He's taught me so much," my face scrunching away tears, "that I could never make it up to him. Rabbi Tichter raised this money from his congregation. He wants you to have it. He asked me to give it to you. Please take it. I know it'll help." I pushed it back to her.

"I…I…" Miz Eldridge dabbed at a tear. She wiped her nose with her cotton handkerchief, one with a small, needle-pointed, red rose in its corner, swallowed hard and sat bolt upright. She grabbed both of our hands at once and cradled them between hers.

"Yes," Nadya said. "This is the least we can do. Please accept it with our love and blessings."

"Thank you so much. Tommy will be so relieved. You have no idea how much this means to us."

But knowing how hard Mr. E worked to make ends meet, and how little he made in spite of all of his skills, I knew.

"I would also be honored to accompany you," Nadya said in her thick New York accent, "if I may, to visit your husband whenever you wish to. Shall we go this week? I can pick you up."

Miz E's head fell to her chest. No one moved. She lifted it, eyes tearful, "Yes. Yes. I would greatly appreciate that, after the boys are off to school. I'd appreciate your company," exhaling relief. "Maybe Friday, at about nine."

"Donala," Nadya said as we drove back to her house. "It makes no sense that Mordechai would allow me to do all of this."

My mind flailed for a sellable answer.

"God sometimes works in mysterious ways," I said.

She said nothing for a moment, then, "Well, then, what else can I do?"

"How about a big banner on the *shul* saying 'Free Tom Eldridge.' "

"Where would I get such a thing?"

"Just kidding. Helping Miz Eldridge is plenty."

A week later, the banner appeared. Four feet high and thirty feet wide, hand-painted in stick letters, three inches thick, by the Hebrew-school kids, with Stars of David on either end of the sewn- together white sheets. It hung across the entire front of the synagogue, above the big, carved, double doors.

Miz Eldridge gasped, knuckle to her mouth, eyes glistening, when Nadya showed it to her as they returned from their second jail visit.

Within the month, it was covered in tomato and egg splatters and riddled with shotgun pellet holes. I could picture Nadya in her nightgown, jumping awake at each explosion.

CHAPTER TWENTY-FOUR

I had no confidence in Uncle Herman's or Clara's father's efforts. Reverend Rampbell's "May Way," idea had been a complete failure. And Mr. E was still rotting in jail. My promises to him were no more than whistles in the wind. I was desperate to find out the identity of the Klanner arsonist, though what I'd do with that information was still a question mark. Still, it was something.

As Nadya and I had been driving to see Mrs. Eldridge, a grungy-looking guy with a large spider emblem on his black leather jacket rode by on a big, noisy Harley. He was like a sign blasting, "help is on the way." And I knew that help's name was Eviatar Gross.

Rabbi Eviatar Gross had roared into the area in 1956 astride his blue-and-white, fringed, saddle-seated, wide-tired, chrome-plated Harley Davidson '74 cubic-inch Panhead with Duo-Glide and custom leather saddlebags. He'd ridden ten hours straight from

New York City on his "where-to-live-near-my-black-soul-brethren" scouting trip.

People looked up from raking leaves or working on cars or hanging laundry and stared. Spooked dogs chased after him as he zoomed through their backwater towns. His long white beard fluttered like bird-wings beside his face. Thick-lensed aviator goggles magnified his green pupils into emerald bug-eyes. *Payas,* braids, sprouted upward horn-like from the side of his head. *Tzit-tzit,* fringes, on his white shirt, flapped out from his bib overalls while his multi-sequined Moroccan *kipah,* skullcap, reflected the sun into a spray of colors. A beaded buffalo-hide holster attached to the side of his bike carried his *mateh,* a big stick topped with an eagle's skull and fluttering feathers.

Reb Gross was forty-eight years old, five feet, five inches tall, with arms as thick as most folks' thighs, and tree stump legs. Short and thick as he was, he was as agile as a deer.

"Yoga," he'd say whenever I'd marvel at nimbleness. "Keeps me young and sprightly."

I'd never even heard of yoga. It was nine years before the fire. I was ten years old. Neither of us even knew Mr. Eldridge.

Reb Gross bought a small farm on the outskirts of Danville and infuriated the adults of both Jewish congregations by refusing to join either. Our Reform rabbi thought he was too traditional, what with his *payas* and *tzit-tzit* fringes. Tichter thought him a blasphemer because he didn't agree with the Orthodox rigidity and liked to hang out with blacks at their churches. Nonetheless, the Jewish community as a whole, because of Reb Gross's sweet countenance and interactions with local Jews over time, ultimately found it hard to deny him when he started inviting their kids to his farm for stories of mystical and comical Judaism, hiking, sleeping under the stars, and donkey-riding.

"I teach donkey-vispering to my Negro farmer friends," he told us. "The donkeys verk harder 'cause they feel loved and both za farmer and za donkey are happier."

Around a campfire one night, he told my group of pre-*Bar Mitzvah* boys about his life, philosophies, and how he arrived in Danville.

I was immediately enamored. He questioned all the calcified Jewish rules. "Vy shouldn't girls, certainly as smart as you fellas, get to read from za *Torah* same as guys? Ridiculous!" He laughed at such absurdities. "Sing, sing, sing," he'd tell us. "Za Orthodox have constipated vocal cords. You zink God doesn't like the sound of his creation making beautiful music. Oy! So sing like zeir is no tomorrow.

"I fought against za Nazis with za Polish underground and against za British with za *Irgun*, za Israeli independence forces, during za British occupation of Palestine. And I am a vegetarian."

We all made excruciated faces at such an awful idea.

"I vitnessed so much violence, against my own people and my enemies, zat I svore myself to a life of peace, unless impossible. I do not eat meat because it involves slaughter and blood. I haf seen enough blood."

The Reb postulated that the American Indians were actually descendants of the twelve lost tribes of Israel.

"Zeir big, beaked noses, just like mine, dark hair and zeir guttural-sounding verds convinced me. I zink zey emigrated across a vanished land bridge from Russia across the Bering Sea and down into vut became za Indian vest. So I vent out zeir to make friends and studied vit several chiefs and reclaimed my long-lost tribesmen. Ve exchanged sacred gifts. I gave zem my grandfather's eighty-year-old holy *tallit,* prayer shawl, to embrace and protect zeir tribe. And zey gave me zis sacred staff. I call it my *mateh*, a Hebrew word vit a double meaning of staff and tribe. It is a truth stick, for speaking and fighting."

It was five feet long, of Douglas fir, the hardest Western wood, about fist-sized in circumference, hand-rubbed smooth and capped with the eagle skull and feathers.

"The *mateh* is much better zan fists or knives," the Reb said. "Za Indians taught me how to use it, first for speaking za truth and only later if you haf to fight for za truth."

After instructing us in the Indian ritual, we passed the *mateh* from boy to boy, saying whatever serious truths twelve-year-old boys considered.

"What about the fighting part?" we said in chorus afterward. We, of course, thought fighting was the better use.

Reb Gross planted the *mateh* upright between two large rocks. In the dark, a breeze stirring the feathers atop the eagle skull made it appear to be flying. The Reb settled himself on a boulder beside the fire. We sat shivering in anticipation.

"When I arrived my first day in Virginia, I stopped at a little diner, Millie's, about fifteen miles from Danville, for zum coffee. It had only five tables and a pretty little red Formica counter vit some stools in front. I vas tired and thirsty from my long ride. Millie's vas out in za country, near small, poor, white-owned tobacco farms, home beauty parlors, and engine repair garages beside dilapidated, unkempt houses. Trash, skinny dogs, and old equipment ver strewn everyvere.

" 'Vun coffee please miss,' I said."

According to Reb Gross's story, Bobby Stillwell, leader of the Tarantulas, the local motorcycle gang, sat nearby, doing a double take when the Reb walked in. Bobby just couldn't stop staring, huffing, and shaking his head. In what Bobby loved to call "Bobby Stillwell Country," nobody rode a Harley without his explicit permission, especially someone as ridiculous looking as Reb Gross.

"As the vaitress poured za coffee and turned to deliver it to me, Bobby got up off his seat, his beer belly straining against his grease-stained t-shirt. He reached out behind za counter vit his big hand, took hold of za vaitress's forearm, grabbed za cup and said, 'Honey, I'll take that,' then vispered something else to her and valked over to me."

"Don't think I've seen you 'round here before," Bobby said.

"I looked up at Bobby's huge bulk, like zum large animal, beamed a big smile and said, 'Vell, I am not from here, young man. I just rode ten hours from up Nort. My name is Eviatar Gross and I am certainly glad to meet you. You are my first new friend. Vut is your name?' "

"Well, sir, Bobby Stillwell's the name," puffing his chest. "And after that long trip, since ah know you must be hungry, ah'm thinking you need more'n this cup'a coffee."

"Vel, dat vud be nice, Mr. Bobby Stillwell. Perhaps a salat too. It is nice to meet you," I said, putting out my hand for a shake.

"Oh, more'n that," Bobby smiled back. "I'm gonna be real nice and feed you some of mah dee-licious, good ole home-made oink, oink, bar-bee-que."

"Vel, that's very kind, Bobby, but I do not eat pork."

"Oh, I know all 'bout that Jew stuff," Bobby said.

He looked back at the waitress, then spit a big, wet wad of brown, thick chewing tobacco cud right onto my outstretched hand.

"How do you know these things about Jews?" Reb Gross asked with a big smile, wiping his hand on a napkin and acting as if spitting on someone's hand was a friendly Southern tradition. "You must be very smart to know just by looking at me that I do not eat pork."

"Well, Mr. Gross-man, you Christ-killin-New-York-money-grubbing-commie-faggot-nigger-lovin-Jew-bastard-mother-fucker, hymies is about my favorite subject other than the cock-suckin-goddamn niggers 'round these parts. So you got a choice," looking back with a chuckle at his stable of buddies, "you kin either eat my pig-sandwich yerself, or I'll gladly shove it down yer throat. Take yer pick!" and he poured the coffee on the Reb's head.

The Reb's head jerked back from the pain. His *kipah* and thick hair offered some protection from a serious burn, but his scalp still sizzled, his face soaked and reddened. Bobby and his friends guffawed as he stood over the Reb.

"Vell now, young man," the Reb said as the coffee streamed on its path, staining his shirt. "I haf done you no harm and vud just like to drink zom coffee. I am tired after my long ride. Vy not? Vut's de harm? Then I vill leave in peace."

"No fuckin way you're leavin here in even one piece," Bobby replied, looking around to see if his crew had caught his clever word play.

"You, my friend," said the Reb, tears welling up, "are a big bully, and I don't like bullies."

"Well, ain't that a shame for you, kike, 'cause this here bully's gonna kick some Jew ass and then..." winking at his friends, "... then I'm gonna do some circumscribin on yo balls and give them to you fer dessert."

Reb Gross looked at the waitress. She only shook her head. The others simply stared back at him.

"I am now doubly impressed by you, Bobby. You even know about za Jewish rite of circumcision."

"That's 'cause you Jews think you're the only ones what know things."

Bobby turned to the counter. The waitress handed him a thick, white, china plate loaded with a hamburger bun stuffed with slices of barbeque, hot, and drippy with brown gravy.

"Eat it, or I'll shove it down like baby food."

Reb Gross shook his head, took a deep breath, and looked up.

"Mr. Bobby, zere are two things zat I do not tolerate. Vun is forcing somevun to violate *kashrut,* za kosher laws against eating pork, vich you zeme to know about. Insulting me, zat does not matter zo much. I am not important. But, since *kashrut* is a direct commandment from God, your insistence is an insult to za Blessed One himself.

"And second, vun should never be a bully, purposefully hurting an innocent, sentient being. America is za land I vill forever zank for destroying Hitler, za biggest bully in history. Though I haf killed many Nazis, Bobby, I find violence abhorrent. I haf fought enough for two lifetimes. I haf no desire to eat your sandvich or to fight vit you."

Bobby spit onto the plate. "Well, ain't that too fuckin bad, 'cause after I fuck you up, I'm gonna kill you. I'll ride that hog of yours with your head flapping top of that stupid stick you carryin."

Bobby grabbed at Reb Gross's *mateh,* almost toppling to the table as the Reb yanked it out of his grasp with a surprising quickness.

Reb Gross sighed, looked up again and asked, "Vill you fight me like a man, zen?"

"What in the hell's that's supposed to mean?"

"Vell, if you are not too scared, let us go outside so ve don't damage dis nice place and you can kill me right out under God's own blue sky."

"Have it yer way, asshole. Inside or out, even Jesus cain't save you now."

The Reb cocked his head. "Jesus?"

"Well, shit, not him nor nobody else."

Bobby followed the Reb out the door.

Reb Gross told us he noticed that it was a fine spring day. "Birds ver zinging. The air smelled of zose lovely Southern magnolia blossoms. A nice breeze through za humid air tickled my beard. A flock of ducks flew through a pastel blue sky, qvacking. It vas a divine day."

"Where the fuck you goin?" Bobby shouted, after the Reb had walked almost thirty feet.

"I stopped and turned to Bobby," the Reb told us. The look in his eyes vas so familiar—like zose of my neighbors in Poland who raped and burned and killed my family and friends ven the Nazis came. I closed my eyes to vun more breath of za magnolia perfume, zen raised my *mateh.* It felt like a dead weight to my reluctant spirit.

"Oh, like yer gonna hit me with yer widdle stick," Bobby chuckled.

The Reb's tears matted his beard, raising a pleasant coffee odor, reminding him of how tired he was.

"I vud rather us be friends," he smiled weakly. "How 'bout it? Please, I beg you, let us not hurt vun another. Let me vish you good luck vit your life and zhen let me leave and you vill not see me again."

Bobby spit another brown wad and almost hit a crow pecking at pecans on the ground. It squawked and flew up onto a tree branch.

"Luck?" Bobby sneered. "Don't know what it is. Never had any. Nor will you, 'cause you're not only a filthy Jew bastard, but yer a coward, too. Jest like all them other Jews deserved to got kilt in the war. Didn't even have the guts to shoot at the fucking Krauts. Buncha pussies."

"Oy oy," the Reb recounted. " 'This man must read,' I thought. I vas utterly amazed that he vas aware of the passivity of the East European Jews in the face of their own extinction. I shouted, 'Yes Bobby, you are correct. They misinterpreted the Sixth Commandment as *'Thou shalt not kill'* rather than *'Thou shalt not murder.'* Self-defense is not murder.' "

"I am a man of peace and ask you to join me, Mr. Bobby. Put your hate aside. Isn't zat vut America is all about and vy ve fought zat var?"

Bobby's face and eyes squeezed hard together. He hesitated and looked at the Reb, his head cocked to the side, as if the Reb's words had sparked something in his mind. Then he shook it off, like a dog after a swim.

"The only piece 'round here," Bobby bellowed again, "is gonna be yer ass hangin from a tree."

He sauntered the first twenty feet and then sped into a rush at the Reb. Hands stretched straight out like a zombie, his big, floppy man-breasts and stomach jiggled and swayed. He snarled like a lion, his flushed cheeks and open mouth framing a rotten front tooth.

The Reb's *mateh* moved with the same instantaneous muscle memory that springs a lightning-quick succession of notes from a great sax player's hands, without even a thought. It slammed against Bobby's ankles and feet, tripping him, sending him sprawling in a belly flop onto the ground before he could say, *"Hymie."*

Bobby looked up, plum-faced, saucer-eyed. He forced a grin and push-uped to standing.

"OK, you wanna fight with sticks, do ya?"

He walked ten feet to the pecan tree, cracked off a low-hanging limb and lunged, arms raised high, swinging the big branch down at Reb Gross like an axman splitting a log. With a dull thud, Bobby's wood hit the ground. The Reb could feel its wind as he stepped back and to the side and swung his *mateh* almost casually. This time it bounced off Bobby's forehead and then down against his nose and mouth.

Bobby wobbled around like a drunk, his body fighting to ignore his brain, then fell like a tree cut through. No one said a word. The only sound was the crow cawing from its pecan tree lookout. Bobby grunted and raised his head and chest up from the spreading pool of snot and blood oozing over his eyes and nose and mouth into the dirt.

"Should we hep ya?" one of his gang called out.

"Fuck you and him," Bobby snorted, the gooey mess dripping down his chin and throat like a turkey's wattle, his eyes blinking away tears. "I wath jest feeling sorry for thith thack a thit old Jew bathtad," he slurred through his quickly swelling lips, "but now I'm pithed off and ith time to teach 'em a lethen."

"Please," moaned the Reb, "let us stop ziss fighting and I vill just leave."

"Please my ath."

Bobby hefted himself up with an un-concealable groan and stumbled a few steps. He wiped the blood out of his eyes with the sleeve of a blue denim shirt with pearl pentagon-shaped buttons that one of his gang had thrown to him. One button edge scraped his gashed lip, making him flinch.

"You ain't neva gonna leave to go back to Jew-ville," Bobby said, casting the shirt away. "Thith here's gonna be yer grave. You can thay yer Jew prayers now, 'cauth you are gonna meet yer maker."

If he were killed, the Reb figured his body would be thrown into a ditch or a stream, perhaps buried in a field. No police called. No investigation. The Harley would be chopped or sold off. No one up North knew where he was—he barely did—and no one would find out.

Bobby reached into his pants pocket. "Fuck," he yelled, as he fumbled to unfold an eight-inch knife from its bone handle. Fingers dripping blood and sweat and slipping off the smooth metal, he finally wrestled the blade open, stood up straight, raised his right, knife-wielding arm high above his shoulder and staggered toward Reb Gross, tripping against an exposed tree root, righting himself, and stumbling the last few feet.

The Reb, with a sad fierceness in his wet eyes, brought his *mateh* full force up between Bobby's legs, doubling him over. Bobby grunted, retched and grabbed his groin with his left hand, knife arm still flag-waving above his head. Reb Gross, with a batter's swing, slammed the *mateh* onto the side of Bobby's skull. Bobby swayed side to side, like a dead moose still standing, then thudded to the ground, the knife still firmly held in a corpse's grip.

"Za sound, ven I hit his head," Reb Gross told us with tears in his eyes, "vas like a vatermelon crackin open. It zickened me."

Bobby lay there, blood gushing from his head and nose, foaming at the mouth, his body convulsing. His friends rushed over and kneeled at his side.

"I am zorry," Reb Gross said to the crowd as he trudged to his motorcycle.

He told us, "I valked to my motorzycle, looked back, and told the boys to call an ambulance. I shoved my *mateh* into its holster and tried to kick the starter, but I was so tired that it took me three tries. Birds still sang, the sky was still blue with fluffy clouds, and the magnolias still perfumed the air. But all I heard or smelled or saw was the ugliness of vut I had done. I had a right and a duty as a human being, and especially as a Jew, to defend myself. Nevertheless, I rode off broken-hearted."

We boys sat in silence, watching the reflection of the fire's light against the Reb's moist cheeks.

"At the hospital the next day," Reb Gross started again, "Bobby was still unconscious."

"He crashed his bike," his gang claimed.

That night, after they had left or passed out in the hallway, the Reb sneaked past them into Bobby's room.

"I put my hand to his head and started chanting, in a visper, *Ana Elna Rafanalah,* the ancient Hebrew healing prayer. Over and over, I caressed his head and face. I vas crying like a baby. I begged God to heal him and to forgive me."

Eventually, his ministrations awakened Bobby's comrades, who ran into the room. After a few moments of puzzled shock, they started to move toward the Reb, who grabbed his *mateh* and held it over his head, like Moses in front of the Pharaoh.

They stopped.

"What the fuck you doin here?" one said.

"Healing prayer," fast-breathed the Reb.

"For the guy you just nearly kilt?"

"I didn't vant to hurt him."

"You cain't hold us all off."

"No," said the Reb. "I can't."

Still, no one moved.

"Wha..." Bobby exhaled like a big fart out of his mouth, eyes fluttering open. "Wha the hell?"

"This fucker snuck in here and we gonna kill 'em, Bobby," one suddenly brave guy said.

Bobby puckered his dry lips in and out, closed his eyes with a big sigh, licked his lips with his swollen tongue, forced his eyelids back open with a wrinkled forehead and whispered, "Fuck...no."

He looked into the Reb's eyes.

"I was dyin. I was floatin in the air, lookin down on mysef in the bed and I know'd that I was dyin," Bobby whispered. "And then, I see'd you come into the room. And I heard these strange sounds, like angels. Like the Lord was beggin me to stay 'round. Like I had somethin more to do in this fuckin world. Next thang I knew, I waked up and you was standin here, singin, and I know'd I'd be OK."

The boys looked around at each other.

"Leave that old fart alone," Bobby said, his nose whistling with every breath. "He might've put me here in the first place, but I fuckin deserved it. I started the fight with 'em and he was only defendin hisself."

A nurse walked in, looked around. "He okay?"

"He is okay," Reb Gross said.

She looked across to Bobby, who raised a thumb.

"Well, please keep the noise down," she said, shaking her head as she walked out.

"And how many people," Bobby strained to say, "do you assholes know who would come back to save a fucker like me after whut I said and done to him?"

His gang-mates couldn't argue with the logic and soon were patting the Reb on the back like he was their long-lost father.

After fumbling with the blankets and taking a few breaths to gather his strength, Bobby said, "Whut the fuck's that stick thang you clobbered me with?"

"It is not just a stick," the Reb replied calmly. "It is a *mateh,* an ancient, holy staff, like the vun Moses used in Egypt. It vas given to me by an Indian medicine man far out vest. Whoever holds it in sacred ceremonies must speak zeir truth. It is passed from generation to generation of chiefs as a zign of za continuation of da tribe and its values."

"How kin I git one and learn to use it like you done?" asked Bobby.

"I am zorry, but you can't," replied the Reb as he bent down, kissed Bobby on the forehead and said, tears flowing, "Please forgif me for hurting you, my zon." He started to leave the room, the boys parting like the Red Sea.

"Wait," Bobby wheezed, reaching his bandaged hand out to the Reb.

Reb Gross turned and returned to Bobby's side.

"Bobby squeezed my hand gently," Reb Gross told us, "tried lifting his head but couldn't. He looked into my eyes—peacefully but sort of vith a qvestion he didn't yet qvite know how to ask but still vanted to try. I held his hand in both of mine."

"You assholes get the hell outta here," Bobby ordered in a sandpaper voice. "And close the fuckin door behind you."

Suffice it to say, none of the boys had ever seen, and probably would never again, anything so out of their ordinary.

Holding tight to Reb Gross's hand, Bobby sighed.

"I got somethin to tell ya—'bout a girl."

"Oy," the Reb said.

"In high school," Bobby spoke softly, "I used to be kinda smart. I liked to read," he said, cocking his head to the side, raising his eyebrows in a 'can-you-even-imagine-it' kind of half grin. "I was clean-cut and a big football star. Didn't drink or nothin, since I seen how tha 'shine my family sold fucked up people's health and minds."

"Yes?" said Reb Gross.

"It's why I use copper tubes now, instead of lead. The leads what did it. Leached inta the shine and was poison."

"Good."

"Was before I got hurt in Korea. And started the drugs and all, first for the pain and then," he took another deep sigh, "well, my mind kinda got messed up over there."

"Yes, I can imagine."

"Her daddy was an Orthodox rabbi here in Danville. I mean he didn't preach or nothin. Just he was educated. Know whut I mean?"

"Yes, yes, I do," said Reb Gross, "a *Yeshiva boychik*."

"Yeah," said Bobby, "that's what she said he called hisself. And, you know, an educated Jew can be called rabbi even if he don't preach and all."

"Yes, I know." Reb Gross patted Bobby's arm.

Bobby flinched.

"Oh, I'm sorry," the Reb said, drawing his hand away from one of the raised, weeping, deep purple welts on Bobby's arm.

"I liked talkin to her, even tho she was kinda daffy-lookin. Didn't even use makeup. Had a big Jew-hook nose."

Bobby stared at the ceiling. Suddenly, his eyes shifted in a start to Reb Gross's face.

"Shit, ah mean, hell, ah mean, you know, Rabbi, sorry."

"Don't vorry. I know I got a good honker too," the Reb smiled, touching his. "Go on, Bobby."

"Other kids couldn't figure why I'd be hangin round with her, bein that I could've pretty much been gettin mah hands in any pussy I wanted. Just that she was so downright curious," his dry throat a parched undertone, "and smart and diff'rent and knew so much.

"An the funny thing is that she just plain and simple liked football. Would sit there all alone in the stands watchin us practice, jumpin up and down and shaking her hands like some puppet on strings when we'd make a mistake or a good play. We just sort of fell in together after she asked me a football question one day in history class."

Bobby pulled his covers up with a shiver and a grunt.

"Shit, she'd git all excited talkin with me 'bout strategy and college teams and players an last week's games. Yeah."

Bobby bounced in a coughing fit. The Reb touched a glass of water to his lips. Bobby swallowed, closed his eyes and took a big breath, a rapturous smile on his face, "like he'd gone to sleep," the Reb said.

Then, suddenly, "And I learned all this stuff 'bout Jews and that Toe-rah from her and it was all so new and interestin and I just couldn't get enough of her. She was so diff'rent from the girls 'round here. They were always all gussied up and just wanted a football hero to strut their stuff with. And ta take 'em dancing and shit.

"But she dug out things and listened to stuff I wouldn't have dreamed of tellin my kind of people or the preenin girls. Wantin to know how I felt. How *I* felt! Shit, whoever cares how a big ol country boy football player *feels*?

"Told me 'bout how Doctor Freud would've loved scrutinizin my clan!"

Bobby laughed and flinched at the pain, then shook his head with a grin.

"That vud be interesting," the Reb agreed.

"Said she knew all about him because of her 'meshugar' family."

"*Meshuganah*," Reb Gross laughed, "crazy."

"Yeah, that's it. You ever read any his stuff? Boys, shit—even kings—wantin to fuck their moms and kill their dads and such crazy shit. Man.

"She'd ask me all kinds of questions 'bout football. Makin me feel smart. But way more'n that, getting me to think 'bout all sorts of things nobody ever even ever thought about or even ever wanted to know 'bout round here. Givin me books that were so fuckin excitin," he said, letting out a big breath. "Like the war and them Nazis and President Roosevelt. And how Jews debate all sorts of ideas. Round her, my brain felt like it was on fire. Made me feel just like them cells in science class—like sometimes a blob of nothin like me could grow into somethin full'a life.

"And then one day, a few months after we started talkin, she just walked up, cryin, and then run away right after she handed me a letter tellin me her daddy had found out and whupped her real good and sayin she couldn't be 'round me no more."

"Vat vas her name, Bobby?"

"Sara. Sara Kushner. Yeah, Sara. I love that name, don't you? From the Bible."

"Yes, Abraham's wife," Reb Gross said.

"Yeah, that's right. Well, I just couldn't think straight after that. Couldn't concentrate on football or nothin else. That's when I dropped out of school, junior year, and signed up with the Marines. When I came back three years later, she was gone.

"And I never even touched her, I swear, 'cept just holdin hands a few times in the hall. First time she let me, she started shakin all over.

" 'My father will kill me, literally,' she'd told me, 'if he ever hears about me being around you, not even to mention holding hands.' Maybe that's what got back to her daddy.

"I still have that blue letter and envelope, hidden away. And sometimes," Bobby gulped, "sometimes I take it out just kinda tryin to smell the perfume. Kinda pitiful, ain't it, after all these years?

"Guess 'tween that and the war, turned me mean and, and..."

"A deep roar of a groan growled up from his belly and he wept," Reb Gross told us. He ran his hand through Bobby's damp, matted, oily locks. He wiped both their eyes with his red and white spotted headband until Bobby rolled over into a fetal position.

"I am zo zorry, my friend. Life is not fair," he said as Bobby's sobs melted into snores.

Forevermore, the Reb was put on a pedestal in the strange world the Tarantulas reserved for their own contradictions.

He was honored and protected, as if there were a sign on him: "Don't mess with that Jew or you will pay."

Only later did the Reb remember to tell Bobby about his ancestor, a third cousin, Colonel Oscar Gross, who fought for the Confederate side in the Civil War.

"You shittin me," exclaimed Bobby.

"No, I haf looked it up in my family tree and it is true," the Reb told him excitedly. "You can look it up. You, ve, do haf zomezing in common. And my family even had its own coat of arms from Medieval Hungary. Ve vas fighters, for better or verse."

"Well I'll be, you little shit—oh, I mean, Rabbi," Bobby laughed.

"Not a marriage made in heaven, perhaps, I thought, but it was progress," Reb Gross told us.

Bobby didn't exactly go the straight and narrow, but he was "never hisself" after that, his friends, and even enemies, would say.

He organized Tarantula toy and food drives for poor kids and families—bewildering the local authorities who could not believe "that white trash" would actually be doing something without ulterior motives, just for the good of it. To this day, they still do it.

Though he didn't exactly hang out with them afterward, the Reb would occasionally see Bobby's gang around the county when out on a ride. Bobby would stop them, get off of his hog and give the Reb a big bear hug.

"Is you all bein good boys?" he'd ask.

They'd nod their heads like teenage schoolboys and say, "Yessuh."

Right after I'd first met Reb Gross—I was eleven—Bobby was shopping at Dad's store for Levi's. Dad's store was the first east of the Rockies to sell them, after Dad saw cowboys wearing them during the war. I mentioned to Bobby that Reb Gross had given me a ride on his hog. "It's as big as yours, Bobby."

"You know that old coot?" Bobby said.

"I just met him. I'm going to camp out at his farm soon."

Bobby shook his head and laughed. "Well, son, that ole guy saved mah ass, so's now I'm his fire-breathin pro-tec-tore. Anybody tries to mess with that old fart an I'll bite off they'se asses like a German shepherd."

After his fight with Reb Gross, Bobby also changed his handle, his nickname. It was very odd, to say the least, to see *Jewdawg* emblazoned on his leather jacket, right above the swastika.

I dropped Nadya off at her house after our visit to Miz Eldridge, then sprinted to the pay phone at the gas station right around the corner.

"Reb Gross," I almost screamed into the receiver, breathing so hard and fast that I could feel the blood rushing to my head, "Will you ask Bobby to find out the name of the arsonist? He must know those types and hear their gossip."

I was sure that he'd be as excited as I was at the prospect of helping to catch the culprit. There was a moment of silence. I felt a headachy rush of confusion. I heard Reb Gross blow air through clenched lips.

"Bobby loves me, Donala, but it is not zo zimple. Asking a favor of a man like him is not zo zimple. Ven I tell him vy I vant his help, that it is because that fellow hurt you and killed our friend, Albert Rippe, Bobby could vant to kill him in my name. He is my blood friend now, but violence is his second nature, and I do not vant him to hurt another person in my name."

"But this could save Mr. Eldridge," I said.

"Donala, these are choices ve must make in life and you are asking me to make one that could be terrible either vay. This Bobby is unpredictable."

"But this is to save an innocent man. You have to help. Bobby would do anything for you. You know it. This is *Tikun Olam*, like you always say, repairing a wrong. You're being a fucking coward."

The words were like a self-inflicted bullet to my heart. The phone line was silent again. I couldn't believe I'd made such a vile comment to one of the bravest, most decent men I knew. But if it would help Mr. E, I almost didn't care. I hated myself.

"Please, Donala, don't continue on this path vith me. Please let your Uncle try his best. Let us zee how he does. Let me know anything else that I can do to help. I vill pray for your friend and ve vil see. Goodbye, Donala."

The phone line went dead.

CHAPTER TWENTY-FIVE

I stood frozen in the booth; the black phone glued to my ear until its crackling static jolted me back, like a nerve shock, to Clara. Her black eye and desperate attempt to help demanded that I not desert her in my plots to save Mr. E, even if I absolutely could not tell her about her father's perversity or my blackmail. And, truth be told, my own wretched turmoil and the possibility of keeping her in my life was a need as strong as hunger.

Like the roar of Mr. E's busted muffler and Bobby Stillwell's Harley, another man's image boomed into my mind, a man who was like a comic book character to me, a man who knew everything, everybody, and everywhere in the county, and therefore a man who might, without his even knowing why, allow me to bring Clara into helping Mr. E and at the same time help give her a panorama into the deeper truths of the South. I was in awe of him and thought Clara would be too.

I originally only needed him because he'd sell beer to anybody without checking IDs at his garage, Blue's Esso, just over the Virginia border on 86 South in North Carolina, only ten minutes from my house.

But, my awe of him, beyond the beer, started because his was the only garage I'd ever been to that blared mostly classical or even jazz rather than hillbilly music. Hearing his country-boy mechanics whistling Brahms, Liszt, and Beethoven was surreal.

"If they don't like the music," he'd say in his Southern drawl tainted by his parents' British accent, "they can fucking work someplace else."

Locally raised, forty-four years old, Harvard-educated William Charles Fairfax, self-mantled "Blue," was a Virginia blueblood with grease under his nails. He drank like a fish and reveled in writing letters to the editor about his disdain for his royal lineage and Southern hypocrisy. In another time and place, I could easily imagine his noble face and six-foot frame in a British uniform on a white horse, sword outstretched, leading his men into battle by the simple jut of his perfectly angled jaw. Somehow, Danville seemed to breed these one-of-a-kind characters.

Since I was old enough to remember, he'd charge into our store to buy mechanic's uniforms, reeking of beer. My father blanched at every "fuck" or "goddamned" that spewed out of his mouth. Finally, Dad had enough after Blue started one of his cynical homages about Thomas Fairfax the Sixth. In 1742, one of Virginia's original counties had been named after him.

"Lord 'Asshole' Fairfax of Cameron," Blue started up, "was proprietor of the Northern Neck. George fucking Washington built Mount Vernon there. The Sixth fucking lord was the only goddamned member of the British nobility to ever actually live in the fucking colonies. I'll give him credit for that. Course, old Georgie boy and he disagreed about whether he should give up his goddamned royal rights to all that land and let us own our own fucking country."

Dad, fuming to us all at dinner that night, said that he was willing to risk the loss of Blue's business. The next time Blue came into the store and started his rant, Dad walked up and said, "Mr. Fairfax, sir, please stop. You are upsetting my staff, my customers, and me. We do not speak like this in my store or in my home. It offends me and I would sincerely appreciate your stopping, please."

Dad always ended his demands with please. I loved him for that, though it always made it hard for me to stay mad at him.

Blue stood silent, then bowed low, his forward leg bent at the knee and the other straightened backward, raised his arm with a flourish of his oil stained cap, stood back up and said, "Mr. Cohen, you are a man of fairness and honor, and I will be happy to accommodate your wishes. Please forgive my rudeness."

Dad was so relieved, he told us, that he almost cried.

As enamored as I was of Blue, I was just as proud of Dad's courage.

The day after meeting her father at the rock quarry, I called Clara.

"Somewhere I want to take you," I hoped her father had lifted her ban as we had agreed, "after school today."

"Weirdest shit," she said over the phone. "Daddy apologized for hittin me and said I could see you as long as we didn't flaunt it all over town—'at least keep it undercover,' he said. I thought him sayin undercover was hilarious even if he didn't realize the irony."

"Hop in and close your eyes," I said when we met in the parking lot after school. "We'll be there in a minute."

"Fun," she said. Her excited smile and twinkling eyes made me sure of my choice.

Percy Sledge's When a Man Loves a Woman was playing on the radio as we drove. Like the song said, I couldn't keep my mind on "nothin else" but her and my good fortune. With the Mr. E situation ready to be settled with her father's help and his "permission" for me to be with Clara, it all seemed perfect. It felt like Percy was speaking directly to me.

"You're the good thing I've found," I sang to Clara as I stopped the car. "Open your eyes."

Clara's sunny countenance turned black as storm clouds when Blue looked up from the car he was bent over and shouted, "Clara darling."

He ran to the door, opened it, pulled her out, put his arm around her waist, and gave her a crooked smile.

"You know each other?" I asked.

They both hiccupped a strained look back at me, then at each other.

"Uh, friends of friends," Clara said.

"Yes, old friends," Blue said, his perfect blond curls bouncing up and down from his enthusiastic head shaking, with a smile as wide as a coat-hanger, and as tight.

"Church," Clara said.

"Church? I thought you never went to church, Blue. You're always saying how anybody who goes to church, much less believes in God, is a stupid asshole."

"Yes. Well, I used to go. Before, when I was younger."

"Oh, so when Clara was a little girl, 'cause I've known you for a long time and you've always said you hated churches almost as much as your British ancestors."

"Oh yes…she was such a cutie. Clara, old girl, you've grown so big." Blue patted her head and kissed her cheek. Clara pushed him away. Not a gentle push—more a shove.

Clara looked down at the greasy parking lot and kicked hard at a few pebbles.

Neither seemed inclined to yak, a strange state for either of them, and a disappointment to me.

"Time for me to get back to work," Blue said in a blink.

I paid for a six-pack of Pabst Blue Ribbon and we left. Clara didn't say a word the whole drive back.

"You okay?" I asked when we arrived back at the school parking lot.

She grabbed my arm, hard.

"Okay, so he fucked me when I was sixteen. I was a virgin. Shit, Donny, you're the only other I've ever been with, even though everybody thinks I've fucked every boy in town. Anyway, I came to buy some beer one day when Daddy and Momma were away at one of their goddamned conventions. All the mechanics had left and he was closin up. He said he'd give 'em to me for free if I'd sit down and drink with him—plowed me with about six of 'em. Then, he took me to his fucking house next door. Was like a museum, full of amazin Revolutionary and Civil War stuff and maps of every piece of land in the county. Family's been here since forever. Started tellin me about it all and how most folks 'round here have their heads up their ass, thinkin they're so close to God while hatin Negroes and thinkin the fuckin Confederacy was so great. Knows all the people around here and geography and history like the back of his hand. 'Tween the beer and his looks and him sayin that I really wasn't crazy to be thinkin the same kinds of thoughts he had, we just kinda fell into each other's arms and did it. I'm not ashamed, if that's what you're tryin to lay on me, Donny," as if I had made a comment. "Just did it once. After my dream, it just felt good to be close to somebody who wasn't a fuckin hate-filled, stupid, goddamned redneck. He wanted to do it again, but once is curiosity, twice is stupid. I mean, shit, Donny, the guy's old enough to be my fuckin father. Wish he were, though. Maybe then I wouldn't be so fucked up. You hate me?"

Her look was a combination of angry and pleading.

I hadn't said a word and was in my not-so-unusual state of bewilderment, especially at the, "You're the only other I've ever been with," revelation. She was right. No one would find that easy to believe. In that split second, another of Sledge's verses assaulted me—about how if a man lets a woman deep into his soul, he can make himself vulnerable to the misery of betrayal, to making him feel like a fool.

"Why didn't you tell me when we got to his garage?" I asked. It wasn't that I felt like a fool exactly. More that niggling feeling a boy gets when the fantasy of a pure love smacks against the reality of, well, reality. That buried not so deep in the consciousness is a fear that it's all been a charade, that something has been going on behind your back that you were too stupid to detect or even imagine—mixed with my constant insecurities about not being handsome enough for Clara.

"How could I fuckin tell you when I didn't even know where we were headin until I opened my eyes? Didn't even have time to hope he'd forgotten or somethin. So do you think I'm a total scuzz-ball?"

It seemed important to say the right thing. In spite of my fear, I could see how Clara could have wanted to be wrapped in Blue's blanket of relative sanity. However twisted it was, it was warmer than anyone's before mine. It was part of the same reason I'd figured to bring her to see him.

"Shit, Donny, say something. You think I'm a cheap whore now, don't you?"

"Mostly…" I said and then went silent. I took a breath and closed and rubbed my eyes with my knuckles—to think for a second—then opened them to a terrified look in hers. "No, I don't mean that I mostly do," I said when I realized that she was reacting to my saying 'mostly' and then going silent.

She let out her breath.

"Mostly, I'm afraid you'll do it again with him, truth be told. He's so cool and good-looking and I'm just..." and I held my arms up, raised my shoulders and frowned. "But, I mean, Clara, if I was a sixteen-year-old girl, I'd probably have done the same thing. I mean, he's handsome and smart and tells it like it is, like you said. You're the best thing that's ever happened to me."

Clara stood gape-mouthed, then threw her arms around me and clamped her lips against mine until I could barely breathe.

"Man, if all Jews are as sweet and nice and...and...forgiving, yeah forgiving, as you, how could people hate them like they do?"

As she continued to hug and kiss and drape herself around me, I almost started crying. Then, I told her why I'd taken her there—that since he knew everybody in the county, maybe we could entice him to help us find the arsonist.

Looking deep into my eyes, running her hand through my hair and kissing me delicately on the lips, she said, "That's a fucking fantastic idea."

We went back the next day toward closing time, Clara's folks still at their revival or whatever it was that fundamental Baptists do out of town, our purpose unsaid. Clara told the "babysitter" that she was going to the library for a few hours to continue her tobacco research.

Blue seemed a bit surprised, but invited us to hang out after closing, around his pot-bellied stove, talking about all sorts of stuff. He seemed to enjoy the repartee, though mostly it was him lecturing and us listening—a break from the normal talk of most of his crowd about tobacco prices and whether Fords were better than Chevys—and flirting with Clara.

It didn't take much beer for him to start up. "My family, and the whole fucking British aristocracy crowd, were a bunch of fucking tight-ass, gin-soaked bigots. Their descendants down here think they're something special because they've inherited the blood of some goddamned nasty ancestor that got rich breaking the tobacco picking balls of a bunch of fucking African ninnies. Hated everybody, Negroes, of course, but any white, too, who wasn't royalty." He threw his hunting knife perfectly between the boobs of Queen Elizabeth's photo tacked to the wall. Which was beside his Harvard degree and another picture of a never-pierced Robert E. Lee. Then, wiping his hands on a filthy rag and popping open another Blue Ribbon, he rhapsodized about Thomas Paine and the dignity of the common man.

Clara said, "Hell, Billy, your hero there," throwing an empty beer can at the Lee picture, "fought so those same cocksuckers could keep their fuckin slaves."

Blue scratched a blue-tip, wooden match against the metal zipper of his Levis and tipped the flame into his Sir Walter Raleigh-packed pipe, then pulled a hefty inhale and let go an apple-sweet, slow exhale.

"Isn't the same, Clara darling. That man," blowing a kiss to Lee, "fought to protect the little guys—most of whom never could even afford to own a slave. He fought for the little guys' God-and-Constitution-given individual dignity and liberty. Those boys were nothing but cannon fodder conned by the rich Southern oligarchy to fight against the Northern oligarchy, also a bunch of fucking English-related, unearned-status, pooh-bah-fucking control freaks who didn't like the competitive advantage we got from all that free slave labor. Those poor boys thought they were fighting for liberty and states' rights when they were really just fighting so our rich Southern sons-a-bitches could keep their fucking slaves.

"But that guy," saluting General Lee, "that guy hated slavery, as far as I can tell from my own research. More than Lincoln, truth be told, who would've probably let our rich Southern assholes keep their fucking slaves had they not seceded—bunch of spoiled idiots.

"Only difference between the two sides was that, to their credit, the Northern bunch, Lincoln at the helm, saw that being broken up into a bunch of independent little hegemonies would lead us down the same historical road as Europe, all sorts of cretinous, power-grubbing little aristocrats fighting over decades and centuries at the expense of the common man, killing their sons and pissing away tons of money that could've been made by being one hell of a big trading bully. They didn't like the slavery stuff, but it was secondary to the economics.

"And that poor bastard, Robert E. Lee, had to choose. His only weakness was that he just couldn't bring himself to fight against his own kind, even if they were wrong. He was a military man, and as such, had to—was trapped into—choosing sides. I can only imagine the demons that must have besieged him knowing that in choosing family, he probably chose wrong. Must've been a fucking civil war inside his own soul. Maybe he fooled himself into believing that he was fighting for the rights of the little man, conned just as much as the fucking poor sons-a-bitches he led to slaughter."

His railings felt like hammers of truth—his British accented and proper completion of the endings of words, never dropping the "g's" from their endings, added to his erudition.

Blue looked like he was going to explode, his face colored like his name, sucking furiously at his now extinguished pipe. He banged its ashes out against a pole and stuffed it into his greasy pants pocket.

"Shit, fucking assholes, all of them," he finally said. "Now get out of here. I have goddamned cars to attend to and beer to drink. Come on over again and God fucking bless you both."

"Blue," Clara finally said, "we came here for a purpose."

Blue gave her a strained look, hoping for a threesome perhaps, but mainly just curiosity.

"Okay, honey, and what would that be—cheaper beer?" Blue laughed, but stopped when Clara didn't.

We told him the whole story, at least what Clara knew.

"We need you to listen, to talk, kind of sniff around and see if you can find out who that asshole is who burned down Donny's temple 'cause they've charged his friend, Mr. Eldridge—do you know him, Thomas Eldridge—with arson and since a man died in the fire, murder too."

"Hooey," Blue said, "heavy. I'll have to be careful. Lots of bad people and they know how to keep their mouths shut around guys like me who they know don't like all that Negro hate shit. Still and all, I'll raise my antennae. What fucking shit."

The next day, we sat around his woodstove on hunks of pine trunks on a chilly late afternoon—more "tobacco research"—Blue offering no new information—"lips tight as frozen pistons, none of these sons-a-bitches saying anything"—but enjoying our company and us his, me still praying he'd come up with a name. After drinking a few, Ravel's *Bolero* or the *1812 Overture* at full blare ("The two fucking greatest pieces of music ever written," Blue said often), Blue went on one of his lectures, Clara following with one of her rants about the Klan and her father's hypocrisy and hatefulness. And this time, she cried a little. And no one else ever did or would see it but Blue and me.

CHAPTER TWENTY-SIX

And then, two days later, the miracle I'd prayed for every day since Mr. E was arrested, happened.

"Ricky Parker's told me he done it," Reverend James said over the phone.

"Just like that?" I asked. Ricky's family shopped at our store. I knew him from the label I'd put on his layaways.

"Well, he actually bragged to me 'bout it at a meetin. All the young studs like bluffing and bragging about killin niggers and runnin out the Jews. Flows rampant as the whiskey."

Not that whites around town need intoxication to hide their truths, I thought.

"Said he'd been helpin his friend Sammy Anderson and his ma get their garden done after school in exchange for Sammy's ma stitchin him a new hood. He'd just left their place, 'bout a half block from yer temple, after dinner. Was walkin to the bus station when he see's yer nigger lockin the door and drivin off in his truck. Gettin closer, Ricky sees a screwdriva sittin in the grass by the curb and says, 'What the hell?' Slipped on his hood. Still had on his work gloves, so he picked up the screwdriva and used it to jimmy open the door. Said the place smelled like 'fire perfume.' He tossed some alcohol on some of the pews from a bottle of it he found when he walked in, touched the cigarette he was smoking to it and let it blow. Said he figured he could burn the Jews and frame a nigger at the same time. 'A *twofer*,' he said. Said he stood there, outside, like an artist admirin his handiwork, callin to his friend to come see the bonfire. Must've been when you snuck up behind him."

Reverend James's voice crooned as friendly and collaborative as if we were buddies working together on a church project; sweet as sugar, artificial as saccharine, like Southerners do when you've got them by the balls.

"For a boy like him," Reverend James said, "it's hard to keep a secret like that when he don't have much else to be proud of. Ricky told me 'burnin down thems kikes' church was almost as much fun as hangin a nigger,' " the Reverend giggled.

"He didn't mean to kill nobody. Though he was crowin 'bout how he later found out he'd done gone and kilt a Jew without even tryin. Said, 'Shit, I got me a *three-fer*.' Damn funny even if the kid's a dim bulb otherwise."

"I forgot to laugh," I said. "Anyhow, now it's time for you to go talk to The Junior."

"To my eternal damnation, you little son of a bitch."

I put the phone down and drifted to my room, thrilled. Duke Ellington's "Take the A Train" steamed from my horn. I was sure my plan was carrying Mr. E on the express tracks to freedom.

I even called Reb Gross and told him the good news.

"Thank God," Reb Gross said.

A day later, Reverend James called me again.

"I spoke to The Junior. Told him I was at the meetin and Ricky's braggin 'bout it right out in the open to me. So I says to The Junior, 'Junior, seems like an open and shut case to me.'

" 'That so?' he says back. 'Well, I ain't 'bout to shoot mysef in the foot by droppin no charges 'gainst that nigga. Don't fergit, I got evidence, his screwdriva and cigarette butt with fingerprints. And even a witness. And you coming up with some story 'bout a shit-faced, poor, good-for-nothin boy tellin stories at a drunken gatherin, wantin to git famous by claimin he done somethin that might make him appear to be a big man hero—nah, Rev'rend, with all due respect, that just don't cut it much with me. Shit, man, why you so interested in settin that nigga free anyway?'

" 'We must stand with our Jewish brethren against this sort of hate, as stated in the Bible,' I said back at him. Well, The Junior almost spit out his coffee.

" 'And fo that matta, Rev'rend, since when you give a shit 'bout the goddamn Jews either?' "

"Now," Reverend James said to me, "that wuz both a good and suspicious question. So I said, 'Too much of this sort a thing can do damage to our city's reputation.' Well, The Junior almost busted a gut laughin at that one.

" 'Fuck that, Rev'rend,' he said, 'cause I know you're up to somethin more than you're tellin me.' "

"I done my best," James said to me, "so why don't you just give me them pitchas and let's be done with this."

"We'll both go to The Junior tomorrow and I'll come forward as another witness," I said. "Maybe having you with me will convince him this time."

"Whatever you say, but I don't think it'll do no good."

The next day, at The Junior's office, he scowled at me.

"You say he had on a hood and you saw his eyes at twilight?" The Junior asked me, smirking. Reverend James and I sat across from him. A freight train passed under his window.

"Damn trains," The Junior said.

"Yes, sir," I said.

"But, you didn't see his face, right?"

"No, sir," I replied.

"And you cain't positively identify him?"

"No, but if I saw his eyes and his height in a line-up, I might be able to identify him like they do on Dragnet."

"Sorry, young man, but we don't really give much weight to identifications based on someone's eyes."

"Well, he sure wasn't a black man, that much I'm sure of."

"Oh, you could tell that in the dark, son?"

"Yes, I wrestled him and his arms and hands were white as mine."

"Son, far as I can tell, you wrastled a guy who was just lookin at a fire, same as I might have if I happened by one. Plus, I know you'd say anything to help your nigga friend."

"I'm not lying."

The Reverend lied, "I know this here nigger. He works for me sometimes, and he's a good nigger as far as that goes. He wouldn't do nothin like this."

"Well, thank you both for comin in," The Junior said as he stood up, took my arm, and started to escort us, really more a push, out of his office. "As I now remember saying once before," he said, holding the door open, slightly grinning, and slowly moving his head in a side-to-side no, "I'll let the evidence speak for itself."

I could understand his skepticism at Jimmy James caring whether a black man went free. Much less the unthinkable idea that the Reverend would actually help convict a Klanner. And bringing me along. No, this could not make sense to The Junior—it stunk of who-knows-what. Though I guess The Junior couldn't figure the why of it all, I imagine he was sure that he would end up skewered like a big hog over the Reverend's barbecue pit if he let Mr. E go.

My A Train had crashed off the high trestle of my hopes just as surely as the Southern Railroad's Old '97 had in 1903 near Danville. And if I couldn't think of something else, Mr. E was approaching his calamity just as surely as engineer Broadey had.

"Don't know what's wrong with him," Jimmy James said to me afterward. "Always been able to mostly get him to do most anything I asked, though I could see why he'd be skeptical of me wantin to help a nigger, not ta mention bringin you along."

Power was Jimmy James' aphrodisiac, and I imagined losing it was possibly even worse than helping a black man. He looked as deflated as a groom left at the altar, even if he hadn't wanted the bride in the first place.

"I done my part. Ain't my fuckin fault it didn't work. So gimme those goddamn pitchas."

He had a point. It wasn't his fault. But I was suspicious that he and The Junior were in cahoots. Still, he was the most powerful minister in town, powerful enough, I was soon to find out, to make the most powerful woman in town, Helen Gant, owner of *The Danville Recorder,* to back down.

"I'll think about it," I said.

"Think hard," was all he said back.

Mr. Eldridge's trial was looming. All of my surefire plans had failed as surely as a badly-designed foundation. Time was running out.

CHAPTER TWENTY-SEVEN

"Donny, I don't really have anything good to tell you," Uncle Herman said to me in his office two weeks before the trial. "The Junior is really pleased with his evidence. And Jim Manza, the city attorney, will hardly do anything without his approval. Not to mention that we don't have anything, *bupkis,* to support Tommy.

"I always send Jim a case of French wine every Christmas. Helped him develop a taste for it, so I called in his appreciation."

Uncle Herman's lips tightened into a frustrated wince. He leaned back in his chair and blew smoke into the air.

"I at least convinced him to lessen the second-degree murder charge to voluntary manslaughter, even though there's absolutely no evidence that whoever did it knew Mr. Rippe was in the building—which is really the only way someone should ever be charged with voluntary manslaughter. Whoever did it really should be charged with involuntary manslaughter, since the way they found Mr. Rippe indicates that the perpetrator didn't know, couldn't have known, he was back in the Rabbi's office."

I could feel my shoulders and gut tightening, anticipating Uncle Herman's final, awful, hopeless conclusion.

He shook his head again and turned his hands upward, smoke drifting up from his cigarette like a metaphor of Mr. E's hopes going up in smoke.

"But voluntary manslaughter is still awful and is the wrong charge. I just couldn't get the Manza to see it my way, to take it any lower. I figure, for once, since we like one another, he probably fought The Junior tooth and nail just to get it down to that. I guess there's only so much even great French wine can do down here in the South."

Uncle Herman looked at me like he expected me to laugh at his attempt at humor. I sat there, still as a rock, grim-faced.

"I'm very pessimistic, Donny. Even though, thank God, Tommy won't go to the electric chair," Uncle Herman's voice going deep and serious again. "He could still go to jail for five to ten years. His initials and fingerprints on the screwdriver are bad enough, not to mention his cigarette butt."

He lowered his eyes to his desk and drummed his fingers on it. Even with the air-conditioning, I was sweating. He looked up at me.

"The Junior thinks the witness seeing him there just before the fire is the clincher, thinks it's open and shut. I don't have anything to help our friend, Donny. And nobody but you really saw this other guy. And you didn't actually see him set the fire, even if you can prove he was there, which you can't."

I was frantic to come up with something to say. Knowing Mr. E wouldn't die but would rot in jail for years left me mute. I wanted to strike out at, to hit, to hurt something or someone.

"Oh, one more thing, Donny," Uncle Herman said as he smashed out his cigarette, "do you know anything about some big brouhaha Tommy and Jane Schneider had at the temple a few weeks ago–about the lights?"

Jane Schneider was the temple's self-designated interior decorator.

"Yeah," I said, "Mr. Eldridge couldn't stop talking about it. I've never seen him so mad. He said: 'Donny, that ignorant woman held back from what she owed me 'cause she said I should've known that the light from those fixtures she ordered and I installed wasn't bright enough.' "

"Oy," was all Uncle Herman said.

I went home and smashed my fist against the wall. I knew Mom would kill me when she saw the big dent. I called Clara's father.

"Clara's got to testify. She saw Ricky Parker running away. It could help."

"First of all, you goddamn shit," he whispered into the phone, "when and if I even did let her, no one would believe her. No jury 'round here would ever believe my daughter would be copulatin—much less sinkin so low as to do it with a Jew. No more'n they'd believe somethin a fuckin teenager says 'bout me if you didn't have those pitchas. And if they did, are you really willin to ruin her reputation and mine. We'd both be goddamn laughingstocks, not that you give a shit.

"Besides the fact that all she saw was the backside of somebody you tied up with and then him runnin away, you might have me by the balls, but I can't see where bringin her into this shit would do any good for your goddamn friend."

He could have been Uncle Herman talking.

And he was just as right.

"Reverend James," I said, my nerves as splattered as fresh road-kill, "I told you at the quarry that this wasn't personal and that my intention was and still isn't to hurt or embarrass you or your family. I just want justice for my friend."

"Well, hangin my daughter out in public with what you two been doin behind my back sure feels fuckin personal to me."

I didn't say anything. I wanted Clara next to me, hearing her voice instead of his.

"You still there?" he said.

"Yes, sir. I think you're right. I'm sorry," I said and hung up.

CHAPTER TWENTY-EIGHT

I collapsed and fell asleep on my bed.

As I lay tossing and turning, the wind raged. The branches of our weeping willow tree flailed against my window. I dreamed a nightmare. The tree's scratching limbs had become the sound of Mr. Rippe's fingernails clawing the floor. The fire licked his crumpled, gray, woolen sport coat, the one he'd worn since I could remember. The flames rose around his upraised head, bulging, then boiling his desperate eye, bursting it against his grizzled, burning face. He reached out to me from the cloud of smoke, empty socket oozing, both trembling arms outstretched, coughing and croaking, "Donala, Donala, save me!"

I awoke, sitting up, arms and hands reaching back to him, teeth grinding, stomach heaving, eyes burning in the room's suffocating darkness. It took a split second for me to realize that I wasn't back in the burning temple. I forced myself to inhale, imagined Mr. Rippe's last breath, then flopped back down onto the drenched sheet. The night's earthy humidity provoked a pungent memory of Mr. Rippe's casket being dropped into its damp pit.

After a macaw-like screech, followed by dog yelping, skunk stink permeated my room through the open window. I thought of Mr. E, buried alive in his jail cell, where the smell never left. And of my stupid whirligig, throwing his initialed screwdriver onto the ground.

I grabbed my headphones from the side of the mattress. The battering branches gave name to my record choice, Dexter Gordon's "Willow Weep for Me," the song's blues lyrics about beaten-down dreams once so full of promise and hope.

It wasn't hard for his tenor's raspy, tender, sad sweetness to bring me to tears. Ever since Grandpa died, when I was sixteen, crying had become my secret habit. I knew most boys and men considered crying a disgrace, almost a sin—something they fought hard against their entire lives. In truth, I'd found it to be upset aspirin—as most girls and women knew by instinct. In my case, perhaps it was the unspoken continuation of a family trait, my father bawling at every sentimental family event.

I couldn't dam my tears. As a Jewish Southern boy, I'd suffered and enjoyed all kinds of emotions. But I'd never felt utter aloneness. I cried for Mr. Rippe, never again to hear his interruptions at services or his grumpy kindnesses. I cried for myself, exiled from real family consolation by my lies about being sick and about Clara on the night of the fire. I cried, desperate for her touch. I cried, insane at the thought that I'd helped put Mr. E in jail and that all of my certain strategies were useless—Don Quixote tilting at windmills.

My clock beamed a waxen light up onto the poster of Miles's taut face.

"I kicked smack," he'd have screamed. "Stop the crying. Be a man. Kick *your* smack. Do what you can do. Find your groove."

I took off the headphones and stared up at the trumpet sage.

Like his pure tones in *All Blues*, the message was clear and true, no vibrato. I fought myself and stopped the tears.

"Donala, Judaism teaches that we are all broken vessels, leaking our Godliness," Reb Gross had taught me. "Our job is to make the glue for repairing the brokenness, *tikkun olam.*"

I cursed my useless efforts and swore that I would not give up.

And then my tennis racquet fell off of its hook onto the floor with a thunk, more like a freedom bell clanging the note of hope for saving Mr. E.

CHAPTER TWENTY-NINE

The thunk shocked my mind back to two weekends before the fire, when I played a tennis game and made a bet with Somelaw Gant, a boy whom I hated and often envied, and of a favor he still owed me that could save Mr. E.

The clang was so resonant that I could almost see Mr. E walking as free and easy as a Grover Washington ballad. This could really be it. Since the fire and Mr. E's arrest, I'd been so consumed with saving him that I'd forgotten what had seemed to be a worse problem.

Somelaw was the captain of our high school tennis team, regional champions his junior year.

The handsome, eldest son of the richest family in town, he ruled the sons and daughters of the local oligarchy. They tried not to kowtow to him, but they'd be mortified if they weren't invited to his annual Christmas party at the Danville Country Club. To be fair, he was usually pleasantly condescending to most, if only with a grunt of acknowledgement or a hallway "Hi."

His mother, Helen Gant, owned the *Danville Recorder*, started in 1855 by her grandfather. She attended every tennis match, home and away, sometimes flying on the paper's helicopter right to the side of the tennis courts. Occasionally, Somelaw would fly in with her, raising a big cloud of dust and awe.

"America was founded by and for the white Christians, and everyone else was a mistake," Dad said she'd say over and over at Chamber of Commerce meetings. It should have been her paper's masthead, which did include the Confederate flag. A statue of Robert E. Lee stood in front of the paper's office. When two white boys beat up a little black boy who refused to give them his swing at Max's Park, the paper ran an editorial, "Respect from Negroes Is Still a Southern Tradition." Next day, the city manager took out all of the swings, including the ones May and I had swung on as kids.

She'd built a clay court for Somelaw and his friends at Homeplace, their 800-acre summer retreat, about twenty miles from town.

I was in debate club with Somelaw. He had a sharp mind and a good sense of humor. Somehow, I thought we seemed to sort of like one another. I'm not sure why. Maybe he was curious about Jews, despite his constant Jew and nigger jokes, followed by, "No harm intended," or "Black at ya" if I shot him the bird.

Usually, I'd just wince on the inside, then smile, trying to be one of the guys. But sometimes I'd summon the courage to say something like, "Boy, put on a white hood and you could tell that at your next Klan rally." He'd give me a "fuck you" look, then grin as if we were pushing some unspoken boundaries and he liked it.

The only boundaries his mother had were how far she could kick anyone she disliked—blacks, Jews, Catholics, Greeks. She was about as hated as she was hate-filled. People expected her to die some day from sheer "nasty-cide."

Somelaw's dad, Daniel, a handsome country boy, was the nominal publisher of the *Recorder.*

"I let him think he runs the goddamned thing," Helen would laugh.

Their loud, glass-smashing arguments were celebrated in elegant gossip circles. Rumors flew that Mr. Gant ran around with women of ill repute. His gambling losses were legendary.

He officially died of liver failure during Somelaw's senior year. Dad said he was a nice guy who "probably died from a combination of alcohol and the 'nasty-cide' of his wife. Doing her bidding poisoned him more than the whiskey."

Somelaw adored him.

"Sorry about your Dad. He was a nice man," I said to Somelaw in class after his father's death.

"Yeah," Somelaw said, with a fleeting wince, quickly covered.

After an awkward silence, I casually mentioned that I'd watched my tennis hero, Pancho Gonzales, on TV.

"I think he's the best in the world. I'm trying to copy his bent arm serve. It works. I've been killing with it."

"Fuckin spic."

"Well, that spic has kicked most white boys' asses."

"And now you got his serve down, huh? The spic-Jew serve. OK, when you wanna show me? Kill me with it, too?" strangling his neck with both hands, to the laughter of his pack.

I hesitated. "You want to play *me*?"

"Seems to be what I said, *don't* it?" looking around the room. He knew better than to say don't instead of *doesn't.*

"Where?"

"Homeplace. Best court in town."

I'd heard about Homeplace. No Jew that I knew had ever set foot there.

Unbeknownst to Somelaw, my tennis life had started eight years before, in fourth grade, with my best friend, Dane, and continued through high school. Dane and I played for years on a hidden court behind the mansion of Mrs. Arial Lorrilard Truelove, a reclusive widow who had played in college and then all over the world with her tobacco magnate husband. She caught us messing around on her neglected court early on and offered to teach us to play—under three conditions. First, we had to clean up and help restore her clay court. Second, we had to learn that the essence of good tennis was "style over powah," which she repeated ad nauseum. And third, we had to bow deeply to each other before and after each game, "like they do so gracefully in the Orient."

At first, we thought she was just a cuckoo old lady, but over the years, we developed a mutual love and affection that continued until she died, six months before my game with Somelaw. Under her relentless tutelage, we developed as players, not to mention learning exceptional bowing techniques.

For eight years, Dane and I fought tooth and nail for every point, but my real love was jazz sax and carpentry. I had no time or need to prove myself at tennis. By junior year, Dane was number two, behind Somelaw on our school team.

"Somelaw wants to play you?" Dane said with a whistle of concern and raised eyebrows. "Holy shit! Don't mean to scare you, Donny, but, most of the time, I wouldn't bet on you or me."

I could feel any confidence I might have assumed draining out of me as quickly as rain down a gutter.

Mrs. Gant's chauffeured, stretch, white limo picked me up and brought me to Homeplace. I'd hoped she'd send the helicopter. The driver wore a black captain's hat, coat and pants with a white shirt and bowtie. Spanish moss-draped live oaks and towering magnolias bordered the hickory split-fenced, half-mile driveway. I saw acres of fields and meadows dappled with grazing horses and cows.

Somelaw met me outside the house, which looked like a reproduction of the mansion from "Gone with the Wind." The black servants were dressed in pre-Civil War outfits. The butler wore formal British tailcoats with split tails, white gloves, and shined black shoes. If you changed their skin color and accent, you could be in England. The inside maids wore bonnets and crinoline petticoat dresses with ruffled aprons. Everything was "Yessum" and "Yessuh."

We walked through the main part of the house to the kitchen for peanuts and a Coke. I recognized some of the help as customers at Dad's store. I nodded to them and they back to me.

"Mornin, Mr. Don."

"Morning," I smiled back.

"You know all these niggers, don't you?" Somelaw said.

I ignored him.

We walked across an expanse of manicured lawn past a heart-shaped pool with a diving board to the tennis court. His mother was sitting on a white, leather lounge chair, talking on a phone with a cord running all the way from the house, sipping a martini and picking at some food on a gold platter set next to a crystal pitcher on a side table. A female black servant tidied up the area and waited behind her.

"Good morning, Miz Gant," I said.

She looked up. A glowing cigarette with an inch of ash hung from her lower lip. Smoke drifted up over her grayish-brown, disheveled hair. She smiled. Her teeth were stained yellow. I couldn't help but think how ugly she was compared to her son.

"Ready ta git yo kike ass kicked?" she croaked.

"Come again?" I said.

"I said," the word sounding like two syllables, 'sa-yad', after a big slug of her martini "Are you ready to get yo kike ass kicked by my son?"

My lips moved, but no words came out.

"Cat got your tongue?" she said, reminding me that Clara used the same expression when I first met her.

White boys do not come of age easily in the South. Its brutish essence infects and warps their male psyche, often making even the best guilty of some degree of awfulness in spite of their fundamental decency. It was as unavoidable as heat and humidity. It's something that those not raised in the South seldom understand and always underestimate. Perhaps it's the result of internalizing and rationalizing the inhumanity, arrogance, and viciousness of slavery over centuries and the ongoing denigration of blacks—it becomes what is considered normal. And despite my determination, that brutish essence, not in my case against blacks but there nonetheless, was buried in me, just under the surface of my Jewish sensitivity and morality like a latent germ needing only a catalyst to trigger it.

"Kike ass," she'd said to me. I'd said good morning. I'd been respectful of her. It was the way I was raised. It was the Jewish way—decency and respect for elders, even if they didn't deserve it. Add in Dad's, "the customer is always right," and I was at pains, always, to stretch for courteousness.

In my best imitation of a black Southern drawl, I replied, "We-yul, ma-yam, I reckin I ain't thinkin 'xactly 'bout mah ass gettin kicked as much as yo son's snow-white Baptist hi-ney gettin whupped like a bad dog."

She choked and coughed on what had been a self-satisfied sip, spitting some on her chest. Her maid's head snapped upward with a fleeting, split-second grin.

Forcing herself upright, "We'll see 'bout that, won't we, Summy?"

"Yes, mother," Somelaw replied, shaking his head up and down, looking embarrassed like a boy does when his mother invades his budding manhood.

"Show that Jewboy what's what, son."

A black man with graying hair, about fifty, dressed in pressed, cuffed, white slacks, a white short-sleeved polo shirt and white suede shoes with pink soles, was just finishing sweeping off and rolling the tennis court.

"Lawson," Somelaw commanded the man, "you'll be the line judge today."

"Yessuh," replied the man I knew from Dad's store as Mister Lawson, nodding his head toward another, slightly younger black man standing outside the manicured lilac hedgerow surrounding the court.

"Thomas tells me you've become quite a good carpenter," he said to me once at Dad's store after I'd been working for Mr. E for a year or so. "Says you're the first Jew, Jesus excepted, who could hammer a nail." He'd laughed and gave me a pat on the shoulder.

"You know Mr. E?" I'd said.

"Oh yeah, been knowin him since I was a boy. One of my all time best friends."

"Guess that explains why you both tell the same bad jokes," I said back to him. We both laughed.

"Sure enough, probably the truth," he said with another big smile and shoulder punch.

Mr. Lawson started toward the white referee's chair on the other side of the net. Another man had been staring at the tennis court for the last several minutes, holding his hedge clippers stock-still over the lilac bushes.

"May as well be the ball boy, Eddy," Somelaw's mother shouted. "You ain't done shit on them bushes after too much time already."

Eddy, wiping leaves and limb fragments from his arms, then sweat off of his brow with a calico rag, shuffled toward the gate.

I'd never played with a ball boy. This "boy," whom I knew as Mr. Johnson, also a customer at Dad's store, was at least forty.

"Wanna bet?" Somelaw shouted to me, to the approving nod of his mother. "Five sets to match, like your spic hero plays in his matches."

"Nah, I've never bet on tennis."

"C'mon. Scared I'll burn you up? Nazi-ize you?" He winked at his mother. "Bet me."

"Might *'holla-cost'* you some of yer Jew money," Mrs. Gant said. They both guffawed. "I'll put some cash on that, too."

"Yeah," Somelaw said, "since your Daddy and you make so much money selling shit to niggers, you must have a big wad too. Shouldn't be no big deal to you."

I was beginning to feel sick to my stomach.

"Ain't kickin a Jew's ass enough for ya, ma'am?" I said, the words oozing out slow and thick, like melting tar on a July blacktop road.

After a long draw on her cigarette, smoke billowing out of her nostrils, staring straight at me, she said, "Well now, even better'n that is takin a Jew's money too." Her mouth slowly crawled upward at the corners, then erupted into a loud, throaty laugh.

Somelaw looked majestically confident. I figured he couldn't imagine me beating him.

I looked at Mister Lawson, then at Mr. Johnson. Mr. Bill Peroe, Dad's oldest salesman, would always say, "Y'all come *black*," to black men like them, always laughing and winking at me, after their careful purchases.

"Just ignore him," Dad would say when I'd complain to him about Mr. Peroe's "joke."

When a white customer would say, "You gonna let me Jew you down today," or something about "those fucking niggers," Dad would say, "The customer is always right. We need their business, so just smile and ignore them."

But this once, no smile creased my face. "Not this time, Dad," I said to myself.

"Fill up my glass," Somelaw's mother shouted at the girl behind her.

"Yessum, Miz Gant."

"Two things the Jewish tribe don't know squat about," Mrs. Gant sneered, "good liquor and tennis. I assume that you are guilty of ignorance in the first case and I presume not much better in the second. So what's the bet?"

I could feel her poison oozing into me, deep, like the smoke of a full inhale. I knew it, hated it, and hated myself for knowing that I couldn't stop my reactions any more than I could stop her from lighting her next cigarette.

If I was going to bet, I thought, it had to be about more than money. Money was too easy for these two. I strained my brain to find something sacred to them, something that would humiliate Somelaw and his mother. It had to be something that would hurt them, shock them, burn them, something that would bring them as much pain as they inflicted on others.

Then it slammed into my mind like a Gonzales serve. Looking at Somelaw, I said, "Okay, I'll bet. But I get to call the terms."

"Up to you," he said. He smiled as if he'd already won.

I knew that everyone dear to me—Clara, Mr. E, May, my family—would be ashamed of what I was about to say, and I of myself, but I couldn't stop—I didn't want to stop.

"OK," I said, "if you win, you can fuck my Jewish girlfriend," whom, of course, I didn't have, "and if I win, I can fuck your pure white, Baptist-dick-sucking girlfriend, JoLene."

"My God," I heard his mother gasp.

I could hardly believe the words vomiting out of my mouth. But the poison had permeated and possessed me, shame be damned. Mrs. Gant and Somelaw were the monsters I'd been fighting inside my soul since I could remember. Now I could fight them for real, without any pretense of Jewish empathy or humanity or smiles. Hate against hate in its purest essence.

Somelaw's face turned scarlet. He lowered his racquet, hung his head to his chest and stood there, arms dangling. Even from the other side of the court, I could see the veins risen in his forehead, eyes narrowed, jaw pulled down tight, and sweat beading on his face.

His mother looked over at him, "You okay, baby?"

Ever so slowly, as he raised his head, a grin spread across his face.

"You mean that?"

"Shit yeah," I hissed.

The grin evaporated.

"Deal!" Somelaw screamed at me. "And she better be ready, 'cause I am gonna enjoy hearin that Jew bitch moan."

"You mean it?" I said, tightening my grip on my racquet to stem the trembling. "No way JoLene would do it."

I could feel whatever goodness was still in me trying to dilute my venom.

"She'll do whatever I say!"

I flushed out the goodness as surely as a good piss.

"Not what I hear from all the other guys she's fucked."

"Fuck you, you kike scum. You have just fucked yourself, your stinking Jew cunt and...and...just fuck you. Let's play."

"Kick that nigger-lovin Yid's ass."

"Shut up, Mother."

I could imagine Clara, Mr. E, and everyone else I loved agreeing, for once in a lifetime, with Mrs. Gant—cheering me to defeat for making such a disgusting bet—and all of them being right.

But it was done. I'd just become as much of a monster as Somelaw and his mother. I'd have to reclaim the other Donny, the one who would never think, much less utter, such vulgarity, later.

I had to win. Neverthess, I knew that whoever won, whoever might ultimately get screwed, I'd just screwed myself.

I heard the swish of air release as Mr. Johnson opened a new can of Wilson Championship Tournament balls. He threw the three balls to Somelaw, one by one. As I inhaled, a slight breeze tickled my nose with a sweet magnolia scent. Part of me wanted to lie down and pass out under the shade of one of those big, fragrant trees, to sleep and awaken to find it all a bad dream.

"Get on up there already, dammit," Somelaw said to Mr. Lawson, who had been standing by the referee's chair.

"Yessuh."

I bowed slow and properly to Somelaw. It was somewhat calming.

"What tha…?"

"Nothing," I said.

I twirled my racquet. Somelaw won the serve.

On his first serve, his power almost knocked me over. The emotional advantage had reversed. He broke my serve and killed me first set, six-one. He was like a mad dog, even better than I'd imagined.

Then, like out of a Bible story, I heard the Hebrew words, *"Baruch Hashem,"* praise God, a prayer-like phrase Reb Gross uttered whenever he needed resolve. I'd never found much practical use for prayers. I figured that if God even existed, he sure wouldn't have the time to worry about whether I won a tennis game or if Jews ate pork. He'd worry about feeding the poor or preventing war, but definitely not me winning a stupid bet. Nonetheless, I did feel a surprising stillness inside myself, a balance to the monster.

I stood there for another moment, a bit shocked, but calm and peaceful. I could hear Miz Truelove almost singing, "Don't forget, style over powah."

"C'mon, asshole, serve," Somelaw yelled.

I stared at him. *"Baruch Hashem,"* I roared, *"Baruch Hashem, Baruch Hashem."*

Somelaw said, "What the fuck?"

"Huh?" mumbled his mother. "Wha'd he say? Serve the fuckin ball."

I served. Ace. Ace. Ace. love.

"Pancho Gonzales spic-Jew serves," I shouted. *"Baruch Hashem."*

"Big talk," he shouted.

He hit the next one back. I sliced it. His racquet face hit it straight and square, sending it into a swerve left and out. I won the game.

Ace, ace, my point, my point, his point, my point, my point—my game.

"Baruch Hashem."

"Jesus Christ, shut the fuck up," Somelaw yelled.

"He's one of my boys, Somelaw."

"Fuck you."

My game.

He won the next two games, then I took the last four. My set, six-two.

One set each.

"Baruch Hashem."

I won the next set, six-three, two sets to one, my lead. I was as surprised as he seemed to be.

"You're crap," Somelaw chimed, "and now you will suffer."

"Kick the Jew's ass," his mother blubbered.

He did kick my ass, six-two.

Two sets each.

"Your girlfriend is already screaming," hollered Somelaw.

"Baruch Hashem," I shouted.

"Baroots Hashit, asshole," he shot back.

His shouting seemed anxious now. I could feel a strange power and energy within myself. I knew I had him—at least for a moment—until terror returned. *I have no Jewish girlfriend,* I thought. And Clara wouldn't even stoop to spit on him, not that I'd ask her if my life depended on it, which suddenly seemed possible. What if he wins?

Stop! I screamed inside myself. *Believe. Use your will. You will focus and beat this creep. And his goddamned mother. For once, the Jew will win. I will stomp on every Nazi, every Klanner, every Negro hater—oh shut up and play. Style over power!*

We didn't say another word. I was hot and sweating. Somelaw was about to serve when Mr. Lawson nodded, and the mother's servant walked to the fence gate and asked, "Some water for you, sirs?"

Mr. Lawson got down from his elevated linesman's chair, walked over to the woman and took the tray. He filled two glasses, gave one to Somelaw, then walked over to me. He looked at me, his back to Somelaw and his mother. "Some water for you, sir?"

It looked like he winked. *Did he just wink at me?* I thought.

"Thanks," I whispered.

He nodded with his eyebrows and a slight smile.

"New balls, Eddy." Somelaw commanded.

Eddy threw three new balls to me, one by one.

"It's my fucking serve, you dumb nigger," Somelaw said.

"Yessuh," I hollered. "Yessuh, Mister Somelaw. Oh please forgive me, please Mister Somelaw, please don't whup me 'cause I is *so* dumb."

I heard murmurs, sniggers as soft as a spring breeze, from the edges of the lilac hedge as I threw the balls back to him. His mother shouted at the hedge, "Git back to work, goddammit," holding her hand up over her eyes against the sun, straining to get a look at the culprits. I heard the shuffling of feet. It was the last set—win by two games. Somelaw's white shorts were smudged at the pockets from the clay on the balls. His white tennis shoes were pinkish from the dust. My legs were chafed from my new Carhartt cut-off carpenter jeans, my black Converse high tops red with clay. Both of our shirts were drenched. My Pancho Gonzales racquet against his Rod Laver, both wood. I adjusted my strings more out of nerves than any useful need.

The first game, his serve, went back and forth. My ad, then deuce, his ad. Over and over, exhausting. Finally, he won. The entire set dragged on the same way—my lead, tie, his lead, tie.

"*Baruch Hashem,* please," I said to myself. "Not for me."

"Baruch Hashem," I shouted.

"Shut up," Somelaw yelled back at me.

"Yeah, shut up," his mother said, drooling.

"And you, too," Somelaw said, glaring at her.

"Oh my, such poor manners," his mother cackled. "Well, stop wastin time and get it over with, son."

"Baruch Hashem, ma'am."

"Go to hell," she said, making hell into a two-syllable word, hey-yull. "Oh, pardon me, you Jews don't believe in hell now, do ya?"

I stopped, my grip on the ball as tight as my clenched jaw.

"Well, ma'am, that's correct. We believe that's reserved for Southern Baptists like you."

She choked on an ice cube. The servant girl behind her stifled a laugh by putting her hand to her mouth and pretending to cough.

I noticed black faces peeking out from various windows and trees. Some were even daring enough to stand there and watch, hats and work gloves in hand, linen dresses and tuxes swaying in the breeze. Seeing me looking behind her, Somelaw's mother woozily raised her head.

"Back to work, everyone!" she shrieked.

Some scurried off, but others stood there, shuffling as if to start moving, but not leaving.

I finally broke his serve in the fifteenth game. He'd started the game with three winners, 40forty-zero. I then noticed his red face. As he was getting ready to throw the ball into the air for his serve, I shouted, "Time out! Water break, Summy? Mr. Lawson, could you get the boy some water? He seems a little unsteady."

"Don't move a fuckin inch, Lawson," Somelaw screeched.

Double fault. Forty-five. The next serve was fast and out. Second serve, I returned deep, his return to my left corner. Somelaw rushed the net. I lobbed it over his head deep into the corner. Forty-thirty. He slammed his racquet onto the net. Next point I hit another deep return. His return nicked the top of the net, hung in the air, and petered down onto his side. Forty-forty, deuce.

"You know I beat Dane last week."

Somelaw stopped. "Dane plays with you?"

"My best friend. All the time."

Somelaw walked to the service line. I won the next two points. I was ahead eight games to seven.

A good ten or so field workers, some with baskets of freshly-picked produce, leaning on hoes or muddy implements, had gathered behind Somelaw's mother, now a muddled heap splayed on her back. She tried to lift her head, but it flopped back down onto her chaise.

We were hitting with every ounce of energy, power, and speed we had left—style seeming to be a distant fourth. I was ahead thirty-fifteen.

And then a second Biblical lesson popped into my head from Jesus's Sermon on the Mount, I later learned: "And the meek shall inherit the Earth."

I held the ball, shook my head, and squeezed my eyes. *What the…?* I wondered. I lowered my racquet and stood still.

"C'mon, serve, goddammit," Somelaw yelled.

"He's kickin yer ass, Summy," his mother slurred.

"Shut up, Mother. Serve the fuckin ball."

I stepped to the line. Then I knew what the message meant. I knew.

I served the slowest, easiest, shallowest serve of my life. It was so slow, so meek, that I held my breath as it barely passed over the net.

He couldn't get up to it. Forty-fifteen.

"Fucking pussy serve," he yelled at me.

Come on, one more time. *"Baruch Hashem,"* I said to myself. One more point to win the game, set, and match.

I looked at Somelaw, knees bent, swaying side to side, shoulders slightly angled forward, racquet perpendicular to his chest.

I stood at the base line, just to the right of center. I bounced the ball three times. Then I placed it on the ground, reached into my pocket, and smacked the extra ball over the fence and into the bushes. I picked the lone ball from the dirt surface, kissed it like I'd seen Pancho do and said, "Last point." I threw it three feet directly above my left shoulder, reached high on tiptoed feet and swung at the apex of the ball's arc.

It landed just inside the outside corner of the midline. A perfect, hard, fast serve. Somelaw turned just twenty-two degrees, not the full forty-five necessary to get maximum return velocity and accuracy, his racquet face slightly pitched upward. His hit soared and hit deep. I couldn't quite tell if it barely hit the back of the baseline, in, or just behind it, out.

Mr. Lawson hesitated, then called, "Out."

"Game, set, match!" I shouted.

"No way, Lawson," Somelaw shouted. "Lawson!" Somelaw glared. "In or out?"

Mr. Lawson paused.

His forehead was a frown of wrinkles. He was sweating. His face got darker. He looked back and forth between Somelaw and his mother.

"Make the fuckin call, Lawson," the mother squealed, suddenly sitting upright.

"Best I can tell," he spoke haltingly, "with all due respect, Mister and Miz Gant, that ball was out."

Silence.

"No way," hissed the mother.

"Sho' nuf," Mr. Lawson repeated, "best I can tell, ma'am."

"Fuck that lyin nigger." His mother sprang up to her feet like a jack-in-the-box playing Dixie, suddenly sober as a nun. I was impressed.

"Lawson wouldn't lie," Somelaw said.

"All niggers lie," she shot back. Then her face cracked a big, almost sweet smile. "Swear, in our savior and Lord Jesus Christ's name, Lawson."

Mr. Lawson gave a startled look.

He wrapped his fingers and his hands round and round one another. He took out his handkerchief and mopped his brow, chewed on his tongue, and puckered his lips, looked at Somelaw's mother, then at Somelaw, then back at the mother, mopped his brow again, puffed out his cheeks, blew out air, and said, "As Jesus Christ is my savior and Lord, Miz Gant, I swear that ball was out. Sorry, Mr. Somelaw." He looked down, beaten, drained somehow of color.

"Baruch Hashem," I said to myself. *"Baruch Hashem!"* I shouted.

I fell down on my back, eyes closed, hands to my face, legs stretched out, breathing fast, soaking into the red clay.

I heard Somelaw's mother yelling, "Shit, shit, shit. That nigger's lyin like a dog."

I heard a chorus of murmurs all around.

I lay there completely exhausted.

After some time, I heard Mr. Lawson say, "You all right, Mr. Don?" as he gently shook my shoulder. I opened my eyes.

"You get yourself back to work or I'll fire your ass as we speak," howled the mother.

"Sorry, missus, just thought..."

"Fuck you thinkin," she said. "I don't pay ya to think. Now get back to work, now."

Looking back behind her chair at the assembled muttering choir, Somelaw's mother yelped, "All of ya, get outta here. Back to work."

They lowered their heads, slowly turned, and shambled off, whispering. I heard, "Woo-wee," and whistles.

"Get the car," she squawked. Her head swung side to side, eyes like bloodshot searchlights, looking for her driver. Her shoulders jerked up as she realized he was standing, hat in hand, right next to her. "Git him outta here," she yelled.

I got up. Somelaw walked up to me.

"Good match," he barely mumbled. He started to extend his arm for a handshake, changed his mind, turned, and walked over to his ranting mother.

"Thanks," was all I could manage. I felt a fury of pride. *For once, goddammit,* I thought, *the meek Jew, me, I hadn't smiled and turned the other cheek.* I started walking the hundred yards to the car. Yes, goddammit, yes—fuck Somelaw and his mother and all the goddamn Jew-hating, goddamn Jew-baiting, goddamn Southern racist and Baptist-Jesus-fucking-preaching assholes who ever lived. Fuck them all, goddammit! *Baruch* fucking *Hashem,* goddammit!

My reverie lasted almost to the car before the other reality hit me like a hammer to the skull—what the hell was I going to do about the bet—about my poisoned soul? By the time I opened the door, I felt dirty, inside and out. I threw my racquet in.

Then I remembered. I turned back toward the court and stood there. I stood there, still and straight and erect. I took a deep breath. The sweet smell of the air was like an infusion of decency, even if I didn't deserve one. I stared until they both looked back at me.

"What the fuck you doing?" his mother screamed. "Get the fuck outta here."

I bowed, deeply.

"Fuck you!" Somelaw shouted.

I felt a deep peacefulness, at least in the moment, as I slowly stood back up, turned, and sat in the back seat.

As we drove away, the driver, whom I didn't know, quietly cleared his throat and said, "You done good, Mr. Don, and we all thank ya."

I exhaled. "My pleasure."

But I suspected a secret, another disgrace, that only one other person knew.

That night at home, my mother yelled, "Phone for you, Donny." She handed me the receiver.

"Mr. Don, that you?" the voice asked in a deep baritone.

"Yes. Who is this?"

Slightly giggling, "It's me, yessuh, John Lawson," chuckling again. "Guess you're wonderin why I'm callin."

I'd never talked to him outside of the store except for a casual hello if we saw one another on a sidewalk.

"It didn't go out, did it?" I whispered.

"No, sir, it sure enough did not, Mr. Don." He was sniggering now.

"Mr. Lawson, holy shit, sorry–I mean, don't you realize how much trouble you could get yourself into if they ever find out you cheated?"

"Lordy, Lordy, Mr. Don, I do know what you mean there, son."

"I mean, Mrs. Gant can't do anything to me, but this could get you in a lot of serious trouble. You could lose your livelihood and who knows what else she might do to you? She does not take kindly to being crossed. She's a mean SOB. Why put yourself in such jeopardy? It was only a fucki…it was only a tennis match. It's too dangerous. Don't you know what they would do if they ever found out?" I was almost ready to cry.

"Now, now, Mr. Don. I'm a grown man with some education. And, if I may say so myself," he purred, "a pretty good actor, wouldn't you say?" He started laughing again. "Son," he went on in a calming voice, "all my life and my daddy's before me and his daddy's too, we been not much more than slaves to them Gants. Now, I do grant that they coulda treated us worse. I do credit them that. Yet and still, that boy has never once called me mister. Me bein old enough to be his granpappy. And his ma—well, you know 'bout her. You seen how she was durin that game. She was just goin crazy. Oh my, my. And worse to us folk, let me tell ya, when no one else be around. I been there long enough that she don't mess with me too much. Yet and still, I'm careful."

"But you swore on Jesus Christ, your Lord. It wasn't worth making yourself a liar or a blasphemer," I said. "I appreciate what you did, Mr. Lawson, but not if it takes away your honor. I am so sorry to have put you in that situation."

At that, he exploded into deeper and deeper guffaws before he could catch his breath.

"Oh, Mr. Don, you are sho nuf a sweet boy. You cut the cake. So can I ask you a question?"

"Uh, sure Mr. Lawson."

"Well, son, you ever heard of Elijah Muhammad and Rev'rend Mister Malcolm X of New York?"

"Well, yeah," I mumbled, "I read about them in my contemporary history class last year."

"And what you learn 'bout them in that class?"

"Well, I know they think white people are the devil class… and that Jewish stores like my Dad's take advantage of blacks and…and that blacks should separate from whites and live on their own and have their own stores. That blacks should lift themselves up."

"Well now, that's not too bad, Mr. Don. You learned good. And, if you don't mind me tellin ya the truth..." He suddenly sounded a little concerned…"Do ya?"

"No, of course not," I said. "With all due respect, Mr. Lawson, I've never really talked to a black person about any of this."

"Well, boy, I love the radio. Always have. My daddy used to shoo me away from it 'cause I listened so hard. That's where I heard Rev'rend Malcolm speak the truth, 'cept the part 'bout Jews, since me and my family's always been treated well by you and your family. Maybe it be different up North." He stopped for a moment. "You okay so far?" he asked gently.

"Yes, I'm okay."

"So's, as I was sayin, I been sendin for and readin all the stuff they send me and I been sendin them back a little money here and there. And I been tellin my friends at church and at my house what he been sayin 'bout respectin ourselves. And how the white man took away our African gods when we was slaves and told us to worship Jesus and to accept sufferin in this lifetime for redemption in the next. And Rev'rend Malcolm says that's the way they could control us. By keepin us thinkin that now don't matter 'cause it'll all be better in the next life. And you know what, Mr. Don? He is right as rain. So that's why I became a Black Muslim brother."

I didn't know what to say.

"Mr. Don, you still on the line?"

"Yes, Mr. Lawson, sorry. I'm just trying to take all this in. So do Muslims think it's all right for you to lie, even if you did it for me, because you wanted me to win?"

"My, my," snickering again, "you is a piece a work, you is, Mr. Don."

My brain felt like it was in a vise.

"Woo-wee," he laughed. "You still don't get it, do ya?"

"What?"

"Well, Mr. Don, when his mother made me swear to her God, Jesus Christ, she didn't even ever consider that he wasn't mine no more. So's I'm there frownin and sweatin and tryin my best just to keep from bustin out laughin, 'cause she was so sure she'd got me trapped and wrapped up. She was right about one thing—we niggas can lie when we has to. Been doin it regular for so many years to save our own sweet ol asses ever since slave times."

"Well, slaves had good reason."

"That's sure 'nuf so, Mr. Don," the laughter building. "But to see the look on Miz Gant's face, Mr. Don. Well that was almost worth losin my job. And to help you beat that spoiled boy, who never in all these years had the courtesy to address me as *Mister* Lawson, like you do, well, I just had to help. And I got no regrets, I swear to ya," trying to restrain himself, "as Jesus Christ," he howled, "is my savior and Lord."

He finally caught his breath. "You still okay with all this, Mr. Don? 'Cause you know I wouldn't do nothin to harm ya? It just felt so good and right and I just couldn't let that chance go by."

We'd both sinned, my solemn Jewish superego chimed in my head. And I was still stuck with the consequences—what to do about winning the bet. But how could there be a God so humorless as to not appreciate this terrific, perfect irony, this wonderful revenge and the joy that it was bringing Mr. Lawson?

"We can't tell anybody else Mr. Lawson. It's just too dangerous."

"Man, I'm tellin every nigga whose got ears. Niggas know how to keep secrets from white folks. And this one's just too good to keep to myself. Don't you worry none 'bout me though, Mr. Don, much as I appreciate it.

"Now, every colored man and woman and boy and girl in town gonna have a grin every time they see that boy and his mother struttin 'round. Not too many times that happens. That's a fact. It's a gift from you and me."

"You, Mr. Lawson, are a piece of work," I finally laughed.

"Good night, Mr. Don," almost wheezing now from laughing so hard. "You rest easy, son."

I didn't.

CHAPTER THIRTY

The next Monday, at school, Somelaw tapped me on the shoulder as I left the lunchroom.

"I owe you, goddammit." He was standing bolt upright, face taut, eyes narrow, fists clenched tight by his sides, lips scrunched together. "You might think I'm an asshole, 'cause I sure think you are, but a bet's a bet. When?" he said, not moving, eyes boring like a hard serve into mine.

"Forget it," I tried to act nonchalantly. I'd forced myself to practice the perfect out. "I wouldn't fuck that white trash girlfriend of yours with your dick."

I was on the ground before I even knew he hit me.

He grabbed my arm and pulled me up.

"Now you listen real good," he said, breathing hard, flame-faced, against mine. I could smell the lunchroom spaghetti sauce on his breath. "You won fair and square and I might be an idiot for bettin like I did. But don't ever, ever, feel sorry for me and don't ever say anything bad about JoLene. Understand?"

He stood there, waiting.

Rubbing my jaw, I knew, for Mr. Lawson's sake, his job and his family's safety, that I definitely could not use truth to free myself from my awful wager.

"Now, when and where?" Somelaw demanded, his breath steaming against my face.

Eyes wide, jaw hurting and almost teary, I invoked my second strategy—"I can't do it with a non-Jew. It's against my religion."

"What?"

"Jews of my denomination can't have their first sex with a non-Jew. It's a sin," I lied.

"You've never fucked?

"No," I lied again. I held my breath to look like I was blushing. Thank God that Clara and I had been forced to keep our affair so secret, and that I could, for the first time ever, actually use being a Jew for my benefit.

"What a pussy religion," he said. "Then what about the fucking bet, asshole?"

"You're right, I was an asshole to make the bet. How about if I need a favor sometime, you'll maybe give me a hand?"

It was two weeks before the fire, so this had nothing to do with anything other than avoiding the consequences of my disgusting bet.

His lips stretched into a forced smugness, like he'd won. "Fuck you, you don't even have the balls to fuck JoLene. Okay, a fucking favor, huh? Whatever the fuck that could be—but not money."

Which was, coming from him, somehow so ironic that I almost had to keep myself from laughing.

Now, with Mr.E's trial looming, what I hoped was the solution to his, my, and even Somelaw's troubles arrived in such a pleasant flash that I laughed as long and hard as Mr. Lawson had.

Somelaw's family was Danville's royalty. Their power had swept dirt and corruption under the rug since the late 1800s. Rumors about the mysterious death of Somelaw's great-grandfather's wife, replaced by a younger one, were followed by decades of buzz about rape by a great uncle and all sorts of other transgressions and dalliances. They were never reported in the paper or prosecuted.

I was convinced that one word to The Junior from Somelaw's mother would set Mr. E free.

At school the next day, I pulled Somelaw over and whispered, "I need the favor."

"Yeah, what?"

"I need you to help a friend of mine get out of his legal troubles."

"Who?"

"Thomas Eldridge. I do carpentry with him and he's honest as the day is long. He's a deacon at his church..."

"Wait a minute. Isn't that the guy arrested for burning down your temple?"

"Yes. No. I mean he didn't do it. Wouldn't. He's my friend."

"You want me to help a nigger?"

"Yes. That simple."

"And you're telling me you'd let that suffice in place of..."

"Totally in place of."

"You people really are nigger lovers, aren't you? So what do you want me to do?"

"Get your mom to talk The Junior into dropping the charges."

"I'll tell you tomorrow," he said.

The next day between classes, he pulled me over into a nook.

"She can't do it," he said. "Seems Mama and The Junior's dad, Senia, were arch enemies. Started about twenty-five years ago. Something about Mother's moonshiner complaining to her about a police protection racket—payoffs to leave 'em alone. So she sent a reporter sniffing around about how Senia managed to buy minks for his wife and nice cars and boats and all kinds of expensive shit on a police chief's salary.

"Senia threatened to expose stuff about my dad if she didn't quit the investigation. Mother told me, 'Your goddamn father ran around on me like a stallion in a breedin pit, with whores, nigger whores, no less.'

"Said Senia was smart. Had pictures of Dad passed out drunk and nekked with a nekked nigger whore kissing his cheek. Told me, 'That idiot father of yours even wrote her and her mulatto son checks every few months. Checks! The fool didn't even have the sense to give her cash. Imagine the headlines in the county papers, *The Gants' Other Boy*. Would've made us a laughin stock. Goddamn son of a bitch. The Junior must have some shit on the city attorney too. I can't even get a parkin ticket fixed.' "

Somelaw stared up to the ceiling, lost in his thoughts. The strain in his voice convinced me of his genuine angst.

"I can't believe you're telling me this," I said.

Somelaw shrugged. "Who gives a shit? People gossip about us all the time. There's more rumors about my family than time to do all the crap they talk about."

"I liked your dad. Mine says that he'd drop by merchants all over town just 'cause he liked to schmooze, to yak, 'cause he was such a nice guy, so friendly."

"Maybe you can't blame him," he said in a suddenly small voice, rolling his eyes and puckering his lips. "Shit, when I think about him being married to my mother..." gazing over my head. "Still, he could have done it all with a little more discretion."

As much as I wanted to just hate him, for a second, it almost seemed that we could be friends, confidants, that our tennis struggle had somehow bonded us.

"Fuck 'em all," he said. "So fuck you and fuck your nigger-lovin deals. I'm tired of this shit. I'll deal with Jolene. She'll fuck you till your dick falls off. And nobody would ever believe all the other stuff I told you. Now tell me when."

"I don't think you'd have told me all that stuff, Somelaw, about your family if you hadn't tried your hardest to do my favor. That's all I can ask. Bet's done."

"I hear one word of gossip..." he said, poking his fingers between my ribs, "one laugh behind my back and I'll kill you. Jolene ever hears and I'll kill you. Can't believe you got me to bet. Can't believe you beat me."

"We were both assholes," I said. "Got caught up in the moment. It's done. I'm sorry."

Finally, "You're not bad for a Jew. But I'll kick your ass next time," and he stomped away.

I was in the clear. My head still intact. But the sword still swung over Mr. E's. I'd failed again.

CHAPTER THIRTY-ONE

"I can't think of anything else," Uncle Herman said to me back at his office the week before the trial. "Your testimony is about the only possibility we have. Weak as that is, I'm going to have to go with it."

"Uncle Herman, Reverend James's daughter is a friend of mine. She told me she heard her father telling somebody over the phone that Ricky Parker, he's a customer at Dad's store, confessed to him that he did it. We could call Reverend James up to testify."

Uncle Herman sat back in his chair, his Gauloise exhaust more furious than ever.

"Now let's get this straight," he said, scrunching his eyes and waving his rigid finger side to side, a habit of his whenever he heard something too Southern, stupid, or useless to believe. He twirled his chair around and pulled a big book off of his bookshelf, *Roget's 20th Century Thesaurus.* "You know what this is, Donny?"

"Yes," I said.

He thumbed through the pages, stopping to lick his finger several times.

"Have you ever heard the word 'hearsay'?"

Before I could answer, he said, "Rumor, gossip, tittle-tattle, idle talk, unfounded information, unconfirmed report, word of mouth. And the antonym—do you know what that means, Donny?" Again, before I could open my mouth, he said, " 'Fact' is the antonym, the opposite, of 'hearsay.' "

He sucked on his cigarette, raised his eyebrows, and cocked his head, then blasted out the smoke and stared at me like I was an idiot.

"Oh, yes, Donny, I can hear the city attorney now. 'Rev'rend James, now we all know how interested you are in helping out niggers, especially at the expense of a good white boy,' which would be accompanied by snickers throughout the courtroom. 'And all you got, whatever your reason for wanting to help that particular nigger, is some ignorant, low-class, white farm boy bragging to his friends that he did it. Whereas, ladies and gentlemen of the jury, The Junior has a screwdriva the defendant has admitted he carved his initials in, along with a cigarette butt of the type the defendant smokes, found right outside the buildin. And a witness who saw the defendant walk out of the temple just before the fire. And he even admits he left a fire burnin inside the building that day. And he was mad as hell about some money some Jew woman at that place of worship refused to pay him. Rev'rend, I do respect you, but in this case, I must say, if it don't walk like a duck or quack like one or in this case, even have feathers, then whatever the reason you are claiming this to be a duck, it just ain't one.' Which would be accompanied by guffaws.

"Knowing how often these self-righteous, bombastic religious fanatics have been caught messing around on the side," Uncle Herman fumed on, "the jury would probably think some black whore had some goods on him and was blackmailing him.

"Without The Junior backing him up," Uncle Herman said, still waving his dead finger, "even if James would get up on the stand and say such things, which I can't in God's good name imagine, no locals that I've ever seen would buy it."

I sat there, dumb-struck. I wanted to punch him.

"Anything else, Donny?"

"No, I can't say there is, Uncle Herman."

"Damn."

CHAPTER THIRTY-TWO

"Justice, justice shall ye pursue."—from Deut. 16:18-20—I'd carved on the lentil of the door to Uncle Herman's office when I was sixteen. He'd paid me more than my bill. Now, walking from that office to the courthouse, any hope for Uncle Herman's route to justice seemed as sure to fail as had all of my extra-legal schemes.

I stepped up to the witness stand after swearing on the New Testament, which, if not for the circumstances, I would have found funny. The prosecutor, Roscoe Moore, senior assistant to the city attorney, had just finished the neighbor's testimony. Out in the gallery, I recognized splashes of black and white, including the man whose Queen Anne trim I'd repaired. I wondered who he was rooting for. I saw that Dad wasn't there—busy season at the store. And Mom had said she was leaving right after my testimony—bridge club.

May looked almost regal in her pale, mint-green, silk, kimono-like dress embroidered with gold, threaded curlicues around her bosom. Her string of pearls shined bright white as her teeth against her almost purple skin. My friend Barry, son of the owners of *Karns,* Danville's high fashion women's store, would brag to me in Sunday school about how much she spent there. "Right up there with the mill owner's wife. Mostly imported Parisian fashions."

Prosecutor: Please tell the court what you know 'bout all this.

I told my whole story about the night of the fire, except for the Clara part. May forced a weak smile and waved to me, moving her hand from the bottom of her chest to the front of her throat in a "keep breathing and relax" motion.

P: Did you see and talk to the defendant just before the temple caught on fire?

I swallowed hard. My Adam's apple bumped against my tie. I reached up and loosened the knot. I pictured Clara running out to say hello to Mr. E before I could stop her.

D: Yes, sir.

P: What time was that?

D: It was late afternoon, before dusk.

P: And then you saw him leave?

D: No, sir, I only heard his truck start up as he was leaving.

And there was no fire then.

P: And how do you know there was no fire? It could've taken a long time for the fire to go from inside to the outside of the building. Could've been burning inside quite a while before it erupted, before it got all the way to the outside of the building, before you noticed it.

D: Well, guess it could have, but I didn't smell any smoke when I heard his truck leave.

P: Okay, then how long before you noticed the fire did you hear his truck start up? Half-hour? Just before?

Uncle Herman: Objection, Your Honor. My client didn't have a stopwatch.

Judge: Sustained.

P: Son, what time, about what time of day, would you guess the fire started?

D: Well, right past dusk, sir.

P: Dusk. So—early, right? Let's see, the sun goes down that time of year 'bout 6 p.m., would ya say?

D: Yes, sir, that sounds about right.

P: And you were alone–no parents, brothers, sisters? Cause, like you just testified, you told your folks you were sick?

D: Yes, sir. They went out of town.

P: And it was about 6 p.m. then. That right?

D: Yes, sir, that sounds about right.

P: And you was, you were, there alone, sick in bed? Now what kind of sick?

I looked over at Uncle Herman. He was nodding his head up and down. He'd insisted that I tell the truth, everything that I'd told him. All of it.

D: I wasn't really sick. I just didn't want to go.

The prosecutor's face lit up. Even though Reverend Rampbell was sitting twenty feet behind Uncle Herman's table, I saw the whites of his eyes widen. My mother's face flushed red.

P: So you wasn't sick then, just fakin it? That right? Why, son?

I looked again at Uncle Herman, then at Mr. E, and didn't answer.

Judge: Son, please answer the question.

P: I ask you again, boy. Why didn't you go with your folks? Why'd you lie?

My eyeballs felt popped out like the pin on a pressure cooker lid. My head rattled like the thing on top that bobbles and shakes and screams steam.

Uncle Herman: Your Honor, could we have a short recess?

Judge: Granted, but git on with it.

Sitting in the recess room, empty except for a few hard back chairs, a table, and a phone, Uncle Herman said, "Donny, what is going on? You promised me you would tell the whole thing.

The truth. Do you want to save him? Because at this point, any credibility you might have is slipping away faster than a drunk on ice."

Even Uncle Herman liked Southern metaphors.

"Sorry, Uncle Herman," I said. "It's just that somebody else was there that night with me, a girl, but I can't tell anybody who. She'd get into too much trouble. That's why I didn't want to go."

"Are you crazy? Are you telling me now that you withheld that slight bit of information from me? This is a man's life—our friend—we're talking about. What the hell were you thinking, goddammit? And why didn't you tell me before? Who was it? I'll subpoena her."

"I can't tell, Uncle Herman, and it wouldn't make any difference anyhow."

"And how the hell do you know that?"

Uncle Herman was apoplectic; his face as red and puffed out as his wife's first place, county fair tomatoes. Her bisque was legendary.

"I'm busting my ass, *pro bono,* at your insistence. You have no idea how much time and effort a trial like this entails. And now you're telling me that you lied to me and you still won't fess up, even to me here in private?"

His hushed screaming snapped my head back like a fist.

"I can't say who. She'd get into too much trouble and it wouldn't do any good. All she saw was Mr. E, just like I did."

Uncle Herman closed his eyes and just stood there for what felt like an eternity, his head tilting up toward the ceiling.

"Damn, missed it," he said.

"What?"

Just then, the bailiff knocked on the door. His eyes knifing me, Uncle Herman pushed me out. I figured he'd never forgive me.

Judge: Is yo witness ready to answer the question?

UH: I hope so, Your Honor.

As I took the witness stand and sat, I saw Uncle Herman whispering with Mr. E. and then passing a note to Mrs. Firestone, his secretary, sitting behind him. She jumped up and scurried, more waddled, out of the courtroom as fast as an overweight, older woman could.

P: I repeat boy, why did you pretend to be sick?

D: Because I wanted to go to the Friday night YMCA dance and maybe pick up a girl.

The white and even some black faces erupted in laughter. I felt like I was melting.

P: OK. So you weren't sick at 6 p.m. then. And you wasn't sick or even in bed neither. True or false?

D: I was in my bedroom.

P: At 6 p.m., you're sayin you was already in bed?

D: No, I was playing my saxophone in my bedroom.

P: So then, you're tellin us you didn't go to that dance?

D: I changed my mind.

P: You sayin you decided, when you could've gone an picked up a girl, maybe even brought her home without your folks bein there, that you decided instead, at 6 p.m., to play on your instrument, in your bedroom, alone?

D: I—I, yes, sir.

P: So, son, you lied first to your folks, then to your lawyer, who's your own uncle, and now, under oath, 'bout being sick in bed?

D: Yes, sir.

P: Why?

D: Because I was ashamed of lying to my folks.

A chorus of murmurs sang out. Reverend Rampbell mopped his face with his handkerchief. May shook her head with a piteous grimace and Mom's eyebrows arched into her scalp. My chest vice-gripped my lungs and my legs clung to the chair like two bags of wet concrete. Mr. E just stared ahead.

P: Well, let's fergit the lie for right now. Except, son, why should I or anyone else believe any of your story now that we know you're a liar?

D: I'm not a liar.

P: But you jest admitted you are.

D: Just that part.

P: OK. Let's pretend you are not a liar. Tell me 'bout your relationship with the defendant.

*D: I've worked for Mr. Eldridge since I was twelve. My father didn't know much about carpentry and fixing things so he asked Mr. E if he would teach me. He's the best teacher I've ever had. I've worked with him for almost seven years now. And he's taught me...*and I went on and on about how patient and kind and loving he was. I ended with, *That's how I absolutely know he'd never do anything like this. He's like my second father.*

The muttering started again. The prosecutor wiped his face with his handkerchief, then massaged it into the side pocket of his jacket. He looked at the jury, took a deep breath, puffed his cheeks, blew out air, walked over to them, leaned on the handrail, and pointed to me.

P: Then would I be correct to guess, boy, that you kind of love him like a father too? Right?

D: Yes, sir, he's a hero to me. There's few finer men.

P: And you love him like your daddy, right?

D: I guess I do, yes, sir.

Shaking his head, lifting his glasses up over his nose, cleaning them with the extracted handkerchief, the prosecutor swung his head at the jury, then the crowd.

P: That boy, a white boy, loves a nigger much as his own daddy. What is wrong with these Jews?

UH: Objection.

Judge: Sustained, shaking his head, grinning.

P: Guess if I loved someone as much as my daddy, I'd say most anything to pertect him. Though lovin a nigger much as my daddy, shit, much as my dog, is beyond anything I could ever imagine.

I saw most of the whites shaking their heads up and down and laughing and the blacks shaking their heads side to side and grimacing.

UH: Objection.

Judge: Sustained. Git it over with, Roscoe.

P: Surely, Judge. Didn't mean to be rude. Son, let me git this whole thang in order.

Roscoe's Southern drawl was getting thicker and thicker as his questions rolled on. Thing became thang, my was now mah. He was slicing my testimony with a redneck blade.

P: Fust, you lied to yer folks. Then you lied to yer own uncle, a lawya. Then you lied 'bout seein some boogie-man in a pillow case, or maybe jist someone goin fer a nighttime walk, so you could save a nigger's ass 'cause you love him much as your own daddy. Do ah have it all purdy much right, son?

D: No. I mean some of it, but I really did wrestle somebody there. And the only fire Mr. E set was done to dry the shellac faster and was in a steel bucket. And Mr. E left before the building caught on fire.

P: OK, then, tell me about this fire that you now admits the defendant started.

UH: Objection. The witness never said that the temple fire was started by the defendant.

J: Sustained. Roscoe, don't put words in the boy's mouth.

P: Okay, then. Son, tell me anything about any ol fire that you know 'bout.

D: OK. When Mr. E and I were finished sanding and shellacking the pews early that afternoon, we lit alcohol in a couple of buckets between the aisles to heat up the place to make the shellac dry faster, so it would be dry when Mr. E came back that night to lay on the last coat. You fill a bucket about half way and then it burns itself out in a couple of hours or so. Mr. E says it's a lot cheaper than heating a whole big building for hours at a time. And denatured alcohol doesn't leave any smell after a while. So the place won't be all fumy the next day during services. When we left, we had about half of the gallon bottle of alcohol left and we put it in the vestibule table because the janitor likes to use it for cleaning when he cleans the windows and everything the morning before Friday night services.

P: That's impressive knowledge, boy. Do you have any idea, then, why there would be that gallon glass bottle of denatured alcohol, empty, lyin on the floor between the pews?

D: Somebody must have snuck in and used it to start the fire.

P: Yes, somebody surely did use it to start that fire.

D: Mr. Eldridge wouldn't have used it to light another bucket after he went back that night to put on the last coat. He said when the last coat has as much as twenty-four hours to dry, it sets smoother without any extra heat as long as the temperature's not too cold. And the forecast was for a not very cold night. No, that doesn't make any sense.

Uncle Herman's eyes shut for a second. I could hear him sigh.

Mr. E's stock-straight back sagged and his head sank into his chest. The white people mumbled, the blacks looked stricken.

The prosecutor looked over to the jury with mocked worry.

P: Oh, son, it makes lots'a sense to me. The defendant's fingerprints on the actual bottle, lying right there 'tween the pews where the fire was. Oh, Lordy, sure makes lots of sense ta me.

He nodded his head at the jury, frowning still, until several nodded back. My head was bee-buzzing. My shirt drenched my sport-coat in a wool stink. My head swung back and forth in a blur to the jury, the crowd, the judge. The picture of Mr. Rippe reaching out for help in my dream popped into my brain. I wanted help now. How could they not see the truth? My proud explanation was incinerating Mr. E's chances as surely as the fire had burned up Mr. Rippe.

The prosecutor rushed over and stood facing me, leaning close. I could smell his Aqua Velva, the same Uncle Herman used. I only knew because he'd once joked that the alcohol content was so high that US sailors in World War II had asked unsuspecting mothers to send them big supplies, which they drank in lieu of booze. He pulled a pack of Camels from his inside coat pocket and tapped it against his palm until one poked out. He slowly slid it from the pack, put it to his mouth, returned the pack to his pocket, dug a shiny silver lighter from his pants pocket, flicked it once with his thumb, lit the cigarette, and casually drew in a breath. He leaned his head slightly backward, held it a second, lowered his head, opened his mouth, and slowly blew the smoke in my direction. He spoke as slow as mud.

P: Now that we know how he started the fire…

UH: Objection, it hasn't been proven that Thomas started the fire.

Judge: Sustained.

P: Okay, let's talk about the cigarette butt, son. Not to mention the screwdriver? Explain those fingerprints.

I wanted to vomit.

D: Like I told you, Mr. Eldridge borrowed it from me and used it that afternoon to tighten the door hinges on the way out. It must have fallen out when I was whirlligigging my toolbox, like I told you before.

P: Son, the only thang spinning round and round like a whirligig here is your stories. No furtha questions.

Uncle Herman called Reverend Rampbell and a few other character witnesses. He asked all sorts of questions, on and on, that felt like a big waste of time. None of it seemed to matter. Jane Schneider said that she was certain Mr. E, "would never do such a terrible thing, no matter what." Uncle Herman kept asking her for minute details about the lights, how much they cost, weighed, why she liked them, on and on. Finally, he called me again, to repeat my version, detail after detail, and finished with a question.

UH: Donny, was there anybody else there at the house with you that night who might have also seen the arsonist?

D: No.

UH: No more questions.

Bailiff: Witness is excused.

My testimony seemed as useless as a watermelon seed bit hard and spit out. Uncle Herman turned his head away from me as I stepped down. "Oy," was all Reb Gross said, fidgeting and twisting his *payas,* then patting me on the knee when I sat next to him.

Suddenly, from the back of the courtroom, "Lordy, that boy's telling the truth, sure as Jesus is my savior. Praise be God. I saw that man shove that boy sure as God is mah witness. He's truthful as a prophet. I helped him raise up from the ground."

Judge: Order, order.

Everyone turned their heads to watch Red being restrained by two deputies.

P: Judge, we've already heard about this crazy nigger's "rescue" after the boy ran in an out of the place. Don't rightly matter who tossed or didn't, even if he did see somebody standing there in front of the fire, watchin it, who the boy attacked.

Judge: Agreed. Bailiff, could you please remove that man from this sanctum?

The doors banged shut after Red, Ditto, was tossed out like a bag of trash, followed by their being opened once more as Mrs. Firestone walked back in and quickly over to Uncle Herman. She and Uncle Herman whispered. He stood, turned, and looked at me with the strangest stare, then turned back to the judge.

UH: Can I approach the bench, Your Honor?

J: Come on.

I couldn't hear their conversation, but I could see the prosecutor angrily arguing until the judge finally said "alright, get on with it then, counselor," as the prosecutor stormed off to his table.

UH: I call Miss Clara James.

I thought my heart would pop out of my mouth. The courtroom was loud with silence and held breaths as the bailiff opened the door to the courtroom once more. Clara, dressed in the clothes she wore from home to school, her "good-girl" clothes, stood there, straight and proud with a serious, scared to my eyes, expression. The bailiff, followed by big, lipstick-smeared, frilly-bloused Mrs. Firestone, escorted her to the witness stand and swore her in, she adding to the "I do," with "as Jesus is my witness." I knew that Clara's life would never be the same and that I would be caught in another lie, not to mention whatever repercussions would be heaped on Clara. I could barely breathe.

UH: Are you the daughter of Reverend Jimmy James, one of Danville's most notable, respected ministers?

C: Yes, sir.

UH: Knowing that and after hearing your oath to your Lord, can I, we all, expect that anything that you say will be absolutely the truth?

C: Yes, sir, like I've been brought up, never to lie.

In any other circumstance, I would have laughed out loud.

UH: Thank you, miss. Now, did you witness the fire at Beth Sholom Temple?

C: Yes, sir.

UH: Do you live nearby?

C: No, sir.

UH: Then how were you able to see the fire?

C: I was visiting a friend who lives right across the street.

UH: Who is that?

Clara pointed to me. I wanted to run to her. The murmurs of the crowd felt like darts.

C: Donny Cohen.

UH: And what did you see?

C: I saw flames coming out of the temple.

UH: And what else did you see that night?

C: I saw a guy push Donny down and then run away.

UH: Can you identify the "guy?"

C: No, sir. It was pretty dark by the time I got over to where Donny was. And the guy had something over his head.

UH: What do you mean?

C: Like a bag or something, you know, like at the meetings.

UH: The meetings?

C: Klan rallies.

Another audience gasp.

UH: So you couldn't recognize him?

C: No, sir.

UH: Did you see him light the fire?

C: No, sir. But I did hear Mr. E, Mr. Eldridge, the defendant, drive away before the fire started.

UH: And how do you know that?

C: 'Cause his muffler was broken and his truck made a lot of noise, like Donny said.

UH: How did you know it was his truck? Had you spoken to him earlier?

C: Yes, sir. Donny works with him—he's like a hero to him—and I wanted to meet him so when we heard his truck pull in, I rushed out to introduce myself.

UH: And what was he doing there?

C: He said he was varnishing some pews so that they'd be dry before the temple's services the next day, their Sabbath services on Friday night.

UH: And how long after that did you hear his truck leave?

C: About an hour or so, late dusk.

UH: What were you doing during the alleged hour?

C: We, Donny and I, were hanging out at his house.

UH: What made you and Donny aware of the fire?

C: I guess it was about an hour or so after we heard Mr. E. leave. Donny asked me if I smelled smoke and then I looked out a window and saw the flames and smoke.

UH: So, Miss James, where were you in the house? I've been in that house many a time—it's my brother's house—and from the first floor, you wouldn't be able to see the front yard of the temple from any of the windows because of the tall hedges in front of his house. I'm just trying to make sure that you could see all of this happening, since I know the prosecutor will think you're making this up to protect your boyfriend and his so-called hero. What made Donny run out in the first place? How were you able to see when the fellow pushed Donny and ran?

Clara looked down and said nothing, everyone waiting.

J: Answer the question, miss. Let's get on with this.

Clara still said nothing.

J: Miss James, darlin, either speak up or I'll be forced to hold you in contempt—that means going to jail yourself.

C: Upstairs.

UH: Which side of the house?

C: Well, the side looking out at the temple.

UH: Which room is that?

C: Donny's bedroom. It's the only room on that side of the second floor.

The courtroom exhaled into a noisy maelstrom, quieting down only after the judge threatened to jail anyone making a sound. I felt like someone was pounding a sixteen-penny nail into my head.

UH: So you were in his bedroom, Donny asked you about smelling smoke, and you both looked out of his window at the temple, and you saw the temple on fire.

C: Yes, sir. Well, I saw it first and kind of screamed and then Donny saw it.

UH: And could you see that Tommy Eldridge's truck wasn't around?

P: Objection, leading the witness.

J: Overruled.

C: I wasn't really looking for it one way or another, but it definitely wasn't there since I noticed what a beautiful truck it was when he drove up in it and when I ran down to meet him. And we'd heard him leave, like I said before, from the sound of his busted muffler. And I don't remember seeing it again.

UH: And how did you see this man push Donny? Still from the window? Where were you when you saw this man push and run? I mean, were you in the house or had you run outside with Donny?

C: No, I stayed in the house. Donny told me to.

UH: Why?

Clara closed her eyes.

UH: Please, Miss James, it's important for you to tell us why?

C: 'Cause we were afraid.

UH: Of what?

Clara looked out at the crowd. I'd have been rich if I could have charged a buck for everyone leaning forward in his or her seat.

C: That my daddy would kill me if he found out I was in a bedroom with a boy, especially a Jew.

UH: Literally kill you?

C: No, but that he'd get crazy angry.

UH: I guess that's understandable around these parts.

Snickers from the audience. Even Uncle Herman seemed to smile.

UH: So you just stayed up there in his room?

C: Well, I did for a while and that's when I saw him fightin the guy and him pushin Donny down.

UH: And then you left?

C: No, I watched Donny just standin there, looking at the fire, doing nothing, until I just couldn't stand it anymore and so I ran down to him and told him to do somethin and he told me to run away before anybody saw me there.

UH: And did you?

C: Yes, sir. He knew I'd be in a heap of …

Clara stopped, looked horrified and lowered her head.

UH: Go on, please.

C: I'd be in a so much trouble if my daddy found out I was there.

UH: So can I conclude that his lies were to protect you, to protect your honor?

C: Yes, sir. He's the nicest, sweetest boy I've ever known.

She looked at me with the nicest, sweetest smile. More murmurs from the crowd.

UH: Thank you, Miss James. It was very brave of you to come here today. Thank you for your honesty. No further questions.

I wanted to jump up and kiss her and hold her. *We did it,* I thought, *notwithstanding my lies and her public shame—a slam-dunk for Mr. E's innocence—that he couldn't have started the fire because she'd heard him leave so much earlier and didn't see his truck when she ran to me, and that Ricky, in his Klan hat, really had been there enjoying his pyric victory.* The prosecutor stepped forward to Clara, his angry facade from Uncle Herman's surprise thrust now transformed into a smirk.

P: A simple question for you, Miss James. Did you see anything other than a man standin in front of a burnin building, your boyfriend grabbin and pushin and shovin at him, and then him throwin your boyfriend off of him and gettin away from the heat and flames and your attackin boyfriend?

Clara frowned, looked at Uncle Herman and up at the judge.

J: Go ahead, girl, answer the question.

C: No, sir.

P: No further questions.

Clara hesitated, her "nicest, sweetest smile" now transformed into a stricken stare. She glanced over at me, her eyes wide, almost pleading. I put my hand to my lips and with a small motion, sent her a kiss. As she walked out, shaken but erect, between the rows of staring, murmuring people, someone shouted "whore" and "Jew slut." Others called out, "Bless you, child." Uncle Herman's eyes followed her out, and then caught my eye with a blank expression. *Bless you, Clara,* I thought, *my brave, beautiful, now-in-awful-trouble-with-who-knows-what-price-to-pay, love of my life.*

With an almost gleeful wink to The Junior, who nodded back with equal sparkle, the prosecutor called, "Mr. John Lawson."

Mr. E cocked his head to the side with a puzzled frown. Uncle Herman whispered to him, but Mr. E shook his head in an "I don't know." He tightened up like a yanked rope.

The Junior motioned to a deputy, standing at the back of the courtroom. He opened the door. Mr. Lawson, followed by another deputy, walked down the aisle to the witness box. He was sweating profusely, head lowered almost to his chest, his eyes squeezed almost shut. I noticed that his hand was slightly lifted off the Bible during the swearing in. I recalled Mr. Lawson's triumphant guffaws about fooling Somelaw Gant's mother by swearing, "as Jesus is my Lord," that he hadn't lied about calling Somelaw's final tennis shot out in my match with him.

P: Boy, did you ever receive the defendant at your home over the past year?

JL: Yes, suh, I did.

P: And for what purpose?

JL: Tom's been a friend of mine from the time we was boys an on up till now.

P: That's real nice, but I'm askin about any special meetins you might've held at your house with him and others.

UH: Objection, Your Honor, leading the witness.

P: Mr. Lawson, did you invite the defendant, Tommy Eldridge, to your house to discuss a violent sect of niggers who call themselves Black Muslims.

JL: I don't believe in violence 'gainst no man, suh. And Mr. Malcolm and Rev'rend Elijah Muhammad only say that Negroes has the right to defend ourselves.

P: That ain't what I asked, boy. I asked if the defendant, that man sittin over there, was present at any of your meetins when you was discussin such matters?

Mr. Lawson's face darkened. He pulled out his thin white handkerchief and wiped his brow, turning his head with a frightened look at Mr. E.

Judge: Answer the question, boy. We ain't got all day.

P: I repeat, was that man at any of your meetins when you was discussin the hatred of the nigger for the white, as they say, devil?

JL: Yes, suh, I have to say he was there once.

P: Once? Well, I have here a statement provided to me by The Junior, written and sworn to by a Mr. Charles Davis, who is a patriotic Negro, former Marine, a Christian preacher who was hired by The Junior to attend such meetins. Mr. Davis swears that the defendant was at these meetins plottin malevolence against white people at least three times, maybe more. Boy, you wanna change what you just said?

JL: Cain't say fer sure. Lot's of folks come to my house. Possible he came more'n once. But we never planned no violence.

Uncle Herman looked stricken, ambushed. He leaned to Mr. E again, whispered to him, then looked down at his table, vacuumed smoke into his lungs, and scribbled onto his legal pad.

P: So tell me, how do you Black Muslims feel about Jews?

JL: Don't have nothin personal 'ginst no man who ain't done nothin injurious to me nor others.

P: That ain't what I asked. Seems you slide 'round certain of my questions quick as a cockroach runnin from a swattin.

The white faces in the rooms snickered and waggled their heads. The blacks sat stony.

P: So, guess I'll have to repeat agin. How do you and your haters of the white man feel about Jews? Maybe I can refresh yer memories with a quote from a spokesman of this group of vile Black Muslims, a Mister Khalid Abdul Muhammad. Am I sayin his name right?

Mr. Lawson didn't have time to respond.

P: Don't matter. And I quote: "You see, everybody always talks about Hitler exterminating six million Jews...but don't nobody ever asked what did they do to Hitler? What did they do to them folks? They went in there, in Germany, the way they do everywhere they go, and they supplanted, they usurped, they turned around, and a German, in his own country, would almost have to go to a Jew to get money. They had undermined the very fabric of the society." Unquote.

The Prosecutor unfolded a newspaper clipping.

P: Now here's somethin even more interestin, actually amazin. A Nazi, one George Rockwell, head of the American Nazi Party, a Nazi like the ones we fought against in the war, Nazis who hate Negroes as much as Jews, this Nazi was actually invited in '61 and agin in '62 by a nigger, that Elihah Muhammad that you seem to like so much, to his congregation. That Muhammad fella invited that Nazi, can you believe it, to one of his meetins 'cause he said that the Nazi was someone who understood that the real enemy is the Jews.

Uncle Herman stood up to make an objection.

P: No further questions.

Uncle Herman: Mr. Lawson, have you ever been involved in any criminal or violent behavior? Ever been arrested?

JL: No, suh. Worked for the Gants since I was a boy. Never got into any trouble at all. Raised three children, all graduated high school.

UH: Do you believe in violence?

JL: No, suh, but I do believe that the Negro has been kept down and that tellin him to put off till the afterlife what he needs now is white Christianity's way of keepin him from seekin a better life and equal rights in this one.

UH: Are you saying that regardless of what any other of these Muslims are saying, that all you took from them and talked about in your meetings was how the Negro in the South has been mistreated and denied equal treatment under the law?

JL: That's surely close enough, plus that us Negroes hafta get better educated and hafta quit thinkin that we somehow less just 'cause of the color of our skin.

UH: Did you or my client ever mention or support any sort of violence against white people or Jews?

JL: No, suh. We all try not to hate nobody, though I do know many a white man who ain't far from the devil. That said, there's Negroes out there I know who ain't far behind neither.

Equal murmuring, quick comments and whistles from blacks and whites.

UH: Why did my client attend your meetings?

JL: He only came 'cause I asked him to. 'Cause he's the kind of friend who could never say no to nobody, 'specially somebody's been a good friend long as we has—an 'cause he stands up for anybody who's down and out, always has, always helpin. As good a Christian as there is in the real way of what a Christian's 'sposed to be like. But ain't no reason he shouldn't wanna hear 'bout how he could stand up fer his own kind and for his kids' future.

Uncle Herman thanked and dismissed him. The light that shone through Mr. Lawson's voice and out my phone during his euphoric call to me after my tennis match was now extinguished. His face swiveled around the room, contorted in a desperate plea for rescue, or forgiveness. He touched Mr. E's shoulder with a "sorry" as he slouched to the back of the room. A chorus of mutterings greeted him. It all felt like a lynching—with my testimony and Mr. Lawson's helping to tighten the noose around Mr. E's neck.

The Prosecutor called Mr. E to the stand. Mr. E had insisted on speaking his truth and Uncle Herman couldn't see where it could hurt him at this point any more than his silence.

P: Boy, are you friends with Mr. John Lawson?

Mr. E: First off, I ain't no boy, sir. And neither is John Lawson, who I do claim as a friend.

Mr. E stared eyeball to eyeball at the man. "Amen to that," I heard several voices behind me say. "Uppity-nigger," others said. The prosecutor looked down at his notepad.

P: Have you been to any of the meetins at Mister Lawson's house, like the ones he described?

Mr. E: Yes, suh, I been to a few.

P: Oh, so then you agree with these hate-filled folks, these Mooslims sayin the white man, and Jews, is the devil?

Mr. E: Just 'cause a man's a friend, don't mean I hafta agree with all he says. Ain't no crime to listen. Though nothins wrong with the black man makin more of hisself, like he talked of.

P: So then, I ask again, do you agree to the idea of malevolence to white people?

Mr. E: Show a man a knife, don't mean he hasta grab it and use it to cut someone. Still, he can 'preciate how it's made and what it's capable of. But nothin 'bout what my friend said had anything to do with violence 'ginst no man.

After further questioning, Mr. E said that yes, he had been at the temple, shellacking the pews the afternoon of the fire and later, just before the fire. Then the prosecutor pointed to me.

P: And did you stop and talk to that young man and his girlfriend, just before you entered that place of worship, just before the fire?

Mr. E: Hour or so before, yes, suh.

As the prosecutor's questioning went on, Mr. E said that, yes, he did smoke Lucky Strikes and that, yes, the initials carved on the screwdriver were the ones he carved on all of his tools to identify them at shared worksites. And that, yes, he had placed a metal bucket with denatured alcohol and lit it in the aisle between the pews.

Mr. E: But I swear, as Jesus is my witness, that I put the remainin half-full bottle of alcohol on the vestibule table so the janitor could use it to clean windas with.

And that, yes, he had recently argued with Mrs. Schneider.

P: Oh, now, she is a Jew, correct? She is a Jew just like the ones you and your Mooslim and Nazi brothers hate and revile, the enemy who undermines Negro society, accordin to the teachins and preachins of Malcolm X and those other hate-filled Black Mooslims that you and your bosom-buddy friend, Mister Lawson, seem to hold in such high esteem. A Jew who happened to be your boss at the same Jew temple you was workin at. What you got to say 'bout the way that Jew treated you?

Mr. E: She hired me to install some 'spensive designer ceilin lights of her choosin. Then she blamed me 'cause they didn't shine enough light. Said I should've known and said she wouldn't pay my bill for the week-long rewiring job on twenty-five-foot ladders.

Dad had intervened on Mr. Eldridge's behalf, but Mrs. Schneider, the chairwoman or the building committee, would only compromise to half his due. Dad made up the difference.

P: Must've made you pretty damn mad, huh? Havin been falsely accused and havin to put in all those hours for nuthin, specially for a devil Jew.

Mr. E: Ain't got no problems with any decent man or woman's religion. God made us all equal in his eyes.

P: But, you must've been spittin mad at how this one particular Jew treated you.

Mr.E: Yes, suh, I must say it upset me somethin terrible.

P: Mad enough to git even, maybe even be a hero to those Mooslim and Nazi friends of yours?

Mr.E: No, suh, never.

Uncle Herman's questions were anemic, not surprising considering his evidence or lack thereof, simply getting Mr. E to reiterate his side of the story, his innocence, his appreciation for the ideas of Negroes educating themselves and being self-sufficient, discarding the notions of black inferiority.

The prosecutor and Uncle Herman summarized their cases and that was it. I was sure that of the two ears on each juror's head, one had perfect hearing for the prosecutor while the other was deaf to Mr. Eldridge.

The jury was sent out for a city-paid lunch at Freida's Busy Bee Café and Kosher Deli, right across from the courthouse. The locals loved her hot pastrami on rye as much as her hickory smoked ham.

"I don't touch the *traif,* the pork," Freida rationalized. "The *goyim* do it. I only touch kosher." It was a Southern compromise.

The jurors sat in the banquet room. I could hear their talking and laughter from the booth next to it. I was as used up and wrecked as the cars sprawled all over redneck neighborhoods. Reb Gross and I silently sipped Freida's hand-mixed cherry Cokes, served in beer mugs that she'd custom-ordered, like the ones she'd seen on "Gunsmoke," her favorite TV western. Freida loved Westerns. The walls were covered with signed photos from her favorite cowboy stars.

May, Mrs. E, and her kids were sitting in the adjoining "coloreds only" room with its separate entrance and pass-through kitchen window.

A wire ran from the jukebox to another speaker in the colored room. With a dime, I punched in "Midnight Special" by Lead Belly. May had told me he'd gone to prison for knifing a white man. The Texas governor liked his singing so much that he'd bring guests to the prison for private concerts and pardoned Lead Belly after he served only seven of his thirty-five-year sentence.

If you ever go to Houston,
You better walk right,
You better not stagger,
You better not fight
Sheriff Benson will arrest you,

He'll carry you down
And if the jury finds you guilty,
You're penitentiary bound
Let the midnight special shine her light on me
Let the midnight special shine her ever-loving light on me.

CHAPTER THIRTY-THREE

"All stand," the court clerk announced an hour and a half later. The judge strode in with the stern face of an inquisition priest in black swirling robes. His white ones, pointy hat, and mask were probably neatly hanging in his closet back home. He raised his gavel, struck it hard against its wooden base, then sat.

Thomas Jefferson Eldridge, he said, looking at Mr. E. You have been charged within the Commonwealth of Virginia with voluntary manslaughter as well as arson. Looking at the twelve white men, he said, "Have you, a jury of peers, reached a verdict?"

The foreman, Mr. Vernon Waddell, a tobacco farmer, wore faded-blue bib overalls, the narrow, vertical pocket holding a sharpened pencil and a hard, rubber, black, pocket comb. His greased hair was combed straight back. He stood up, spit a stream of brown liquid into the copper spittoon located on the floor to his side, then wiped his mouth on the back of his hand.

"Yes, suh, Yo Honah. We have," his head rotating toward the squirming, murmuring assemblage. The wood floor creaked with scraping chairs as folks adjusted themselves to attention.

I felt as broken as the Confederacy. My knuckles pressed white tight against the front of the bench. The yoke of hope I'd pulled trying to save Mr. E felt more like a hangman's knot.

The bailiff took the papers from the gnarled fingers extending from Mr. Waddell's red and white checkerboard flannel shirt and handed them to the judge.

The judge glanced at the verdict, nodded back to the jury, handed the papers back to the bailiff, who delivered them back to the foreman.

"This jury," Mr. Waddell drawled slowly, saying 'jew-ree,' the corners of his mouth raised into a simper, like a confident man waiting for some sort of special approbation for delivering a foregone conclusion, "has found that nigga," pointing to Mr. Eldridge, "guilty as charged."

Mr. Eldridge's striped, cotton prison pants vibrated as if a fan was blowing against them. His chest humped against a sob, shoulders slumped. He turned to look back at his kids and Mrs. E. Along with many others, she screamed, bundling the kids in her arms. Rachel sobbed. Tommy Junior stared, blank-faced, stoic like his dad. Mrs. E reached out, stretching into empty air as if to pull Mr. E into a cocoon of solace.

"This court," the judge quickly went on, "sentences you, Thomas Jefferson Eldridge, as prescribed within the Commonwealth of Virginia's penal code, to fifteen years at hard labor, with no chance for parole, to be served startin immediately." He slammed his gavel once more, turned, and marched out.

Two big deputies pulled Mr. E up by the armpits. He struggled against them to reach back toward his family, arms flailing like branches in a storm as the deputies attempted to jerk him forward and out of the courtroom.

"Dottie," Mr. Eldridge called. "Tommy, Isaac, Rachel," he howled, eyes darting from one to the other, a feverish hysteria I'd never witnessed in him melting his normally placid face.

Mrs. E ran the ten steps to him, pushing at one of the deputies, reaching to her husband, before the other deputy shoved her away.

"Let 'em touch her a minute, Harold," I heard one of the deputies say to the other. I was amazed at his empathy. Then he snickered, "Might be the last time this nigga gits ta touch a woman fer a long, long time."

I wanted to grab his gun and kill him.

Mr. E stopped and planted himself, rooted, thighs inflating, his face in a fierce stare, reaching to her, immovable against the tugs of the deputy.

"Treat me any way you likes," he roared, eye to eye with Harold, "but don't never touch my wife that way or you'll find regret the least of your worries."

The deputy flinched in that way that bullies do when stood up to, looked around, red-faced, to see if anyone else had seen him talked down to by a black man, then, "move on, nigger, or we'll hog-tie you, and carry you out." But he relaxed his grip on the chain to let Mr. E reach to his wife and caress her cheek as her tears met his hand.

"It'll be awright, honey," he said without conviction.

I'd never heard him tell an outright lie before. It hit me like a scratch on a perfect record.

He lifted his arms, chains clanking, and cupped her face with his palms, his long fingers encircling her head. "Oh Dottie," he said. He kissed her lips and closed his eyes. When the deputy pulled his hands away, she collapsed to the floor, her kids rushing to her. Mr. E bent over, struggling to reach down to her, but was stopped, yanked upright by both deputies pulling again behind his back.

"Let the man tend to his wife," a huge black woman called out, furiously waving a woven straw fan down low in front of her sweating bosom.

My chest cinched up like a heart-stricken lover as I watched the man who could do anything, who could fix any problem with concrete certainty, finally face his own unfixable situation. Mr. E's face sagged along with his body as he surrendered to the power of the deputies' efforts.

"Help yer mama up, kids," he croaked. "It's up to you from now on."

"Now," he said in a resigned calm, looking back at Harold, "I'll come along without no trouble."

"Thomas, we haven't given up on you," Reverend Rampbell shouted out, others joining in a chorus of "Stay strong, Deacon" and "We love you" and similar encouragements. A twenty-ish black man wearing a white Nehru jacket, probably sold to him at Dad's store, raised his fist and barked, "Black Power, Black Power!"

Some white spectators, faces flushed and scared, started to hurry out while others stood around, muttering, anger painted on their faces like makeup, pointing at the agitated Negro crowd or to Mr. E.

His youngest son, Isaac, five years old, yelped, "Daddy, Daddy" as he ran up and wrapped his arms around Mr. E's leg. One of the deputies jerked the boy off by the collar and flung him back. Isaac fell onto his butt and slid three feet on the slick wood, wailing.

"Isaac, Isaac," Mr. E bellowed, hurling the two deputies away like scattered bowling pins. Stepping to his son, he tripped on his ankle chains and sprawled face down onto the floor, his arms swimming toward Isaac. One of the deputies, now also belly down on the ground, grabbed the connecting chain and dragged him back. Mr. E pawed at the floor and kicked his feet, while the other deputy jumped on his back, pinning his arms behind him and snapping on handcuffs. Mr. E winced and grunted in pain.

"Quit hurtin the man, goddammit," Mr. Lawson hollered. Reb Gross sobbed.

Mr. Waddell ran over, snagged Mr. E under his arms and lugged him up to standing.

"Isaac, Isaac, Isaac," Mr. E kept screaming, Isaac screaming back, "Daddy, Daddy," the other kids joining in cacophonous squeals and tears.

The crowd surged, black against white, a dozen or so blacks moving the melee toward Mr. E and his captors, arms reaching, stretching out to him. Most of the remaining whites, including the jury, pushed and shoved back against them. The Black Power man chanted, "Free Deacon Eldridge, Free Deacon Eldridge," repeating it to the pumping of his fist, as his group joined in. "White justice is no justice," he added over their chorus.

The white bailiffs in the courtroom joined the white crowd. Hearing the commotion, the hallway door opened and two more white deputies rushed in.

Uncle Herman stood motionless and mute at his table, then flopped into his chair, shaking his lowered head side to side. I recognized the same spent expression that I'd seen in his office. He stamped out his cigarette on the clear glass ashtrays provided at each table. As quickly as he had flopped down, he jumped back up to his feet.

"Stop, stop it!" he yelled, banging his fist so hard on the tabletop that the ashtray bumped up and crashed to the floor. "Stop it, goddammit, and go home. Enough already."

It was as if a silent hammer had smacked them all, the abrupt quiet as soundless as the melee had been loud.

"He's right," Reverend Rampbell spoke up, looking squarely at the Black Power shouter. "This won't help. Let's leave now before more evil befalls us."

With a final body shake, Mr. E lifted his head, blinked hard against his emotions and flared his nostrils for a deep breath. He stood stock still, gathering himself, forcing himself erect, and looked at the throng.

One tear leaked out of his right eye and drained down his face. Ever so slowly, he clenched his jaw and squeezed his eyes into dryness as he tried, in spite of it all, one last time, to leave us with a vision of dignity.

"Y'all go on now," was all he said.

As Mr. Waddell and the deputies spun him around and dragged him to my side of the courtroom, his back now to the mass, I looked into his eyes. Their dead vacancy and his slumped, encumbered gait reminded me of the creatures Clara and I had seen in *The Plague of the Zombies* at the Rialto Theatre on Main Street before the fire.

The ankle chains clanged against the hard oak in a sequential, sliding drag rhythm—clunk, shhh, clunk, shhh—as they led him away. The thick, wooden, courtroom door, emblazoned with *Sic Semper Tyrannis,* slammed shut.

CHAPTER THIRTY-FOUR

3,4,5,—the golden rule of carpentry perfection—popped into my head.

"It'll always make things work out right," Mr. E had said when he taught me to square a foundation perfectly. But all my carefully measured plans toward his house of freedom had built only failures. They flashed across my mind: Somelaw Gant and his mother, a flop. Reverend Rampbell's appeal to May, impotent. The Junior, untouchable. Clara's father, quixotic. Uncle Herman's court trial and my testimony, useless. At least, I'd thought, my pictures would have been a useful plank, the 3 on the way to the perfect angle for Mr. E's freedom. But even with Clara's testimony, 4 was still a blind carpenter's mystery. And 5, Mr. E's deliverance, was never even close to square.

Reb Gross, Rev. Rampbell, and a few others hung around after the trial, like muddled mourners at a funeral, then shuffled off until May and I were left alone in the courtroom. We sat in our seats, anchored in our grief, until the bailiff said, "Y'all gotta leave now. Everybody's long gone, and I'm closin down."

"I have another idea for four," I mumbled in a fog to May as we staggered out and sat in front of the post-Civil War courthouse, the last of the low fall sunlight sinking to dusk. The streetlights flickered on above the empty street. The stoplight changed to a blinking yellow warning. I leaned against one of the Greek revival columns, balancing my feet on white marble steps worn down through time into slippery slopes. The musky pleasantness of May's sweat and gardenia perfume only magnified my opposite mood.

"For *for*? What are you talking about, honey?" she said.

"I just don't know what else to do. I'm sorry."

"Apologizing before you even tell me why. Do you need me to give you another lesson?" she said with a tearful smile, flicking her butt at me, trying to lighten the mood.

"It's not for me, goddammit, May!"

"Well, spit it out then, sugar! And don't you curse at me."

"I'm sorry," I said, stifling a hiccoughing moan.

"There's that sorry again," May said. "What are you talking about?"

I explained the whole thing to her. The fire at the temple, the whirligig, Mr. Eldridge falsely accused, Reverend Rampbell's asking her to sleep with The Junior, Reverend James and the pictures, The Junior refusing to drop charges and arrest Ricky Parker, and my dead-end plans with Somelaw.

"I know all that ad nauseum, so what are you running your mouth about?"

"I have a new plan," I said.

"A dull blade is like a coarse man—makes objectionable noises and injures whatever it touches," Mr. E had told me in his careful instruction in the art of sharpening. I knew my idea was a dull knife before the words even touched May's ears.

"You have to have sex with The Junior. I'll even pay you."

She slapped me hard across my face.

"Fuck you big time! Offering me money. Even if I did agree to let that jerk have his way with me, it wouldn't have anything to do with money. So shame on you for even thinking that I wouldn't help Deacon Eldridge for free if I could."

Rubbing my cheek, "But you could, with my new plan."

"Having sex with The Junior is not a new plan. You know that. So what on earth are you talking about?"

"You've told me how The Junior wants you so badly it hurts. And you've told me that you can't stand him. And you told Reverend Rampbell that you wouldn't do it because even if you did, there would be no guarantee that he would honor his part of the bargain." I was rushing my words to keep her from slapping me again before I finished. "But I have a way that would work. I'll hide and get a picture of him having sex with you and then threaten to make it public if he doesn't help us get Mr. Eldridge free. He'd be so afraid of the bad publicity that he might agree to drop the charges."

It didn't take a second for May to turn her nose up.

"You know I can't stand that man, and for all the right reasons, Donny. And you know it could ruin my business if other men got scared that I might do this to them. You know all that and you still ask me?

"And, Brother Don," she steamed on, "what you don't see here is that a picture of a white man fucking a black whore is not going to do diddly-squat to make white people not like him. Sure, it might be a little embarrassing. It might even cost him a few votes here or there, mainly the Jewish vote, which is doubtful he would get anyhow. But overall it just wouldn't matter much in the long run. It might even help him.

"You got the right key, baby, but the wrong keyhole," she sang in a slow and bitter whisper.

"What?" I said.

"Bessie Smith—big hit. Seems appropriate to your stupid idea."

My hands ran across my face and scalp like they were chasing fleas.

"I'm desperate, May. I just can't think of anything else. They're taking him away. Who knows what they'll do to him in prison."

I leaned my cheek against her shoulder, the wet growing a stain on her dress.

"What an awful world we live in," she said, sobbing along with me, arm around my shoulder. "Oh Lord, what a cruel, awful place it can be."

I felt so stupid. I could see the yokels the way May said, grinning through their tobacco-stained teeth. "Po-lice chief done got him some hot, nigger pussy. Haha. Dumb sonabitch got hisself caught doin it. Betta be mo careful next time else I won't vote fer 'em jest 'cause he's too stupid to hide it proper."

"Sorry, May." I stood up to leave. "Another one of my pitiful, stupid ideas."

"Jewboy, where the hell do you think you're going?" she said, tugging at my pant leg, pulling me back down. "You think I could leave Deacon Eldridge's ass hangin out in the breeze?"

"Hanging," I said on automatic.

"Fuck you. I fuckin know how to say it. This is low-down time and I'll fuckin tawk like a nigga if I wanna."

"Jesus, May, sorry," I said, looking down at the steps.

She touched my reddened cheek, kissed my forehead, raised my chin, and looked right into my eyes.

"And I just love you, you crazy white boy, all the more for wanting to help a black man so much.

"Donny, you know Deacon Eldridge and Dottie were my folks' good friends. We all went to Reverend Rampbell's church ever since I was a baby. I spent many a night at their house baby-sittin their kids when I was young. Mr. Eldridge did handyman work at Daddy's farm in return. They treated me like one of their own. When my folks died, they were like second parents. Their place was too small for me to live there, and that's why I asked your folks to put me up. But if they had said no, Deacon and Dottie would have slept on the floor so I could have had a bed to sleep on. Not just for me, pretty much for anybody who needed help.

"When I was getting my house ready, I couldn't not tell them what I was up to, even though it went against all their Christian beliefs. They didn't hesitate to help me for even a second."

She squeezed my arm so hard that I winced.

"As Jesus is my witness, Donny, I'll not rest until the Deacon is free, no matter what it takes. But whatever it is, it has to work or it's just another waste of time. And it's gonna take a hell of a lot more than you or the Reverend think. Your and his ideas are just too stupid to work, no insult intended. You're thinkin too much like men. This type of situation requires a woman's delicate touch. And that is something I know all about.

"Ever since you and the Reverend came to me, I've been thinking. I'm sorry it took this long. Sometimes it almost feels like God, forgive me, enjoys watching Negroes suffer. But sitting in that courtroom today, watching the Deacon get crucified, it hit me like an epiphany. God finally spoke to me. *He* said, 'May, you are here for more than your sinful ways.'

"Reverend Rampbell and your ideas were wrong, but not all wrong. Donny, men are the spark, but women are the fuel. Men want our heat, but if they're not careful, we can scorch them. And I'm ready to do some terrible burning.

"But we can't talk here, Donny. Come over to my house."

As I drove over, Clyde McPhatter sang, *"We had plenty of love but still nothing."* No matter her certainty, I had none that May's idea was more than another nothing.

I walked into her parlor. It was decorated with European art, a hand-woven Moroccan rug on the polished oak floor and fine furniture throughout, all purchased on her trips abroad.

Sitting, shoes off, staring up at the ceiling in an old-fashioned, wicker rocking chair with a bright red crocheted pillow, a white knitted shawl on her shoulders, she was singing a song I'd never heard.

Oh mama,
Pray for me.
Lord, I got a long, oh a long walk,
To go free.

"It's called "Murder's Home." Negro slave and prison call-out song," she said.

Well, I gonna leave my baby cryin,
Lord knows Mr. George,
You gave him too long.

"Man, Donny, your heart just aches with the beauty of the agony those black prisoners could express in song."

"Where'd you learn it?"

"My old great-uncle taught a bunch to me when I was a little girl, after they let him out of Parchman Farm Prison in 1948, down in Mississippi. Some white farmer who hired him to help butcher hogs claimed he was taking too much fatback as part of his pay. Called him a 'son-of-a-bitch-nigger-thief.' So Uncle Sumer smacked the guy in the face with a big rib slab, broke his jaw. Judge didn't even let Uncle Sumer state his case. Anyhow, he'd chop wood and I'd hit the tree trunks with a stick and sing with him."

She pushed herself up with a weary effort and walked over to her stereo, then put a record on the turntable and closed her eyes. The stereo speakers at either end of the room, each about four feet high, boomed with a clarity and separation I'd never heard. *Klipsch* was written on the nameplate.

"It's called "Carmen." When it was first introduced in 1875, it got terrible reviews. The composer, Georges Bizet, died three months later, never knowing it would be one of the greatest operas of all time. Now if that music doesn't make you cry, Italian suffering, just as deep as our blues, Donny, then you don't have ears or a heart."

I'd never listened to opera.

She started messing around with a new toy I'd never seen before. The hammered copper and hand-tooled silver fluting and ornamentation of the machine looked like something ancient and remarkable, something from castles like the ones I'd seen in my medieval history textbook. I thought maybe it held some exotic liquor.

"Sit down, honey," she said, handing me a small cup.

I had no idea what it was.

"I brought this back from Italy. Espresso maker. One of a kind in Danville, as far as I know," she said with a pleased smile. "Try it."

I gulped it, a hot and sweet palliative, as we forced ourselves to try to relax and listen.

After the overture, she changed her mind, got up, and replaced the record.

"Remember this?" She put on an old forty-five. Out sang "Your Precious Love," the 1958 gold hit by Jerry Butler and The Impressions. "Dance with me, sweetheart."

"Now?"

"We've got time," she smiled, reaching out to me. As I took her into my arms, she said, "We've both come a long way since your basement, haven't we?"

"Yeah, mostly you." I looked around. "You're highfalutin, just like you said you wanted to be."

"Cain't hardly believe it mahsef," she said in a self-mockery.

"I, myself, find it difficult to believe," I fired back.

We both laughed and wrapped our arms around each other.

Feeling her warm, muscular body swaying so slowly against mine, enveloped by her perfume, as delicate as her touch, I felt embraced in a soul-goddess waltz. Without another word, the icy tension from the trial started to melt away.

"Did you see the Rebbetzin sitting in the back?" I asked.

"She's the one?"

"Yeah."

"I figured she'd be..."

"...younger and better looking?"

"Well, since you put it that way, yes. She looks even more worn down than Dottie Eldridge."

"Yeah, she's in a prison of her own."

After the last verse, May was trembling.

"Hold me another minute Donny. I'm scared."

I was shocked. She'd never been scared of anything.

We danced in the silence, barely moving. I remembered her asking me years before, down in that basement room, "Can your heart be as big for me from now on as the rest of you was before?"

I pulled her tight against me, our tears melting together down our clenched cheeks.

"OK, I'm ready," she finally said, inhaling and letting it out slowly, her lips skating across my slippery cheek. I didn't want to let her go. She wiped away her tears, then mine, with a silk hanky and took the skating needle off of the finished record. We sat on her velvet sofa. I noticed a small picture frame, flipped face-down, on the side-most cushion.

"We know," she said, "The Junior is one big-time bastard. So if we're going to try to change his mind, we'd better do it right because we have only one try. It'll take a battle a lot more devious than your and Reverend Rampbell's pansy-assed ideas to get that man to let go of Deacon Eldridge."

She picked up the picture frame, turned it over, ran her hand across the glass, caressing it like a treasure, took another deep breath, and handed it to me.

"Read it. It's the last page of the speech Dr. King gave two years ago at church during the '63 civil rights riots here. Said the police brutality in Danville was the worst he'd seen in the South."

I looked at it. It was the original, typed on onion-skin paper. It was signed in black ink, "To May, a light in the darkness. Martin."

I was staggered. "May, did you and Dr. King..."

"Hush now," she said. "Just read it."

"Fight. Fight through it. Fight to find the half-full rather than the half-empty. Fight for the beauty rather than the ugliness. Fight for your highness rather than your lowness. Fight for curiosity rather than boredom. Fight for depth rather than shallowness. Fight for the light rather than the darkness. Fight to understand and learn rather than be befuddled and ignorant. Fight for love of self and others rather than bitterness and self-negation.

"And through all the fighting, you will find your strength, your heart, your cleverness, your thrill, and your will. Fight."

Before I could comment again, May said, "I'm ready to fight Donny. It's fightin and rightin time." She touched her eye with the pink hanky. "Time to get things right. So don't you go getting depressed, love, because I'm ready. Jesus has shined his light on me. It's time for the only plan that will work, and that is May's Plan. So listen to me.

"Sitting in that courtroom, it hit me like that shaft of light that struck Moses when he got the Ten Commandments. Maybe it was Jesus speaking to me, or maybe not. I don't care. And for it to work, I don't *need*, but I definitely *want*, your help."

"Whatever you need, May. Anything," I said, still reeling from Dr. King's words.

"But you have to agree to do exactly what I tell you to, no questions asked. Otherwise, I'll have to find somebody else."

"Oh thanks. You don't trust me?"

"It's not that. I have my good reasons and you'll understand when the time is right. Please, just trust me."

"If you say so," I growled.

"Then swear on your Jewish God, 'cause we could use both him and mine, whoever might be list'nin, to help us with this. Swear that you will show up here when I tell you to, won't interfere, won't give me a fuss, or do anything other than what I tell you, when, how, and where I tell you. Swear!"

"Shit, May."

"Swear, Donny, or walk out of here right now."

"OK, I swear," I mumbled.

"Didn't hear you," she smiled.

"I swear, dammit!"

She cupped my chin in her hand, looked deep into my eyes, and tried to sweeten me up with a kiss on the cheek she had slapped.

"Now listen," she said. "We've talked about how I didn't ever want to be a farmer's wife or a maid, and most of all a maid."

"So?" I said, still fuming.

"So I've never been, other than my time living with your folks, which doesn't really count."

"Okay," I said.

"A while ago, I started to realize that to really prosper, a business needs to grow. So an opportunity came out of the blue to branch out," her face suddenly beaming with the satisfaction of a true entrepreneur. "Maybe it was God's hands."

"You mean you're adding new employees?"

"Well, no, not yet."

"And how does this help save Mr. Eldridge?" I grumbled.

"One day, Donny, I got a call from a white woman who told me she wanted to hire me. I figured she wanted a maid. But then she said she knew about me from one day overhearing two men at her church bragging about being my customers and commenting at the same time at how expensive I was, but worth it. She said she lived with a man who didn't love her, emotionally or physically, and whom she had come to realize she didn't love either. In fact, she said, she had come to suspect that she didn't much love any man. She said that she was starving for affection and couldn't stand living a lie any longer. 'Would you come over?' she asked me."

"So?" I said.

"So she said she couldn't ask any white women who were like her, even if she knew any, which she didn't—because there was always the chance that with another white woman, they might have loose tongues or try to blackmail her. But nobody, she told me, would ever believe some nigger woman making such claims. She was sobbing, Jewboy, and I felt sorry for her, even if she and her husband were shitheads and deserved suffering each other's existence. Plus, she said she would pay double my normal rate."

"And…" I said, my head spinning like a *dreidal.*

"There was one condition she insisted on," May said. "She said that I had to come to her house dressed as a maid so that no one would ever be suspicious of why I was there. And, to be honest, other than the money and new opportunity, I was curious. You know, I have grown and changed since I started all this and I just wondered what it would be like to love a woman. It's maybe like your dad looking for new merchandise."

My mouth gaped as wide as the Red Sea when Moses crossed, fleeing the Egyptians. She'd certainly learned to seize opportunity.

"And who would this be and how was it?" I was so agog, I could barely whisper. "And what exactly does it have to do with saving Mr. Eldridge?"

May beamed, enjoying my torment.

"None other than the honorable Mrs. Reverend Jimmy James. Becky James," she said triumphantly.

The entire Red Sea disappeared. My mouth was sand.

"And it was interesting, from an educational point of view," May said almost academically. "But try as I might, I can't say that women are my thing." She shook her head side to side in a no. "Know what I mean?"

My mind didn't want to come close to knowing what she meant—to picture Clara's mother and May naked, doing *it.* I squeezed my eyes shut, trying to keep from thinking about what May was telling me—which is why it was the only thing I could think about.

"Anyhow," May went on nonchalantly, as if telling me about having lesbian sex—no less with my girlfriend's mother—was normal, "I was surprised how sad I felt for her. She's just like a lot of my white male clients, out of touch with their bodies and just lonely as all get out. She wears the stinkiest perfume and cakes on makeup like a bordello whore. Her skin looks so pale I don't think she's ever spent a day in the sun, and she doesn't even know how to have an orgasm. I don't think she ever has. Her vagina smells like store-bought douche medicine since she figures she needs to keep 'down there,' as she calls it, clean. Like it's a dirty, terrible thing. I've at least taught her to start using my Granny's old vinegar and water natural douche, but only if she has an infection.

"I'm trying to teach her the things that a good mother would teach a daughter about enjoying and taking care of her body. Her mom never really talked to her about female things. She's like this little girl dressing like a woman, with all her makeup and clothes and social postures. It's really pitiful."

"And so," I croaked, totally exasperated. It was way more than I ever wanted to know about my girlfriend's mother—not to mention another secret I'd have to keep from Clara.

"So I have slowly tried to give her some real Christian love, to get her to relax and enjoy herself, as much as that might be possible, all things considered. I've even started giving her massages and getting her to give me some, so she can learn to feel. It's pretty miserable, all in all. But as time has passed, I've seen that she really isn't a bad person. She just got off to a bad start, raped when she was a girl by her two uncles and watching her dad beat her mom.

"Then she made a lot of bad decisions. Like marrying that asshole because she thought a man of God might make her feel whole and loved and cared for, kind of like, ironically, that rabbi's wife. That maybe her shit wouldn't stink if it was dressed up in mink, but instead—being stuck with him, and him being mean like her father, much less not having any love for a woman, as we now know from your pictures, and her not knowing how to escape and live a real life."

May said the whole thing with hardly a breath between sentences.

"Dressed in mink?" I said.

"Never mind that, darling. It's just an old saying."

"Okay," I said, again in a dizzy kind of haze. "So?"

"And so," May said, taking more of a gulp than a breath, "that is how I've figured how to get Deacon Eldridge out of his troubles."

"To help Mr. E?" I asked, letting out the breath I'd been holding until my face was turning red.

"Well, like I said, she isn't a bad person, in her heart. She's just very confused. And I can see why. I've told her that she deserves a good life. She can't quite believe that she's listening to a black woman, much less one who does what I do. But she's realized that she can't keep living this way. She takes tranquilizers because she feels like she was going insane. I told her she wasn't crazy and she needed to get off of those vile things and start living. I told her what Reverend Rampbell has said for so long, that 'a real Christian is true to himself, or herself, and that only by first letting God's loving presence into your own heart, no matter how low down your life is, can you then do Christ's work of loving and helping others.'

"And I told her about her no-good, lying, hypocritical, blowjobbin husband. No wonder you've never felt loved, I told her. You were just window dressing for him so he could make a bunch of money lying to all those people while he was giving his sex to men. He never loved you, he just used you."

"You told her? Jesus, May. If he finds out anyone else knows, it could blow any chance I still might have of using the pictures to help Mr. E."

"Doesn't matter now, with my plan."

"Yes, it does. She can't even mention to him anything about him being a homo."

"Okay, okay, sorry. I'll make her promise."

I was beyond shock. A sort of documentary of *This Could Only Happen in the South*, played in my mind: a homosexual rabbi fucking a Klan minister, whose daughter was screwing a Jewish boy—almost funny that both were attracted to Jews—both the rabbi and Klan minister in sham marriages and now, the minister's wife deciding she might also be gay and trying it with a black prostitute. No one outside the South would believe such impossibilities. But the South made such aberrant and weird situations somehow plausible. It was almost as if Southerners celebrated the creativity of their perversity.

"And so?" I finally mustered.

"And so," she proclaimed, "I'm going to ask her to help me with my plan to free Thomas."

CHAPTER THIRTY-FIVE

"Hello, Junior."

"That's me, who's this?"

"Jimmy James. Got a minute?"

"Always do fer you, Rev'rend."

I was sitting in Reverend James's office. It was impossible to keep from picturing him and Tichter lying naked across his desk. He'd said to me, "Come over quick, and listen to my phone call to The Junior."

As I'd walked over, I remembered one of Mr. E's lessons about executing a difficult cut: "Course it's fearful to cut into an expensive piece of finish trim that has to be just right. Ain't 'bout not having fear. It's 'bout layin the saw on the wood in spite of it."

I took a deep breath and walked into his office.

"Got an idear," he'd told me when I walked in, just before the call. "Seems The Junior craves a certain sweet nigger pussy. Happens to be mah wife's new maid."

He looked like a cat that'd caught a bird in midair. It was almost as if he really wanted to help—was even enjoying helping—free Mr. E, like a willing partner. Until I reminded myself that his help was only due to his terror of the film stuffed under my mattress.

"After a while, this nigger maid starts complainin to Becky 'bout how The Junior's always pawin at her, and beggin and threatenin her if she don't fuck him. Wants her so bad, won't leave her alone. The maid starts asking if Becky'll help her, maybe get me to talk to The Junior, to let her be, leave her alone." He looked at me, silent, expectant.

"Uh, yes, sir, uh..." I tried to stammer with my best confused look, as May had instructed.

"Well, goddammit, don't ya git it, son?"

"Get what?" I said, with a dazed look any high school acting teacher would have applauded.

"Sure thang not all you Yids as smart as you think, if you any 'xample," he snarled. "Don't you fuckin git that I kin maybe use this information to git him to let that nigger go?"

In his frustration, his elevated Southern accent was devolving into plain old yokel.

"Oh," I dug up an even more befuddled look. "Uh...how?"

"Shit, you are one stupid Jew." He slowly shook his head side to side, jowls swaying like the swings at a park. "OK, so I'll try to explain it to ya real slow now so you kin wrap yer little brain 'round it. The maid tells mah wife that she wouldn't sleep with that man fer a hunnerd bucks. Well, then, Becky, God bless her soul, says, 'Well, whut would you sleep with him for?' That Becky ain't dumb, ya know. She knows we kin always use a favor from that idyit po-lice chief.

"Well, now, the maid kind'a smiles a nasty little grin an says, 'Well now, Miss James, I'm not that kind'a girl.' Well, Becky smiles back and says, 'Well, if you were, whut would it take?'

And that nigger smiles agin and says, 'Well, jest 'tween you'n me, Miss James—you ain't gonna say nothing to nobody, is ya?' Becky smiles even bigger and says, 'Course not, shuggah.' And that sweet piece of nigger cunt laughs and says, 'Well, it sho 'nuf would take at least a couple hunnerd.' "

I looked at him, acting almost stricken, choking, "Even if she would, I don't have 200 dollars to give to her to get her to do it," I said. May had prepared me for this one too.

"Fuck the money, son. The point is that I think we have the solution."

Reverend James looked hard at me, shaking his head side to side, his face blotched with frustration.

This was almost getting to be fun.

"Do you mean that we, you, would pay that maid 200 dollars to have sex with The Junior?" I said, giving him the eyes of a boy making contact with space aliens.

Reverend James snickered, "Well maybe you ain't so dumb after all. Now we just gotta pray that The Junior will take the bait."

In spite of being a nervous mess, the idea that the two of us would ever pray for the same thing almost made me laugh.

After his call to The Junior, as May had tutored me, I asked Reverend James, "Did The Junior promise to drop the charges against Mr. E if you set this up for him?"

"Well, he didn't 'xactly promise. Said he'd think hard 'bout it."

"That's it? Think hard about it?" I said.

"Fuck you, shithead, I'm doin mah best," Reverend James shouted, slamming his fist onto his desk. "I should just call yer bluff and see if you'd really put out them pictures and embarrass and disgrace mah daughter even more than you did after you lied and got her to testify."

"I swear, Reverend James, I didn't know Uncle Herman was going to do that. I never told him about Clara and me. He figured it out. I think Mr. E told him in the courtroom that she was with me that night even though he'd sworn to me when he met her that he never would."

"Fucking liars, all you Jews and niggers."

I took a deep breath, realized that my job was done for the moment, turned around, and walked out.

When I told May there was no concrete deal, she said, "Can't trust either of those creeps' word as far as I can throw them. But it doesn't matter. Jesus be thanked, my plan doesn't depend on their integrity."

CHAPTER THIRTY-SIX

As May had commanded, I was hiding, completely concealed, behind the plush, floor-to-ceiling, velvet curtains that separated May's living room from her dining room.

"Donny, you swore on your God to do exactly what I want you to do and to ask no questions. Right?" she'd confronted me again at her house a half hour before The Junior was to arrive. "Can you keep your oath? Do nothing, no matter what happens. Don't move. Don't step out. Don't talk. Don't do anything but take pictures with your movie camera once it starts."

"But the camera will make noise."

"He won't notice, I assure you."

She'd looked at my worried face, gently pressed her hand against it and said, "Don't worry, my beautiful friend, this plan will work and our friend will go free."

"But what exactly is the plan? I thought you weren't going to have sex..."

"Hush now," she said, handing me a pair of rubber gloves. "Hold on to these until I tell you."

"Are you afraid?"

"I'm ready," was all she said.

Not late by a minute, The Junior pulled up in his customized black Pontiac Bonneville cruiser. The rest of the force drove drab, white Dodge Darts with small, red dome lights on the roof and "City of Danville Police" in black block letters on the sides.

Inscribed on the doors and hood of The Junior's car was "Chief of Police" on one line and "Eddie Baker, Jr." below it, both written in gold-leafed cursive. Blue, red, and yellow lights adorned the roof and rear trunk. Just above the headlights, a pair of spotlights raised up like chrome-plated horns. The Bonnie's dual, Lake's Pipes snorted like bulls in rut.

"My big-assed P-O-N-T-I-A-C," he'd spell out loud with a wink and a grin, slapping the back of anybody when they first saw his car. "Impresses or scares the shit out of most people, whites or niggers."

He rang the doorbell.

May put the needle on Aaron Copland's "Fanfare for the Common Man." She said, "It's one of my current favorites." The drums boomed.

"Take off your shoes and come on in. It's open," May sang her friendly greeting over the music into the intercom.

The chief opened the door, hesitated, looked all around, and walked in, his dick winning out over his caution.

Over the previous spring and summer, four years after May had turned on her red light, Mr. E and I, supervising an army of helpers, had connected her small, lovely, two-story, ash-green home to the one she'd purchased next door. The two houses were so close that, after knocking out adjacent walls, it only took a few feet of boards to connect them.

"In anticipation of expanding my business—or having a family," she'd said.

"How can you afford all of this?" I'd asked.

"Remember that 200-dollar suit? Well, my friend, that would barely cover half of me anymore."

One who had never seen the two houses would assume that this was one original Victorian, with a classic wrap-around porch, stone corbels supporting Greco-Roman style columns, and shuttered windows, the flower boxes overflowing. Its corner gingerbread-detailed, octagonal turrets, multiple rooflines, and clapboard exterior oozed Southern sophistication. Except for the thin, delicate, latticed screens we constructed from pictures in books she had about India. Placed in front of the second-level bedroom porches, they allowed "for privacy, shading, and air circulation—comfort," May had told us, "and the occasional cigar."

The Junior entered the hallway entrance and tugged off his boots, smiling.

"Maybelline Matthews," he shouted above the ascending music, "this here house is the finest nigger house in town."

May, dressed in her starched maid's uniform, stood in the living room, behind the carved oak French doors that separated the living room from the long hallway.

"My, my, don't you look fine," The Junior said when she opened the doors. "Ooo-wee," beaming, whistling, licking his lips like a drunk looking at a full bottle, intoxicated by the notion that finally, May Matthews, *Miss* May Matthews, was going to let him have his way with her. "I know you ain't no maid no more, so I guess you put that tight thang on 'cause you figgured it would get my testicles all raised up." He laughed.

"What the fuck are *you* doing here?" May yelled, with a look of shocked revulsion. "I was expecting Reverend James."

The Junior stopped.

"But, but, but...Jimmy James told me he set...he set this whole thang up."

Then he smiled big.

"Don't play no hard-to-git cat 'n' mouse with me, Maybelline," grinning ear to ear. "I been waitin to stick my big old thang up yo sweet black pussy fer too long a time," he hollered. "Now turn off that damned awful music, sweet thang, and let's git it on."

The trumpets and French horns blasted.

"Well, today's your unlucky day Junior," May shouted, the music building right along with the argument. "I don't know what the hell you're talking about. I wouldn't fuck your ugly-ass white dick if that bastard paid me all his collections for a year. You're nothing but a fat, rotten-toothed, nigger-hatin, shit-stinkin piece of white trash."

For a few moments, The Junior just stood there in the hall, frozen. His face, ruddy and pocked like a yam, drooped. He reminded me of the pudgy twelve-year-old boy I'd known in elementary school who shyly gave a girl a Valentine's Day rose and hand-drawn card only to have her stick out her tongue and say, "You're fat and ugly," as she threw them back at him.

If I didn't hate him, I'd have felt sorry for him.

May was unrelenting.

"You're so full of it, if I squeezed your head, shit would come outta your ears. I'd sooner fuck a pig, you pitiful excuse for a man, and it'd probably do a better job than you anyhow. I don't think even the ugliest black whore in Danville would fuck your sorry white ass, you so ugly and disgustin. They laugh at you behind your back. I'd rather fuck that asshole Jimmy James under his white robe and hood in front of his Klan friends than let you touch my little finger. I'd let a mangy dog fuck me before I'd let you."

The volume and speed of Copland's *Fanfare* intensified.

"Turn off that damned music and come on over to me girl," The Junior said with a pained smile. "You can quit this jokin now honey. You don't need ta make no mo excuses. Yer daddy's been waitin a long time fer this," putting both hands together like a supplicant praying, with a little boy's trying-to-be-cute wink. "Reverend James done told me he's paid ya well," he said with a pleading laugh. "Ah got a receipt!" trying to make a joke.

May screeched back, hollering above the music, playing him like keys on a humiliation piano.

"You can turn your fat fuck ass around right now and get the hell out of my house. If you'd be the last man alive, I'd die before I'd fuck you," jabbing her finger into his belly. "Get the hell out of here, right now," pushing her hand against his chest, "you fat-assed loser." She spit into his face, turning her back on him.

The Junior stood shock still, fists clenching open and closed by his sides.

"You black-cunt-shit-ass-bitch-whore," he said. He reached at her like he'd done to centers as nose tackle on the same championship high school football team as Bobby Stillwell. Even then, with all of his fame, the good-looking girls just couldn't bring themselves to get near Junior Baker. I could smell the sweat glands soaking him with the same acrid stench that probably had driven them away back then.

When he grabbed her arm, turning her to face him, May kicked him in the shin and spit again.

"I said get the fuck outta here, you stinkin cocksucker," she barked.

"We'll see whose suckin cock today," The Junior growled back.

With his prized championship ring with the big, dark red ruby in the center, he backhand slapped her mouth, knocking her against the wall, bursting her lip, the blood flying like sparks from a grinding wheel.

"Donny, don't you move an inch from your hiding place, no matter what. Agreed?" **she'd demanded**.

"But..."

"No buts!"

He ripped at her chest, opening her one-piece uniform, popping the buttons from the top down to the bottom. The uniform dropped to her feet. With the palm of his other ham-hock hand, he struck her face, once, then twice. He grabbed her bra, ripped it off from the front, held her by the waist and yanked off her panties, then pulled her body to his and bit into her left breast. Blood dripped down her nipple.

May screamed, kicking and gouging.

Her blood smeared on his face, he grabbed hers in both hands, forced her mouth open with his thumbs and pushed his tongue into it until she gagged. She bit it. He screamed, "Goddamn you." Her long nails dug into his face, drawing blood and leaving three long, parallel gouges. She beat at him. The thuds sounded like a kid punching a big wad of Play-Doh. Her five foot, four inch, 130 pounds seemed no more than a gnat pecking on a bull.

"Don't do anything, Donny," she'd sworn me. "No matter what! You hear me? No matter what. Period!"

He grabbed her buttocks, pulling them apart, and stuffed one fat finger into her anus as he lifted her up until her head smashed into the antique tin ceiling tiles, let her down, now dazed, ramming two fingers of his left hand into her vagina, twisting and slamming them as deep and hard as he could, ripping at her from the inside.

She shrieked. The trumpets from the stereo blared.

At about the same time, Mrs. Becky James was walking up May's front sidewalk with a bag of clothes. She was prepared, if need be, to tell whomever asked that it was for her maid's collection for poor black children, about the only plausible reason a white woman would ever visit a black's home.

The Junior dropped May to the floor, held her down with one hand while unzipping his pants with the other. He jammed his penis between May's legs. May beat and scratched at his arms, chest, and shoulders, drawing more blood, but not slowing him. Sweat boiled from his body, his face contorted in rage-full pleasure. May puked.

"You don't fuck with *me*," he said, without a hint of the irony, as he started humping and grunting like a bull in heat.

May's shrieks barely registered against the trombones blasting.

"May, May, honey?" Mrs. James's knock and call was lost in the cymbals and timpanis crashing into the climax of the "Fanfare". She walked through the open front doorway and into the living room and screamed.

As The Junior turned to her, she screamed louder, "Oh mah God in hevvin. What is goin on here? What are you doin? Hel-l-lp," she screeched to no one. "Oh, Jesus Christ, it is Chief Eddie Baker. Whut have you done to this girl? Hel-l-lp."

May let out a moan and a wail. Tears streaming down her cheeks, she yelled through her swollen, bloody lips, "He done beat and waped me, Miz James. Hep me, hep me," she cried.

The Junior, his head flinging beads of sweat-stink back and forth, back and forth between Becky James and May, jumped up, tried to zip himself, failed, pushed Becky James against the wall and ran out the door, bootless, dick bobbing. His torn, stained shirt hung out of his pants—blood dripped from his hands and face.

"Are you all right, May?" Becky James cried. "What have we done? How could you let us do this? Talk to me, honey, please, talk to me. Are you all right, May? Talk to me, honey, talk to me," kneeling down to May's limp body, lifting and stroking her blood- and vomit-spattered head. "Turn off that damned music," she said to me just as it ended.

It took a minute for May to collect herself. She puckered her split lip, spit out some blood, dry heaved, took a deep breath, swallowed, then looked into Becky's horrified eyes.

"Can't…thay," May whispered, spitting out more blood and almost, it seemed, sort of smiling, "that-I-haf eva been betta. Now help me up."

May looked to her side, to where I'd been hiding.

"Did you get it all?" she slurred, her lip now swollen to twice its normal size.

"Yes, yes, I did, damn you, May," I answered over my tears and terror, holding my dad's Kodachrome Super 8 movie camera. "I got it all."

I was full of rage at, and admiration for, her. I'd done nothing to help her.

"Good," she sputtered now, blood dripping down her chin, vomit all over her chest. "Now put on the rubba gloveth and put hith boots and his shirt in a plathtic bag, give it all to Mrs. James." She looked at Clara's mother and said, "Pleathe take me to the hothbital."

I carefully put the boots and a piece of his shirt she'd torn off into the bag and handed them to Mrs. James as they walked out the door.

CHAPTER THIRTY-SEVEN

When May first introduced me to the blues, in her little basement room at my folks, she'd said, "The blues are sometimes happy, ironic as that may sound, because sometimes down ends up being up." She was about to prove it to me.

Late in the afternoon, two days after the attack, May called me, so excited that I could barely understand her fast-paced, swollen lipped slurring.

"Donny, come ova here fast ath thu can. Big newsth."

I jumped on my bike, rode like a demon, jumped off, and slung it away before even stopping and, without knocking, barged in and ran across the blood-stained hall carpet to the living room. May and Mrs. James were sitting on the couch, quietly talking and drinking coffee, May more slurping through her swollen lips.

May's left eye was swollen shut. Cotton strips protruded from both nostrils. A big bandage covered most of her forehead and scratches and bruises ran down and across her face and arms.

Becky James stood up as I ran in.

"We visited The Junior today. Sit down," she said as she poured me a cup of coffee from May's ornate Italian machine. Her face was flushed—her smile so big with triumph and worry that I could see tiny cracks in her cake makeup.

I sat down and took the cup, then ignored it as May started telling me the story.

"We walked into the police station, Donny. Everybody there looked shocked—probably as much at the sight of Mrs. Jimmy James walking in with a black woman, much less a known prostitute, as at my horrible looking face."

"I want to thee the chief, right now," May demanded to The Junior's secretary.

"Got an appointment, girl?" She huffed.

Becky James stepped forward.

"Just mention my name, dear. An lets not waste any time doin it, honey," she said in that thick talking-down tone an important Southern woman could command.

"Let 'em in," came back quickly over the squawk box.

"When we walked in, that man turned whiter than a bleached Klan sheet," Mrs. James said to me, laughing, "then redder than a flaming cross."

This came from a woman who had probably Cloroxed those sheets and watched those crosses burn, I thought.

"The Junior heaved a weighty sigh," she said, "closed the door and said in that snail-paced Southern drawl of his, 'So-what-do-y'all- want?' "

He motioned for them to sit down on the stiff, black, cushioned, steel office chairs in front of his desk. Becky helped May sit.

"From the beaten look on his face, you'd have thought he was the one who'd been smacked down," May said to me. "I did enjoy, if that is an appropriate emotional description, the parallel claw-lines of scabs running down both sides of his face."

May got right to the point.

"Junia, I got your boots, some pieces of your bloody shirt, a doctor's report and a witneth, as you can see," May said, turning her head to Becky.

" 'All you saw,' he said, ignoring me and jutting his chin at Becky, 'was me fuckin a black whore. Could say I just ran out 'cause of embarrassment. Ain't no crime nobody 'round here cares much about.' "

" 'Well, then, Junia, what about the movie pictures?' At whith point, Donny, his tough-guy smirk, slacked off ath quickly ath a kicked dog's bark."

"Whaddaya mean, movie pittures?"

"Remember how loud the music wath, Junia? So you couldn't hear the camera. All you did to me ith on film too."

"The Junior's eyes bulged like cotton balls," Mrs. James said to me.

"Who took them pittures?" he yelled.

"None of your goddamn bithness," May replied.

"You tellin me this whole damn thang was a goddamned set-up?"

May stared at him. "A smile would've hurt too much," she said to me.

"Could pour ketchup all over his face and it wouldn't have looked any redder," Mrs. James said.

"Goddamn you, Becky. Always knew I couldn't trust that sum-bitch husband of yers. But bringin you into it all," rubbing his eyes hard with his knuckles, "that breaks all the rules," as if some unspoken law of treachery had been violated.

Mrs. James blurted out, "Junia, my good friend Helen Gant is gonna be trippin all over herself in excitement to publish all of it in her paper, since everybody knows how much you two love one anotha. Tells me you won't even fix a parking ticket for her. Not to mention the exclusive interview I'll give her with me, who just happened to be bringin to May's house some used clothes for the poor Negro children that she helps.

"Helpin to send you to jail is about the only thing that would taste better to Helen Gant than her goddamn gin and tonics. 'Bout the only way I could ever fuckin imagine her helpin to put a white man in jail, even a shit-faced dog like you, for rapin a black girl. Not to mention that you can kiss ever bein mayor goodbye."

"Man, Donny," May said to me with as big a smile as her lips could manage, "Becky blushed like a schoolgirl when she saw both me and The Junior staring slack-jawed at timid-never-cuss Mrs. Reverend Becky James," May laughed now. She looked at Mrs. James and said to me, "Becky lowered her gaze and head almost to her chest in embarrassment, then straightened herself upright just as quickly, looked right back up into The Junior's face, narrowed her eyes, folded her arms across her chest, and glowered at him. I was so surprised and proud of her that I would have jumped up and hugged her if it wouldn't have hurt so much."

Not that, regardless, The Junior didn't have Southern jurisprudence on his side, I thought. Uncle Herman had often lamented about the statistics against his black male clients accused of raping a white woman. "Twenty black convictions to every white found guilty. All a white woman discovered having sex with a black man had to do to save her reputation was to accuse him of rape—worked like a charm. But to get a white man convicted of raping a black woman, I'd need incontrovertible proof."

As May had lain bloodied and fractured on the floor, I'd held that proof in my hands. I'd said, "Let's send the bastard straight to jail."

"Not jail," May slurred through her dripping lips. "Come on Jewboy, I antithipated all thith kind of shit. That's why I made thure I got all the physical evidenth as well ath a docta's examinathon—and tha timely vithit of Becky. Plus, your movie picthures, if I need them. But not for thending him to jail. What good would that do?"

I frowned at her.

"I may be a lot of things, Donny, but I'm not dumb and I knew how the thystem works around here, as does The Junior. Only he never figured in hith wildesth imaginathon that a black whore could beat him at hith own game."

"So what part of my ass do y'all want?" The Junior said to May, running his fingers through his close-cropped hair.

"A spark ignited in his eyes," May said to me. "Sweat beaded all over that pocked face of his like fat drippings on a roasting chicken. I almost puked when the smell hit my nose. Even with all the cotton stuffed up my nostrils, I could still smell it. When he was beating me, that smell was almost as bad as his fists."

"This is about that nigger, ain't it?" he said to them. "You all in cahoots about that nigger, ain't ya? Jimmy said as much, but I never promised nothin. Goddamn his soul, I thought I could have my cake an eat it, too."

"Then," May said, "his whole body flinched—like he realized that his thoughts had popped out of his mouth before his mind could stop them. He looked up at me like a boy slapped trying to steal candy at the store, kind of sorry, but more mad that he'd been caught."

"I want Deacon Eldwidge's convicthon overturned..."

"...matter of fact," The Junior interrupted in a hurry, "I have been re-examinin the so-called evidence against that nigra..."

"...and a convicthon of whomeva really did it," May interrupted back.

The Junior's head snapped back.

"Whoever that is, I don't know," he lied.

"Whomeva," May corrected him, "did it is your problem to dithcova," even though she knew all about Ricky Parker from me.

"The Junior paused," May said to me, "cracked his knuckles and raised his eyebrows at both and Becky and me."

"I guess, then, this terrible attack, Miss Matthews, by some unidentified intruder will then just go unsolved and forgotten. And then you'll just go on with your life, fergit about all this, and give me all of the possible evidence, in case, by some miracle, we ever do find a suspect. Oh," sucking air and looking straight at Clara's mother, "an you, Miz James, will, of course, swear on the Bible to not mention this to anyone, includin your husband and that otha friend of yours."

"Junia, we both did what we needed to do," May said. "If you do the right thing now, I thwear on Jethuth Chrith ath my thavior and witneth, that no one will eva menthon what happened again," and May looked at Becky, who nodded.

"You bastard," Mrs. James said.

" 'Huth now!" May said, turning to her in front of The Junior.

"The Junior's eyebrow flinched," May said to me. "Guess he'd never seen a nigger scold a white woman like that."

With that, May and Mrs. James laughed together, looking at my bewildered face.

" 'Then, I guess we got oursefs a deal,' The Junior said with a nervous smile, as he held out his hand for me to shake on it," May said.

"You got my word, Junia," May said to him, "but I won't take your goddamned hand till my friend *Mithta* Thomas Eldwidge, ith free and the real pupetwator ith convicted."

With that, May stood up, turned, winced at the pain in her hip, and limped out, Mrs. James holding her arm.

"Exthept for the pain I wath feeling, Donny, it wath almoth worth the beating to see that white thcum turn even paler, even though it wath definately going to hurt my buthiness for a while…"

May took out a handkerchief and wiped some drool from her mouth and a tear from her left eye. I was probably as pale as The Junior had been.

"…but worth it, worth it in thpades to save Thomas."

The next day, Reverend James called me.

"Jewboy, I just got a call from The Junior. That son-of-a-bitch police chief said, 'Jimmy, you son of a bitch—guess you mighty proud of yersef fer this. Guess I got no choice but to have a change of heart 'bout that nigger. You still willin to testify?'

" 'Well, sure,' I said back to him. 'You know, Junior, that I am always happy to help you uphold the law.'

" 'I'll remember how I owe you one, Jimmy. So in any case, fer me to pull this shit off, I need ya to do somethin tonight.'

" 'Happy to—what is it?'

" 'Bring me a book of matches with fingerprints on it.' "

Before he hung up the phone, Reverend James said to me, "Two hunnerd dollars well spent on that nigger whore, eh boy?"

CHAPTER THIRTY-EIGHT

The next day, at two thirty in the afternoon, The Junior stood in front of a few reporters and deputies outside the courthouse. Mr. E used to say, "The lazy man'll do and say 'most anything to keep from doin an honest day's work. And he'll brag the most 'bout the least of accomplishments." The proof of it was about to unfold.

"I have an impotant announcement regardin the burnin of the Jew house of worship. The most honorable Reverend Jimmy James has come forward out of the blue with a first-hand confession from the true perpetrata, Ricky Parker. To have someone of such stature stand up fer justice, even if it means freein a nigra, is indeed righteous citizenship and a gift from the Lord.

"Reverend James knows Tommy Eldridge personally, since the man has worked for him many times in the past. He knew that man couldn't never commit such an awful crime. So the Reverend, on his own time and effort, decided to find the real culprit. Even got Mr. Parker to tell him the bushes under where he throwed the book of matches he used to light the fire.

"So, in the name of fair justice, which is my lawful mission, I went and looked and found the evidence which indeed had Ricky Parker's fingerprints on it."

The Junior triumphantly held up a plastic bag holding a book of matches emblazoned with Sonny's Bar-B-Q on one side and a giant flaming pig on the other.

"As po-lice chief of Danville," he almost sang, "I must admit that we have arrested and convicted the wrong man. And due to the high-minded actions and courage of the Reverend Jimmy James, we have found the real perpetrata of this heinous deed. God bless Amurica, where the law applies whether to niggers, uh, negras, or reds, whites, or blues." He paused with a satisfied smile.

"I have talked to the city attorney and the judge and they have agreed to vacate the judgment against the Eldridge fella and to set him free immediately."

The Junior looked almost giddy. He must have come to realize that in one fell swoop he could get the Jewish and black vote without alienating the whites, since their own Reverend James had turned in the criminal. If Machiavelli had been a redneck, he would have been proud to call The Junior a peer.

"Donny," Uncle Herman's voice exploded into the receiver just before The Junior's announcement. He'd called the principal and demanded that he pull me out of class to take the call. "Tommy's been exonerated. The city attorney just called. He's filed a motion to free him based on some new evidence The Junior apparently found that resulted in a confession, and the judge has agreed to vacate the verdict. I can't believe it. There'll be an official announcement today. You know anything about all this?"

"Uh, no."

"Well, whatever happened, I'm just thankful and pleased as all get out. Other than being mad as hell at you, I respect how hard you pushed all this."

All my time in the South and I've still never quite figured out "all get out."

"So am I, Uncle Herman. You have no idea."

"Well, the important thing is that Tommy is free."

"Yeah," I agreed. "I can't thank you enough for how hard you tried too."

"Guess I'll have to forgive you then, whatever the hell was up your butt in court."

At Ricky Parker's sentencing hearing, Reverend James was in oratory as high and bright as his church's golden dome.

"In the name of truth and justice, which everyone in America deserves, even niggers, I have testified against the perpetrata of this awful crime. We here in Danville are good Christians, and we cain't let such evil deeds go unpunished when we know the truth. We must stand with our Jewish brethren, as Jesus would have, against hate as in the Bible. I must therefore admit that the defendant braggadociously told me at a meetin that he set the fire to the Jews' church."

At this point, the Reverend slipped in a brilliant lie, one that simultaneously covered his ass and fulfilled our agreement.

"Judge," he proclaimed righteously, "I personally sat down with Mr. Parker after his braggin and asked him if he wuz ready to ask Jesus fer forgiveness fer this terrible crime. To be honest, Yer Honor, it took him a while to see what I was talkin 'bout. He thought he wuz a hero, and to some, maybe he is." He turned to and quickly gave a little wink to his flock. "But we kept talkin 'cause I was sure that there was good in his heart, havin known his mama and daddy fer years, and that if

I preached to him long enough, he would see the error of his ways. I called them over right then and there at that meetin and we talked all night.

"At 3:00 a.m. Ricky started cryin like a baby, Yer Honor, and as Jesus is my witness, he has since made peace with the evil that wuz inside of him. He did not know that there wuz anyone in that buildin and wud neva have lit that match had he known. For all we know, Yer Honor, that man coulda died of a heart attack befo' the place even caught on fire. Ricky tolt me that I had shown him the light and that he would be a changed man and live the rest of his life as a servant of our Lord, Jesus Christ. He is now one with the Lord!"

The Reverend then took a long pause to let this revelation sink in.

"He swore," he continued, "that he would foreva be a good Christian and would neva do any more evil deeds. Judge, he is saved and I beg you to show mercy to this fine Christian man. As Jesus said, 'Let he who is without guilt cast the first stone.' Judge, we are all guilty of somethin in our own wicked ways. Ricky Parker has asked fer the fergiveness of the Lord. Isn't the least we mortals can do is show the same fergiveness and mercy we ask of God fer ourselves?"

As he went on, Reverend James's voice rose into a booming crescendo. "As the Lord punishes the sinner, he also fergives him. The sooner Ricky Parker walks a free man, the sooner he can live a life of penance, with love in his heart fer Christ and his fellow man, and become a productive, God-fearin citizun!"

With his arms stretched up to heaven, he then let out a thunderous "AMEN!" He walked over to Ricky, hugged him, and made the sign of the cross. Ricky looked a bit befuddled, since, as Reverend Rampbell later told me, Baptists almost never make the sign except at Baptisms. I guess Reverend James knew that the judge was Catholic. In any case, Ricky followed suit. Reverend James then sat down, to the applause of the audience, handkerchiefs at their eyes.

One innocent man, Mr. Eldridge, and two bastards' asses—The Junior and Reverend James, three if you count Tichter—were saved that day.

And, I could almost see the judge sighing in relief. Judges in Danville were elected. He extolled Reverend James as "one of Danville's most important and pious leaders, one who would never say things were they not true."

To Ricky's guilty plea to arson, and in consideration of the city attorney's Uncle Herman-wine-bought reduction of second degree murder to voluntary manslaughter, the judge actually reduced it to what Uncle Herman had said was the proper charge of involuntary manslaughter and gave Ricky one to three years at the city farm minimum security jail.

And The Junior and the judge were re-elected in the next election.

CHAPTER THIRTY-NINE

Reverend James called me the next day.

"Time fer you to deliver yer part of the deal, boy. My office in an hour."

He was right. Mr. Eldridge was a free man, and the trash who torched the temple was going to jail, thanks in part to Reverend James's "two hunnerd dollars well spent" and his eloquent testimony.

As I stood before the door to Clara's dad's office, I noticed again the brass plate attached to the middle of it saying, "Door never locked to the righteous." Between my blackmail and Reverend James's general nefariousness, I thought that neither of us qualified for that door to be unlocked.

I could hear the breakneck, ferocious fiddle of the Martha White Country Music Hour blaring from inside—"Goodness gracious, it's good. Martha White Flour."

I knocked, then walked through the "He Has Arisen" doorway. Clara's father stood up, stiff and hard, his arm extended, palm open, parallel to the floor. Without his even asking, I placed the film canister in the middle of it.

"I still cain't believe it worked so well," he said. His face relaxed and he chuckled, stroking the cylinder like it was a pussycat. "An I'm guessin The Junior's still in bafflement as to why I cared so much 'bout saving that nigger's hiney."

So sudden my breath had to catch up, he grabbed me by the shirt collar.

"This all?"

"I never developed the pictures," I told him honestly, croaking against his choking fist. "It's the original film."

"You not lyin to me, is ya, boy? You nevah made copies to pass around? Nevah gave any fer safekeepin to anyone like you said you was gonna do?"

"No, sir, that was just a ruse. I've never even developed the film into negatives."

I never needed to. And fair was fair. Whether he wanted to or not, Reverend James had done his part. I felt honor bound to do mine, whatever honor remained to me after what I'd done to him and Tichter. "Useless Jewish guilt," Reverend Rampbell would have said to me.

The vein in Reverend James's nose brightened. His face tightened into a mean look, a look like the one he gave me at the quarry when he found out I was his daughter's Jewish boyfriend. He reached into a drawer in his desk. I hoped it was for his flask—a parting drink? He pulled out a Bible.

"Antique Old Testament, book of you Jews. Gift from Rabbi…a gift. Take it!" He shoved it into my hands.

Imprinted in gold leaf on the black, pimpled, leather cover was the word *Torah*, in Hebrew. I opened it. It was all in Hebrew.

"Now, keep holdin it. Do you swear, right now, on your faith's Bible and on all that is holy to you…"

He hesitated. His eyebrows lifted up as if in a sudden epiphany.

"...and on the soul and spirit of that nigger you love so much, that you never made any pitchas and are tellin me the whole, entire truth and are givin everything that has to do with them pitchas to me?"

"Yes, sir, I swear," I answered without pause.

"Look at me, boy!" he said, his eyes boring into mine. "Swear it again!"

"I swear," I felt weak, drained of life.

A slight, almost imperceptible grin cracked the corners of his clenched jaws.

"This was never about you and me, Reverend James," I said. "I'm sorry for forcing you to help, but I just didn't have any other choice. You were about the only one who could've pulled it off. So I've gotta say thank you." I reached out my arm for a handshake.

"Yeah, okay, and I've gotta say fuck you!"

He pushed me away.

"Boy, I'm gonna have to work mah ass off to figure out how to git mah people to understand and fergive me for helpin to free a nigger, much less for testifyin against that Parker boy. I shoulda just kilt you. And if you're lyin 'bout making copies, I'll kill you no matter whut."

"I didn't make any copies."

He shoved me toward the door. "And one more thing–don't you neva git near my daughter agin or I'll kill the both of you. Now get the hell outta here, you little piece of shit."

We were both happy to see me leave, though I was stricken, like a slap hard to my heart, at the idea that Clara and I were done.

One of Reverend Rampbell's favorite sayings was, "Shake hands with the devil and you'll leave with only one." Mr. E's version was, "Make a deal with tha devil, ya git two things: what ya want and what ya don't want."

I was experiencing their truth—though I didn't yet know its entirety.

CHAPTER FORTY

At the celebration in the basement of his church, Reverend Rampbell sang *Hava Nagila* while Reb Gross played his flute and showed everyone how to dance the *hora,* the Jewish circle-dance, with inevitable soul variations. Except for Red, who bounced around like a jumping jack to his own internal rhythms.

"Where's May?" both of the Eldridges asked me.

This was the moment I'd dreaded and been practicing, at May's behest.

"She fell down some steps and broke her nose. Didn't want people seeing her with black eyes and cotton stuffed up it and scratches all over her face. Told me to tell you she'd come by in a few days. Wouldn't even let me bring her soup—said she looked too ugly. You know how vain she is." The soup part was to anticipate and keep Mrs. E from doing just that.

"I'll call her tomorrow. Poor thing," Mrs. E said, Mr. E shaking his head in agreement.

The entire gathering moved in a big circle, the upright piano plinking along once the pianist got the hang of it, the Eldridges waving and smiling in embarrassment from chairs lifted high by the men. Then the Reverend and some others hoisted me up. I waved a Confederate flag hanky and everybody broke up laughing, especially the guys in the corner taking slugs from their flasks, tipping them to me in guilty headiness.

To protect May and her agreement with The Junior as well as my blackmail of Jimmy James, Reverend Rampbell had spread the word that I'd heard some men talking at Dad's store about Ricky and had persuaded Reverend James to help free Mr. E. It was all flimsy, but in their happiness at Mr. E's being freed, no one was in any need to question his version of the truth.

"Colored folks all over town are just smiling inside in pure puzzlement at what you must have done to get that man into a position to have to argue for a black man's freedom," Reverend Rampbell had told me in his office. "But, as you insisted, I've kept my mouth shut regarding the details. I hinted that you agreed to quit seeing his daughter and that seems to satisfy."

It was almost the truth, only not due to my choice.

"And don't think you two can sneak around any more," Clara's father had told me as I was walking from his office after giving him the film. " 'Cause I'm yankin her out of your school and putting her in the Christian Gospel Academy out in Yanceyville and watchin every step she takes between school and sleep."

The party went on for several hours, until Mr. Eldridge reminded everyone, in a commanding voice, that they had to go to work the next day. A group groan chorused around the room.

"Me, especially," he said, an involuntary heave of his chest, suppressing tears.

He looked down at the scuffed linoleum floor. Folks grinned at him, flailing their hands in the air, high-fiving, yelling, "Amen!" and "Bless you, Deacon!" and such. A strained seriousness clutched his face, his eyes moist, as he raised it to look back at them. Everyone went silent.

"I usually try to measure my words as careful as my wood cuts," he said into the expectant quiet. "But, now, tonight, all that seems to want to come out of me is...is…I can't tell you…" He put his hands to his face, unable finally to refuse the tears that he'd held in since his arrest. He wept for the first time I, or probably anyone else, had ever seen.

More "Bless you, Thomas" and "Praise God" rang out, tears flowing in streams of caring.

Mrs. E wrapped her arm tight around his shoulder and looked out over the crowd.

"What Thomas is trying to say…and none of us has ever seen him to be at a loss for words…" she laughed through her own tears, as we all did "…is that we are so grateful for all of your love and kindnesses. We will never be able to give enough thanks. We are so blessed by all of you."

More refrains of "amen" and "bless you" echoed around the hall. Reverend Rampbell started "Amazing Grace," to which all joined in, hands interlocking in another big, sweating, swaying circle. Smiles and congratulations and whooping and hollering abounded.

I looked around with a thousand-mile smile, thinking that this was what religion and a religious community was supposed to look and feel and sound like—spirited celebration and humility and warm embrace and loud, unashamed singing and praising and whooping and thankfulness all wrapped together. It didn't matter what image or name you used for God—only that you celebrated being alive and free. For many there, mired in poverty, that was about all they had to celebrate.

In the midst of it all, a familiar sadness, in addition to being Clara-less, struck me. Why weren't Jews more appreciative and expressive of all that we had to be thankful for—certainly a lot more on the material level than most present?

As the crowd started to disperse, Mr. E walked over to me, put both hands on my shoulders and held me at arms' length, face to face. He lowered his arms, looked at me in a way I'd never seen from him—straight in the eye, without mischief or orders—and extended his hand. "Don't know how or what you did, but…" He stared deep into me, again losing his ability to speak.

I grabbed his hand. We gripped tight, like men do to show real affection. He put his other hand on my shoulder.

"Donny, ta be honest, I never thought I'd be free. I heard all your screamin 'bout getting me out, but black men don't go free just 'cause they're innocent."

I flashed on Uncle Herman saying the same thing.

Without thinking, I pulled him closer, into a real hug, my arm crooked around his neck. I had his strength now. I could feel his body start to go rigid, then felt him let go and hug me back. It was a hug seven years in the making. How could I not cry? But I didn't. I forced myself to savor the moment, to feel what unadulterated gratitude felt like, to appreciate the honor of his surrender.

Mrs. E came over and wrapped herself around us. That's when I cried, as did she. After less time than I wanted, Mr. E shook himself loose.

"Time to go home," he said, standing tall, rearranging his dignity. "There's only so much of this I can take."

We all laughed through our tears.

I was so tired when I got home that I tumbled onto my bed and woke up the next morning, fully clothed and still smiling, "Amazing Grace" still singing in my mind.

PART 2

The Revenge

CHAPTER FORTY-ONE

As I was walking home from school the next day on my normal shortcut through the city cemetery, still whistling the song, a van stopped beside me.

"Whut you doin out here in the graveyard?" the driver asked.

"Just walking home from school." I didn't think much of it.

I figured he was just some guy visiting a grave, on his way out of the cemetery.

From his radio, I could hear a wailing, twangy, high-pitched man's voice singing a country song, the kind I'd told May I hated years earlier, and still did, something about a teardrop on a rose.

"Man, them songs just shoots right through yer heart, don't they?" the guy asked.

More like straight through my intestines, I thought.

"Where you live?"

He had a crew cut, work-dirty jeans, a plaid, worn, flannel shirt, leather construction boots, and tobacco-stained teeth. No different than a lot of guys in town.

"About a mile away, over there," I pointed north. "Forest Hills, by Max's, uh, Ballou Park."

"Hell, I'm headin there to wax my van," he said with a friendly grin. "The air don't stink so much over there. Wanna ride?"

People hitched rides around town all the time. I was feeling tired and lazy from the night before. Plus, he was right about the air. It hung with the cloying odor of tetrachloroethylene, toluene, and whatever other unnameable mix of chemicals Dan River Textile Mills constantly belched out. I'd studied in chemistry that even one part per million of the compounds created a sweet smell in the air and possible cancer. However, with ten thousand textile employees in a city of forty-five thousand, no one, including myself, questioned their right to spray that perfume.

"Sure, thanks." I opened the passenger door as the verse sang, *"I loved, I lost, my story ended..."*

I stepped in, sat down, closed the door, and leaned back against the seat. Before I could even start directions, someone grabbed my arms, pinned them against the seat, wrapped me with duct tape, slapped another piece over my mouth, and put a scratchy burlap oat sack over my head. The duct tape taste was somewhere between rotten canvas and industrial solvent.

As we started moving, I heard the announcer on WDVA excitedly say, "The Hank Williams Tribute Show. Folks, we're gonna play ev'ry dang Hank Williams song ever made, all day long, sung by him and anybody else.

As if being taped to the seat and having to listen to Hank's high, nasal, out-of-tune voice wasn't awful enough, I started hyperventilating from the suffocating oat sack and the tape over my mouth. I forced myself to take long, deep breaths, like my sax teacher had taught me when nerves gripped at the start of a jazz improvisation. But I quickly collapsed into full heart-banging terror when a voice in my head screamed, "When you don't show up at home, your folks will figure that you've gone to a friend's for dinner and forgot to call." Had happened a million times. I'd show up at seven or eight.

The van raced along for what seemed like an hour, Hank Williams still singing his doleful songs. I heard and felt the van turn from paved road to bone jarring washboard dirt and gravel. After another few minutes, it scratched to a stop. I felt more than one pair of arms haul me out. I struggled a little at first, but my thrashing was as useless as a chicken's about to have its neck snapped by the local *shechet,* the kosher butcher. My handlers felt like big, strong farm boys, with a faint odor of moonshine in concert with strong BO. Theirs was from hard work, mine from adrenalin-infused dread.

From the smells and sounds, I assumed that I was in a barn. I could hear the cows chewing their cud. The men used coarse, scratchy rope to tie my waist and legs to some kind of post. They splayed my arms, one to each side, and taped them at the wrist to a horizontal piece of wood. *Another Jew on a cross,* even then my mind said. My feet touched the ground so my arms weren't strained by the weight of my body. Someone lifted the bottom of the hood draping my face and ripped the tape off of my mouth.

"Thank you," I said.

I smelled oats and country cologne, cow shit pies. I'd always liked the smell. It had a sweet, earthy scent, as opposed to horse-shit, which has a bitter, urine pungency. It calmed my trembling a bit. The air was cool, but not cold. I was dripping sweat. At first, I heard feet shuffling on the muddy, hay-strewn, dirt floor, mumbled snippets and the occasional spitting of chaw. After a deep throat clearing, a wad landed on my pants. It crawled down my leg like a slug of depression. I thought I would puke.

Nothing else happened much—just occasional whispers when someone came in to check on me, and the Hank Williams songs from the nearby van. Smells of fried chicken wafted in, like at a picnic. It smelled so good. I imagined their plates full of mayonaisey potato salad, biscuits and gravy, and glasses of Coke. My mouth watered. It made me hungry, and desolate.

Everyone seemed to be taking their time, milling around.

It was dusk outside. Crickets were chirping. I heard an owl hooting. Inside the barn, a flickering light that penetrated the thin cloth of the oat sack brought the smell of kerosene lanterns. Against my parents' wishes, I'd always enjoyed studying with my own small one in my room. Something pleasant about the soft, close light, except for now. I fought against a moan.

A hissing breeze snaked its way through the barn's loose boards. Cows kept shuffling and chewing and barn cats mewing. One rubbed against my leg. Pigeons cooed somewhere above. I could hear the coughs and breathing of a few people standing close to me. I figured they were staring at me like I was some freak show at the county fair.

Then Hank shot a poor-me arrow straight through my heart in a song called *The Lonesome Whippoorwill.* When I heard the line about being so lonesome he could cry, I felt like he was singing it at that moment just to me.

Something tuned inside me, like finding the perfect, static-free radio channel, as I pictured some poor, minimally educated, Southern white boy, maybe like Ricky Parker. I could see him sitting on a splintered, worn porch, a hand-rolled cigarette dangling from his mouth, tired and lonely after a day of hard labor eking out pennies on a hardscrabble farm, wondering when the American dream, which I and other successful, pampered Jews took for granted, would come his way. Or working, day after day, in the mill, ears ringing from the noise of the machinery, covered in cotton dust, wondering how his destitute life could ever bring him a lover or wife. I could see what that boy saw as if his eyes were mine.

For the first time in my life, I could see why he might hate my tribe as we invaded his world and figured it out and grabbed what he wanted. And for the first time in my life, I could appreciate country music and how it spoke to and for that boy—how he must ache in his soul at, and love, Hank Williams's songs. It was so beautifully, poignantly sad and dignified that a tear leaked out of my left eye. *The song's wail might be mine for the duration of my torture,* I thought, *but the tears were everyday for that country boy.* Apart from that understanding, I also realized that my mouth felt like it was filled with his mill dust.

"Can I get some water?" I asked quietly.

"The only water round here is gonna be when you piss down yer leg," one of the gawkers said, followed by laughter and back slapping.

After what seemed like hours, I'd given up struggling against the rope and tape. Dirt dust drifted up my nose from the assembling, shuffling crowd. Hank kept crooning, something about a cold, cold heart.

I encouraged my rational mind to convince me that they might beat me up a little, then let me go. It helped my shivering from turning into useless whimpering. The Klan did rant against Jews and Catholics and non-black minorities, but after all was said and done, we were white.

Someone ripped the seed sack off of my head. I saw a guy with his back to me pulling his white hood down over his head and flashing a big hunting knife. Musical hoods. Almost funny, if I wasn't so scared.

"You really think I was just gonna drop this like wiping shit offa my shoe?" he said. *I knew the voice, so why the hood,* I wondered? He slipped a quart jar of moonshine under his hood and took a big swig. I couldn't help but wonder if it was from Bobby Stillwell's still.

Turning to the crowd, he said, "Brethren and sisters, here is the man who put our brother Ricky Parker in jail for settin a little fire." His voice went louder, with a boozy slur—"another Jew on a cross," he snickered, "but this one's the son of Satan, sent up to despoil and destroy our way of life.

"My daughter told me this Jew bastard drugged her and had his way with her, I'm distraught to say. Even though she was half unconscious, she tried fightin him off. Then he took pitchas of her nekked. Told her he'd beat her if she didn't sit still while he took 'em. Then he came to me and he told me he wud send them pitchas all 'round, as if she'd done it all on purpose, and leave my po, precious darlin, not to mention our family, disgraced, if I didn't hep him git that nigga free and even made me let her disgrace herself at the trial. Ain't that jest like them Jews, nigger lovers one and all."

A chorus of "preach the truth" and "amen" now clucked from the crowd.

The reality of Clara climbing all over me with her passionate kisses flashed in my mind.

"Wouldn't y'all do anything to pertect the reputation and dignity of yer own dawta, if she wuz in that situation?" He took another big swig from the moonshine, half the jar now empty.

"I want ya to know, here and now, that Ricky Parker and his folks and me made a deal. He wuz happy to do his part to pertect my daughta, and in return I have personally hepped him and his folks to pay off their farm, which Jew bankers was about to foreclose on. Ain't that right, Mr.'n' Miz Parker," he asked, as two pointed hoods in the crowd moved forward and back in a yes.

"Right as rain, Rev'rund," they said, the crowd clapping dull thuds into the damp acoustics of the barn.

The payment for the farm was probably the most money that Ricky had ever earned, so to speak, and serving a few years at the city farm with fellow Klansmen would be like a paid vacation.

Why the hoods, if they're using names, I couldn't help but think again.

"And how'd you like that preachin at the courthouse to git his sentence knocked down to almost nothin?" he crowed.

"Ya done good, Rev'rund."

"He had to do it," a plant, I figured, hollered to muttered consent.

"My poor, innocent daughta's very life and reputashun wuz at stake. I did whut any fatha had to do, with the approval and hep of our heroic brotha, Ricky Parker. It is our very basic purpose in life to pertect our women frum the heathen Jews, Cathlics, and devil niggers. There is nuthin mo' sacred then the protection of our women and children, now is there?" he intoned.

"No, nuthin," echoed the crowd. "Preachin to the choir, Rev'rund," someone yelled.

"Let the boy alone now, Rev'rund," a woman's voice. "It's settled now. He cain't do no more harm. You've scared him enough."

Reverend James took another swig.

"Hush, woman," he shouted back. "As his poor folks can now attest, that special man, Ricky Parker, knows he is a hero servin the Lord's mission of preservin the dignity and honah of white people everywhere."

The Reverend was right about one thing. Ricky would now be considered a hero and martyr within his community.

"Praise him, praise God, and God bless the only true protectors of the original white heritage that was and is Amurica," he bellowed. "We are the last of the true patriots, and if we disappear, Amurica will be left to the Jew-black-commie-faggot conspiracy and will descend into the pits of hell. We will not go down without fightin," he stormed.

And with that, he led them all in a drunkenly garbled singing of "God Bless America," just like my family did at Passover, to celebrate the Hebrews' deliverance from slavery in Egypt.

For one of those strange moments, moments out of time and space, when one objectively appreciates someone's special skill or knowledge, even an enemy's—like Reb Gross's appreciation in that diner of Bobby's knowledge about Jewish history and culture—I was impressed by the way Reverend Jimmy James spun and controlled and impassioned this crowd. This man had charisma even in his drunken stupor.

He was the ultimate carnival barker, convincing a crowd that a woman with a beard was one of the most exciting things they would ever see. He worked the crowd like a beautiful, young sales girl could an old man—"Buy it and I'll give you my phone number." He built a picture of a Jew-less paradise, even if it only translated into kicking a teenage Jew's ass. He raised his jar. "Let's take a toast to restorin our white heritage." A wave of pint jars rose above the hooded mass. He guzzled another mouthful. I waited for him to close the sale.

In a hippoesque whirl, he smashed his big, diamond-encrusted ring, the one he'd worn at the rock quarry, against my mouth. My big, front tooth cracked horizontally in half like a piece of chalk. A 220-volt lightning bolt crashed through my skull in a thousand points of pain, spreading and sizzling like the static on the black and white TV screen at the end of the night's programming. Silent courage lost to my scream. I slumped down the wooden post in a daze, my shoulders feeling like they would pop out of their sockets.

"Fer defilin the pure daughta of a true white believer and fer causin damage and harm to our brother, Ricky Parker, we sentence you to the loss of what is most dear to you, scum of the earth Jew bastad, so that you will suffa and feel what you done."

Someone offered Reverend James the knife. As he grabbed it, I remembered how stubby his fingers were against his large palms.

For a moment, in my delirium, I floated over myself, watching my suffering body below, the impartial observer of my own demise. *Fuck, if you're going to do it, get it over with already,* some practical part of my brain shouted inside.

"Ain't done this since I left the farm. Yessir," he almost squealed in delight. "Ain't done this in a long time. Good to be back out here in the country with my people."

He took another chug, almost emptying his jar.

"Nice to have ya back out here with us, Rev'rund," a man said.

"Do it real slow," a voice drifted in.

"Let's take some pitchas," someone said. "We can send 'em to his muther." Everyone laughed a deep, rumbling, nasal kind of hee-haw.

"Or his Jew girlfriend," someone else hollered, which drew an even bigger laugh.

Somelaw Gant's flaming, angry face, ready to fuck my non-existent Jewish girlfriend, shot into my mind.

"It's enough now, Rev'rund," another woman said. "Let the boy go. Cuttin him'll only make trouble for us."

"Shut up, woman," a chorus of men's voices answered. "Nobody here'll ever talk."

As my head cleared a bit, I thought about screaming again, but knew no one would care. I pushed my feet hard against the ground to relieve my arms and shoulders.

"Well, at least let me tell my side of the story. Isn't a man allowed to have one final say?" I shouted with a convulsion as the cool air blazed into my tooth like a soldering iron.

"Well this ain't no movie made by one of them kikes out in Holly-Jew-wood, Ca-ly-for-nie-aye. This the real thang, and I don't rightly give a good petooyee what the fuck you got to say," the Reverend said, his cocktail breath of tobacco and whiskey warming my face—a Klan moisturizer.

"If anything happens to me," I bluffed, "Reb Gross has a set of the pictures."

"Sorry, Jewboy, but you done blown that one. That lie won't stand. You got yerself into a game you had no bizness bein in, then you were too stupid to get insurance. That's why I asked you so hard and made you swear on yer own Bible 'bout did you give me everything?"

Now I remembered that strange gleam in his eyes after I'd told him I'd never even developed the film. That I felt honor bound to give him everything. I remembered seeing the corners of his lips quivering upward in a Cheshire cat grin as I handed him the tin can. I could hear Mr. E warning, "Always ask yourself where your hands and feet are before making any cut." In the glow of freeing Mr. E, I'd failed to check where I stood in reality. *Stupid asshole,* I thought. I'd ignored the obvious saw blade of revenge in those eyes.

"And nobody's gonna think I'd be gnashing my teeth at you, since we was on the same side as that nigger! You dealt the cards, boy, but you didn't know how to play the game. You might be a little brave, that I will admit, takin on someone like me," turning to the crowd, which mumbled a slightly confused *hmmmm,* "but mainly, you stupid."

He finished his jar in a last gurgling swig, staggering in the slippery mud.

"Yeah, stupid fer sure," they concurred.

"And tonight, I'm cashin in yer chips."

He stood up, but tripped on his own feet.

"You will lose the a-bi-li-tee to eva mess with anotha woman, of any kind, much less a good, white Christian one. I'll leave the tool but it won't have no power. Here's one Jew won't rise again!"

Hoots throughout the din, some women's hands flitting over their mouths.

The woman's voice said, "Enough, Rev'rend. We've hurt the boy enough. He's shakin like a nigger at a hangin. He won't be botherin your daughter no more, much less no other Christian girl. Let em go. It's gettin cold out here anyway."

"He's lucky I ain't killin him," Reverend James huffed in a drunken slur, lifting the corner of his hood with a spit into the muck. "It'll be a livin hell for him after I cut him," Reverend James hissed like the devil himself. "Oh, that's right, you Jews don't believe in hell, now do ya?" he cackled.

"No," I spit at him, remembering my comment to Helen Gant, "that's reserved for your people."

James's fist hit me right in the *shnoz*. I heard and felt the cartilage crack. I could taste the blood in my mouth.

He whispered, close again, in his drunken wobble, barely able to position his face near my ear, "I might just kill you anyway. You'll just disappear like happens to niggers 'round here sometimes. Body never found. Nobody'll suspect me, like I said, 'cause we was allies, and nobody here will talk neither."

I had no trouble believing him because the Klan was famous for its practiced silence. I recited my own *Kaddish,* the prayer for the dead.

Some of the men started pulling at my pants legs while another fumbled with my belt. I kicked and squirmed. My pants fell to the ground. Only my white Hanes 100% pure cotton jockey underpants, manufactured in Greenville, South Carolina at my grandfather's textile factory, stood between me and that knife. It gave me comfort that they hadn't taken them off. Maybe he was just bluffing, trying to scare me, and succeeding. Or, in some desperate hope against hope, I hoped that he was being considerate of the modesty of the women present.

"Gimme the leatha strop. I want it to be nice an sharp."

He reached for it and slipped to his knees, struggling to right his moonshine clumsiness as he stood up, his white sheet now a muddy mess.

James started rubbing the knife back and forth, back and forth against the leather. It sounded like Sam's razor sharpening at his barbershop. He placed it into a pail full of red-hot coals.

"Cut and seal it," he said in thick-tongued drunkenness. "Don't want ya to bleed to death. Least not right away. Want ya to have to live with it. Yessuh, Jewboy, we gonna cut and close you up nice 'n' clean. Make a surgeon proud."

I wasn't sure if I'd rather be killed.

"He's a liar," I shouted, nose blood specking his hood. "He's fucking your sons. He's stealing your money. Look at his house and car and clothes. Any of you have such nice things?"

There was a moment's silence and hesitation. But it passed, disregarded by the men as easily as their wives' harpings.

"What we waitin fer?" a man hollered. "On with the show."

I felt myself about to cry, but for once fought it off. *I will not share that disgrace with these scumbags,* I thought. Then I cried, trembling like a man with palsy.

A couple of guys duct taped my hips and upper thighs tight against the wooden pole. My feet were yanked around the back of the pole and taped together. My shoulders sagged and strained.

Reverend James, barely able to stand, gripped the handle and pulled the knife from the coals, almost falling into them.

"Come on, Reverend, let me take ya home now. You cain't barely stand much less make a good cut," a man who sounded just like Dad's banker said close to him. "You proved your point and righteously defended your daughter. Let's get outta here."

The man put his hand on James's shoulder. James shoved him away.

He held the knife high above his head like a knight's sword. The blade glowed fiery red in the dim. He fell to his knees in front of my groin, wobbling side to side, struggling to gain his balance.

"Time to cut the devil outta this here Jewboy," James shouted.

In an instant, I imagined myself castrated—a castrato, like May had told me about—the boys who, until up to the twentie[th] century, had been castrated before puberty. As they grew into manhood, their voices never deepened. The power of their manhood went into their voices. They became the most powerful sopranos—often playing the female part in operas. I imagined myself dressed as a woman, singing, singing so high that audiences shuddered at the power—as Hank Williams's voice drifted into the barn.

Then the crowd's chorus started, a few at first and then increasing to many, "Cut, cut, cut, cut, cut, cut…"

My breath was coming in gulps, heart pounding, slamming against my ribs, my skin cold and hot at the same time. *Maybe this was just a terrible charade and he's finally ready to stop,* my mind screamed. *He's the master of performance. Okay, I am scared shitless, you win and I'm sorry for what I did, but I did it for a good reason and I'm sorry that Clara had to be involved and, oh God, please, let me go.* My mind raced around, searching for an escape. I was a salesman's son—there was always another angle, something else to say, to turn things, to make the sale. I could see the newspaper headline: *Jewish Boy's Head Explodes.*

I remembered reading about a small-town kid and his family getting lost while visiting New York City, wandering into a bad neighborhood on a moonless night and being cornered by a gang of guys with knives. I remembered the boy saying that he had read that bullies often could not handle someone going insane, someone having a heart attack, someone having an epileptic seizure—anything that inserted the unexpected, craziness, into their brutishness. So he fell onto the ground, spitting and shaking and jerking his body and screaming incoherently until they ran away.

I started singing, singing at as high a register as I could, straining my vocal cords, castrato, until my voice was a wire-thin screech. Notwithstanding all of my musical knowledge of soul and jazz, I started singing the only song that came to me, a song from my childhood, a song that a little boy would sing—*I'm a little teapot, short and stout, here is my handle, here is my spout*—I sang—*When I get*—as loud and high pitched as I could—*all steamed up*—I sang—*I just shout*—over and over, even after James's fist landed again, splitting my lip into bleeding slivers. The crowd stood motionless—I imagine with mouths wide open and faces scrunched into question marks under their hoods—staring at the boy they'd driven insane. I sang—*tip me over and pour me out*—as the blood spurted and spilled all over my and Reverend James's face and chest. I sang against James's "shut ups" and others, "that boy's gone crazy." I sang until I forgot that I was forcing myself to sing, to sing in high-pitched agony, until I forgot that I was even singing, until nothing could hurt me, until I forgot who or where I was.

I sang until I smelled my hair and flesh burning as Clara's father laid the glowing blade high and flat onto my inner thigh, then slid it up against my underpants and scrotum. I heard myself go silent as my song turned into a scream.

I passed out to the radio's, *"Jambalaya, crawfish pie, and a file-a gumbo..."*

CHAPTER FORTY-TWO

"Is this Reb Gross?" she stammered.

"Yes, who is zis?"

"This is Clara James. Oh Jesus, oh Jesus, you're the only one I could think to call."

From my stories, Clara knew all about Reb Gross.

"I heard my Daddy talkin on the phone, and he said he was gonna teach Donny a lesson, and he was drunk, and he beat my mom and me and called some men, and I just didn't know what to do or who to call except for you."

As much as a Southerner can, she was babbling as fast as a New York minute.

"Oh God, this is my fault, 'cause I told Daddy about Donny and testified. Oh, Jesus, you got to figure how to help him. I've never seen my father so mad or drunk. He's mean, Rabbi, and he's so mad about that trial. He said on the phone that Donny figured a way to make him turn on Ricky."

"Now calm down, my dear. I vil listen betta if you vud tell me more slow."

"At Butch Johnson's barn," Clara willed herself calm. "I heard him say. In North Carolina, somewhere outside of Yanceyville."

"And vat road is zat on, Clara?" Reb Gross asked, forcing himself not to sound overly concerned.

"I'm not sure," she said. "Oh, Jesus Christ, I don't know. Somewhere off of old 86 South. That's as close as I can guess. I've never been there. Can you help him, please, oh please, Rabbi? Oh please, Jesus, oh please."

"I vil do my best, and zank you, you are a brave girl, just as my Donala has tolt me."

"You know about me?"

"He has tolt me zat you are filled with za light and beauty of a true Christian in all of za deepest, most loving vays zat Jesus vud haf intended. Don't cry," he said softly. "I vil go right now. And, Clara-la, I hope ve may meet at a better time."

"Oh shit, sir. Me too. Hurry."

Ten minutes later, Clara answered the doorbell and insistent knocking at the front door. She hoped, and feared, that her dad had returned.

"Can you show me where the farm is?" the man at the door asked, showing her his credentials.

Clara stared, mouth agape. "I don't understand," Clara said. "What are *you* doing here?"

"Reverend Rampbell called me," he said. "Told me about the kidnapping. He's heading out with some of his old army guys. I need to get there as quickly as possible. I figured you could show me the way."

"But I thought you were…" she stammered.

"I'll tell you in the car," he said. "Will you show me the way? We don't have much time."

"But I don't know exactly where…" And then she froze, stone still.

"You all right?" he asked.
Her head shook in a spasm.
"I know who can find it, Blue. Let's go."

CHAPTER FORTY-THREE

"Our friend Donny Cohen's been kidnapped," Reverend Rampbell told his former army buddies over the phone. "Reb Gross called me. Throw on your old uniform shirts and bring some item of armament and get on over here post haste."

The Reverend used the quick-response telephone tree he'd developed to round up supporters during the first sit-ins protesting against blacks being forced to sit at the back of buses. The police, on horseback, had savagely beaten the protestors with heavy wooden truncheons.

The vets gathered at the BVFW, Black Veterans of Foreign Wars Lodge, the one Reverend Rampbell had set up in the basement of his church because the local VFW didn't admit blacks.

Of his Danville Buffalo Soldier army cronies who showed up that night, Johnny Milburn, Nate Manning, and a couple of others had been with the 370th. They all worked at the local textile mill. Jake Nelpok, 'Doc,' had been a medic with the 317th.

Tiny Hankins, all 350 pounds of him, owner of Tiny's Downhome Bar-B-Q, the best in town, served in the 365th while

Jimmy Johnson and Bert Russell, tobacco farmers, had served with the 371st Infantry Regiment.

Tommy Hankins, Tiny's brother, brought his war-booty-captured, rusty, Italian army revolver with its equally rusty unused ammunition. He'd suffered such severe head wounds fighting in the 599th Field Artillery Battalion that he received permanent disability. A metal plate held his skull together, giving it a significant dent on one side and a bulge over one sagging eye on the other. He looked so misshapen that some people were afraid of him. But if you took the time to talk with him, you'd find that he was a nice guy. He told great war stories when he'd come into our store if one had the patience to listen to his slow, slurred speech.

Enid Harper of the 92nd Cavalry Reconnaissance Troop lost an arm in the war. Even with only one arm, he could still shoot ducks better than anybody.

Jimmy Townsend, who'd been with a maintenance battalion, had an auto repair garage that earned complaining refrains like "Bring in your heap, leave in a weep." Mr. E had said of his work, "Sorry to say, proves black skin don't necessarily translate to honest."

Once they'd all arrived, the Reverend told them, "Rabbi Gross called me and said Jimmy James got some Klan boys to do it. Probably just going to scare him, but with that crowd, who knows what they might do? We've got to go out and try to help him. You boys comin with me?"

"Well, whut about Dr. King and our pledge of nonviolence?" Jasper Reid, former army cook, asked.

"That's for civil rights. This is about kidnapping and maybe killing. Plus, don't forget," Reverend Rampbell said, "Gandhi was Dr. King's inspiration, and Gandhi once said the only reason he chose nonviolence was because he had no guns. We got guns."

"So what we gonna do?"

"Well," replied Reverend Rampbell, "I guess we'll just go out there and see what happens. Guess I'm hoping that white trash will be so shocked by our guns that they'll high-tail it outta there." He gulped and offered a weak grin.

"You kiddin," Enid snuffed. "We jest a bunch of crazy niggers to those folks."

"Unless, Enid, you've got a better idea, and let's hear it quickly if you do, that's about all I can think of. We can't just do nothing after all Donny's done to help get Tommy free."

"You sayin you actually willin to shoot a white man?"

"Hell, Enid, we shot white Germans."

"Yeah, but at least we had a chance against them—an we was legal soldiers."

"Well, hellfire, Enid, are you willing to do nothing then?"

"Shit," Enid said, with a grimace. "Let's go!"

Tommy rode with Reverend Rampbell in his Cadillac. Enid and Jimmy drove their pickups, Johnny and Nate sitting inside with them, the others sitting outside in the beds of the trucks.

Once they got to the Yanceyville area, ten miles over the North Carolina border, they drove the dark county roads, up and down, back and forth for about fifteen minutes, not quite lost but not quite sure where the farm was either.

Eventually, they found Butch Johnson's roadside mailbox, situated high above his bottomland farm, turned off their lights and parked. Looking down from the woods above it, Enid quickly reconnoitered the area, taking in information from Johnny Milburn, who knew the basic layout because he'd picked tobacco and helped slaughter and smoke pigs there.

From the parked trucks and cars, they figured the Klan crowd had gathered at the tractor and livestock end of the big red barn. To avoid being heard, Reverend Rampbell and his crew used army hand signals to sneak to the other end. They gathered close to the ropes dangling from the cantilevered hayloft bale pulley and hoisted one another up to the second floor loft, emitting whispers of, "Shh, shut the fuck up!" when the pulley squeaked or someone grunted from the exertion of long unused muscles. After a few minutes, all were safely up.

Enid and Reverend Rampbell silently directed the men to fan out into positions behind hay bales above and around the crowd.

The first thing Reverend Rampbell saw when he looked down from his hiding place between three stacked hay bales was water being thrown onto my face, splashing me back to consciousness. Jimmy James was kneeled in front of my groin, my scrotum in one hand, his Bowie knife, burned into my thigh, in the other.

I felt an icy burning on my thigh. My underpants lay crumpled on the ground, singed and sliced through. But my brain somehow registered that there was no blood running down my legs, just plain old, *thank you, God,* pee.

"I order you, in the name of the United States Army, to release that boy," Reverend Rampbell's deep base voice, sounding like God's own command from above, shouted to the mass below and into my foggy brain.

The hoods swayed in unison, eyes frozen upward.

Tommy, Tiny, and the rest of the Buffalo men rose from behind their bales on either side of the barn, their weapons still concealed.

"What the fuck?" was all Jimmy James could get out at first as he looked up from between my legs. And then a complete sentence, "Whut the fuck you niggers doin up there?" he shouted. I could smell the alcohol on his breath.

A chorus of "Whut the fuck" echoed around the barn. After a few minutes of motionless confusion, the Klanners rushed toward the hayloft ladders, shouting, "Git them niggers."

Reverend Rampbell ordered, "Raise arms and prepare to fire," at which point three World War II army-issue assault rifles, four twenty-two rifles, three shotguns, one rusty, captured, Italian-Army-issue side arm revolver, and one long ax handle

("Couldn't find my fuckin ole carbine," Tommy said later) were raised up from the hay bales and pointed down at the white mob.

"Stop where you are or we will shoot to kill," Reverend Rampbell barked.

The back of the surging crowd splashed over and knocked down those in front. They hadn't brought any guns, figuring they wouldn't need them for one bound-up boy.

"Well, mah God," Jimmy James stammered from between my legs, then snickered when he spied Tiny, who had gained about 200 pounds since he last wore his uniform, his big belly folds erupting from his old shirt and pants like mounds of jiggly chocolate pudding. "You is the most pitiful lookin bunch of niggers I ever seen. And you 'bout to git yerselves kilt here, ya hear me, 'cause you might get a few of us, but then we'll kill you all and feed you to the hogs."

"Yessuh, let's kill them niggas, boys," someone shouted.

"WAIT. RIGHT. THERE!" Reverend Rampbell ordered in a stentorian tone honed from years of commanding men against the Germans and by even more years of charismatic preaching.

"I've—we've—," he took a quick glance around the loft, "faced far worse than you in the big war. And we're all expert marksmen, I can assure you." His face was shiny with sweat.

The crowd froze into a murmuring field of pointy hats.

Their "discussion" was broken by a rumbling noise, getting louder and louder.

Then Reverend James barked, "What the fuck is *that*?"

Everyone turned in one motion toward the barn doors.

In my fog, the rumble seemed like distant thunder, moving closer and closer until it was deafening. My tooth seared with every cold breath. My thigh boiled blisters from where Jimmy James had laid his knife. The skin of my scrotum tingled from the heat and anticipation of the kiss of the blade's edge. Red drool seeped from the corner of my mouth onto the sweaty hand of the hairy-armed man covering it.

Guns pointed and fists clenched. Sweat, hate, confusion, adrenalin, barn animals, and hay conspired to create a pungent stink. I peed again onto Reverend James's hand.

"Goddamn," he yelped, pulling it and the knife away, standing up and shaking off the wet indignity. He struggled to his feet, wobbled in the mud, and stepped forward to the edge of the crowd.

It seemed like an hour, but it was really only half a minute. The noise came right up to the barn—roaring, revving—then silence.

No one moved.

I saw an arm rise above the throng, launching a pocketknife up at Reverend Rampbell. The small blade penetrated the left shoulder of his hard leather jacket. He grabbed it and yanked it out with an impressive flourish and sneer as if nothing could hurt him.

In the next moment, the big barn doors opened. In stepped a huge, bearded, sumptuously gutted, greasy-blond-haired man, holding a long, metal pipe. An unkempt gang, wearing black leather jackets, followed. *Klan reinforcements,* I thought. Reverend Rampbell and his boys were in deep shit.

Blinking through my soggy mind and eyes, I noticed a word in big, embroidered letters on the bearded man's sleeve, above his swastika: *Jewdawg.* I blinked again. Yep, *Jewdawg.*

Up from behind, skullcap bobbing on top of his wild curly hair, *tzitzit* swirling out above his pants, ran Reb Gross, *mateh* held high, tears flowing.

"What the hell you boys doin here?" Bobby Stillwell shouted. He looked up to the hayloft. He looked down at the Klan horde. Back and forth, up and down, back and forth he looked, just shaking his head, until he lowered it and settled on the conehead in front of me.

"Care if we join in the fun?" he asked, grinning through two front teeth with the most beautiful decay holes I'd ever seen. A dribble of chaw juice stained the corner of his mouth. "You know we party animals, don't ya? Cain't have a big shindig like this without invitin us, can ya? Kickin nigga ass 'bout as fun as it gits, ain't it? Though it looks like you fellers might be at a slight disadvantage 'bout now," he said, chortling and flicking his head up once more at the black army, "what with them guns pointed at ya. Lettin a bunch of niggers—" But he caught himself and looked sheepishly back at Reb Gross, who'd elbowed him and given him a dirty look, then pointed to me.

From the confused stillness, one of Bobby's crew, staring up, hollered, "Get them niggers."

For a second, all eyes turned to him. Then Bobby said, "Not them, you idjit. Theys here to help the boy."

"Oh," the guy said with frown.

Reverend James, like everyone else in the county, knew Bobby as the championship football player and war hero gone bad after having been awarded the Purple Heart and Silver Star for rescuing five injured men in Korea, the last survivors of his squad, under heavy enemy fire.

"Now, Bobby," he said, "this ain't none of yer affair, so you can just leave right now and nobody's gonna have any trouble. We'll handle them niggers just fine on our own."

"That so?" Bobby answered with a gleeful giggle. "Well, trouble seems to be mah middle name, big feller. And I reckin that there's a friend of mine you cutting on, so why don't you just let him go and we'll be out a yer hair. Then you folks can finish yer little fight with them niggers up there." He chuckled and looked back at his gang, who snickered with him, except for Reb Gross, who looked grief-stricken.

Clara's father looked around. There were about forty of his guys to Bobby's fifteen. But that's like comparing a high school football team to the pros. The Klanners were used to sneaking up on isolated, lone blacks. The Tarantulas liked to fight, even if they got beat up–it was like a gladiatorial epic. Fighting was just part of the fun and rock 'n' roll of life. Still, they preferred fights that were at least a challenge, like good athletes who want to face the best competition to see how they measure up. And Bobby, I'm sure, was almost disappointed by this group.

But Reverend James didn't seem to understand the equation.

"Now, listen here, son," he said, chest puffed out but the knife shaking in his hand. "Why don't you all just look 'round and see all of us and then just get on yer way and mind yer own bidness? It's only a fuckin Jew. And we'll take care of them niggers ourselves, too."

"Well, that may be," said Bobby, grinning and looking up at Reverend James's crew—in seeming agreement with Jimmy James that a Negro army of guns was irrelevant—"but that just happens to be a Jewboy," pointing to me, "who's a friend of the ol Reb's here, who's a friend of mine." He gave an affectionate nod to Reb Gross.

Reb Gross, tears racing down as fast as his Harley, pleaded, "Please, sir, ve just vant Donala back and no more trouble. Please."

At that moment, a big knife flew right at Bobby. He wobbled backward one step as Reb Gross, with a sad and indignant look of defiance, lunged against and in front of him. *WHACK!* With hairbreadth precision, just inches in front of Bobby's face, the Reb had snagged the knife with his *mateh*.

"Well, shit, Reb," stammered Bobby, "that's the second time you saved my scrawny ass."

With that, the melee ensued.

Reverend Rampbell and his pack, mouths agape, stood frozen in the hayloft.

I saw a man sneak behind Reb Gross—about to hit him. But, in an instant, the Klanner was on his back. Bobby beamed his decayed grin at Reb Gross, holding up his metal pipe and yelling, "Got him with *my* mah-tay, Reb. What you think? Pretty good, huh?"

The Reb managed a weak smile.

The mob migrated in a cacophony of slaps, grunts, yells, and moans toward the open barn doors, leaving me at the stake with my hooded guard. Suddenly, he crumpled to the floor. Reverend Rampbell had jumped silently from the hayloft to the hay-padded barn floor and thwacked the man's head with his rifle butt.

"Haven't done that since '45," he said, his rifle held in front of him, ready for the next assault.

As before, in a grimy about-face, heads turned in unison and motion stopped, this time at the sound of sirens and flashing lights blaring through the open barn doors.

The Junior and a few deputies, guns drawn, rushed in. Seems Clara had called more than Reb Gross. The chief looked around with the amazed expression that was becoming commonplace.

Many of the Klanners were on the ground. The Junior looked up and did another double take.

"What the…?" was all he could manage as the Buffalo Soldiers, guns awkwardly held, waved meekly, sort of smiled, but mainly shuffled side to side.

"Evenin, Chief," Reverend Rampbell spoke, "I—we…" He looked up into the loft, back at The Junior and shrugged, raising his free hand palm upward, letting his rifle butt settle back to the ground.

The Junior, scratching his head with the end of his gun barrel, slowly looked down at the fallen sheetsters, then at Bobby and his boys, and once more back up to the soldiers.

"I guess I have seen it all now," he said, shaking his head.

He walked right up to the still-hooded Reverend James, ceremoniously tore off his hood, tossed it into the muck with a dramatic flick of his wrist and announced, "You," poking his finger against Reverend James's chest, "you son of a bitch, are under arrest fer kidnappin, assault, battery, and maybe even attempted murder of this boy."

I watched The Junior's face tense, struggling to stifle a smile—but he couldn't hold it back. I could see his satisfaction at paying back Jimmy James for luring him into May's web of deception.

As the clumps untangled, The Junior asked a few questions while his deputies arrested a few more Klanners.

"You all right?" He winced as he looked at the mess of my face and down at my groin. I was glad he didn't know I was the one who filmed his rape of May.

Doc, who had continued his family tradition as a country healer, jumped down and cut me from the tape as Reverend Rampbell held me up.

"Well, I been better," I slurred, my hand jumping to the fire in my mouth.

"Better get you to the hospital," Doc said.

The Junior looked at Bobby and his crew, "Fer Christ's sake, Bobby, y'all get the hell outta here now, before I arrest you, too."

He fell silent at the sight of Reb Gross, staring at the hunting knife imbedded in the eagle's skull atop his *mateh.* The Junior's mouth opened as if he was going to say something, but no words came out.

"Zank you, Sheriff." Reb Gross smiled, holding out his hand.

"I'm the Police," pronouncing it po-lice, "Chief, not sheriff, but sure nuf, yer welcome." He shook the Reb's hand with the puzzled look of a man coming late to an inside joke he'd never understand.

"An you boys, uh men, what the fuck you think you was doin here, anyway?" he said, looking over in stupefaction at Reverend Rampbell and up at his soldiers. "And what on earth is you doin in them old uniforms pointing them old fuckin guns?"

I think his exhilaration at arresting Jimmy James must have put him into a tolerant, or at least generous, mood.

Reverend Rampbell smiled.

"Just helping a friend," he said. "Best we could think of."

"Well, now, how 'bout just getting the hell on out'a here along with all the others."

Just as the exodus commenced, everyone once more turned toward the sound of horns blaring. A parade of big cars—Cadillacs, Buicks, Lincolns—rolled toward us down the long driveway, headlights flicking on and off.

"Now whut?" said The Junior.

When the cars stopped, out popped Rabbi Mordechai Tichter, Nadya, and a dozen or so Orthodox Jews. As they rushed into the barn, we all stood there, dumbfounded at the sight of a bunch of men in suits and fine leather shoes, most, I later learned, WWII vets too, carrying carving knives, rolling pins, heavy mops, and even a big salami, *tzit-tzit* hanging out of their shirt bottoms, *kipas* on their heads, accompanied by a woman in a shawl and plain black dress.

"Is he all right?" Reb Tichter dully asked The Junior. Even in my current state, I couldn't help but think that he probably hoped otherwise.

"Five minutes ago, I thought I had seen it all. What in the hell?" said The Junior, looking at Nadya, "Scuse my profanity, ma'am. Whut did you folks think you could possibly do here? I mean, whut? A meat stick? Mops? Now, if you don't mind, how 'bout just gettin back in them fancy cars and gettin the hell, sorry agin ma'am, outta here."

The Orthodox posse looked at each other, looked at all of the others looking at them, looked back at The Junior, raised their eyebrows and shoulders and started to turn around to leave.

The Junior, I guess, realizing that this was a "Jew vote" opportunity, turned back and shouted, "I thank y'all fer comin, even if I didn't need ya. You is good citizens. I got nothin 'gainst you Jews. I'm truly thankful we caught the man that burnt yer church."

"It wasn't ours," Tichter sneered, just as a white Dodge sedan with a blue, blinking bubble on the roof raced, zig-zagging across the field north of the barn, the only way to avoid the crowded car lot.

As the car slid to a stop by the barn door, the driver's door and the two back doors snapped open. Out rushed three square-jawed, serious-looking white men in dark blue suits and one other white man, Blue, the mechanic, in a greasy mechanic's uniform—and one crying, cringing, bruised, blotchy-faced girl, my Clara. With guns drawn, the three men ran to The Junior and his assemblage of Klan prisoners, flashing badges, Clara right behind them. Blue stumbled over in drunken clumsiness.

"FBI, stay where you are," one of the agents shouted.

I blanked into some sort of trance and saw, instead, John Coltrane jive-talking, *Ah, the FBI note, the resolution. It's a fucking musical farce,* he cackled. *The sacred culmination of the major scale and the satisfying, uplifting, unifying, climactically explosive final note in the arpeggio of Donny's rescue chord.*

"Wow," I heard myself mumble.

"What?" Clara said, standing there hugging herself, staring at my charred nakedness and glaring at her dad. She stepped forward, put her hand to my face, looked down, and feather-touched my thigh, looked up at me dewy-eyed, then wrapped her shawl around my legs in a fever of modesty. I yelped.

Still held by one of The Junior's deputies, Reverend James's mouth opened as if he was about to say something, but stopped when the passenger door of the sedan opened.

He and the throng stared, bug-eyed.

Dreadlocks jiggling, bells tinkling, walking calmly, almost casually, a concerned smile on his face: Red Combs.

I snapped back to…reality?

"Whew, almost missed all the action." He looked at me, winked, winced, and shook his head. "Didn't mean to let it get quite this far," carefully caressing my face with that same gentle touch I'd felt at the temple fire. "Took us a while to find this place," he said.

"Had to stop on the way to pick up a friend," Red said with a grin, looking over at Blue, who looked hard at Clara's dad and said, "Fucking asshole." Red walked over to The Junior and flashed his badge.

"Lincoln Perry, Special Agent, FBI, Civil Rights and Hate Crimes. We'll take over from here, Chief, if you don't mind."

The Junior stood, slack-jawed, staring from the badge to Red.

"But…but," he tried, but gave up without a fight as he kept staring at the badge, then back at the "crazy nigger."

"Clara, darlin," Jimmy James said as he reached out to her, "that nigger force you to come out here with him? Baby—"

"Fuck you," she said and spat into his face—a nice, big *lugee* landing on his nose, dripping to his lips.

Red walked over to Jimmy James. "James Wilkes James, I arrest you on the charge of kidnapping across state lines, assault, battery, and attempted murder."

"Fuck you, nigger," Reverend James spat at him, more spray than Clara's success.

Special Agent Perry wiped the moisture off of his face, moving the inside of his sleeve across it in one slow, fluid, graceful motion, followed by a fast, furious, whip-like recoil backhanding James across his face. Nose-blood washed Reverend James's face as the agents held his arms firmly at his side. Red, serious as a Calvinist preacher for once, shook his head.

"I'll be sure to send you some cinnamon sticks in prison, Reverend."

The agents led him away.

Red? Special Agent Perry? My pain suddenly ran a distant second to wonder. He turned to me.

"We've had him under surveillance for the last two years. You too, Donny, since the fire. Klan activity, racketeering, money laundering. Just been waiting until we could catch him in the act. It's why I came to town. He's the big *kahuna* of this whole area. He's slick, but when he took you across state lines, we knew we could at least get him on federal kidnapping. That's enough to put him away for a good many years by itself. We'll throw a few of his other pals into jail, too, enough for us to bust up his little group here. Sorry I got here so late, Donny. Really sorry."

He gently smiled again at me.

"Me, too," I managed to slur, wanting to hear more.

He reached out to shake the hand of Reverend Rampbell, now standing at my side. "Sorry, Linc," the Reverend said. "Got so excited I forgot to call you until we were out the door and halfway here. Maybe could've saved Donny-boy here some grief."

"You knew about him?" I said, sort of pissed.

"He swore me to secrecy—oath on the Bible," Reverend Rampbell shrugged. "Sometimes, you've got to keep secrets, even from your friends, to save the world. What's next?" He looked back at Agent Perry for relief.

"Didn't really think it would end this way, but we got the bad guy in any case. Guess I won't be making any more appearances around here," he said. "I'll kind of miss this place. Enjoyed myself. Met some nice people. Got to exercise my thespian chops. Coming from Detroit, I never really got to experience my Southern heritage. So it's been nice for me, connecting with the black community and just feeling what it's like down here for them. Always wanted to sing in a gospel choir, too. Didn't hurt to get to know Maybelline, either," he winked and laughed.

"So Red was all an act"? I said the obvious.

" 'Fraid so," Red, Agent Perry, answered. "That's what undercover's all about. Pretty convincing, eh? Stepin Fetchit's always been my hero. And Stymie in "Our Gang." That boy could talk his way out of anything. I must admit, though, it will be good to get back to my old self. Still, I will miss seeing and whistling at Sylvie's beautiful mammary displays outside her church every Sunday," at which point he couldn't help himself and starting cackling, slapping Reverend Rampbell on the back, laughing together. "She *is* a mighty fine white woman. Some parts of this job are just about as good as arresting bad guys. Whew!"

After they stopped laughing, he carefully took my arm, holding me up as I stumbled, and moved me a few feet away from everybody. Clara reluctantly moved to the side. He put his head close, right in front of my face. With his deep, watery eyes, he looked into mine, like he had at the fire, and whispered, "You've done well. Be proud. I know most of the story from—" He turned his head toward Reverend Rampbell and they exchanged smiles. Red hesitated, then, audible only to me, said, *"Yasher Koach. Tikkun olam."*

I frowned, narrowed my eyes in astonishment.

"What?" I said. I assumed that in my muddled state, I must have misheard him.

"Tikkun olam," Red, Special Agent Perry, repeated. "You've repaired a bit of the world." He put the palm of his hand on my heart—his face shined with a golden smile. "Raised since three by Murray Hill, my Jewish stepdad. Wish you could've been at my *Bar Mitzvah.* Maybe the first black one in Detroit. *Shalom,* my brave friend."

He rubbed the top of my head, giggled just like Red would have, turned around, looked back at me, grinned that Red grin, winked, jumped up, clicked his heels, and walked back to the car.

I stared, then went wobbly. Clara stepped over to me and gripped my arm.

Seeing this, Nadya shook off Reb Tichter's hand on her arm and ran to me.

"Oh, Donala, are you all right?"

I tried to smile through my tooth's pain, the oozy slobber of snot, caked blood, tears, sweat, and my swollen eye.

"Thanks for comin," I said.

From the sleeve of her blouse, she pulled a handkerchief, spit on it and started to wipe away the mess on my face. She smelled so fresh and clean. I wanted her, like a mom now, to hug me and kiss away the pain—but she scrubbed hard, leaning heavily into me to balance herself as she slowly sank into the wet, muddy, cow-shit muck we'd migrated to. I flinched at the pain and turned my head away.

"I'm OK," I said to stop her.

Reb Tichter slipped me a vicious look, then a side glance at Jimmy James.

"Let's go," he demanded, yanking Nadya's arm again and pulling her outside. She was weeping, hitting him with her free arm, struggling to turn back to me. Once again, I felt helpless.

"Let's go, too, Donala," I heard Reb Gross say softly, like out of a dream. My legs suddenly went rubbery. Reverend Rampbell grabbed me under one arm, Clara the other.

"Oy, oy, oy," the Reb kept weeping as we walked, me more stumbling. "Vat haf dey dun to you?" he moaned as they loaded me into Reverend Rampbell's big red Caddy for the ride to the hospital. Clara was kissing my cheek, her salty tears stinging.

"That scumbag," she kept saying.

Abruptly, she stopped. With her hand, she turned my face to hers, squeezing my cheek, hurting me.

"Goddamn it, tell me why. Why'd Daddy do this?" she said, tight-eyed. "Truth time."

I hesitated and closed my eyes for a second.

"Can he tell you later?" Reverend Rampbell asked, rescuing me. I wanted to kiss him. She looked at me, demanding, angry.

"Tomorrow, I promise," I answered.

"Goddamn right," she said. I shook my head up and down in a big nod. She started crying again, kissing and caressing my gooey face. "That fucking scumbag."

In his car, Reverend Rampbell opened his glove compartment. "Wait a second."

I was expecting Kleenex.

He pulled out a fifth of Southern Comfort.

"Take a slug. It'll make you feel better until we get there."

I did, he did, she did, and it did. The whiskey anesthetized the exposed nerve on my tooth for a few seconds.

"Jesus Christ," Reverend Rampbell said when he saw me in the light of the car. "You really got yourself into a mess. You look like shit, I must say."

"Oh, thanks," I slurred over my swelling, blood-caked lip, taking another slug. I flinched against the sting, then relaxed into its warm comfort. "You don't look so great either—pretty fat in that old uniform," I slurred through my swelllen lips.

He pretended to scowl at me.

"My, my, that sure was some scene," he giggled.

"If I wasn't so scared," dabbing at my leaky nose, trying not to inhale, "I would've laughed at you guys myself."

"Did you see the look on Jimmy James's face when my bunch of Negroes and I stood up with our guns?" he chortled. "I don't think I've ever seen the word bafflement better described."

I started chuckling too, wincing with every breath.

"In the name of the US Army?" I said. "Where did that come from?"

Now the Reverend was really starting to laugh. "Well, I…I was at a loss for words. Never happened before. But I had to say something, and fast, what with that knife about to end your love life. Oh, my Lord," he said, his laughter now a roar.

"Never known you to be at a loss for words, either." I slobbered. "But still, it did—" and we were both choking on laughter now—"make them stop and think."

Clara, face scrunched up like a dried-up crone, looked at us like we were demented.

Reverend Rampbell took another big gulp from the bottle, then I did and then Clara.

"How'd you like me pulling that knife outta my jacket and snarlin like I was Clint Eastwood? Truth is, that tiny knife barely made it through the leather." Reverend Rampbell was starting to weave back and forth on the road from cackling so hard. "Man," he said with a Southern accent, "they ain't neva seen no nigga snarl like that, I 'spect."

I had to grab the wheel to keep him from running off the road.

"You guys are nuts," poor Clara said, having a hard time getting into the spirit.

"And the look…that look, oh my, the look on The Junior's face," the Reverend was definitely losing it now, "when he came in and kept looking back and forth, back and forth between us and the Klan boys and the Tarantulas…oh my, it was better than the Keystone Kops," he hooted.

I was getting worried about our safety because the Reverend was bending over and swaying and convulsing so hard that he could barely catch his breath. And I was almost as bad, even though I kept wincing and grabbing the wheel.

"And then…and then…when Rabbi Tichter…" he was snorting now between the words and laughs, "and his Jew posse came with their suits and wingtip shoes in those fancy cars—oh my Lord and savior."

At which point his head fell sideways onto my shoulder, the Reverend guffawing.

"The Jew Klutz Klan," he screamed.

Clara reached over me and grabbed the wheel.

"I thought The Junior was gonna start crying," he whooped.

"And the one with the salami…" the Reverend roared, tears rolling down both our faces.

"Oh Jesus God, pull over, pull over," Clara begged. "You're gonna kill us."

Reverend Rampbell finally took back the steering wheel, pulled to the side of the road, and stopped the car.

Reb Gross, riding his motorcycle at the head of the Tarantula pack escort, saw us pull over, did a 180, got off of his bike and came back to us.

"Are you OK?" he looked in, worried.

We were laughing so hard, Clara moping, we were flopping onto the seat, hands slapping our thighs, wiping our tears on our shirts, wailing, not able to stop until we almost couldn't breathe.

"Vat?" The Reb looked incredulous. "Vat's so funny?" he asked, almost indignant.

"Niggers and Klan and Tarantulas and The Junior and the Jews and…and," Rev. Rampbell said between our gasping whoops, "and …" Reb Rampbell pointed at Reb Gross, "…and you," as he handed the Reb the booze bottle and screamed in another spasm of laughter.

It took a minute for it all to register. But slowly a smile spread on Reb Gross's face, then he let out a bit of a giggle. He took a swig and finally started laughing, more and more, until we were all about to pee in our pants. Well, I already had, several times, in Clara's dad's hand. After shaking her head and fighting against it, even Clara started to get into the spirit.

"You're all nuts," she laughed. "Gimme that fuckin bottle."

As Little Stevie Wonder's *Uptight (Everything's Alright)* blared on the radio, Bobby's head bobbed into the open window.

"Whut the hell's goin on?" he asked, taking a good look at Clara's heaving chest, raising his eyebrows, and winking at her. Reb Gross handed him the bottle. Bobby automatically took a big swig.

"Black minister...white boy...rabbi...and you guys on Harleys—Jewdawg," was about all I could say. Gotta hand it to Bobby, it didn't take anything else for him to break out in a bellowing laugh, too.

On the side of a lightless, county dirt road, in the middle of nowhere, all of us, like drunken fraternity brothers, kept laughing and howling and drinking and crying and wheezing, snot and whiskey flowing.

Finally, "Vait, vait," said Reb Gross when he noticed a snail of bloody mucous ooze from my nostril. He willed himself to stop, took a big breath, returned to his worried look, and said, "OK, now Donala, you look terrible. Let's get you to za hospital."

That's about when I crossed back from the Comfort's numbing relief to searing tooth pain and fried ball-sack shock. Suddenly, the air felt cold and my mouth and thigh felt like they had been hit with a branding iron.

In a unison of nodding heads, everyone concurred with the Reb.

CHAPTER FORTY-FOUR

Hospital workers, though accustomed to random commotion, stopped in their tracks and gaped. Reb Gross and Bobby's gang on their Harleys, a police car with lights flashing, and a big, red Caddy driven by Reverend Rampbell, with Clara and me beside him in the front seat, arrived in a parade Christmas would have envied.

As we got out of the car, big ol blubbery Bobby held me up on one side and Rev. Rampbell on the other, Clara and Reb Gross bringing up the rear.

"Sing that song, Reb," Bobby said as we walked toward the emergency room entry, "the one ya sang fer me. Bring in them angels."

Reb Gross, holding the rear, frowning, crying, started his angelically out-of-tune healing prayer, *Ana elna refa na la,* Bobby accompanying him with a surprisingly nice bass.

Reverend Rampbell, still laughing, brought the cacophony of concern under harmonic control with his tenor until a nurse put her finger to her lips in a grave looking, "Shh."

The Reverend poked Bobby in his belly.

"You gotta admit, Bobby, we both got that Jimmy James and The Junior into a confused state of mind—and you weren't far behind." He bent over in laughter again, accidentally twisting my arm and almost dumping me to the floor.

Never before had either come so close to the other without thoughts of savagery. Bobby had never hung out, much less laughed or joked around with, a black man before. Or been poked! He tried to scowl, but the Reverend kept laughing.

"Come on, boy, lighten up," the Reverend howled as he poked him again. Bobby gave him a serious look, certainly never having been called "boy" by a black man. He looked at the Reverend, the Reb, who was giggling again too, at me, grinning and groaning, and at Clara, now laughing too. He finally just swatted The Reverend on the shoulder and boomed guffaws heard all over the emergency room.

In a fit of impaired inspiration, I shook off everyone's grip, hobbled to the counter and said, "Me and my friends were wondering if you had any rooms available for tonight."

We were all at it again—the Reverend beside himself in laughter, Reb Gross, giving up on *Ana elna,* Bobby gasping, his belly heaving like an earthquake, and Clara, wiping blood and snot off of my face while giggling and crying—and me, wincing in painful chuckles, slaver dripping onto the floor.

After I was taken into a room, a busty young nurse's aide leaned low over the examination table to ask my name and insurance. Without even thinking about it, my head lifted slightly to sneak a peek down her billowy blouse. Reverend Rampbell, noticing, elbowed Bobby again, nodding his head toward me so that Bobby would see too.

"You must be okay, Donny-boy," he laughed, "pain's not hotter than she is."

"Woo-wee," Bobby chimed in. "Hot stuff."

"Oy," was all Reb Gross managed, as Reverend Rampbell and Bobby blew on their hands as if they were on fire, laughing their asses off.

If I hadn't been so flushed already, I would have blushed.

"Men!" Clara said, shaking her head along with the nurse.

All of that night's terror transformed itself into a bizarre brother and sisterhood of caring and affection, Clara stroking my head and the others standing around with concern, Bobby even rinsing a washcloth in cool water and swabbing my face.

The doctor came in, looked around at the crowd in a state of befuddlement paralleling that of The Junior, my friends refusing to leave the room, shot me with Demerol, and started to patch me up.

For the first time, floating in anesthetic reverie and looking at the faces of my strange band of cohorts, I saw the threads of the South sewn beautifully into the fabric of the Jew and the threads of the Jew sewn elegantly into the cloth of the South. Together, it created a canopy, a *chupa*, large enough to shelter all that stood beneath it. As I drifted away, I could swear that I heard a tenor sax wailing one of May's happy blues, Coltrane laughing in the background.

I thought, like May had said after her beating, that it was all "worth it, worth it in spades."

PART 3

The Deadly Healing

CHAPTER FORTY-FIVE

After a few days of healing, I realized I still had some "righting" to do.

Before my affair with Rabbi Tichter's wife, I'd never really had to think much about Orthodox Judaism's laws judging homosexuality an abomination. But to me, his choice to marry was without doubt a sin—and he'd driven Nadya insane, with me her apostle of madness.

I called to make sure her husband wasn't around.

"I need to talk to you. There's something about Mr. E's story that you need to know."

She shuddered at the first sight of my damaged face—the bruises now turning black and yellow and blue.

"Oy," she said, her hand starting toward my black eye, then stopping herself and putting it to her mouth. "Come in, Donala."

I stood there, in a kind of dread-daze. I didn't want to do what I knew I had to. Without a word, she took two fingers of my hand and led me into the house. It again carried the satisfying fragrance of matzoh ball soup. In the kitchen, the table was already set with a steaming bowl, challah, and a spoon.

I opened my mouth to speak, but she held up her hand.

"Eat first," she said. I took great comfort in that time-honored Jewish edict.

The soup was an elixir. I slurped it loudly between my swollen lips. It wasn't hard to notice my struggle to fit the spoon into my mouth under the white gunk blobbed over my broken tooth.

"Thanks for trying to help me," I said, slurred, through my swollen lips.

"How could I not?" she answered softly.

"Well, I sure didn't expect to see you there."

Though Nadya's campaign to free Mr. Eldridge had not produced much in the way of legal results, Reb Gross had called her anyway after Clara's call.

Nadya's face flushed with excitement through her normal gloom.

"We were at the weekly lox, cream cheese, bagel snack and *Torah* study session at the back of Freda's deli when Rabbi Gross called. I took the call because Mordechai was speaking at the time. I repeated Rabbi Gross's worried message and said to the men, 'We've got to help that boy.'

"When they acted uninterested, I shocked all of them by screaming at the top of my lungs, 'He's in trouble and I could never forgive myself, or you, if we don't at least try to help a Jewish boy in trouble. I'm going with or without you.'

"I think they were so astonished at hearing meek old me speak to them that way, that they jumped up like someone had stuck knitting needles up their…."

She stopped herself and looked at me, her face again flushing. After a moment of silence, we both started laughing. It hurt my lip, but I didn't care.

"Freda's husband, Simon, grabbed his butcher knife, then threw whatever other implements he had around him to the other men," she started laughing again, "and even the big salami he was about to cut. Donala, it was very exciting. It was like a movie. We had no idea what we would do when we arrived, but we went anyway."

In less than a breath, her countenance shifted back to worry. She touched the periphery of my damaged eye. "Are you okay?"

"Getting better. They're gonna fix my tooth soon. Do you want a *get,* a divorce, from your husband?" I blurted out.

"What?"

I repeated the question, slurring almost as badly as May had.

"I am the adulterer," she sighed.

Even if she accused him of having a homosexual affair, a potentially divorceable offense in an Orthodox Jewish court, neither Nadya's husband nor Jimmy James could be forced to acknowledge the accusation. Why should they? The safety of their choice of one another was strategically brilliant. Who would ever believe that a white supremacist could stomach, so to speak, a Jew, or vice versa. Just too outrageous. Still, with a picture that showed them in the act, it would be hard for the court not to grant her the *get.*

I swore her to confidence. If the story ever went public, who knew the legal and/or social ramifications for any of those involved in my and May's plots. As I told Nadya the details about her husband, she turned pale and silent, pursing her lips and taking and releasing deep breaths.

"I wondered why my husband was so willing to help and to let me help," she said. "My mind no longer trusts my intuition. Why did you not tell me before? How could you not tell me?" Her face turned red and contorted—not so much in anger, she was too sweet to allow anger with me, but more with frustration.

"I was afraid you or Clara might somehow mess up the chances of helping free Mr. Eldridge. I'm sorry."

After another strained silence, she patted my head.

"You are just a boy," she said. "And there was no blueprint for what you had to do. What you did was a *mitzvah*. I understand."

She wasn't crazy anymore, didn't swat at imaginary flies or fidget. She simply sat with closed eyes.

Still, to my surprise, a wry smile slowly crept across her face. Less a smile than a prisoner's first breath after release. She tried to subdue it, raising her hand to her mouth, eyes alternating between cloudy and bright—then tears, face in her hands.

"Thank you," she said in a dripping whisper. "Now I know I wasn't just imagining. I know I am not insane. I stopped dreaming that I would ever be free of him. I have been bound by my upbringing to honor my marriage vows and would be rejected from my family if I left without a *get*. That would be too much for me."

She placed her hands on either side of my head and kissed me on the forehead. I cringed because I knew I was about to shatter her momentary reverie.

"But I don't have the pictures," I said.

When I told why, her body slumped.

"You'll have to fake it, to claim that I have them," I said. "I'll even come over and claim I have the pictures. But if he calls our bluff, I can't deliver. I'm sorry, so sorry, but I gave them to Reverend James. It was part of the deal."

We sat in silence. I ached as much on the inside as I did on the outside. I wanted to say something else, anything else, that might be helpful—but I had nothing to offer.

"I…am…not…a…natural fighter," Nadya said, patting me on my shoulder between her convulsions. "But now, I will have to be if I am ever to be free. As is said in the *Torah*, 'Misery is the weak sister of defiance.' "

She helped me as I stood with a groan and walked to the door.

"I'm sorry," I said again.

Nadya kissed me on the cheek.

"You are a hero, to Thomas and to me. Thank you, Donala."

Standing there, looking back at her, I was again faced with an all too familiar question—had I done any good at all?

Days later, she called me with what she had done:

"When he came home, I *ordered* him to sit down and listen to me. 'I have disgusting pictures of you in carnal embrace with another man. I will destroy them and will allow you to preserve your honor and your profession if you will grant me a *get*. We will follow *Halacha*, (Jewish law). You may say that I refused to follow you to Israel to live. Or that I am incapable of giving you children. It will be that simple. It doesn't matter if people don't understand how you could let me go. I promise on the *Torah* that I will never utter anything again about this to anyone as long as you are alive. Your secret will be protected by me as long as you do not molest children."

" 'How dare you imply...' he roared."

"I apologize," I immediately interrupted. "One does not necessarily follow the other."

"He stared daggers at me. But, for once, I met his gaze.

" 'You have no power over me anymore with those terrible stares of yours that you have used to intimidate others, and me. That is the past and it is gone forever.

" 'From now onward, you must renounce your hateful and cruel attitude toward the Reform Jews here and announce that you are leaving for a new congregation. This detestable intolerance violates the very fabric of Judaism.'

"His eyes bulged and his face drained so white and tight that he looked like a ghoul. He clenched his fists and stretched his arms against his sides.

"I feared that he would strike me—but, he only slumped back onto our couch and hung his head in his hands."

" 'I am ashamed of my weakness,' he confessed, breaking down into tears.

"I'd never seen such vulnerability in him. I never suspected it even existed in him.

" 'Ever since I realized at a young age that I was this way, I have been tortured,' he said, blubbering now with tears. 'I was a loving boy, full of the love of God and *Torah.* I wanted to share God's joy with the world and bring it to other Jews as a rabbi. *A nahr bleibt a nahr,* a fool remains a fool. There was no question to me that it was my calling. But I knew that I could never resolve my carnal feelings with the beliefs of our faith. I was doomed, enveloped in darkness, and I could not hold my anger and sense of betrayal at bay. I see now that I have become that anger. Please forgive me, my sweet Nadya.'

" '*Gait trev zich,* go fuck yourself!' I screamed at him. 'If I had a gun, I might kill you. I will never forget what you have put me through. You are so evil and perverse that I do not know if I believe a thing you are saying. I hate you. *Gai in drerd arein,* go to hell, you *mumser,* son of a bitch.'

"Donala, I was shocked at the dark gruel spilling from my pot of rage. I'd never spoken or even thought those kinds of words before.

" 'You are a thief who has robbed me, not just of love, but of my innocence,' I screamed at him. '*A choleryeh ahf dir,* a plague on you for what you have done to me.'

"Donala, I couldn't stop sobbing and cursing. He just sat there. Perhaps he wanted to scream back, to kill me. The simple fact of my femaleness, and his being forced to bond with it, must have represented all of the suffering and deceit and self-loathing that the laws of Orthodox doctrine had foisted on him."

As she was telling me, I imagined how he must have hated all the parts of her anatomy that I had so enjoyed and her *her-ness*. But mostly, he must have hated himself.

"Eventually, watching him weeping and moaning," Nadya told me, "I couldn't help but feel his pain. I finally pulled myself together and stared at him.

" '*A sof! a sof!* Enough, enough,' I told him.

"He looked totally desolate and lost. Against all of my hate and disgust, I looked inside myself for some redemption. I couldn't only hate him. I forced myself to search inside my heart. A door opened and I heard myself speak with a clarity and wisdom that surprised me, and him, as much as my venomous tirades had.

" 'I do not hold your sexual orientation in and of itself against you. If you are a homosexual, then I believe that God made you that way in his love and for his own reasons, and it is not therefore an abomination. It is not fair or right that our religion judges you so. That is the true abomination. If Judaism cannot honor all of God's loving beings, then it is inherently blasphemous in its essence. I believe that it is the narrow, misled, and lost souls within Judaism who hold these hateful views. People...oh God... people like you,' I said, as I realized this sad irony. 'But, I reject that it is the word of God. It is the misinterpretation of his words that make them believe that he would ever feel this way. But you, Mordechai, you must not hurt another woman as you have me, and you must not take out your rage by making so many others suffer.'

"His weeping and groaning grew even greater.

"It took a moment, Donala, but then I watched myself, almost like another person within me, reach out, touch his hand and hold his weeping face to my chest. And for a moment, we loved one another, even if only because we could relate, through our own pain, to the other. And, at that moment, I had an epiphany. It shocked me. I suddenly knew that God was moving through me, allowing me to caress him even as I wanted to kill him. And that this suffering in my life must therefore have had a purpose. So it was up to me to find out what it was and would be. I forgave him, and I was washed clean. I became a woman again. I reclaimed myself, my Judaism, my optimism, and my femininity. Then I knew that I could keep living."

Afterward, Reb Tichter stumbled out of their house. Nadya didn't see him until three days later. She looked for the gun in their house, but couldn't find it. She frantically called everyone she knew, including The Junior and Reb Gross. His body was found by a man who went to check why his dog was barking in a field of high weeds, just outside of town, by the river.

Tichter was without parents or siblings, and no one from up North volunteered to take his body. So Nadya buried him at our local Jewish cemetery. Reb Gross officiated at the funeral.

Nadya wailed, as is customary for an Orthodox widow at such a time. She never told anyone else, except Reb Gross, nor did I, until now, about the circumstances leading to his death. Suicide is even more of a sin in Orthodox Judaism than homosexuality. She begged The Junior to list his death as a hunting accident. It didn't matter to him, since they didn't suspect foul play, so he did.

"May he rest in a peace he never knew while alive," Nadya said to me at the funeral.

I left the cemetery in a panic, I went out to Reb Gross's place.

"I killed another man," I moaned. "If I hadn't told Nadya and taken those pictures, he'd still be alive. Oh God, Reb Gross, I killed him. It's my fault that he's dead."

Reb Gross tried to console me. I was shaking and crying.

"I didn't have to tell her about those pictures. It was none of my business. It was between them. I just wanted to be a hero."

"He vas not a nice man," said the Reb. "Your actions saved Mr. Eldridge, an innocent man. But Rabbi Tichter violated Jewish and civilized law. He deceived and hurt his vife, community, and zo many ozhers. He sewed za zeeds of hate. Dis is not just your fault, Donala."

"What do you mean 'not just?' " I said.

"His life, his misery, his karma, his lies all created za atmosphere for all of dis to happen to him. And, yes, truth be told, my zon, you haf zinned, too. I von't lie to you. You knowingly stepped into zheir lives in violation of her vows, Jewish law, ethical conduct, and morality, no matter how you justify it, no matter if you were only a boy. Your lust vas a zin in dis case. You must ask God for forgiveness. At za same time, you mustn't blame yourself for trying to help Mr. Eldridge or the Rebbitzen. Learn from dis mistake of yours, not by hating yourself but by forgiving yourself and loving everyvon. Because zen you can understand forgiveness and can teach ozhers about it."

His peaceful, doleful eyes stilled me.

"And ve must have *rachmannas*, compassion, for Rabbi Tichter, and forgive him, too. He vas forced to live a tortured life because of how God chose him to be. It vud never have been his choice. Religion is supposed to show us God's love, not deny it ven ve're different, harmlessly zo, from the norm. Rabbi Tichter zimply reflected za hate zat had been heaped on him by zose who should have loved him. His Judaism failed him. If anything, Judaism killed him. May he rest in peace. And may ve all learn from dis tragedy. I am so sorry, Donala. Religion is often not just and life is not fair."

"Amen," I said, as he cradled me, let me cry, and sent me home.

CHAPTER FORTY-SIX

At our variously designed construction jobs, Mr. E used to always say, "One man's idea of ugliness is, a lot of times, another's of beauty. An I'll be damned if I can tell the diffrence most of tha time."

A week after the kidnapping, Reverend Rampbell asked me to visit him at his office. When I arrived, Reb Gross, Mr. Eldridge, and May were there too. We all sat down and sipped Cokes. They asked me what they could give me to honor what I had done. I didn't want anything. Besides, May looked as bad as me.

"May's the real hero," I said to them, choking up as usual. "What you did..."

"You shut up, now," she said, her smile, even through her bruises, so sunny it could toast a piece of bread. She'd told Mr. E the whole story and sworn him to secrecy.

"I might have gotten my butt whupped...uh whipped," she laughed with a head shake, "but you pushed us all to really do something more than we thought we could. And your parts, seen and unseen," looking toward my crotch, "don't look very good right now either."

Everyone stood there nodding their heads up and down like bobblehead dolls. I couldn't help but think that it was me who was humbled and honored by being able to help. It was its own reward, *tikkun olam*, I insisted. But they wouldn't stop insisting, *hocking*, me even more.

"Now, Donny-boy," Reverend Rampbell spoke in his most resolute tenor, "It's time to let us bestow our love on you. We won't take no for an answer. Just like you wouldn't. So you calm down and accept our loving embrace."

But what more could I want? Helping Mr. E certainly wasn't about things. Getting things for what I'd done only seemed to cheapen it. I was blank. Mr. E sat there, his moist eyes like a blessing to me, grinning with a big, happy, gold-capped-front-tooth smile. Then, Red's ridiculously amazing tooth popped into my head. That's when I knew.

Dr. Manny Kaplan, our family's Jewish dentist, bragged of bravely hollering, "Fuck you" when he passed a Klan cross burning, failing to mention that he was a mile down the road at the time. He was famous in the black community for his one-of-a-kind, made-to-order, custom gold crowns. I'm not sure if he'd made Red's, but I wouldn't be surprised. Together we designed my special crown, a white gold background fronted with a hammer over a golden quarter note.

It has graced my broken front tooth since then. I am, and will always be, proud of it. Strangers are often shocked, even repulsed, by the white guy, a Jew no less, with the gold front tooth who plays the blues. They never quite know what to think about me. I can understand their reactions. But Mr. E was right about beauty or ugliness being in the eye of the beholder.

To me, seeing my glorious tooth in the mirror or feeling it with my tongue or against my reed, constantly reminds me of my amazing Danville adventure and of the love of my friends and how fortunate and happy I am just to be alive. And above all, it reminds me to keep looking for ways to help repair, as May says, "this woeful, wonderful world."

PART 4

Whatever Happened To…

Clara, dear Clara: After the kidnapping, I explained everything to her—all of it—including how I couldn't bring myself to tell her about her dad.

"Fuck you!" was, of course, her first reaction. "You didn't trust me enough to tell me. Fuck you again!" she shouted.

"I didn't want to hurt you," I tried to explain.

"Well, you fuckin failed that one, buddy."

Our relationship was never the same. At the end of the school year, she and her mother moved to Atlanta. Six months later, she wrote me that after some therapy to clear her diseased father from her mind and soul, she had forgiven me. When she finished high school, she attended Emory University and found her calling in her deep belief in Jesus Christ, eventually going on to become an Episcopal minister, tolerant and open to the true living love of Christ. She married a Jew named Norman Greenbaum, who had written and recorded one of the first Christian-themed, cross-over rock singles to win a gold record, "Spirit in the Sky." He said in an interview that he knew it would never be a hit as a Jewish-themed song—another Jew seizing opportunity—and so marketed it to the Christian market. I still love that tune.

May: Ever the clever businesswoman, supporter of black empowerment, financial improvement, and women's liberation, she expanded her business to five ladies, becoming Danville's wealthiest black woman. She insisted her employees graduate high school, learn and practice strict hygiene, eat healthy diets, and regularly attend church. To become cultured women with a good future in and outside their profession, they had to enroll in and make decent grades in college correspondence courses, since blacks weren't allowed at Stratford, the local women's college. By the way, their intellectual and cultural improvement didn't hurt business. Seems most of the clientele found smart girls more alluring.

"They're all 300-dollar suits, Donny," she told me.

" 'Heck, anybody can fuck a stupid farm nigger,' my wealthy customers laugh and say to me. 'But, yo' girls are clean and have class.' "

After almost fourteen successful years in the business, under circumstances she never would disclose, she met, fell in love with, and married Danville's first black city attorney, Daniel Worley. She soon sold her business to her employees. Her twin boys are named Joseph and Donny.

Nadya Tichter: The Rebbetzin moved to Israel, remarried, and joined a *kibbutz*, running its day care center. Five years later, she wrote me that her life was rich and sweet, even though her family had little money. She again asked me to forgive her. Her husband was a learned man who'd chosen life on the land, growing oranges and raising chickens while studying *Torah* on the side. Their four children grew up wild and free. She said she hoped my life had become as happy and blessed as hers had.

The Reverend Jimmy James: Paroled after ten years in Canon City, Colorado's federal prison, James was nowhere to be seen, thank goodness. Clara heard that he was trying to resurrect his career as a traveling tent revival preacher. Reverend Rampbell said he'd heard that James had started a fundamentalist Christian congregation in Colorado Springs.

Ricky Parker: Ricky became a full-fledged hero of the Klan. He learned to run heavy equipment in a jail program and was released after one and a half years, and that's about all I know or care to know about him.

John Lawson: When Helen Gant tried to fire him, he told her she couldn't, " 'cause I quit." He hired on as a janitor at the black high school and became a Black Muslim preacher through a correspondence course. After a year, he was informed that he was excommunicated because he refused to preach that *all* white men were devils. Eventually, the school upgraded him to guidance counselor.

Reb Gross: He married the widow of one of Dad's rich merchant friends. She was ten years younger than the Reb, but she struggled to keep up with his endless energy. She took to country living on the farm, except that she refused to deal with his beloved donkeys. She quickly learned to love riding with him on his motorcycle and going to black gospel churches with him and was warmly embraced by her new friends. She and the Reb built a nice lake on the farm and had many fine summer swimming parties and picnics for Jewish, poor black, and white kids.

With Reverend Rampbell's help, he started a new movement, *Jewish Revival,* embracing the best of Jewish traditional liturgy and music with the pulse of black gospel rhythm, dancing, and singing. The Danville area became home to some of the funkiest "Heebs" in the South, his vision eventually extending to Boulder, Colorado, and even out to California.

Mr. Eldridge: When Mr. E went back to his handyman business, both Jewish communities adopted him as their official institutional and personal handyman. Mrs. Schneider felt so bad that she sent him a personal check for twice the amount she'd withheld, along with a note saying, "Sometimes even a woman can be a *shmuck*." His business grew, prospered, and expanded. He hired several employees and eventually brought his sons into the business.

And he quit smoking, the gift I'd asked of him in private.

"Youth teachin old," he'd said to me. "Guess dyin young wouldn't be too useful to the wife and kids." With a laughing slap on my back, he added, "Not to mention the trouble I seem to git in throwin butts around."

I'm still using his initialed screwdriver and toolbox.

Uncle Herman: By the time he died of Lou Gehrig's disease at age sixty-eight, he could only communicate by hunt and peck on a talking typewriter. Until his dying day, he refused to buy a Mercedes, unlike most of Danville's Jewish professionals. He'd always plead, "Why give those German killers your money when a fine, American-made Cadillac," and then he'd wink and say, "or a shitty Citroen, will do just fine."

In his will, he left me that by-then-antique French car, with the codicil, "For keeping a secret to beat the system," a secret he never asked me to divulge. I still wonder if he'd discovered what May and I had done to convince The Junior to free Mr. E or if he'd simply guessed.

Becky James: After her own therapeutic cleansing, Becky came out as a Christian lesbian. She told May that, "I'd never known that love was more than just a four-letter word." She founded a mission for the poor in Atlanta, specializing in helping abused women and children, funded by the substantial money she received from her divorce. She met a wonderful woman, a black Indian activist. They are reportedly very happy. Her daughter, Reverend Clara, officiated at their wedding.

The Junior: Now called by his Christian name, Edward Baker, he became Danville's three-term mayor. After he'd dropped charges against Mr. Eldridge and gotten Ricky Parker convicted, he discovered he was a hero of sorts to the black community, the moderate whites, and the Jews for his courage in freeing a black man and admitting that he'd been wrong. They never questioned his motive and May kept her promise to remain silent. He won his first mayoral campaign by a wide margin. Even Uncle Herman voted for him.

Nothing changed much during the first year of his two-year term. But at the start of the second year, he "found the Lord, Jesus Christ."

Soon thereafter, he asked May to meet with him.

"I started havin bad dreams 'bout a year after the incident with you," he told May. "Devil was a woman with a knife. Chasin me and slashin at my e-rect manhood. Kept lickin her lips and sayin, 'Might take forever, but one day, you son of a bitch, I'll git to it and it'll be mine in a bun with mustard and relish.' I'd wake up in a stinkin sweat, my wife telling me to stop all my screamin. So I went to my minister. He told me I was possessed and had to beg all who I'd wronged to fergive me. Wasn't too hard to know where to start.

"I've been *saved*," he told her, "and now I want to live the Christian life."

May told me, "He said that he'd realized that he had to find his inner grace and beauty or forever be damned. And that he had to serve all the people. He started weeping like a big baby. He poured out his heart to me like he'd never done, even to himself, totally out of control and out of character. It surprised him as much as it did me."

"I cain't do much 'bout bein born ugly and repulsive," he said to her, "but I sure can do something 'bout actin ugly to folks."

"I was so hardened and vengeful that I almost laughed at him," May told me. "But I told him I'd think about it. And back at home that night, I found my answer in one of Dr. King's speeches. He said, 'In the process of gaining our rightful place, we must not be guilty of wrongful deeds. Let us not seek to satisfy our thirst for freedom by drinking from the cup of bitterness and hatred. We must forever conduct our struggle on the high plane of dignity and discipline.' "

So she called The Junior the next day.

"For your own gain, you knowingly and falsely accused Deacon Eldridge. And you beat and raped me," she started, "but, I admit, I trapped you into doing it. Christ and Dr. King says we have to forgive, so I guess we both have some forgiveness to ask of one another."

"Well, what do I do now?" The Junior asked her.

"You live the rest of your life healing, not just yourself, but this whole damned community."

Under his guidance, Danville became home to a peaceful, though not perfect, coexistence and cooperative spirit between all races that still remains today. The Junior established better community services for the poor and fair treatment of black prisoners. And he kept his thumb on the Klan's worst elements. He also hired Danville's first black city attorney, Daniel Worley.

It's hard for me not to still hate him, but May says it only poisons me.

Reverend Rampbell: The reverend went on preaching and teaching. He remained a shining light in the black community.

"Never picked up another weapon after that night," he said when I visited him years later in the hospital, toward the end. Pancreatic cancer. Diagnosed and dead within six months.

"Boy, that was an exciting night, though, wasn't it Donny-boy?" He laughed. "You sure never were a typical white boy."

Thousands attended his funeral when he died at age seventy-eight, including, I'm sure, a cadre of his re-chargers.

Bobby Stillwell: Jewdawg changed more than a little, too—from a neo-Nazi biker to simply a biker. He and his Tarantula pals tore off their swastikas and replaced them with crosses. They rode their bikes in the Christmas parade, tossing out candy, with Bobby and Reb Gross in the lead. The gang would rev their engines, take off at full throttle, leaving Reb Gross in the rear, and surround the decorated Cadillac Coupe de Ville convertible of the waving, smiling Reverend Rampbell. The first time, the white crowd expected, probably wanted, trouble. Bobby sidled right next to The Reverend's car. They gave one another a big scowl, followed by a big laugh and a high-five. Most folks never did figure out how they came to join forces—they just shook their heads in surprise and disbelief. Bobby still makes the cleanest, purest moonshine in the area.

Finally, I received a letter on FBI stationary two months after the conviction of Clara's father:

Dear Donny,

I know what I did might feel awful and you might be thinking that you hate me, but I hope you believe me when I tell you that if I'd thought it could have saved Mr. Eldridge, I would have discarded my cover before the trial. Maybe I made the wrong choice. But Donny, I don't think it would have mattered.

I tried within the confines of my disguise, but I knew it was useless. I made the judgment that blowing two years' worth of undercover work all over the South on a fish as big as Reverend James would not have resulted in a different verdict for Eldridge—because I really didn't see anything more than a man throwing you down and running. Even had I revealed myself as an agent, it would not have been enough to compensate for the evidence The Junior had at the time against Thomas.

And no matter what I said or did, a Southern white jury probably would have only seen and heard a "lying nigger," and even worse, an uppity, Northern, FBI, carpetbagging one.

I'm still not sure why The Junior changed his mind. It is very unusual after a verdict, but as Red would say, "Praise God, amen."

Shalom,

Lincoln "Red" Perry

At the bottom of the manila envelope was a cinnamon stick.

PART 5

A Note From Donny Cohen's Son – The Origin Of This Book

In our brokenness, we find our wholeness.

—Reb Gross

After sitting the seven-day Jewish mourning period, *Shiva,* I was given the manuscript you've just read. It was written by my dad, Dr. Don Cohen.

"Your father told me he promised this to you," the executor of his estate told me.

I'd pestered my father all of his life for this story. And I wasn't the only one. Nearly everyone who ever met him or watched him play sax on stage thought his strange gold front tooth was certainly not something normal to white people, much less a Jew. But he was stubborn.

"Nobody's business but my own," he'd say to me or anybody else who asked.

He'd even sworn Mom to secrecy. She took it to her grave a few years before him.

But I pushed hard, just as stubborn as him.

"You even gave me a name that means truth seeker," I'd harangued him.

"It would embarrass people, son, innocent people," he'd repeat year after year. "But I'll tell you before I die, I promise."

It was the only time he ever lied to me.

Dr. Don, Danville's long-serving family physician, was a civil, women's, and gay rights activist. He was shot dead in 2007, at age sixty, on a fine, sunny, late-spring afternoon. It was the kind of day Dad said reminded him of his times swimming, praying, and yakking, *kibbitzing*, with his friend Reb Gross, my godfather, who died a few years after I was born.

On the day that Dad died, he was so happy that I was bringing his two-year-old grandson, Thomas, to his band's annual Martin Luther King charity fundraising concert. May's gospel group, The Soul Stirrers, always headlined the three-hour gig, with Dad's old-guy jazz band, The Hip Replacements, warming up the crowd. He'd always say, "The Hip," pausing, "Replacements," making sure I heard the hipness part, whenever I'd tease him by saying The Hip Replacements, like the operation.

One hundred percent of the money went to The Reverend Joseph Rampbell Fund, Danville's largest black charity, dedicated to the nourishment and education of poor, pregnant black women and their children from birth through college. The concert was held at the new city bandstand, built along the Dan River, right by the Southern Railway Yard.

Dad walked to the stage, his gleaming tenor sax slung across his shoulders, ready to introduce my little son to Miles Davis and John Coltrane, still Dad's deities of jazz.

"Today," he said with his gold-toothed smile as bright and shiny as that spring day, "we're gonna try to cover most of the tunes on my favorite jazz album, *Kind of Blue.* It's a challenge for us old farts, but then what's life if you don't do things every now and then that scares the bejeesus out of you a bit? Hope you enjoy it."

Murmurs of "Right on" and "Sho 'nuf" echoed throughout the black and white crowd.

He put his horn to his lips, looked out at us with a wink, then hit the head of *Freddy Freeloader,* just as the bullet ripped into his.

My wife grabbed Thomas and ran to the car with him as I rushed to Dad's side. I thought I would die myself as I knelt beside his bleeding body. He never opened his eyes or said another word. I miss him everyday and will never recover.

The crowd instantly jumped on the shooter. A day later, the authorities charged Ricky Parker, the same man who had burned down our temple decades before, with first-degree murder. He apparently couldn't help but brag, once more, to his sheeted friends in prison, that he'd gotten a "four-fer—killing a Jew, a fag, and nigger-lover and a baby-killer, all in one."

After his conviction, pumping his fist into the air as he was being led away to the cheers of his Right to Life supporters, I stepped in front of him to look into his eyes, as Dad had done the night of the fire. Of course, the deputies shoved me aside, but in that brief instant, I was able to see the empty pride that Dad always said "flourishes in the soul of fundamentalist certainty."

If death was the price of my father's *tikkun olam,* doing to the end what he believed in and helping those in need—trying to repair the world—then I believe he at least died at peace with himself.

At the funeral, with trumpet, drums, a clarinet or two, and even a tuba, Dad's musician friends, black and white, played *Just a Closer Walk with Thee.* The pallbearers lifted the Jewish-mandated, plain wooden coffin above their heads, then let it droop waist high, then swung it back and forth, high to low, again and again. Dad had told his band mates that he wanted a New Orleans jazz funeral if he went before they did.

"Those folks celebrate the joy and beauty of life even in death, just like our *Kaddish* prayer," he'd always say when we'd go to New Orleans. "That's what I want—to cut a groove of happiness when I die. Makes Nazis and Klanners shudder in their graves."

Quite a few of the folks at the cemetery—blacks, whites, Jews, and Gentiles, as well as those buried below us, were also probably shuddering, as I, holding his cherished sax, along with those who understood, danced and wiggled to the music in the slow processional.

As requested in Dad's will, May stood beside me at the gravesite, her husband and sons at our sides, and sang *Amazing Grace.* Even at sixty-five, her voice was strong and pure enough to pierce the hearts and raise the spirits of all present.

Mr. Eldridge, eighty-seven years old, helped by his daughter, hobbled up to the coffin with the aid of his magnificently carved, cherrywood walking stick. The corners of his lips lifted into a weak smile as he nodded to me. His eulogy shined with the same precise simplicity that had been a beacon for Dad's morality:

"At the end of it all, when you walk away from a job well done," Mr. E said in his whispery weakness, "yer not thinking much 'bout the money earned nor the praise received from those that benefited. It's more the unseen and unspoken, the contentment you've built inside yerself from knowledge, hard work, patience, doin yer best, and the joy of creatin durable beauty. Real usefulness. I'm proud to have been a friend to a man who lived those principles."

He walked back to his seat, plopped down, stared ahead, bolt upright as always, and dabbed his face with his red-checkered handkerchief.

The rabbi said the final blessing, the *Kaddish,* which celebrates life and the beauty of the world God has bequeathed to us, and doesn't even mention death.

We buried Dad in our family plot, right next to the Rippe plot. After the coffin was lowered into the pit, I placed his beaten-up vinyl record of *Kind of Blue* on the coffin and his sax on top of it. Some musicians, possibly including Dad, might have thought that burying such a fine instrument was blasphemous—leave it for others to make music. But to me, it was such an integral part of Dad's life that I wanted it to keep him company into eternity.

I then helped Mr. Eldridge to his feet. At my insistence, he dug the first shovelful of dirt from the pile and threw it into the hole with a moan. May went next. One by one, relatives and friends and I did the same until it was filled.

Leaving the cemetery, I placed a small rock on Mr. Rippe's headstone, in the Jewish tradition, as Dad had done each year since the fire.

I remembered the Jewish saying, "Let their memories be for a blessing." I said a *Schecheheeyanu,* the prayer of gratitude. I felt blessed to follow in the steps of the men in our family as I broke into tears, May's arms holding me like she had held Dad so long ago.

Emet Cohen